**Praise for the novels of
USA TODAY bestselling author
Victoria Dahl**

"This is one hot romance."
—*RT Book Reviews* on *Good Girls Don't*

"A hot and funny story about a woman
many of us can relate to."
—*Salon.com* on *Crazy for Love*

"*Lead Me On* will have you begging for a reread
even as the story ends."
—*Romance Junkies*

"[A] hands-down winner, a sensual story filled with
memorable characters."
—*Booklist* on *Start Me Up*

"Dahl has spun a scorching tale
about what can happen in the blink of an eye
and what we can do to change our lives."
—*RT Book Reviews* on *Start Me Up*

"Dahl smartly wraps up a winning tale
full of endearing oddballs, light mystery
and plenty of innuendo and passion."
—*Publishers Weekly* on *Talk Me Down*

"Sassy and smokingly sexy,
Talk Me Down is one delicious joyride of a book."
—*New York Times* bestselling auth

"Sparkling, s
Victoria D
—*New York Times* be
on

**Also available from
Victoria Dahl
and Harlequin HQN**

*Real Men Will
Bad Boys Do
Good Girls Don't
Crazy for Love
Lead Me On
Start Me Up
Talk Me Down*

And coming soon

Too Hot to Handle

VICTORIA DAHL

Close Enough to TOUch

WITHDRAWN

HARLEQUIN®

entertain, enrich, inspire™

If you purchased this book without a cover you should be aware
that this book is stolen property. It was reported as "unsold and
destroyed" to the publisher, and neither the author nor the
publisher has received any payment for this "stripped book."

Recycling programs
for this product may
not exist in your area.

ISBN-13: 978-0-373-77688-7

CLOSE ENOUGH TO TOUCH

Copyright © 2012 by Victoria Dahl

All rights reserved. Except for use in any review, the reproduction or
utilization of this work in whole or in part in any form by any electronic,
mechanical or other means, now known or hereafter invented, including
xerography, photocopying and recording, or in any information storage
or retrieval system, is forbidden without the written permission of the
publisher, Harlequin HQN, 225 Duncan Mill Road, Don Mills, Ontario
M3B 3K9, Canada.

This is a work of fiction. Names, characters, places and incidents are
either the product of the author's imagination or are used fictitiously,
and any resemblance to actual persons, living or dead, business
establishments, events or locales is entirely coincidental.

This edition published by arrangement with Harlequin Books S.A.

For questions and comments about the quality of this book,
please contact us at CustomerService@Harlequin.com.

® and TM are trademarks of Harlequin Enterprises Limited or its
corporate affiliates. Trademarks indicated with ® are registered in the
United States Patent and Trademark Office, the Canadian Trade Marks
Office and in other countries.

www.Harlequin.com

Printed in U.S.A.

This one is for Jodi.
Thanks for keeping me company and making me laugh.

Close Enough to TOUCh

CHAPTER ONE

THIS MADE IT OFFICIAL: Grace Barrett's life was over. Or, at the very least, it was so irrevocably screwed up that a quick death would be a blessing at this point.

She was twenty-eight, in debt to an angry ex-boyfriend, she had exactly $37.40, and she was *here*.

In Wyoming.

Well, she'd been in Wyoming for hours, actually. Hours of endless beige hills and barren mountains. Hours of cows. And sheep. And some strange creature she'd thought was a deer until she'd gotten a better look. Deer didn't look as if they had exotic black masks painted on their little faces. What the heck were those things?

Grace shuddered a little as she stepped out of the bus. Her feet touched the ground and there was no taking it back now. She really was in Wyoming. She was standing on it.

"Damn," she muttered.

The elderly man in front of her turned with a concerned smile. "Sorry, ma'am?"

Grace crossed her arms in defense. "Sorry about that. I was just…"

He smiled and put a hand to his balding head as if he meant to tip a hat. "Beg pardon."

No one had ever begged her pardon before. Grace crossed her arms more tightly, unsure how to handle this situation. Thankfully, the man moved away before she was forced to respond.

Grace glanced warily around. After her years in L.A., she knew to keep her guard up against anyone who approached her on the street, no matter how kind and polite the people here might seem. Nobody did, so she edged toward the driver as he unlocked the luggage compartments of the bus. She was used to being alone, but she'd been surrounded by people on this bus for nearly two days. She felt almost panicked with the need to be free.

The driver began unloading the bags, laying them out in neat rows. Grace kept a sharp eye on his hands, waiting for her ancient camouflage duffel bag to appear.

No one else seemed to be watching as closely. The other passengers were hugging friends and family or idly chatting with each other as their eyes traveled along the horizon. She spared only the barest of glances toward the view of the mountains. Someone could walk up and grab a bag and be gone before anybody even noticed.

These folks were obviously not from L.A. Or…maybe their bags didn't contain every ridiculous, precious thing in the world that belonged to them. Maybe their bags were just filled with dirty clothes and cheap souvenirs from a beach vacation. But when Grace's bag appeared and was set on the ground, she jumped forward and dragged it away like a feral animal with a piece of precious meat. It was nearly too heavy for her to lift, but she'd have to find a way. She had no car, no spare money for a taxi—if they had such things here—and she hadn't told her great-aunt when she'd be arriving. So she was hoofing it.

"Hoofing it," she breathed, managing a laugh as she glanced around to see if there were any cows standing next to her. Unlike the rest of Wyoming, the town of Jackson seemed to be blessedly cow-free. It was also slightly larger than she'd expected, dashing her hope that she could simply wander down the main street until she spotted the address she was looking for. She'd have to ask for help. The idea made her grimace as she took a deep breath and looked around. Maybe she could just find a free map.

"Bingo," she muttered as her eye fell on a big sign that spelled out *Jackson Hole Information!* in old-timey wooden letters. Grace had lived in Hollywood a long time. If there was one thing she knew, it was how to work a tourist trap.

She dragged her bag across the asphalt and onto the wooden...sidewalk? Grace blinked and looked down the street, then turned to look in the other direction. Yes, as far as the eye could see, the sidewalks were wooden, like an Old West town.

"Wow," she muttered. These people were really trying hard, even if she had to admit that it was cute. Shaking her head, she pulled her bag down the sidewalk until she got to the brochure stand.

"Do you have a free map of the area?" she asked the matronly woman who'd turned away to straighten papers.

"Oh, hello!" the woman called as she spun around. "Good afternoon!"

"Hi. Um. I just need a map of the town. Something simple."

The woman's eyes flicked up to Grace's hair for a moment, and Grace wondered what she must think of a purple-haired girl in combat boots asking about Jackson, but the woman's smile didn't waver. "Well, I won't lie. There are a lot of choices. Here's the official town map." She laid out a folded brochure. "But—and don't tell anyone I said this—I actually like the one the restaurant association puts out a little better."

"Thanks." Grace took both the brochures and opened the one the woman had recommended.

"What are you looking for, sweetheart?"

Sweetheart? Grace glanced down at her T-shirt. Yep. It still advertised an old L.A. burlesque club. "Just a street," she said softly, hoping not to invite more questions.

"Which street?"

Grace cleared her throat and shifted, her gaze desperately boring into the map, hoping she could just find it herself. "Um, Sagebrush."

"Sagebrush. That's a long one. What's the address?" The woman's pink fingernail pointed toward the map, but it moved before Grace could register which street she was pointing to.

"Six-O-five West Sagebrush," she said, sighing.

"Oh, that's way over here!" The woman pointed again, and this time Grace saw it. A long line that meandered all the way through town and then followed the curve of a stream before it ended. It looked like quite a haul.

"Thank you," Grace said. She folded the map and hefted her bag up, biting back a grunt as she worked the strap over her shoulder. "This way?" She tilted her head in the direction she thought she needed to go. She'd always been pretty good with that sort of thing.

"Yep!"

Grace took a deep breath and started walking. Her boots clomped on the wood.

"Oh, honey!"

Grace pretended she didn't hear.

"Sweetie, stop! You can't walk all that way."

"I'm fine," she called.

"But there's a free bus!"

Her boots stopped clomping. "Free?"

"Totally free. In fact, it'll stop right here in a few minutes. Comes every half hour."

Grace turned back and eyed the woman suspiciously. "Will I have to go tour a new condo complex or something?"

"What? Oh, heavens no. It's the town bus. It'll stop just a few blocks from where you're going. Six-O-five West Sagebrush. That's the Stud Farm, isn't it?"

"The what?" She dropped the bag. She'd heard tales that her great-aunt was a crazy old lady, but… *"What?"*

"Oh, never mind me." The woman laughed. "That's just a silly local nickname."

"For *what?*"

"The building."

Just as Grace was opening her mouth to demand a real answer, a hiss of brakes sounded from the curb. The bus had arrived, and she didn't have time to get more information. She hauled up her bag, wrestled it onto her shoulder and jogged for the bus. As promised, there didn't seem to be a fee. The driver glanced at her impatiently, and she felt a small jolt of comfort at that. The bus might be free, but the driver was just as jaded as every bus driver in L.A.

Slightly less suspicious, Grace took a seat close to the front so she wouldn't have to haul the bag any farther, then dug the map back out to see which intersection she was looking for.

A few blocks later, the wooden walkways were replaced with cement, and the two-story buildings with front porches became less common. By the time they reached the right intersection, they'd passed a strip mall and a big grocery store. She felt slightly less disoriented as she grabbed the bellpull and hauled her bag down the steps.

She didn't dare stop and look around as the bus pulled away. Her shoulders were already aching and the bag wasn't getting any lighter, so she set off down the side street with her head down. Sagebrush was only four blocks down. No problem.

By the time she reached the next street, she was gasping for air. "Good Lord," she muttered, stopping to take a few deep breaths. It didn't help. Altitude, she reminded herself, finally giving in and setting the bag down. Closing her eyes, she concentrated on oxygen, and without the weight of the bag, she was breathing normally within a few moments.

Had she really thought she was going to walk all the way from the bus station to the apartment? Laughing at the image of herself crawling down the street with the bag balanced on her back, Grace opened her eyes and took a deeper breath.

"Mmm," she hummed. The air smelled…nice. Really nice. Crisp and fresh and clean. Maybe she could live with less oxygen. Just for a little while. It wasn't like she was going to stay in this ridiculous little town.

It was cute, though. The Old West part of town had morphed into a slightly Victorian feel. Little gingerbread houses, separated by the occasional 1960s ranch house. Grace had never lived in a small town before. Maybe it would be okay, temporarily.

As if to show her just how wrong she was, the jingle of a bike bell interrupted her thoughts. A bicycle passed by. An honest-to-goodness bicycle built for two. Both riders waved as they rode away. Grace grimaced at what looked like an advertisement for happiness. This town was going to rub her own misery in her face.

Once the bike had passed, she lifted the bag and trudged on. Another bike appeared, this one with only one rider, but with an old-fashioned bike horn that the rider honked before he waved. Yeah, L.A. was bad enough with all the sunshine, but this town was just too much.

Vancouver would be better, hopefully. There was a big enough movie industry there. She had a job waiting for her if she could get there in six weeks. And if she did a good job, maybe she could get steady work as a makeup artist up there where nobody knew she was difficult to work with. *Difficult,* as in she wouldn't put up with handsy actors or abusive bosses. That seemed totally reasonable to her, but in L.A., ass kissing was a way of life.

Grace turned onto Sagebrush and started watching the addresses.

When she finally spotted number 605, she was pleasantly surprised. The Victorian building didn't look like it had anything to do with a farm. Or studs. It wasn't the prettiest house on the block, but the paint was fresh and bright royal-blue. The trim around the windows and the porch was vivid white. The place looked perfectly respectable.

Then her eyes slid to the building next door.

The *saloon* next door.

She knew it was a saloon because of the wide plank of wood over the door that screamed SALOON in big black letters. Barstools lined the ancient porch and, unlike the building Grace was standing in front of, this place looked as though it hadn't been painted since 1902. In fact, it looked like a *barn* that hadn't been painted since 1902. She was pretty sure that was some sort of hayloft door near the roof.

Grace's shoulders were protesting the delay, so she adjusted the bag's strap and walked up the sidewalk to the house. As soon as she stepped in, she saw two doors marked A and B. The only other possible route was a wide staircase that led to the second floor. Grace dropped the bag and dug out the letter from her great-aunt, praying that her apartment was on the ground floor. She wasn't sure she could make it up the stairs without passing out.

"Apartment A," she breathed. "Thank God."

She was reaching for the door when she realized the mistake and paused. She didn't have a key. And—she looked at the letter again—her aunt hadn't given a phone number.

Feeling stupid for even trying, she reached for the knob and tested it. It didn't budge, of course. Who would leave a vacant apartment unlocked?

"Crap."

Grace stood on her tiptoes and ran her fingers above the door frame. Nothing.

"Shit."

When she looked down, she saw that her black boots were planted right in the middle of a doormat that said Howdy! inside a circled lasso. Her last hope was this rectangle of Western kitsch. Holding her breath, she stepped off and picked it up. Nothing.

"Damn it," she groaned, letting her lungs empty on a growl of frustration as she glared down at the envelope in her hand. Her aunt's return address was a P.O. box. She'd communicated only via letter to the friend's address that Grace had used for return mail. And Grandma Rose never answered her cell phone.

On the off chance that it was the one time of day that her grandmother turned her cell on to check messages, Grace pulled out her crappy pay-as-you-go phone and dialed Grandma's number. A few seconds later, Grace heard the beep of the voice-mail message starting, and her heart dropped. However Grandma eventually went, it wasn't going to be from "radio wave brain cancer," at least according to her.

Grace looked back to the letter in her hand, feeling

hopeless. What was she going to do? Wander around town asking everyone if they knew her aunt? She'd been on a bus for two days. She'd thought she was about to get a break. Just a few hours to rest and let her guard down.

"Damn it, damn it, damn it!" She hauled back one boot and kicked her bag as hard as she could. It wasn't hard enough. She pulled back her foot to do it again. The bag held everything she owned in the world, but right now, that seemed like the perfect reason to kick it. This was her life. Right here. Her whole crappy life in this beat-up, dirty camouflage bag.

"Damn it!" she screamed one more time as she kicked it hard enough to slide it six inches across the floor.

"That bag must've done something really shitty to get a little thing like you all riled up."

Grace stomped her foot onto the floor and spun to face the low drawl, her heart slamming into a crazed beat. A man stood in the doorway of the other apartment. He leaned against the doorjamb, arms crossed and mouth turned up in an amused smile.

"Excuse me?" she snapped.

"Just wondering why you're kicking the tar out of that bag, darlin'."

"First of all, I'm not your darlin'. Second, it's none of your business."

His smile widened, revealing dimples in his tanned face. His tanned, granite-jawed, handsome face. "Really? None of my business? When a crazed banshee of a woman stands on my doorstep cursing her heart out on a beautiful Friday afternoon? Tends to pique my interest."

"It's my doorstep," she corrected, hoping she was

right. Hoping her aunt hadn't decided to lease the apartment to somebody else in the week since she'd written.

His eyebrows shot up, and the man pushed up to his full height. "*Your* doorstep? Are you sure?"

Grace went for bravado and snorted. "Of course I'm sure."

He shrugged one wide shoulder, and Grace was suddenly very aware that his plaid button-down shirt wasn't actually buttoned down. It looked as though he'd just shrugged it on to come investigate the commotion in the hall, and when he moved, a long strip of skin showed from his neck all the way down to his waist. And then there were his jeans and the affectionate way they clung to strong thighs.

The Stud Farm, she suddenly remembered. What kind of place was this?

She shook off her thoughts. The man was wearing cowboy boots, for godssake. He was wholesome and homey. His thighs were none of her concern. But the sight of his boots reminded her that she was in Wyoming, which reminded her why she was in Wyoming and what a mess she'd made of her life. "Anyway," she said with a scowl, "still none of your business."

She grabbed the handle of her duffel bag and pulled it up with shaky arms. She couldn't leave her bag here, but she didn't know what she was going to do with it. She didn't know what she was going to do with *herself.*

A surge of anger gave her the strength to bounce the bag higher in her grip, but she wasn't going to make it to the curb, much less walk to… Where, exactly?

"Let me get that." A large hand closed over the handle and lifted the weight from her grasp.

"Hey—" she started, but he'd already transferred the bag to his possession. He held it with one hand as if it were a pocketbook. Even more skin showed past his shirt now. Skin and muscle and golden hair.

While she was staring, he reached past her and opened the door.

He just…opened the door.

"What the hell?" she bit out.

He shot her a puzzled look. "You did say it was your place, right?"

"Yes, but…" She felt like smoke was about to come out her ears, and wanted to snatch her bag away and tell him to get lost. But her arms were so tired. "The door was locked," she said past clenched teeth.

"It sticks a little. You have to pull back on it before you turn the knob."

"So it was just open? Unlocked?"

"Nothing to steal here," he said, gesturing with his free hand. "Where do you want this?"

Where, indeed? Now that they were inside, the apartment looked like an old converted place she'd once rented in L.A. White walls, scuffed wooden floors, a nondescript kitchen. But with little touches from the past, like a fireplace and built-in bookshelves. And not one single piece of furniture.

Somehow that hadn't occurred to her.

"Right there is fine," she murmured. "Thanks." It didn't really matter, after all. Living room, bedroom. They were equally empty rooms to her.

"Here?" the guy asked doubtfully.

"Yes, there. Thank you. I appreciate the help."

"Yeah?" He smiled wide enough to show his dimples again. "Then why did you look like those words hurt coming out?"

She tried frowning at him, but he just stuck out his hand.

"I'm Cole, by the way. Cole Rawlins."

"Grace Barrett," she said. His wide hand engulfed hers, and though he didn't squeeze hard, there was no mistaking the strength in those rugged hands. His calluses rasped against her fingers.

"Grace," he murmured, his gaze rising momentarily to her hair.

"Yes. Grace." She enjoyed the contradiction of her traditional, gentle name and her physical appearance.

This man recovered more quickly than most. "A pleasure," he said simply. Then added, "Grace."

She pulled her hand away at the intimacy of hearing him say her name as if it truly were a pleasure.

Cowboy freak. Though her hand tingled and she tried not to smile.

"You're not from around here." The understatement of the year.

"Look, I really do appreciate the help, but I need to find my aunt, so…" *Give me some space?*

He didn't seem to hear that last, unspoken part of the conversation. "Your aunt?"

"I'm renting the apartment from her."

"Wait a minute. Old Rayleen is your aunt?"

"My great-aunt, actually."

"Ah. I get it, then."

"Get what?" she asked.

"Why she'd rent this place to you."

Grace straightened her shoulders and scowled. "Why exactly wouldn't she rent this place to me, huh? Real nice, cowboy."

She assumed he would stammer and shift and try to find some excuse, when what he really meant was that she didn't look like a girl who belonged here. But instead of clearing his throat or changing the subject, he just grinned again.

"Let's just say you're a little smaller than the other renters here."

Grace glanced around as if those other renters had just joined them. "I thought you Wyoming folk were supposed to be plainspoken. How about you try saying what you mean?"

"Talk about plainspoken. They don't make 'em timid where you come from, do they? All right, here's the deal. Your aunt has a reputation for renting only to men. Says that they're easier to deal with." The wry tone of his voice implied something different.

"Uh, is there something going on here I should know about?" When she shot an obvious look down his body, his eyes widened in horror.

"No! Absolutely not. But, hey, if she likes my face enough to give me a hundred-dollar discount on rent, I won't argue with her. But that's the extent of her quirkiness. I swear."

Even the most cynical person could tell he was offering the truth. And his face? Hell, that was enough to inspire generosity. It was lovely in a very masculine way. A jaw like steel. Strong nose. And blue eyes that crinkled with warmth fairly often, if the laugh lines were any indication. And his short brown hair had just enough wave to make it look unruly and disheveled. He was gorgeous, and his body called for further attention, too, but Grace kept her eyes on his face.

"Isn't it illegal to rent only to men?"

"Beats me. But I guess she gets away with it."

"Regardless," she finally said, "I need to find my aunt. Get a key. Let her know I'm here."

"Well, that's easy. She's probably next door."

"At your place?"

"No! Come on. I meant next door at the saloon."

"Is she a big drinker?"

"She runs the place," he corrected. "And she's a big drinker."

"Got it. Thanks. I'll just go see her then." She was clearly implying he should leave. She even raised an impatient eyebrow and glanced toward the door. But Cole didn't notice because he was pointedly looking around her apartment.

"You got some furniture coming?"

"Sure. Of course. Thanks for the help."

He turned his grin on her again. "All right, then, Grace Barrett. Even cowboys can take a hint when you're bashing them over the head with it. But let me know if you need any more help. I'm only a few feet away."

"Great. Thanks."

The sound of his boots on the wood floor of the apartment was softer than Grace would've expected, but his steps still echoed against the bare walls. If she were the kind of person who had ever planned to stay in one place more than six months, Grace knew what she would be thinking at this moment. *I'll need to find something to put on these walls.* Or at the very least, she would've been painting them some warm and inviting color in her mind, and wondering where she could find some rugs. Instead, she just took pleasure in the fact that the white paint was still white and was marred by only a few nail holes.

At least she'd learned to appreciate the small things in life. And the big things, like the sound of the door closing behind Cole Rawlins as he finally left her alone.

"Whew," Grace breathed, letting the air ease out of her lungs. The place felt a lot bigger without him taking up all her space.

Okay, maybe a little too big. But without him here, she could see the small ways that the apartment wasn't quite like an old place in L.A. The beautiful, dark wood window frame hadn't been painted over, and instead of miniblinds, there were white curtains. It also didn't smell like roach spray.

She strolled over to the window and pulled aside the curtains. Here was another difference. Instead of a view of a parking lot or traffic or a million other apartments, Grace was looking at a huge pine tree. Past that, she had a view of the small street, and a green house with a yellow porch on the other side of it. A snowmobile sat in the open garage.

Grace crinkled her nose at the strangeness of the

sight. That was something she'd never seen in L.A. Jet Skis, sure. But the snowmobile looked like a real machine. It looked dangerous and powerful, gleaming black and red in the sunlight. It looked...fun.

Too bad she'd be long gone by winter. She had to get to Vancouver in six weeks and make some money, or she was going to be in even bigger trouble than she was now. Way bigger.

COLE GRABBED A COKE and leaned against the kitchen counter, eyes on his front door. That had been a surprise. Opening his door to find a raging tornado of a city girl assaulting a stuffed duffel bag. Not at all what he'd expected during his quick run home to shower and grab a sandwich after his half day at the ranch.

The female voice in the hallway had caught his attention. The female herself, spewing curses and kicking things? Whew.

That girl was going to be trouble. If the purple layers in her dark, choppy hair didn't make that clear, the hard glint in her eyes certainly did. He knew that look. He'd seen it before. And despite his image as the wholesome and friendly good ol' cowboy, that look stirred something in him. It was like a dare. A challenge.

And he did love a challenge.

Speaking of... She'd basically pushed him out the door, claiming that she needed to find her aunt right away. But five minutes had passed and he still hadn't heard her leave. Rude little witch. It seemed like she'd taken his attempts to help as some sort of insult.

He should've let her stand out in that hallway all afternoon, trying to figure out how to get into an open apartment.

Cole imagined her increasing anger and frustration. That look of hot rage he'd glimpsed when he'd opened his door to find out what the noise was about. She hadn't even been embarrassed. She'd just glared at him as if he was intruding.

"Trouble," he murmured as he finally gave up his vigil and stood. Shane was waiting at the saloon to grab a beer, and Cole had nothing to do until physical therapy the next day. He managed not to linger in the entryway, but only because he figured he might see her at the Crooked R soon.

He'd forgotten about this type of girl during the past decade. But he was remembering everything now. The way they made his heart beat faster. The way they seemed to dare him to act on his impulses. He'd once had a thing for dangerous city girls. And he'd ended up in a bad way because of it.

He shoved the thought away as he walked into the saloon and spotted Shane setting up a game of eight ball. "Hey," he said as he grabbed a cue.

"Hey. When are you getting your lazy ass back to work?"

Despite the rude words, Cole noticed the look of concern that Shane shot him. He ignored it. "I'm part-time at the ranch now. It won't be long."

"Yeah?"

"Definitely."

Shane watched him for another long moment. "Good,"

he finally said. "Because I want my first-floor apartment back."

"The stairs too much for you, old man?"

"You're one to talk." He gestured toward the table. "You want to break?"

"Was that a joke about my leg?" Cole asked, but he was immediately distracted by the door of the saloon opening. The flash of daylight obscured the person, but as soon as it closed, he saw it was a blonde. No black-and-purple hair in sight.

"You ready to play?" Shane asked.

Yeah, he was ready to play, but he wasn't thinking about pool. Instead he was thinking about his new neighbor.

"Hey, did you hear the news?"

Assuming Shane was talking about Grace, Cole just raised an eyebrow and leaned over the table to break.

"There's a big film production coming to town."

Cole forced himself to pull the cue back as if those words didn't affect him. In fact, he managed to sink two balls with a perfect break.

"You know anything about it?" Shane asked.

"Why would I?"

"I thought maybe you were going to go Hollywood again."

Cole forced himself to smile, even though his mind was spinning. That couldn't be why Grace was here, could it? "That was a long time ago," he said calmly.

"Not that long ago," Shane countered. "Ten years?"

"Thirteen," Cole said. Thirteen long years, but not even close to long enough. Thirteen years since Hollywood had come to town and he'd jumped in feetfirst. If Grace was part of that crowd…

But no. She was renting an apartment, not staying at one of the fancy resorts. Grace wasn't part of the film team. No way. But maybe this was a warning that should be heeded. A reminder that city girls had led him astray before. And he'd followed willingly.

This chick was bad news. And she was living across the hall. And he wasn't the least bit inclined to avoid her.

She should've scared the hell out of him, and instead, he was smiling in anticipation.

Somehow that only made him smile harder.

Bad news, indeed.

CHAPTER TWO

THE FRESH AIR STRUCK GRACE as soon as she stepped out, the cleanness of it startling though she'd been outside just a few minutes before. Almost against her will, she took a deep breath, drawing in the beauty of it. Even if she'd been surrounded by stucco buildings and ten lanes of traffic, there'd be no mistaking that she wasn't in L.A. anymore. The air was too crisp, and when she moved, it hardly even touched her skin. She felt lighter as she headed for the faint sounds of music leaking from the saloon next door.

"The saloon next door," she murmured. That was something she'd never said before. *Bar,* yes. *Liquor store,* sure. And on one occasion even a strip club. But never a saloon.

The strip club had actually made a pretty good neighbor. Unlike bars and liquor stores, no one wanted to hang around outside a strip club. The interesting parts were inside, behind blacked-out windows and plain cement walls. And once the place shut down for the night, the girls dropped everything and left as if the building made their skin crawl.

Grace had always told herself she couldn't imagine doing that. Pretending to like a man for money. Using her body to win favors. But in the end, she'd done the same thing, hadn't she?

As she opened the heavy saloon door, she shook that thought from her head. What the hell did it matter? She'd done what she'd done, and now she was just as miserable as she deserved to be.

Old country music filled the saloon, though it wasn't particularly loud. A friendly buzz of conversation overlaid the music. Even at 3:00 p.m., several of the tables were filled, though not with the usual miserable types she associated with afternoon drinking. Two of the groups looked like young and scruffy college kids that you'd see in any other town. But at the closest table, all five of the men wore cowboy hats. Each man touched the brim of his hat as she passed. Grace felt her face flush at the unexpected courtesy and hurried past them to the long bar that ran along the side of the building.

She hadn't seen her great-aunt in almost twenty years, but the blonde woman behind the bar was clearly not Aunt Rayleen. This woman was somewhere in her thirties, probably, though her skin was fresh and so pretty she could pass for a younger woman.

"Hi," Grace said, catching her attention. "I'm looking for Rayleen. Rayleen Kisler?"

The woman kept polishing a glass, but offered a wide smile. "Of course, sweetie. She's right over there. Usual table."

Grace followed the gesture to a table at the far corner of the bar. An old woman sat there playing solitaire, an unlit cigarette gripped tightly between two thin lips. Yeah. That was Aunt Rayleen. She looked as mean as ever.

"Thank you," Grace murmured, thinking those weren't quite the right words as she headed across the bar. What she should have said was "Never mind" or "Pretend you never saw me." She should have turned around and grabbed her stuff and kept moving. Grace hadn't even wanted to ask for help from her grandmother, much less this sour-faced woman who'd never had a kind word for anyone, even when Grace had been a child.

And her face had only gotten more sour in the meantime. Though her hair was still beautiful. Pure white and flowing past her shoulders in a gorgeous wave. Rayleen's one and only vanity, according to Grandma Rose.

Grace finally stood before the table, but the old lady didn't look up. She just scowled down at her cards, flipping over three at a time in a slow rhythm. Her pale chambray shirt looked about three sizes too big for her.

"Aunt Rayleen?" Grace finally ventured.

The old lady grunted.

"I'm Grace. Grace Barrett." Still no response. "Your niece?"

Her silver eyebrows rose and she finally looked up. A sharp green gaze took Grace in with one flick of her eyes. "Thought you'd be knocked up."

"Pardon me?"

Her gaze fell back to the table and she resumed her card flipping. "A grown woman who can't keep a job or support herself and has to write to her grandmother to ask for money? I figured you were out of commission. But you look perfectly fine to me."

Grace's skin prickled with violent anger. "If you—"

"Aside from the hair."

Grace stiffened and cleared her throat. She didn't have the right to tell this lady off. God, she wanted to, but maybe a free apartment gave Rayleen the right to get in a few insults. Which was exactly why Grace hated asking for help.

"I was living with someone and it didn't work out. With the economy—"

"Who told you you could ever depend on a man for anything?"

"I... No one told me that."

"You probably learned that from your idiot mama. That woman doesn't have the sense God gave a dog. And dogs ain't exactly nature's Einsteins, are they?"

A strange, hot wash of emotion trickled along Grace's skin. Fury, certainly, but it was mixed up with shame and the awful burn of truth spoken bluntly.

"Listen," she pushed out past clenched teeth. "If you don't want me here, say so and I'll leave right now."

"Yeah? Where are you going to go?"

"Anywhere. I'll find a place. I don't need your charity."

"Sure you do, or you wouldn't have taken it in the first place. Your grandma is living in that old folk's home in Florida, and you can't stay there, can you?"

No, she couldn't stay there. Though she'd rather have stayed there than have asked Grandma Rose for money. Unfortunately, her grandmother hadn't had any money to spare, but she'd called in a favor from Rayleen. If Grace hadn't been so utterly desperate, she'd never have hopped on that bus.

"I can see you've got a spine in you. Must've skipped a generation. You want the place or not?"

The burn sank deeper into her skin. She'd always hated that her paleness showed her emotions so clearly. Not that she often tried to hide her anger, but she wanted it under her control. She wanted to be in charge of who saw it and who didn't. And what she wanted right now was to show this woman nothing. To be calm as she turned around and walked out with her chin held high. Sure, she had nowhere to go, but a city park bench would be better than politely asking this bitch for a key.

"Listen, honey," Rayleen said, finally setting down the cards. "It's not a question of me *wanting* you here. I don't know you from Adam. But I'm willing to have you here because I have an empty apartment and Rose asked me for a favor. You pay the utilities and you can stay. But just through ski season. August is one thing, but come December? I've got my eye on a handsome snowboarding instructor I had to turn away last year."

That broke through Grace's fury. A handsome snowboarding instructor? For what? The apartment or an affair? Jeez, this woman really was crazy. But that didn't mean Grace wanted to accept her grudging handout.

She was opening her mouth to tell Aunt Rayleen to do something foul to herself, but the old woman grinned, showing off perfectly white teeth past the cigarette dangling from her lips.

"You're pissed, ain't ya? I like that. Pride's a beautiful

thing, but you've got to ask yourself where your pride has gotten you up to this point. Because as far as I can tell, it's gotten you homeless and bitter. You enjoying the taste of that?"

Good Lord, the things she wanted to do to this woman would constitute elder abuse, but Aunt Rayleen was just so rude. And mean. And *right*.

That was the worst part. The hardest to swallow. She was right. Grace had too much pride. Hell, sometimes it was all she had. But pride didn't fill your stomach or keep the cold out. So she swallowed hard. And swallowed again, tasting every bitter molecule of it. And then she nodded.

"Thank you for the place to stay," she managed to growl. "I'll be out in a month."

Rayleen laughed. "Oh, big words. We'll see. For now, just don't knock out any walls or leave a window open when it rains. No smoking. No pets. The key's in the cash register. Jenny over there will give it to you."

"Thank you," Grace managed one more time. The words tasted just as bitter the second time around, and she wished she had the money to spare for a beer as she approached the bar. Wished her life was as simple as sitting down and washing the day away with a cold one. Better yet, a double of whiskey. God, yes.

"Hi, again," the bartender offered.

Grace made herself smile back. This woman gave off a good vibe. She probably made a lot of money as a bartender. It was a skill. Grace knew that because she'd tried her hand at it and failed. People just didn't like her. But this woman… She was comforting. "Are you Jenny?"

"I am."

"Rayleen told me to ask you for a key to apartment A?"

"You?" Jenny asked. Her eyes nearly disappeared when she laughed. "You'll be quite a change."

"Do I need to check the place for hidden cameras?" she asked, only half joking.

"You're probably safe. She just likes to collect them, I think, not spy on them. Nothing too creepy." Jenny hit a button on the register and the drawer popped open.

"It seems plenty creepy," Grace muttered.

"She's pretty harmless. They like to come over here and tease her, but she calls them puppies and tells them to leave her the hell alone." Jenny held out the key and dropped it into Grace's hand. "Welcome to Jackson."

"Thank you." That was it. No paperwork. No contracts or legal indemnification. "Do you know anyone who's hiring?"

"Summer's a little tight and we're getting to the end of it. What do you do?"

Grace shrugged. "Waitressing. Busing tables. I've done some cleaning."

"Anything else? You look like a woman who might have other skills."

For a moment, Grace's blood froze. What did that mean? Other skills? Stripping? Turning tricks? She knew she looked a little harder than people in Wyoming, but she hadn't expected to be confronted with the same shit she'd lived with on the streets of L.A.

"Have you worked in clothing stores?" Jenny continued, as friendly as before.

Grace blinked. Is that what she'd meant? Something so innocuous? "Uh, sure. I worked in a vintage place when I was young. And I do makeup."

"Makeup?"

"I work as a makeup artist. In L.A."

"Oh." Jenny's eyes widened. "That's really cool."

"But not very useful in Wyoming."

"Maybe, but it's got to pay better than waitressing in a tourist town."

"That depends," Grace said.

"On what?"

"On whether you can avoid pissing off the fifty different people on a movie set who can get you fired."

Jenny laughed. "Well, maybe you should go see Eve Hill. She's a photographer and she's pretty nice. She might have work for you."

Grace made an effort not to look doubtful, but she'd almost rather be a waitress than do bridal makeup for wedding shoots. "What kind of photography?" she asked warily.

"I'm not sure. She does some landscape stuff on her own. Sells it in town here, but she does other things, too. Photo shoots for magazines."

"Here?"

The doubt must've been showing clearly now, because Jenny shook her head and offered a look of friendly patience. "We might be in the middle of nowhere, but there's money here. Lots of money and lots of those people you know from L.A. They like to come and ski and play dress-up, and they like to have a reason to be here. Film shoots and fashion campaigns provide that."

"Right. Yeah. Okay, I'll look her up."

"Do that. And if that doesn't work out, I'll let you know the good places to be a server here, and the places you want to avoid."

"Thank you so much."

Jenny winked with the natural friendliness of a really great bartender, then moved on to serve the two men who'd just pulled up to the bar.

"Eve Hill," Grace murmured. It probably wouldn't work out. The woman likely had no need for a makeup artist. But if there was any chance Grace could avoid working tables again, she'd suck up her pride. Maybe she'd even volunteer for bride duty. After all, there was a common denominator among all these people Grace wasn't very good with. Customers, bosses, lovers, brides. The common denominator was Grace. She was the problem.

She clutched the key tight in her hand and walked out of the bar without meeting the eyes of any of the patrons.

People didn't like her.

Well, that wasn't exactly true. She had friends. She even had really good friends, like Merry Kade, who'd been her best friend for ten years. So some people liked her. Just not the ones who controlled her pay. Although up until a few months ago, that hadn't been a problem. She was good enough with makeup that she didn't have to kiss butt to keep her job. She'd done just fine. She hadn't had to ask anyone for help.

But that was before.

It didn't matter. She'd asked for help this time, hadn't she? And she hated it. She hated it like she'd never hated anything else. Somehow it was worse than the time she'd spent on the streets as a kid, accepting food from soup kitchens and charities. It was worse than crashing on a friend's couch for a few days, because she could say she'd done the same for them at some point. This was out-and-out asking for help, and it stung.

But it was better than going to jail.

She stood in front of the pretty blue house and opened up her fist. Her skin showed the exact shape of the key. Every ridge and angle pressed red into her palm.

"Just a few weeks," she whispered. "Just a month." And if she didn't like the feeling of begging for scraps, then she'd better get used to the idea of keeping her mouth shut around people who controlled her paycheck. Because it was one or the other, and she'd be damned if she'd ever ask for charity again.

CHAPTER THREE

COLE GLARED AT THE TOP of his physical therapist's head, cursing her for an ogre and a devil and a nasty, power-abusing son of a bitch. Farrah looked up and smiled. "You doing okay, Cole?" She pressed his knee tighter to his ribs, resting all her weight against it. Not much heft considering she had the size and appearance of a benevolent fairy. Just another of her evil tricks.

"I'm great," he ground out between clenched teeth.

"Easy says you're bugging the tar out of him again."

"I need to get back to work."

"You want this to heal right or not?" She finally released his knee, but his hip joint screamed as she slowly lowered his leg to the ground.

"It's healing fine," he said.

Her eyes slid away. "You're strong and healthy. You were in excellent shape before the accident, but there's still a chance…"

"Sure."

"When are you going back to the orthopedist?"

"Two weeks."

"Okay." She stood up, dusting her hands as if Cole were a pet project. "I bet a new CT scan will have more answers. But I can definitely tell you've been doing the exercises."

He stood and stretched his back. "Thanks for coming by this morning. I know you don't have to do that."

"You're a special case." She rolled her eyes, but then smiled brightly. "Really, Cole. I want to help you get back in the saddle as much as Easy does."

"Oh, yeah? Your uncle isn't offering much help."

"You mean he's following doctor's orders because you won't?"

"Jesus, I haven't ridden, have I?" Cole grimaced as he realized he'd snapped at this girl who was like a little cousin to him. "Sorry, Farrah."

"Please. You wouldn't believe the things I hear from my clients. Combinations of words that I shouldn't even know." She grabbed her bag. "Take a hot shower. Loosen everything up. And you're making progress."

"Sure," he murmured as he gave her a farewell hug and let her out the door.

He was doing great. Of course he was. Despite what the experts were saying, he was sure he'd be fine.

As fine as could be expected for a cowboy who might never ride again.

Cole shook his head and ran a hand over his sore thigh. He'd be okay. The doctors were hopeful. The shattered femur was healing and the pelvic fracture would mend. Just in time for him to get back out there to round up the stock for fall.

It would be his last roundup for Easy. Oh, he loved Easy like a father, but Cole was ready to own his own ranch. And Easy was ready to sell. Next year, Cole would be rounding up his own cattle, and Easy would be sipping piña coladas on a Mexican beach.

Chuckling at the thought of Easy relaxing on a beach in his Stetson, Cole headed for the shower.

He made the water as hot as he could stand it, hoping no one else in the building had put too much of a strain on the water heater. One of these days he'd do his exercises, take a hot shower and suddenly feel good. Great. Back to normal. He knew it. But for now, the ache hadn't left. Sometimes it faded to something bearable. Sometimes it swelled into a giant thumping heart in his thigh. The pain was normal, his doctors said. Nothing to be concerned about.

Half an hour later, the ache beaten back to a dull roar, Cole found himself sipping his morning coffee and staring at his door again, waiting for some sign of life from the apartment across the hall.

He hadn't seen her since he'd watched her talk to Rayleen at the saloon. Grace hadn't even noticed him over in the alcove that housed the pool tables. He'd been half irritated by that, and half thankful that he'd gotten the chance to watch her openly.

She was a small woman, with delicate bones, but she held her body as though she was coiled to flee at any moment. Or pounce, maybe. He hoped it was the latter.

But as intriguing as she was, she seemed to have disappeared. He hadn't heard her even once, and they shared a common wall along the hall and bathroom. Jackson was pretty quiet at night, and he'd often heard his previous neighbor moving around, but Grace was silent as a mouse.

Of course, the previous tenant was a drunken college dropout whose number one hobby had been juggling three different girlfriends. At least it had given Cole a soap opera to listen to on sleepless nights.

But where was his new neighbor?

Maybe the deal had fallen through. Maybe Old Rayleen had somehow been under the impression that she was renting the place to a hot nephew. Though... Cole shook his head at the wrongness of that thought.

The old woman was harmless. Eccentric, but harmless. Even the jokes in town meant nothing, which was why everyone thought they were funny. Obviously nothing was going on between Rayleen and her young renters, but with the house being part of the old Studd homestead, the jokes were too easy. Too damn perfect.

And she really never did seem to rent to women.

Cole heard a car door close outside and cocked his head, waiting to see if it was Grace returning from... Where? A boyfriend's house? A very, very late night with a new acquaintance? He found himself slightly irritated at the thought, and couldn't help but smile at his own stupidity. That woman was all passion and attitude. If she wanted to sleep with a different guy every night, she damn sure would, and there'd be no apologies either. He'd be a fool to let it get to him.

Raising his cup to his lips, he realized it was empty. He wanted to have another one, but somehow one cup of coffee made his leg feel better and two made it feel worse. And it was already primed for feeling sore as hell today, between working the day before and physical therapy this morning.

Even during the worst of it, just after surgery, he hadn't been expecting that. That the pain would be so overwhelming. That the injury might be so bad he'd never ride again. He'd been on a horse since he was three. It felt more natural to him than walking. And now, now it felt as though his muscles couldn't quite remember the way to walk naturally, much less direct a horse with the barest of tension. But his muscles weren't really the problem. The problem was the crack that went from his hip joint and halfway up his pelvis. With the shattered femur and the metal holding all that together...

"We're going to have to see," they'd said. "You could do permanent damage in a saddle."

But Cole couldn't accept that. He didn't know how to accept it.

He'd been completely out of work for eight months, and he'd been cleared to work half days only a month before. But for a cowboy, a half day should've been eight hours, with no such thing as a weekend. Cole didn't know what the hell to do with himself.

It was worse now that he was up and around. He was at the ranch most days, watching his old friends do the things he couldn't do. Cole was relegated to the yard and corrals, limping from job to job until Easy told him his four hours were up and he had to leave.

Four hours a day, five days a week. It was shameful.

And how was he supposed to be ready for the roundup when he wasn't allowed to push himself?

He wasn't supposed to go in today, but if he snuck into the tack house and worked a few hours on repairs while everyone else was out checking cattle, he could sneak out before lunchtime. Hell, Easy wouldn't know anything about it. Cole wouldn't get paid, but this wasn't about the money. It was about being where he belonged, doing something useful. And getting his body ready to get back to work full-time.

The front door hadn't opened yet, so Cole assumed the car had been stopping at another house. Which still left the mystery of his new next-door neighbor. He eyed the coffeepot, then the clock. He still had two hours to waste before he could safely sneak onto the ranch.

So, what the hell? A little curiosity never hurt anyone.

He laughed at that. Curiosity had nearly ruined him once. But he'd been a boy then. Stupid and easily controlled by his sense of adventure. And his dick. One and the same, sometimes, and not exactly a moot point when it came to curiosity either.

After all, Grace was beautiful.

Well, not beautiful. That wasn't the word. Not pretty either. Or cute. Not with that wild, choppy hair in chunks of brown and black and purple. And those dark eyes that looked like they absorbed everything and let nothing show through. And her pale, flawless skin. She wasn't pretty—she was striking. Like a kick to the gut. And he hadn't felt that since...

Hell, he hadn't felt that since he was an idiot boy getting his first taste of a girl from the big city. So maybe he hadn't grown up so much after all.

But regardless of where she was from, this wasn't L.A. and he wasn't signing up for a life of debauchery. He was just checking on a neighbor.

So, Cole stood up—purposefully not pressing a hand to his thigh as it screamed—and walked out to knock on her door.

The silence that followed wasn't a good sign. Eight o'clock was late by his standards, but too early for a girl like her, maybe. But the more likely truth was that she wasn't there. She'd disappeared as quickly as she'd shown up. Seemed about right. Rayleen had sent Grace on her way. Those two would probably get along like a couple of feral cats.

Convinced that the place was just as empty as it had been two days before, Cole started to leave, only to swing back around when a muffled voice interrupted the silence. "Who is it?"

"It's Cole," he said, a smile springing so quickly to his face that it startled him. When she didn't respond, he added, "Your neighbor."

The door opened. Not all the way, of course, just enough to reveal Grace standing there glaring at him.

"Good morning," he offered, his eyes dipping to take her in. She was dressed in jeans and a black hoodie, but her feet were bare, aside from the deep blue polish on her toenails.

"Somebody painted over the peephole," she muttered, running a hand through her crazy hair. It stood up in wild layers that somehow made her look younger. Or maybe that was the faded, smeared makeup. But he noticed that her lips were still a deep pink color, even first thing in the morning. That wasn't lipstick. That was just the sweet shade of her mouth.

"The what?" he finally remembered to ask.

"The peephole," she gestured at the door.

"Oh." He looked over his shoulder at his own door. "I guess I never noticed."

"I guess you wouldn't. Did you need something?"

"No. I just wanted to check on you."

"Me?" Her eyes narrowed. "Why?"

"Well, we're neighbors. And I hadn't heard so much as a door shut since I saw you yesterday. I thought maybe Old Rayleen had sent you on your way."

She started to shake her head, and then seemed to be caught by surprise by a huge yawn. Her hand clutched the edge of the door and swung it farther open. The place looked the same as yesterday. Not one piece of furniture or sign of life. The kitchen was dark and quiet.

Cole was craning his neck to look around her when Grace seemed to realize what he was doing and narrowed the opening. But he'd seen enough. None of her stuff was here yet.

"Want a cup of coffee?"

For a second, her dark, fathomless eyes flared with emotion. Something close to lust.

"It's already brewed," he coaxed.

"Mmm." She glanced toward his door, and he knew

she was hoping he'd offer to bring her a cup and leave her alone. Fat chance.

"Come on. We can leave my front door open, since I make you nervous."

"Ha!" Her laugh was rusty and gorgeous. "Why would *you* make me nervous?"

Cole wasn't sure he liked the emphasis she'd put on *you,* but he just smiled. "No idea. But I obviously do."

"That's not nervousness, cowboy. It's called being smart enough not to get behind closed doors with a strange man."

"Strange, huh? I hope you haven't been listening to the stories about me. Half of them aren't even true."

"You wouldn't know strange if it bit you on the ass," she said, but she waved him back and stepped into the hall with a small smile. "Are you going to give me coffee or not?"

"Yes, ma'am," he drawled, tipping an imaginary hat before he moved across the hall to open his door. "I was just about to have breakfast," he lied. He'd eaten almost two hours before, but she didn't seem to have done much shopping yet. "Will you eat bacon and eggs? If you're a vegetarian, I can whip up some toast."

She didn't answer for a few seconds. Cole heard her close the door softly as he headed for the coffeepot.

"Bacon and eggs would be great," she finally said. "And toast, too, if you're offering."

"Sure." He poured her coffee and refilled his own cup. What the hell. A little aching in his thigh was worth spending some time with her. He didn't have anything else interesting going on. And it wouldn't be the first time he'd endured aching for an attractive woman.

Cole put sugar and milk out on the counter, tossed a pan on a burner and grabbed the bacon and eggs. He felt her gaze on his back as he worked. "Over easy okay?" he asked as he laid bacon on the cast iron.

"Great," she answered. "You look like you know what you're doing."

He glanced back to find her seated on a stool, hunched over her coffee as if she was cold. Mornings were chilly up here if you weren't from the mountains. He reached past the fridge to turn up the thermostat. "We all take turns cooking in the bunkhouse."

"Oh, the bunkhouse," she said, making the word sound mysterious. There was nothing mysterious about it, unless you thought cooking and sleeping in what was essentially a live-in locker room was mysterious.

"So what are you doing here?" she asked. "Did you get tired of bunkhouse living?"

Hell, yeah, he was tired of bunkhouse living, but that hadn't been the problem. As a matter of fact, he'd become ranch boss and moved into the boss's house less than a year before.

Cole finished frying the bacon, then set it on a plate and covered it before breaking the eggs into the hot grease. "I was hurt last year," he finally said.

"What happened?"

"A horse landed on my leg."

"Ow."

"Yeah." He wanted to reach down and rub his leg, but he concentrated on the eggs instead.

"So they made you move out?"

The whole complicated story loomed before him. Cole rolled his shoulders. "There's not enough room for guys who aren't working, so, yeah. But I'm getting back to work now. I won't be here much longer."

"Me either."

He put bread in the toaster. "You just got here."

"I'm passing through."

Cole blinked at that, tension tightening his shoulders, but he tried not to let it show. "Who could've guessed you didn't want to settle in Wyoming?"

One of her perfectly sculpted eyebrows rose. "You telling me I don't look like a Wyoming girl?"

"You know damn well you don't look like a Wyoming girl. And that's the way you like it."

Now both eyebrows rose as if she was surprised. Cole piled two plates high with eggs and bacon and toast. He slid the plates across the counter, added forks and knives and paper towels, and joined her at the barstools to find out exactly who she was.

THE MAN WAS SMARTER than he looked. She'd been trying to bait him, force him to say something that she'd find insulting. Instead he'd spoken the truth as if it were obvious to him. Grace wasn't sure what to do with that.

"So how long are you staying?" he asked.

She took a bite of egg instead of answering his question. The flavor melted over her tongue and she hoped

Cole didn't hear the way her stomach growled at the sudden pleasure. "Wow. The eggs are amazing."

"Bacon grease," he said. "What are you doing out here? Working?"

Grace cleared her throat and told herself not to stuff the food into her mouth, but damn, she hadn't had a real meal in days. On the bus, it had been granola bars and chips. She took a bite of bacon and spoke past it. "I already told you. I'm passing through."

"On your way to where?"

"Vancouver."

"Oh." He smiled. "This is a strange route to Vancouver."

She shrugged and made a point of changing the subject. "Thanks so much for breakfast. And coffee. The coffee's great, too. Strong."

She felt his gaze on her, but caught the movement of his head when he finally looked away. "You should try it after it's been sitting at the edge of a campfire all day. That'll wake you up."

She was glad he'd given up the questions, because she wanted to grab her plate and run back to her place so she could shovel the food in the way she wanted to. If he pushed her anymore, that's exactly what she'd do. But he dropped the subject, so she slathered too much butter on the toast and managed to get nearly a fourth of it into her mouth in one bite.

God, she'd been really hungry. Now she wanted to groan in pleasure. Maybe he wasn't so bad. As a matter of fact, at this moment, Cole Rawlins was pretty awesome.

She didn't register how many eggs were on her plate until she dug into the third one. "How many eggs did you make?" she asked.

"Four for you, four for me."

She laughed. "Do I look like I eat as much as you do?"

"You look like you're doing okay, actually."

Grace laughed so hard she almost had to stop eating for a moment. "Didn't I tell you I was a lumberjack back in L.A.?"

"Ah. Of course. You've got that look about you."

Jesus, he was funny. A funny cowboy. Who'd have thunk it. She'd thought they were all silent and brooding. Hell, they'd all definitely been silent and brooding in *Brokeback Mountain*. But she tried not to think about that when she looked at Cole.

"So, you're from L.A."

"Unfortunately."

"What do you do for a living?"

"Nothing right now."

"Did—"

"I think I'm getting full," she interrupted with an apologetic wince. "Want my last egg?"

"No, I'm full myself." He reached for the plate, but Grace couldn't quite bear to let it go, so she snatched the last piece of bacon before he could whisk it away. He put the plate back down. Full or not, her mouth still watered when she bit into the bacon. She tried not to think about how long it had been since her last hot meal. It didn't matter. She'd get a job today. Or the next day. She'd have a check within a week. She'd start paying back the money she owed so she'd never have to think about her ex again.

"You want help moving in?" Cole asked.

"No, I'm fine." Now that she was full, Grace really needed to escape. He kept asking the wrong kinds of questions. Not that there were any right questions. Not about her.

"Come on."

"I don't have much." Or anything. "Anyway, you're injured."

"I think I can handle moving a futon." He gestured as he said that, and Grace could see he was right. His hands were wide, and scars stood out white against the tan. And she was pretty sure she'd never seen such *nice* forearms. Assuming one thought thick and muscled and masculine was nice. She had a brief temptation to touch his arm, to see if the hair was crisp or soft.

"So you'll let me help?" he pressed.

Shit. She hopped off the stool and edged toward the door, away from him and his questions. "I'm good. But thank you for the breakfast. And coffee." She forced herself not to ask for another cup, but it was hard. She'd already taken too much from this man. "I'll see you around."

"Hey."

She stopped halfway out the door, but only because he'd fed her. Anybody else and she would've kept walking. When he didn't say anything, she stuck her head back in to see him writing something down.

"Here's my phone number," he said when he crossed the room.

She didn't reach for it, feeling immediately wary. "You live across the hall. I think I can find you if I need you."

"You know anybody here except Rayleen?"

She met his pale eyes and didn't answer. *Yes, I'm alone and vulnerable. Good for you to know.*

"This isn't L.A." he said. "If you get stuck somewhere at night or your car breaks down in the middle of nowhere, you might not see another car for an hour. So, take my number, all right?"

No, this definitely wasn't L.A. And if he thought she was afraid of something like being alone for an hour, then he didn't know what real fear was.

But he took one step closer and pressed the paper into her hand. When her fingers closed over it, he winked. "In case you need me," he said again, this time with a hint of amusement.

Grace nodded. "All right. I'll call you if I have any cows that need branding, stud."

"Stud? My God, you L.A. women are forward. I think I'm blushing."

She closed the door in his face, and scowled at his laughter as she crossed the hall.

Did he think she'd been flirting with him? He probably did think that. He was undeniably handsome, though totally not her type. Too clean-cut. Too chiseled and…

Okay, he was pretty fantastic-looking, but too confident for his own good. He probably thought she'd add a little exotic city-girl spice to his bed. And he probably thought he'd have no trouble getting her there. But Grace wasn't interested in being his little curiosity. Even if she had any interest in getting laid right now—and she didn't—she wasn't going to be his experiment in edginess. His walk on the wild side. He could just sit over there and wonder.

Wanting to get the coffee taste out of her mouth, Grace headed toward the bathroom, where she'd already unloaded her few supplies and one giant box of cosmetics. But when she flipped on the light and got a look at herself, she froze. She'd forgotten to take off her makeup last night, and it had smeared into a crooked mask around her eyes. She suddenly had to consider that Cole's laughter hadn't been flirtation at all. Maybe it had just been pure amusement.

Damn.

CHAPTER FOUR

GRACE WAS NERVOUS. She didn't like being nervous. It made her grumpy and defensive, which wasn't the best attitude for a job interview.

Not that this was exactly a job interview. She'd caught the bus to the other side of town and was now sitting in Eve Hill's photography studio, waiting for her to finish reviewing proofs with someone. Or she assumed that was what was going on behind the closed door at the far side of the room. That's what the sign on the front door had said. The low murmur of voices was a soothing sound, at least.

So far, so good. There were the obligatory bride portraits on a side wall, but for the most part, the pictures were a mix of landscape shots, publicity stills for businesses and some truly amazing fashion shoots that had been done with the mountains in the background and frost covering everything except the models.

This woman was good. Really good.

Grace smoothed down her tight black pants, wishing she'd had an iron. She'd hung her nicest clothes up in the bathroom and turned the shower to hot, but now she felt self-conscious about the slate-blue sweater. Maybe it was the wrong choice. It had been knitted to look ancient and torn apart and shot through with muted grays as if it had faded in the sun. Slightly risky for a job interview, but Grace was counting on the complex beauty of the wool to catch the photographer's eye. The sweaters normally sold for three hundred dollars a pop at the upscale farmer's market in La Jolla, but the knitter was a friend who'd given Grace one as a present. It was her favorite piece of clothing. Ever. But maybe it had been a mistake. Maybe in Wyoming a raggedy sweater was just a raggedy sweater that no one would pay two dollars for. Maybe it looked like something she'd pulled from the trash can behind an L.A. soup kitchen.

God. She should go home and change.

Grace stood up, but then froze without moving toward the door.

Change into what, exactly? The signed Dead Kennedys T-shirt she'd bought at a garage sale last year? The silk tunic with the hand-screened Vargas pinup girl that curved up the hip in vivid colors?

Actually, maybe. Maybe a photographer would appreciate Vargas. Or maybe she'd consider it no better than soft porn.

"Damn it," Grace muttered softly. She didn't like this. Trying to *please* people. Worrying how to make a good first impression. She'd put up with this sort of thing for the past year, thanks to Scott, but what the hell did it have to do with how great she was with makeup? And she was great. Anyone in L.A. would be lucky to have her as a makeup artist, much less someone in Jackson, Wyoming. So why was her confidence shaking like a leaf?

Maybe because this felt like a last chance.

It wasn't, though. She could work at a restaurant. A gas station. She could clean hotel rooms. Anything. But those jobs would all pay minimum wage. How long would it take her to pay back an eight-thousand-dollar debt at that kind of wage?

The white door opened and a pair of female voices swelled through the room. Grace decided to bolt. This whole thing was a ridiculous idea. But when she started to move, her boot hit the portfolio she'd set on the ground. She caught herself, but wobbled on the four-inch heel of her nicest boots. In that moment, she had to make a decision, and instead of falling face-first in her attempt to escape, she settled on flopping back into her chair and staying put. She had just enough time to straighten up before the women glanced her way.

Grace took a breath to steady herself, then grabbed the portfolio and stood. A woman with a long brown ponytail offered a smile before saying goodbye to the older woman she was with. "I'll call you with the numbers tomorrow, all right? Hi," she said as she walked toward Grace. "How can I help you?"

"I'm Grace Barrett." She held out her hand and thought very hard about the pressure of her handshake.

"I'm Eve Hill. It's nice to meet you. What can I do for you, Grace?"

"Jenny from the, um, saloon? She gave me your name."

"The saloon?"

"I'm sorry. I don't know what it's called. It's right next to the…" She swallowed. "Stud Farm?"

"Oh, *Jenny!* Of course. That's the Crooked R Saloon.

After Rayleen, I think. Anyway, are you looking for a photographer?"

"No, actually. I'm a makeup artist. I don't know how much work you'd have for someone like me, but I brought my portfolio, if you'd be interested in taking a look. I've been working in L.A. for almost ten years. I just got to Jackson yesterday."

Eve took the portfolio. "You're planning to stay?"

"I'm not sure yet." It was a lie, but at least she wasn't promising to settle down.

"Why don't we sit down and I'll take a look."

"Sure. Thank you."

She followed Eve to the conference room and sat across the table from her, watching as she paged through the book of photos. This part didn't make her nervous, at least. Her work was good. So she was free to study the photographer. Eve looked about thirty-five. Pretty in an unassuming way. She didn't wear much makeup, but didn't really need it. Her dark hair contrasted nicely with her faintly tanned skin. Her hazel eyes were wide-set and interesting, though she looked the slightest bit tired.

"You're really good," Eve said when she looked up.

"Thank you."

"So, what are you doing in Jackson?"

Well, she wasn't subtle. Grace liked that. "I needed a change."

Eve nodded, and her gaze roamed unself-consciously over Grace, taking her in. The wild hair. The tattered sweater. "I'm not sure I have steady work for you in makeup. Brides, sure. Right now they just get their makeup done at local salons, but they don't always understand what's best for photos. I spend a lot of time touching up the prints."

Grace was nodding already. It was what she'd expected to hear, after all.

"But…" Eve said just as Grace was about to pitch herself for whatever freelance work she could get. "A lot of these are modeling shots and movie stills. You obviously know the industry."

"Yes."

"You know how the business works?"

"Yes."

"So maybe you could do something more for me."

"How so?"

"I do some work setting up shoots for the industry. Magazines. Movie stills. That kind of thing. Right now, I have a lot of that and then some. More than I can handle. You know the players. You know the language and politics. If you'd consider taking some of that on, in addition to the occasional makeup job, we might be able to try something out."

Grace was too shocked to say anything for a few long seconds. This woman wanted to give her a chance? This woman wanted to take a risk on a girl with purple hair, a bad attitude and a completely unknown past? Why?

When Grace didn't answer, Eve cleared her throat. "If you really don't want to do the other work, I'd be happy to call you when I need a makeup artist for weddings. And sometimes there are big charity events that—"

"No! It's not that. I've just never done that kind of work before, but I'd be happy to try." Would she? She had no idea.

"How much do you charge for freelancing?"

"In L.A., I charged a hundred dollars an hour for freelance beauty work, but I'm quick, so I'm never more than thirty minutes. Usually less. But here…forty dollars a session?"

"I think that's fair. You'll be totally freelance. I won't ask for a cut. But there's no way I can pay more than fifteen dollars an hour for the office work, and the hours will be part-time."

"That's fine," Grace said. Fifteen dollars an hour was a hell of a lot more than zero. And more than she'd make as a grumpy waitress. She knew that from experience.

"Great!" Eve said, reaching out to shake Grace's hand again. "I'll do a background check, so I hope that's okay. With all this equipment and so much seasonal employment, I make it standard practice."

"Of course." In L.A., a criminal check was assumed. And Grace's record was surprisingly clean, or it had been since she'd turned eighteen, anyway. But now… Oh, God. She hoped she'd been able to appease Scott. What if he'd changed his mind since she'd called him? What if he—

"Thank you so much," she made herself say. "When do you want me to start?"

"How about Monday? Come in at nine. I can't always promise you a lot of hours, but I've got an unexpectedly busy week, so can you stay until five?"

"Yes. Absolutely." Grace left feeling…excited.

Maybe Wyoming wasn't so bad. Maybe she'd have good luck while she was here.

Maybe the man she'd left behind in L.A. had been the last stupid mistake of her life.

CHAPTER FIVE

OR MAYBE NOT.

She walked around town for a while, avoiding the tourist area for streets lined with lower-end shops, hoping to find a used sporting-goods store where she could buy a cot. Though she finally found a store, apparently used camping gear was in hot demand here in the summer, just outside the boundaries of Yellowstone and the Grand Tetons. The only cot she'd found had been way over her ten-dollar budget.

In the end, she left with a cheap camouflage sleeping bag more suited for sleepovers than outdoor use. Fine with her. She just needed a little padding between her and the floor.

When she got her first paycheck, maybe she'd come back for the air mattress she'd spotted. Maybe even a folding chair. But nothing else she wouldn't be able to take to Vancouver when she left.

By the time she'd stopped at a grocery store for bread and peanut butter and walked all the way back to her apartment, it was after three. And the saloon next door was already hopping. Grace dropped her bags in the apartment and walked over to thank Jenny.

Before she got down the front steps, the tones of an unfamiliar ringer cut through the air. She frowned for a moment before realizing that it was her own cheapo prepaid phone and dug it from her bag.

"Hello?" she asked with obvious suspicion.

"Grace! Oh, my God, we haven't talked in almost a week. Are you in Wyoming? Do you have any minutes left?"

Grace smiled as the voice of her best friend traveled from a satellite and made her sound like she was standing right there. "Merry," she said in utter relief. "Yeah, I've got minutes. What's up, chick?"

"What's up? Oh, my God, tell me what's going on! The last time I talked to you, you had some sort of plan to go be a mountain man or something. And I haven't been able to get through since!"

"It's this phone," she said, which was only partly true. Mostly, she'd been avoiding her best friend. "I have to keep it off or the battery dies. I'm sorry. Everything's good. I'm in Jackson. It's beautiful."

"Beautiful? Really? Where's Grace Barrett and what have you done with her?"

"Ha. Yes, the mountains are pretty, the people are friendly in an almost noncreepy way, and I just got a job."

Merry squealed. "I'm so glad! You actually sound happy!"

"Bite your tongue. But happy or not, it's really still me. I plan to ditch this joint in a month or so."

"Are you coming to Dallas? Please tell me you're coming to Dallas."

"Merry, we've discussed this. Texas is not the place for me."

"Oh, my God, you're in *Wyoming,* for godssake! And you love it, apparently. How can you dismiss Texas?"

"I don't love it," Grace insisted. "I just have a free place to stay. So stop pouting."

"I'm not pouting," Merry said, very obviously pouting.

"You are, but it's cute."

"I just don't understand why you couldn't come live with me."

"I need to be in Vancouver in a few weeks," Grace explained. "Texas is a little out of the way. Listen, I should go—"

"No! You haven't told me anything!"

Grace winced in guilt.

"Please tell me what happened. You were trying to get organized so you could get work at L.A. Fashion Week. Then all of a sudden you were leaving town."

"Nothing happened," she lied. "I lined up this job in Vancouver and then my aunt offered me the apartment, so I decided there was no point hanging around L.A. That's it."

"Grace." Her flat voice made Grace's throat burn with shame. Merry knew it was a lie, but Grace couldn't tell her the truth. She just couldn't.

"I'm good," Grace said. "Really good." That might be an exaggeration, but she embraced it. "In fact, I'm on my way to a saloon to celebrate the new job."

That distracted Merry, as Grace had known it would. Merry loved shiny things, and a saloon was awfully shiny. "What?" she chirped. "A saloon? You're lying!"

"I'm not. It's literally next door to my apartment. There are cowboys in it."

"In your apartment?"

She laughed. "No, not at the moment."

Merry missed that little hint, and Grace couldn't help but grin. If she knew Grace's new neighbor was a sexy hot cowboy with thighs of steel, Merry would squeal loud enough to break the cheap phone. Grace was going to save that little tidbit for a day when she needed cheering up. Merry's joy was medicine for Grace. Something she needed to take like a vitamin when she was feeling low.

"All right," Merry huffed. "Go flirt with some cute cowboys for me. But call me soon, okay? I miss you."

Grace was smiling as she hung up. Merry had wanted Grace to stay with her, but Grace had stayed with her twice when they'd both lived in L.A. Accepting help once was too much. Twice was unbearable. A third time? No. Never. She'd rather sleep in the bus station.

In fact, she *had* slept in the bus station. But only for one night. Before that, she'd managed to find an old friend who'd owed her a favor. Unfortunately, staying at his place had been the worst mistake of all. He'd had an insane party, and someone had stolen her purse and everything in it, including Scott's money.

Why the hell had she taken it? She should've just walked away with the lie that he didn't owe her anything.

She'd really screwed herself over now. But she couldn't tell Merry this time. At some point, Merry would decide Grace was a loser with too many problems who needed to be ditched.

Merry didn't need someone like Grace hanging around, after all. Her name actually matched her personality. She was sweet and happy and kind. And a little awkward in a cute way. But for some reason, she loved Grace. In fact, aside from Grandma Rose, Merry was the only person in the world who loved her, and Grace would be damned if she'd ever do anything to damage that. Ever.

Grace tucked her phone away and walked over to the saloon. She didn't plan on having a drink. But Jenny offered her a celebratory shot of tequila. And then a beer on the house.

"I can't," Grace protested.

"Come on. It's not every day I find someone a job."

Grace started to shake her head.

"And it annoys the hell out of Rayleen when I give away beer."

"Well, in that case."

Jenny laughed and slid her a beer. "I'm so happy for you."

"You don't even know me!" Grace said, shaking her head in exasperation.

"Of course I do. You're Rayleen's grandniece, Grace."

"That's not what I mean," she said, but she took the beer. "Thank you. Really."

"Maybe sometime you can teach me how to do my makeup."

"Your makeup is fine."

"I never know what to do with my eyes," she said. "My eyelids are fat, and now that I'm getting older, they just look puffy."

Grace laughed and shook her head, but it was the kind of thing she heard all the time. A lot of women felt helpless about makeup. "Let me know when you want some tips."

"I will. I feel self-conscious around you!"

"That's ridiculous," Grace said, and she meant it. She was the one who always felt self-conscious. Not about her looks. She wasn't pretty, but she didn't mind. She did what she could to make sure people knew who she was before they even approached her. She wanted them to know that she wasn't like other girls, so they wouldn't be surprised by that. She wasn't soft or sweet or comforting, especially these days. She didn't know how to be taken care of, much less how to take care of others. She took care of herself. She always had.

No matter what the cost, apparently.

When her thoughts veered back to L.A., Grace gulped down half her beer. She didn't want to think about that. She didn't want to, but how could she avoid it?

The truths she'd known about herself, the few things she'd been proud of… She'd thrown all that away.

No, that wasn't right. She hadn't even been strong enough to throw them away. She'd just dropped them, let them scatter in the wind. Her pride, her strength, the weapons she'd armed herself with every single day of her life. All the success she'd carved out of this world through blood, sweat and tears—she'd given that up.

Grace Barrett, a girl who'd never needed anyone… she'd let herself need *him*.

The worst part was, she'd be in the exact same place right now if she'd left him on her own terms. She'd have nothing and no one, just as she did now. But she'd also have her pride. And everything she'd ever believed about herself.

She'd have that.

Now she had less than nothing. Now she didn't even know who she was. She certainly wasn't the tough, kick-ass girl who wouldn't take shit from anyone. She'd taken plenty of shit from Scott. She'd put her head down and kept her mouth shut, and she'd taken it. And on top of everything, she'd been reduced to living on the edge again. Just like when she'd been sixteen.

One stupid mistake on top of all those others, and ten years of progress had vanished in a snap.

Fuck.

Her beer wasn't quite finished, but Grace was. She stood, meaning to rush out, but as she turned, her head swam as though the floor was tilting beneath her. "Oh," she breathed, reaching toward the large shoulder that entered her blurry vision.

"Careful, darlin'," a deep voice said.

"Sorry. I…" She blinked and her vision cleared. And there was Cole, smiling at her, his eyes shaded by an honest-to-goodness cowboy hat. Or maybe all cowboys looked alike.

"Grace? You okay?"

Yeah, it was definitely him. She jerked her hand away and stood straight. "I'm fine."

"More than fine, I'd say."

"I'm not drunk! I only had one beer." And a tequila shot.

"It's the altitude. You've got to be careful."

"I'm fine," she protested, even though she wasn't sure. She did feel awfully tipsy. Maybe it was the altitude. Or maybe it was that she hadn't eaten anything since breakfast. Or had a drink in weeks.

Damn. She was drunk.

"You look great," Cole said, his eyes traveling quickly down her body.

She was suddenly glad she was wearing her heeled boots. They gave her four extra inches of leg. But what did that matter? She wasn't trying to impress this man.

Then she had a sudden flashback to that morning. To looking at herself in the mirror and seeing the mascara under her eyes and her hair standing up in clumps. Oh, my God. "This morning," she stammered. "I didn't realize…"

A man cleared his throat from somewhere close by. "This morning, huh?" he said.

She shot a glare at the man who now stood at Cole's shoulder. His mouth was serious, but his eyes tilted up a little in subtle amusement. She was opening her mouth to tell him to fuck off, when Cole interrupted.

"Grace, this is Shane. He lives upstairs. Shane, this is Grace. Our new neighbor."

"Oh!" His brown eyes widened. "Pleased to meet you. I heard there was a woman amongst us. Welcome."

"Thank you," she said stiffly, still prepared not to like him.

Cole elbowed his friend. Hard. "Apologize. You pissed her off with your stupid attempt to be funny."

"Sorry," Shane said, touching the brim of his hat. "I'm an idiot."

He grimaced so sincerely that Grace almost laughed. Almost. But she didn't want him to think he was off the hook.

"So what were you saying about this morning?" Cole continued. "Something about how the breakfast was spectacular, but the company far surpassed it?"

"No, I..." She looked from him to his friend and narrowed her eyes.

Shane put up his hands. "All right, I know when I'm not wanted. I'll be over here. Out of firing range."

She watched him walk away, and suddenly Cole's voice was in her ear. "I think he's scared of you."

She turned and felt his chin brush her hair before he drew back. "He should be scared of me. So should you."

"Yeah? How come? The purple hair?" He carefully reached up and rubbed a lock of her hair between his thumb and finger, then withdrew before she could knock his hand away.

"No."

"The black suede pants?"

"They're not suede, they're just brushed to look... No. Not that either."

He leaned closer again, and she felt very alone with him beneath the shadow of his hat. "Is it the way you look like you could punch me and enjoy it? Or the way your dark eyes get even darker when you're really mad?"

Grace inhaled sharply at the husky appreciation in his words. She thought she might have swayed closer and hoped it was only the beer affecting her vision. "No, I...I just meant that if you weren't nice I'd come by and hang out in the morning again."

"And why would I be scared of that, Miss Grace?"

Yeah, his voice was definitely husky. And she was definitely swaying. Damn those drinks. She cleared her throat and stood as straight as she could. "You should be scared because of how I looked this morning."

"You looked fine. Cute."

"Cute? You've got to be fu—"

"Cole!" Jenny's voice called from behind her. "You look tired. Want the usual, babe?"

"Thanks, Jenny," he said, his smile widening when he looked past Grace's shoulder. It was just the moment she needed to escape the pull of his low voice and warm smile. And the intimacy of looking up at him under the shadow of his hat. Secret cowboy trick, probably.

Had she actually been succumbing to the flirtations of a *cowboy?* Wow. Altitude, indeed.

She steeled her spine. "Anyway, I'll see you around, all right?"

"Hey, where are you going? I was about to buy you a drink."

"After you just warned me to take it easy?"

A moment of male confusion flashed over his face, but he recovered quickly. "A soda then. Or just some water. It's important to drink lots of water here or you'll get headaches."

"Thanks, but I was going to buy myself a glass of water back at my apartment. Maybe see if I get lucky. Afternoon, cowboy." She touched a hand to an imaginary hat, mimicking the movement she'd found so amusing yesterday.

As she walked away, she was aware of his eyes on

her. She knew he was watching. She knew it because he'd noticed her boots and the soft fabric of her black jeans within moments of saying hello. What she didn't know, what she couldn't even begin to comprehend, was why the knowledge of his eyes on her filled her chest with such a hot burn of satisfaction.

"WELL, NOW," SHANE drawled when he stepped up to join Cole at the bar. "Somebody likes playing with fire."

Cole took a swig from his waiting beer and shot a look at the saloon door that had just closed behind Grace. "I'm not playing with anything."

"Oh, but you'd like to. By the way, you've got a little drool on your chin. Might want to wipe that off."

Cole rolled his eyes.

"You really like that girl? She looks kind of tough."

"She is tough," he said, smiling at the memory of her kicking the shit out of her own bag.

"She looks like she could cut my balls off without flinching."

"As long as it's your balls she's cutting and not mine, she can amuse herself any way she likes."

Shane shook his head. "To each his own, brother. I'm just saying there are plenty of nice girls around here who you don't have to wear a cup around. That woman looks like trouble."

Hell, yeah, she looked like trouble. Cole's eyes skimmed over the room, taking in only vague impressions of the women at the tables. They all looked so dull. Nice, yes. And normal. Blondes and brunettes and the occasional redhead. Not a strand of purple among them.

No smoky-black eyeliner that made them look dangerous and vulnerable all at the same time. No black and
gray and blue outfits that covered everything but somehow looked sexy as hell.

Yeah, Grace looked tough. Which had made it that
much sweeter when her black-brown eyes had softened for a moment. When she'd looked up at him and
swayed the tiniest bit closer. Her lips had parted as if
she'd needed more room to draw a breath.

Cole cleared his throat and shifted on the barstool,
wondering if he really did have drool on his chin, because his mouth was sure as hell watering. He downed
his beer and signaled for another. Jenny winked and
grabbed another mug.

"What do you hear about Grace?" he asked when she
brought his second beer.

"Cole Rawlins, are you fishing for information about
another woman from your *ex-girlfriend?* Don't you
think that's a little rude?"

He smiled at her mock outrage. "We dated for all of
two minutes. Now, spill it."

"Grace, huh?" Her eyes sparkled. "She doesn't exactly seem like your type, Cole."

"No?" He didn't bother correcting her. He wasn't sure
he had a type, but girls like Grace just pushed his buttons. Or they'd pushed the hell out of his buttons thirteen
years ago. As often as he'd been able to talk them into it.

"She just got into town yesterday, but you know that
already, right?"

"Yeah."

"She's Rayleen's niece from L.A. A makeup artist."

That got his attention. Maybe she was part of the film industry after all. Shit. "A makeup artist? Like special effects and stuff? In the movies?"

Jenny frowned. "No, I think the kind that make women beautiful. Maybe she worked with models? She just got a job with Eve Hill, and I don't think Eve would have any demand for zombie makeup."

Cole felt a warm wash of relief. She wasn't with a film crew. She wasn't part of that world.

And no wonder she'd been so embarrassed about her smeared makeup that morning. He'd have to tease her about it now. See if he could get a rise out of her.

He chuckled at the thought. Not *if* he could get a rise out of her, but just how pissed off he could make her.

"Cole?" Jenny said softly. "You're smiling to yourself. You really like this girl?"

"Hardly know her," he responded.

"Yeah," she huffed. "And that usually deters men, right? How's your leg?"

He pressed his hand to his thigh automatically, then realized he hadn't thought about it once since the moment he'd seen Grace sitting at the bar. He hadn't even thought about it when he'd taken a seat, and usually he had to concentrate on not wincing. "Great," he answered, telling the lie he always told.

"Back to normal?"

"Just about."

"Well, you look tired."

Truth be told, he hadn't had a decent night's sleep in nine months. His leg and hip throbbed every time he closed his eyes. "I'm back at the ranch now."

"Speaking of…" Jenny said, raising her chin toward the door.

Cole turned and narrowed his eyes against the daylight. The shaft of light narrowed as the door closed, and Easy was walking toward him. Though the man was only sixty-five, he looked closer to seventy. He was still lean and wiry, but all those years under the open sky had weathered his skin and turned his crew cut silvery-blond. His pale eyes locked on Cole and he glared.

"Were you out at the ranch today?" he demanded.

Ah, shit. Cole stood up and set his beer on the bar. He wouldn't lie to Easy, so he kept his mouth shut and crossed his arms.

"Damn it, Cole! You know what the doctor said."

Quiet fell around them. Cole tipped his head. "Let's talk outside."

"We're not talking about anything. Come in on Tuesday. You're taking Monday off."

"Goddamn it," Cole snarled. "I can handle it. I'm doing fine."

"What you're doing is fooling yourself. But you're not fooling me. If you don't do what—"

"I get that, all right? I'm not a child, Easy. Let me do it the way I need to."

"Tuesday," Easy said. "And if it happens again, I'll do the same thing."

Christ. This was outrageous. Easy walked away, though he paused to tip his hat to Rayleen on the way out. Cole glared, but he let Easy go without cursing him out for being a mother hen instead of a ranch boss.

Easy cared about him. He knew that. But Cole knew his body and what he could handle. Sure, his thigh hurt. And now his back and his hip, but what the hell was he supposed to do? Lounge around in bed? It all hurt there, too. May as well make himself useful. And he needed to get back in shape. Quick.

He had insurance that had paid for the surgery and hospitalization. But half the physical therapy was coming out of his pocket. Not to mention rent and food and drugs. He had the money to cover it, but that money was supposed to be locked up in a safe for the day he bought Easy's ranch. He'd finally saved up enough, but every month out of work was one step backward. Cole wanted to be ready the moment Easy said he was ready to sell.

If his leg hadn't quite healed yet, it could heal on the job. Hell, how many old cowboys did he know who limped around for forty years? Easy himself was a damned pile of old breaks and busted-up joints, and he could barely sit in a saddle for an hour. That was the way it went for old cowboys.

"Maybe you're pushing too hard," Shane said, interrupting Cole's internal diatribe.

Cole pressed his lips together.

"You were looking better last week. Now you look tired."

"Just getting back in the swing of things," Cole said. "And maybe all that snoring from your place upstairs is keeping me awake."

"I don't snore. At least, your mama never said anything about it."

"Really?" Cole asked, forcing his shoulders to relax as he leaned against the bar. "A your-mama joke, huh?"

Shane tipped his beer. "I know how to bring it."

"That's not what my mama said."

"Touché." Shane signaled for another beer, but Cole held up his hand to let Jenny know that he wasn't joining in. It was only four o'clock, and he was so damn tired. If he had another beer, he'd go home and fall asleep. And he knew from experience that meant he'd wake up around midnight and not get another wink the rest of the night.

The two beers ensured his anger wouldn't quite bubble over, anyway. He was too tired and too relaxed. But he couldn't believe the way Easy was acting. The man knew how much the work meant to Cole. Jesus.

He needed to get back out there. For the money, yes. For his savings and his plans and dreams. But he also needed to get his life back.

For the past nine months he'd been a patient. Doing nothing but reading and watching TV and *waiting* to get back to work. And now he was so damn close, and the one person in the world who'd always supported him was blocking his way.

Jenny came to take the cash he set down. "You sure you're okay, Cole?" she asked quietly.

He smiled at Jenny and offered a wink. "I'm good."

"You're quiet, is what you are. That's not like you."

"Come around the bar and I'll slap you on the ass. Will that make you happy?"

"Nah." She laughed. "But I bet it would brighten your day."

"Damn straight."

When he stood to leave, hiding his wince, Jenny patted his hand. "Take it easy out there, all right? I don't want you falling off a horse again and rebreaking that leg."

"I didn't fall off a horse," he growled. "It fell and pinned me."

"Fell?" Shane interrupted. "I hear that horse went down so slow it looked like a dog taking a seat. I don't know why you didn't get out of the way."

Cole elbowed him hard enough that some of Shane's beer sloshed out of the mug. "You weren't even there."

"Pretty sure I'm right, though."

"Hey, Cole," Jenny said as he turned away. "There's a big group of Hollywood people in town up at Teton. You know any of them?"

Cole made sure he didn't stiffen. "Why would I?" he asked with a deliberately puzzled smile.

"You lived out there for a while, didn't you? You were in a movie, even. Some Western?"

"That was a long time ago, Jenny. And nobody lasts in Hollywood. Anybody I knew is long gone by now."

"I'm sure you're right." Jenny sighed. "I just think it'd be neat to meet someone famous. Nobody cool ever comes in here."

"Hey," Shane responded. "What about me?"

She slapped Shane with her towel and winked at Cole. "Bye, then. Have a good evening."

"I will."

Hollywood people. He felt another moment of anxiety as he stepped out of the saloon and into the blindingly

"Yeah?" She hunched over the cup, and Cole reached for the thermostat again. "Who'd you hear that from?"

"Jenny." He figured it wouldn't hurt to be extra sure, so he asked again. "So, what are you doing out here?"

"Seeing the world."

"Yeah? And you decided to start with the middle of Wyoming?"

She glared at him through the steam that rose from her cup. Today, her makeup was perfect. Apparently, she'd already been up and put it on. A secret vanity. Interesting.

"What kind of work did you do in L.A.?"

"The makeup kind."

When she didn't elaborate, Cole just looked at her until she slumped a little and conceded. As if telling him about herself was a defeat. "I worked in fashion a little, but mostly in the movies."

Ah, shit. It didn't matter, he told himself. It wasn't like the movie industry had screwed him over and broken his heart. It had been a woman and his own poor judgment. And if Grace's toughness and edginess reminded him a little of his ex-lover—not to mention a few other women he'd met in L.A.—then he just needed to be aware. Aware that he shouldn't trust people who hadn't earned it. Aware that he shouldn't let himself be used. Aware that sometimes strength meant hardness, and coolness was cruelty.

But right at this moment, Grace didn't look hard or cool. Her brown eyes seemed lighter against the black liner this morning, but still fascinatingly deep. Unknowable. Which only made him more determined to know her. "Why'd you leave L.A.?" he pressed.

She shrugged one shoulder as if it didn't matter to her in the least. "I got fired. I decided to move on."

"Fired? What'd you do? Punch someone?"

"Not this time, no."

Cole was glad he didn't have any coffee in his mouth. He choked on nothing instead. "When did you last punch somebody?"

"At work? Probably five years ago."

He looked down at her small, pale hands. They didn't look like much, but she was wearing a couple of clunky rings that might do damage. "I had no idea Hollywood was a more glamorous version of a cage fight. Or a bunkhouse, come to think of it."

"I don't like it when men stick their hands up my skirt."

"They do that often, do they?"

"Not after that," she said with a grin.

He winked and turned away to finish off the eggs. What idiot would be stupid enough to try something like that? Grace Barrett looked like she'd shove a makeup brush up your ass if you touched her without invitation. Then again, he knew firsthand that some people in Hollywood were so arrogant and narcissistic that signals ceased to exist for them. A fist across the jaw was the most subtle thing they could understand.

"So this time?" he asked as he piled two plates high. "What happened this time?"

"I said I'd already eaten."

Her words didn't match up with the light in her eyes

as he slid the plate toward her. He wanted to tell her she wasn't in L.A. anymore and she could eat real food now. But he knew enough about women to lie. "I was already cooking. It's the light plate today. Only three eggs and no toast."

"You really do eat like a lumberjack," she said, though she dug into her eggs right away.

"Lumberjacks are pussies."

She slapped a hand to her mouth to cover her laugh, and that made Cole smile so hard he felt like a fool. It felt like triumph, making this girl laugh. Like a prize. He couldn't imagine what it would feel like to make her moan. Damn.

"So what got you fired this time?" he pressed. He didn't have to be told that she was an expert at dropping subjects. But she gave in more or less gracefully this time.

"I was working on a movie set. I'd been doing pretty well this year, trying to keep my head down."

"No punching?"

"No punching. And I got an amazing gig, working on a big film. Working with the stars of a big film, not just the secondaries, you know? I won't say who it is, but the starring actress is one of America's sweethearts. And she seemed perfectly nice. Quiet. Polite. And with a couple of fading bruises on her neck. Whatever, though. People are kinky. If she liked a little choking during sex, it's none of my business."

Cole coughed and reached for his coffee as his eyes watered. "Sure," he finally managed to say.

"But one day the producer came to the trailer while

I was working on her. He was her boyfriend. It was an open secret. And she flinched when he gestured. That was it. Just a tiny flinch I wouldn't have noticed if I hadn't been working on her eyes. The next week, her lip was a little swollen. And when he came to the trailer and started berating her about something, I couldn't keep myself from calling him on it."

"The producer."

She glared at him. "An abusive ass is an abusive ass."

Cole raised a conciliatory hand. "I agree. I'm just impressed you were brave enough to say something."

Grace snorted. "It's not bravery. I don't think about it. I just blow up. Anyway, I cursed him out and told him what I thought of him. He fired me immediately."

"And?" he asked, aware of the weight in her words.

"And I told him I'd file a complaint with the union. He said he'd ruin my career, and I said I'd tell the press. Unfortunately, I was the one who was bluffing."

"You didn't tell anyone?"

"Nobody would've cared. I could've told the tabloids about what I'd seen, and who would it have hurt? Her, maybe. Definitely me. And definitely *not* him, because he would've found some way to prove it wasn't true. So here I am."

"You couldn't get another job?"

"It was complicated. And the word is out that I drink on the job."

His eyebrows flew up. "Do you?"

"No. Never. I rarely even drink at parties."

"Only in saloons?" he asked.

She smiled. "Only in saloons."

"Lucky me."

"Yeah." She'd stopped eating, and when her smile faded, she stared at her plate.

"Hey, Grace?"

"What?"

"I'm sorry about that. You being fired by that asshole."

When she looked up, he saw surprise in her eyes. Just a brief, bright flash, and then it was hidden by old anger. "It's no big deal. Nothing new. I've got to learn how to keep my mouth shut."

"Maybe not. You did the right thing."

"Ha. The right thing. It didn't help her. I probably made it worse. You should have seen her scrambling to defuse the situation. Begging me to stop. It was all about me, wasn't it? Me telling myself that I'm not the kind of person who'd just stand by while a man treated a woman like a worthless dog. The worst part? Turns out I'm exactly that kind of person."

"No, you're not. You said something. You didn't just sit there and ignore it because you were scared."

She smiled again. A grimace of a smile, bitter and hurt. And then she jumped to her feet. "Thank you for breakfast. Again."

"Hey, wait. What are you doing today?"

She was already walking toward the door, her bare feet silent against the wood. She was so much smaller without her heels. "I'll probably walk around town some more. See what there is to see."

"Ah. The antlers."

She stopped with her hand on the doorknob. "The what?"

"The antlers. Haven't you seen the antler arches yet?"

Her expression defaulted to grumpy again. "I have no idea what you're talking about."

"I don't know how you missed them. They're right in the town square."

"Antlers?"

"Yes. Elk antlers. Thousands of them. The National Elk Refuge comes all the way up to the city limits."

"And there are elk there?"

"Not right now, but they're around if you drive up into the mountains. They come down to the refuge during the winter."

"And bring their antlers?"

He grinned. "Something like that, yes."

"Oh." She didn't leave. Her hand was still on the doorknob, but she just stood there looking thoughtful.

"Want to go for a drive? I'll show you around. There's a lot more to see than just the town, you know."

She glanced in the direction of the Tetons, even though the blinds were closed.

"Come on. It'll be fun."

"Aren't you busy?"

"Nope. I'm off work today, so it's either you or laundry."

"I win out over laundry, huh?"

"Only because I did a load last weekend. Otherwise it'd be laundry all the way."

That relaxed her. An insult. That was what soothed her prickly stance and made her laugh. Another thing that set her apart from the women of his past. "Then I'd better take you up on it. I might not be so lucky next weekend, and I'll go crazy if I stay cooped up any longer."

"Come back when you're ready, then."

She was back in three minutes. Cole was still washing the dishes and shouted for her to come in.

"I'm sorry. I should've stayed to help, right? People don't cook for me very often. Let me…"

"Believe me. It's no big deal. A lot easier than cleaning a stew pot on the trail, I can tell you that."

"I'm sorry," she said again, sounding as if the words scraped her throat as they came out.

"You can make me dinner sometime."

She looked slightly panicked. "I hope you like sandwiches."

"Peanut butter?" he asked.

Grace's cheeks flamed red. "I haven't had time for a real shopping trip," she said sharply.

Yikes. "I was just kidding."

She crossed her arms and wandered over to look at the books on his coffee table. By the time Cole dried his hands, her cheeks had faded to pink. He was glad he hadn't been standing next to her and made a note to himself that she had some sort of peanut butter trigger. Maybe peanut butter was her secret high-calorie indulgence. If he was going to piss her off—and he wasn't averse to that—he wanted it to be over something worthwhile.

"Ready?" he asked.

She put down the book she'd been looking at, but her eyes stayed on it.

"You like horror novels? I'm done with that if you want to read it."

"Yeah?" She picked it back up again and opened it to the first page. "Was it good?"

"His best in years."

"Okay, sure. Thanks." She slipped it into her purse and shrugged her jacket on. "I'll bring it back tomorrow."

"Tomorrow?"

"I read fast."

"An expensive habit."

"Yeah," she said. "The library. Anyway, I'm not a resident here, so…"

"I'll check some out for you if you like. Give me a list."

She glanced at him as she passed him on the way out the door. "You've got a library card?"

"Sometimes they let cowboys in on free range days."

"With fair warning to the public, I hope."

God, she made him laugh. He wanted to push and goad her just to see what she'd say next. She might be a touch prickly, but, hell, talking to Grace, he felt more awake than he'd been in months.

WHAT THE HECK was she doing hanging out with the cowboy again? When she'd walked out of that saloon yesterday—being very careful not to sway or trip over her own feet—she'd given herself a little talking-to.

Yes, she was bored. Yes, she was a little lost. But

flirting with a guy just to pass the time? That was stupid. Especially when he was hot and lived a few feet away from her bed. It wasn't as if she had a history of restraint. Or wise choices. Or self-control.

Case in point? Less than a day after telling herself to stay away from him, she was climbing up into his big black pickup and settling into the leather seat.

But despite her self-recriminations, Grace felt a thrill of satisfaction as she buckled up. She was going somewhere. Getting out of the house. How many days had it been since she'd even ridden in a vehicle that didn't have dozens of seats? Even in L.A., she'd been taking the bus or train for weeks.

As Cole started the truck, she rolled down the window, breathed in the cool morning air, and she felt *free*.

"Where do you want to go?" he asked.

Where? She had no idea. She should go to the store. She should get to know the town better. She should find the post office and the bank and the library. But she took a deep breath and said, "Just drive."

"You got it," he said softly.

Cole turned toward town, which surprised her, but she watched the streets pass with new eyes. It was different when you were driving. Everything so quick and temporary and new as it passed her gaze. The Western shops were cheesy but charming. The wooden sidewalks so different from anything she'd ever seen. They passed the bus station where she'd first set foot in Wyoming, and then she saw them: the antlers.

"Oh, my God. There are thousands of them." There were. They formed a wide, tall arch at the corner of a square park. When they turned, she saw that there was another arch on the next corner. And another on the other side of the park. And there was a carriage parked there, the horses shaking their manes in the bright sunlight. It really was amazing that she'd missed them.

"Did you want to stop and look?"

"No, keep going." The tourist shops slid past her, the tourists already out in their shorts and sunglasses. They passed another carriage rolling along, two small children looking slightly stunned and unsure as the carriage rocked around a turn.

Then suddenly the crowded blocks of hotels and shops were gone. There was a green park, and then... nothing.

Nothing but a huge expanse of rolling meadows and a tumbling stream and flocks of birds rising up into the bright blue sky.

"Wow," she said. She hadn't expected this at all. Somehow it was all invisible from inside the town, but now she couldn't imagine there was a town anywhere nearby.

They drove along the bottom of a ridge for a while, Grace staring hard over the fields that stretched out from there, watching for elk or anything else she might see. Then the ridge fell away and in the distance, the mountains rose up.

"Wow," she breathed again. "It's amazing."

Cole caught her eye and grinned. "You know, this is what most people do the first day. Jackson's nice and all, but nobody comes here for the small-town charm. It's the mountains. The parks. The wildlife. The sky."

The sky, yes. Something so simple as air, and yet it was beautiful. Magical. Stretching for miles of impossible blue before falling behind the mountains.

She wished she had a camera. It was almost an ache inside her, the need to try to capture the beauty of the moment. They had mountains in California, and she'd passed plenty on the bus ride here, but this moment was just...stunning. A perfect contrast to how screwed up and dark and complicated her life was. She felt insignificant, and that was a relief. That whatever mistakes she'd made, all the things she'd managed to mess up were all meaningless and small.

She wanted to capture that, somehow, in a picture, but she'd pawned her camera the week before. And the kind of cell phone that let you buy sixty minutes at a time definitely didn't come with a camera.

But for the moment, Grace let that desire go and simply took it all in.

"Where do you want to go?" Cole asked, seemingly unmoved by the amazing sight. Then again, he saw it all the time. Maybe that was why he smiled so easily.

She looked around, searching for a place she wanted to get closer to. A sign at the side of the road pointed the way toward the national parks. They were completely surrounded by beauty. How could she possibly choose? What did she want?

"Take me somewhere no one else goes," she said.

He was quiet for a moment, looking out the window as if he could see something puzzling up ahead. Finally, he nodded. "All right. I can't promise no one goes there, but I don't think many tourists get that far off the path."

She glanced down at her boots. These were sturdy, but she wasn't sure they were good for hiking.

"Don't worry. I don't mean that kind of path."

"I can handle it."

"I'm sure you can handle anything."

She felt a warm rush at his words. He said it as though he admired that. Most guys didn't. Most guys wanted to feel needed. They resented that she didn't need them. And she didn't.

The warm rush dropped away like falling water.

She couldn't say that anymore, could she? She couldn't pretend that she didn't need anybody and never had. But she'd never let anyone else know that. She'd rather die.

So she smiled. "I'm pretty tough. But I'm not sure if the boots are."

He glanced down to her feet. "They look pretty tough to me."

"Yeah?"

"Yeah," he said, the appreciation in his tone obvious even before he glanced at her with heat in his eyes.

Wow. Grace cleared her throat. He liked the whole tough-girl thing, huh? Wanted a little edginess in his life, maybe? She told herself she didn't feel flattered. She wasn't traveling entertainment for a small-town country boy.

Then again...he wasn't just a small-town country boy. He was a man who worked with his hands every day. His dimples were sweet, but his hands were scarred and strong. She snuck a look at the steering wheel, at the fingers wrapped around it.

Cole slowed the truck and took a right turn, distracting her from thoughts of his hands. This road cut through a field. She couldn't tell if it was hay or wild grass or something else, but the wind rippled over the golden stalks, and it looked like an ocean. It was beautiful, and the shushing sound of it filled the truck.

Grace spotted something moving through the grass and choked on excitement. "Is that an elk?" she gasped, pointing.

"That's a deer."

"How can you tell the difference?"

Cole looked at her and a smile spread over his face. He chuckled. "They're totally different animals."

She slumped a little in her seat and crossed her arms. A strand of purple hair blew into her eyes and she shoved it out of the way. But there was no way to stay mad. Not right now. The world was too beautiful in that moment. She knew it would be crappy again soon enough. She couldn't waste this, so she turned away from Cole and watched the strange view sliding by her window.

They passed more deer. Probably. How could she be sure when he wouldn't tell her? Then the land got a little hillier. They were driving higher.

Deer jumped out of some bushes at the side of the road and raced away. But they looked a little...

"Holy shit, what are those things?" Grace yelled, grabbing Cole's arm.

The brakes screeched for a moment. The truck jerked right and then left again. But Grace was too busy watching the freakish deer to care. They were the ones with the black masks again. The creepy black masks tattooed over their little deer faces.

"What the hell?" Cole snapped.

"Those things! What are they? They're bouncing! And creepy!"

"Creepy?" He pulled to the side of the rode and shook his head. "Those are pronghorn. And I almost rolled the truck."

"Pronghorn?" She craned her neck to watch warily as the herd headed away.

"Antelope."

"Antelope? Like in Africa?"

"No, antelope, like 'the deer and the antelope play.' You know? The song about America? Maybe you've heard of it."

"Oh." The animals had finally bounced out of sight, so Grace gave up her vigil and looked at Cole. "Those are antelope? American antelope? Are you sure? Because they've got little masks and pointy black horns and they look like they should be grazing next to giraffes."

He frowned. His mouth opened. Then closed again. He blinked several times. "You're really damn weird, you know that?"

"Oh, *I'm* weird? Have you gotten a good look at those things?"

"Grace… You…" He couldn't seem to get any words out after that.

She shrugged. "I'm going to do some research. I'm pretty sure those things aren't native. They're probably an invasive species."

"What?"

"Like killer bees. We've got a big problem with those

in L.A. now. Some genius brought them over from Africa."

His eyes were wide as he stared at her.

"Africa," she said, raising her eyebrows in exaggerated alarm. "A coincidence? Or a clue?"

His eyes narrowed. "How long have you been screwing with me?"

She grinned hard enough that her cheeks actually hurt. Apparently it had been a while since she'd used those muscles. "Not very long, I'm embarrassed to say."

"So, you really didn't know what they were?"

"Are you kidding me? Those things are not right. But I guess I have to believe you when you say they're antelope. And I'm sorry I scared you."

"Come on," he huffed. "I wouldn't say you *scared* me. You just startled me. Thought there was a buffalo on the road or something. Oh, sorry. Bison. I don't want you worrying that someone's accidentally introduced African water buffalo into the ecosystem."

Grace laughed. She laughed so hard she had to press her hand to her mouth to try to stop it. That didn't work. In fact, she laughed harder. Laughed until tears overflowed her eyes. "I'm sorry," she gasped. "They just freaked me out."

"I guess they might be a little odd-looking compared to mule deer."

"You *think?*" She laughed even harder when he smiled. "God, stop making me laugh. Just drive."

"I'm still a little shaky."

She hit his arm and relaxed back into the seat. "So, where are we going? The mountains are the other way."

"Don't worry. There are plenty of mountains to go around. We're taking a back road into the Gros Ventre River valley. There are campgrounds and trails here, but it's not one of the main tourist stops."

As they worked their way higher up the hill, the shrubs and grasses were occasionally interrupted by groves of aspen, their leaves pale green in the sunlight. The only sounds were the truck engine and the shushing of leaves in the breeze. She breathed in and sighed. "It's amazing here. So quiet."

"Yeah."

"You wouldn't believe how noisy the city can be."

He raised an eyebrow. "I've been to a city before, you know."

"Yeah?" she teased. "Like Boise?"

"Something like that."

She smacked his arm again. "I'm kidding. But really. L.A. is just heat and cars and…hunger."

"Hunger?"

She hadn't meant actual hunger, but when he frowned, her cheeks burned, and she scrambled to cover the truth in her words. "Everyone is starving for something there. Fame or fortune or sex or beauty. Even when you have what you need, the next person is always showing you why it's not enough. Everyone feels desperate." And then there was the actual hunger. Plenty of that to go around, too.

She wasn't sure why kids with nowhere to go gravitated to Southern California. Maybe it was because it rarely got cold, but she didn't think it was that logical. Maybe it was as simple as following the line of other souls who thought they were too jaded to hope, but somehow found themselves wishing for more. Or maybe it just felt like a place where things were possible.

Unfortunately, things *were* possible in L.A. Anything was possible. From your wildest dreams to a darkness you could never have imagined for yourself. She'd seen it all. One old friend had ended up on the number-one sitcom in the country. Many others had ended up dead. Or worse. Maybe she should be thankful she'd found some middle path.

Cole finally broke the silence. "Does that mean you're happy you left?"

Happy? She looked at Cole and then back out the window. A tiny creek flowed along the road here. It looked happy, but Grace wouldn't truly describe herself that way. But right at this moment, at least, she felt peaceful. "I'm relieved," she said softly. And she was. She was also scared and worried and pissed off and bitter. But underneath all that, she was relieved. "I haven't spent much time outside L.A., and I'm not sure I would've left on my own. But now, now it's almost like I've broken free of something."

It was. She was in Wyoming, after all. It was impossible not to feel as though she'd stepped out of her real life and was watching it from afar. You couldn't get much farther than mountain wilderness, after all.

She couldn't help feeling lost, though. For so many reasons, and all of them were her own fault.

"I know what you mean," Cole said.

"Yeah?" She didn't turn toward him. She didn't want to meet his eyes. Not when she felt so vulnerable.

"I've felt that way before. Like you escaped something just in time. You can feel it brushing past you. Danger you just barely managed to dodge."

Forgetting her need to stay removed, Grace turned to him with a frown. "That's it, isn't it? What did you step out of the way of?" She couldn't imagine. He was a cowboy. He lived in Wyoming. He worked on land like this, with creeks and trees and blue, blue skies. She knew there were problems in small towns. Plenty of her friends on the streets of L.A. had come from small towns where a parent beat them or an uncle raped them or schoolmates tormented them or people just couldn't find jobs. But Cole was talking about a whirlwind. A larger danger.

His face showed nothing as he stared straight ahead, but when he finally looked toward her, he winked. "You know. Bucking horses. Panicked cattle. I've managed to dodge a lot of things in my life."

He was blowing off her question. Ignoring what they'd both meant. But that was fine. She wasn't planning on telling him her secrets either. Better that he didn't try to get close. The last thing she needed was a big, sweet cowboy confessing his emotional scars and wounds. In fact, the thought made her shiver with fright. She had too much to carry as it was. She didn't want anyone else's burden.

She should've realized that a long time ago. She was better off alone. Her own mess was too complicated, even without letting someone else thread their issues through it.

"Where's your ranch?" she asked, ready to change the subject.

"I just work there—it's not actually my ranch. But it's not too far from here."

"Can I see it?"

"Oh. Sure."

Sure? He didn't exactly sound enthusiastic.

"We'll drive by on our way back. But right now there's something prettier to see." He took a right onto a dirt road that wound through the trees. Actually, it looked more like a trail than a road. Branches dragged over the windshield. Shrubs scraped the bottom of the truck. She cringed at the sight of the road falling away ahead of them and curled her fingers tightly into the door handle.

"Uh, Cole..."

He took the turn easily and she tried not to look down to see how far it dropped.

"Yeah?"

"Nothing," she rasped, then yelped when the truck dipped abruptly into a pothole. She could deal with navigating the back alleys of a big city and all the scary things that lived in them, but this was a bit much. The truck rocked. She wanted to ask Cole to turn around, but he couldn't do that. It would be a three-point turn into oblivion.

"Damn," she whispered, closing her eyes. "Damn, damn, damn." She didn't like this. Someone else being in control of her life. Someone else deciding how close was too close.

The truck slowed to a stop. The engine cut off.

Grace opened her eyes, expecting to see something worthwhile. Something worth risking her life for. But all she saw were aspen trees and undergrowth that looked a lot like poison ivy. Then again, anything leafy and green looked like poison ivy to her, which was why she tried to avoid it.

Cole's door closed and suddenly he was opening hers. "Come on, tough girl."

"Are you making fun of me?" she snapped.

"Absolutely not. Your whimpers of terror were the toughest I've ever heard."

"Screw you," she muttered, ignoring his hand to jump down from the truck.

"You're cute when you're grumpy."

"You know, nobody knows I'm with you. I could kill you out here and just walk away."

"You could kill me out here and then wander around in the woods until you died of exposure."

Grace crossed her arms and tried to frown at his smile. "I could take your truck."

"You'd never make it back to the road. That's a ten percent grade on gravel around a curve."

He had a good point. She'd be stuck here if she killed him, so she shrugged. "Did you want to show me something?"

His lips parted, but his gaze slid to the side and he shook his head. "Come on. The trail's this way."

He started walking, so she followed. It was that simple. She wasn't going to stand around waiting for a bear to attack or some of those weird pronghorns to wander up. Cole held branches out of her way and occasionally told her to watch her step. Then the path opened up and they were standing on a bluff.

Grace skidded to a halt with a sharp gasp. The whole world looked spread out before her. Or at least the only part of the world she'd ever want to see.

Rocks tumbled away into treetops. The trees rose up from a steep cliff face that went down and down and down until it disappeared into a dark green jumble of pines. And at the very bottom a silver river cut a path through the earth, tracing its way out into the distance. Far below, she could see a waterfall. Past that, another. And then the river disappeared into the V-shaped valley.

"Oh, my God," she breathed.

"You like it?" Cole asked.

"What kind of question is that?"

He laughed and turned to gaze out over the valley with her. "Some people don't care about things like this."

"Some people are idiots."

"True enough."

"It's incredible." The word seemed wholly inadequate, but she couldn't think of something that captured the miracle of this view.

They stood in silence for a long time, and Grace tried to absorb as much of it as she could. The beauty, yes. But the peace, as well. And the wonder. It had been a long time since she'd felt wonder. But standing before this expanse, she felt like a child, as if there were millions of things she couldn't know and never would. It was a relief from the feeling that she'd seen everything already and found that none of it was very good.

"Do you think there's anyone out there?" she whispered.

"People? Sure. There are a couple of campgrounds by the river. Fly fishermen stay there. And people who hate the crowds at the bigger parks."

"It feels like we're totally alone. It feels like not one person has ever been here before."

"Yeah." She felt him turn to look at her. "It sounds like you like that."

"I do. I've never seen a place like this before."

"Never?"

She shook her head and had to swallow a lump in her throat. It wasn't sorrow or even something as simple as joy. It was more like that relief again. The feeling that she was small. Tiny. Minuscule. And all the stupid things she'd done, and all the mistakes and all the pain didn't mean anything at all. It was all too small to matter.

Some people would hate the feeling of being insignificant, but she felt filled with it. Overcome. "It's beautiful. Thank you so much for showing me this."

"It's nothing," he said, but, God, he was so wrong about that. Right at that moment, it was everything.

They watched in silence for a long time before they went back to the truck.

Cole drove back up to the road. He took her farther down the valley, every curve revealing another view, another breathtaking wonder.

When she could think again, Grace reminded him that she wanted to see the ranch where he worked.

"Sure. Of course. You've got time?"

"I do."

He took her back a different way, and in between two big hills that would've been called mountains in L.A., he slowed the truck and turned onto a dirt road. They passed under a sign that said Easy Creek, and then he pulled to a stop.

"Is this it?" she asked as she looked over the wide valley that flattened out in front of her. "Easy Creek?"

"It is."

She could see ranch buildings a quarter mile away, and behind them, the mountains rose in the distance. It was beautiful. He worked here every day. This was his life.

"It's going to be mine one day," he said softly.

"Is it owned by your family?"

"No. But Easy's like family to me. I'll buy it when he's ready to retire."

"That's amazing." He probably thought she meant the land, which *was* amazing. Beautiful and quiet and so peaceful. But what she really meant was that kind of security. Cole was a cowboy. Just that. He'd lived in Wyoming his whole life. He worked here on this ranch with friends who were like family, and someday the land would be his. What would that be like? To have always known where you belonged? Her life felt like it had been a series of bad places and rushed decisions.

For a while there, it had gotten smoother. But it had never been anything like this. It had never been safe.

"Thank you for showing me," she whispered.

He drove a little closer, and she could make out a low, long house with a front porch and dark wood walls. A big barn stood nearby, a wooden fence circling out from it. It looked like something out of a John Wayne movie. Two cowboys rode along a trail farther on.

He turned around before they got any closer.

It wasn't until she got home and closed her own door that she realized what had happened. Cole hadn't wanted to drive up to the ranch, because he hadn't wanted to be seen with her. He hadn't wanted to introduce a purple-haired girl to the other cowboys.

She told herself it didn't matter. And it didn't. After the beauty he'd shown her today, Grace could forgive him such a small, human failing.

And anyway, she was tough. Just as he'd said.

CHAPTER SEVEN

GRACE WAS BACK IN THE THICK of L.A.

That's what it felt like anyway, all these people rushing through the hotel with expressions that made clear they were important. Really important. Certainly more important than anyone who actually lived in Jackson Hole.

"You doing all right?" Eve asked.

"I'm great."

"I know this is a lot for a first day."

"I've worked on a lot of movie sets. I'm used to it."

Eve let out a deep breath. "Good. Because I'm not. I'm really glad you're here. I didn't expect to have this whole mess dumped in my lap. The guy who worked with the studios on Jackson location scouting disappeared two weeks ago. Apparently he left behind a mess of screwed-up paperwork and some unhappy leasers. Nobody told me about that part of it when I agreed to take this on. I thought I was just going to take care of a few details."

Eve ran a hand across the back of her neck and grimaced. "I've only done a little scouting before," she murmured. "But, okay. Here's the deal. One of the locations has fallen through. This was supposed to be the final recon on sites they'd already contracted, but

now... Jesus. The director is here and everyone is totally freaked out."

"Who's the director?"

"Madeline Beckingham."

Grace blinked. Wow. Director, indeed. Beckingham
was a powerful, beautiful woman who'd made her mark
by directing fiery, fast-paced action movies. She was the
daughter of Hollywood royalty, and at first, the brass
had treated her like the child of Joseph Beckingham.
A woman to be coddled and amused but not taken too
seriously.

Not anymore. Now she was the heir apparent. Now
she got whatever she wanted, and she wanted a lot, if
the rumors were true.

"Have you worked with her?" Eve asked.

"No. Never."

"Well, here's your chance. I need you to track down
the location coordinator and get the location list I was
promised. I'm going to find the manager and find out
exactly what's going on with each site. None of my files
are up-to-date, and from what I've heard, the scout took
all his files with him. They're going to need new photos,
the specs reverified..."

"Got it. I'll get everything I can from the coordinator."

Grace had never done anything like this, but she approached it the way she did anything else. She jumped
in and dared the world to screw her over. Sometimes
that didn't work out very well and the world happily
called her bluff, but she wasn't sure how else to get

through life. She figured if she was going down, she'd go down swinging.

In this case, it worked out fine. Three hours later when everyone broke for lunch, Grace could barely catch her breath, but she had a notebook full of scrawled instructions, copied reports and a head full of ideas.

"Tell me everything," Eve said as soon as Grace joined her at a tiny round table in the restaurant bar.

Grace went through everything while Eve ate her lunch. Finally Eve stopped her and waved toward the other sandwich. "Eat. This is all beyond my pay grade, but I think the river site is fine. They've got all the photos on it, and the paperwork has already been filed. I'll call Carly on the county council to be sure. The ranch shoot, though… Shit. Uh, sorry. Pardon my language."

Grace nearly choked on her food. "I think I can handle it."

"I'm sorry to have thrown you into all this."

"It's fine. And they'll only be here for a week or so, right? Filming won't start for a little while?"

"Oh, sure. But you know how that goes. They're already behind schedule. Nothing's going right. I might have to bring more people in. Maybe one of the employees from the old company has some ideas for—"

"Wait. I think we're going to be okay. It's just a new ranch site that's needed?"

"Yes. That idiot never finalized the deal, and now the property has changed hands. We need a new ranch site with power and accessibility, but it can't be too modern.

It's for the opening scenes in the movie, and they take place in the fifties."

"That shouldn't be hard to find."

"It depends how difficult Madeline Beckingham will be about what's modern and what's not."

"Well, let's try it at least."

"Yeah?" Eve cocked her head and studied Grace. "You're up for that? We're talking full-time hours. Overtime, probably."

"Yes." She was up for it. Surprisingly up for it. She would've thought she'd hesitate after the past few months. Work had been bad enough, but then Scott had started twisting her arm, making her go to industry functions with him. The parties had been full of fake, grasping, ambitious liars who swarmed like insects around producers and directors. They'd always made her skin crawl.

But somehow this felt different. She didn't know why. Maybe it was the sense of independence. A feeling that they were on her territory now. Stupid, of course. Wyoming wasn't hers. She'd only been here a few days, and she obviously didn't belong.

So maybe it was just the pay. A week of working like that, and she could actually send Scott some money. Enough to hold off his threats until she got to Vancouver.

"It's some kind of Western, right? They said they wanted an isolated ranch with panoramic views for the sky shots."

"Yeah." Eve chewed her thumbnail and stared across the restaurant. "It's a big-money cowboy monster movie. I've got a couple of ideas. A place I did a magazine shoot at a couple of years ago, but it's probably a little too modern-looking."

"I have an idea for a place."

"You? I thought you just got to town."

Grace took a deep breath and told herself to ignore the self-doubt that rose up, telling her to be quiet. "I did just get to town. I'm sure you know of a dozen other places, but… I went for a drive yesterday. Have you heard of a ranch called Easy Creek? It's rustic and beautiful. A little brutal-looking and isolated enough that you can do panoramic shots with no interference. I know they said they could eliminate other buildings in editing, but the isolation of this place might make things a little simpler."

"Depends on how far away it is."

"Not far, from what I remember."

"You know how to get there?"

"Yes." Probably.

Eve grabbed her purse and stood up. "Then let's go check it out. I need to get out of here for a few minutes anyway. You might be used to this, but I'm not."

"It gets easier," Grace said.

"Really?"

"No, not really."

Eve's face broke into a wide smile, and her bright laugh surprised Grace. She hadn't realized how tense Eve was until she'd relaxed for a moment. She looked younger and softer, and Grace found herself wondering what her story was. Oh, well. None of her business.

"Come on. Let's save Madeline Beckingham's ass."

THREE HOURS LATER, Grace left the Easy Creek Ranch in shock.

They'd done it. They'd really done it. Because of *her*.

She'd never experienced anything like that before. She'd come up with an idea, put it out there and everything had just fallen into place.

Well, it had taken a little more work than that.

Somehow, she'd managed to direct Eve back to the Easy Creek Ranch with only two false turns. And as they'd driven down the long ranch road, Grace had realized she'd been right. The place was perfect. Exactly the location that had been described in the location list. Low hills obscured any views of civilization, but didn't rise high enough to block out the Tetons. The buildings, clustered in a loose circle at the end of the drive, were sturdy but ancient-looking. Dark wood aging to gray. Easy Creek looked like a symbol of American ranching.

And somehow...somehow it had worked out.

Granted, the production people still had to approve it, but how could they possibly walk away from such an ideal location?

Mr. Easy, the owner—and, she assumed, Cole's boss— had initially been skeptical. In fact, he'd said no. They'd laid it out for him, offering the same amount of money that had been offered to the previous site owner. Then they'd upped it. But he hadn't seemed tempted until Eve had mentioned Madeline Beckingham by name. The man was obviously a fan, because he'd perked right up.

"Three weeks," they'd explained. "One week now and then two weeks of filming in a month or so. That's it." There would only be two scenes filmed here, after all. The rest of the movie would be filmed in California and on soundstages to accommodate the special effects.

Easy had finally agreed. Now they were armed with crude measurements and dozens of pictures Eve had snapped. If Madeline Beckingham liked it, the place was theirs.

As soon as they pulled away from the ranch, Grace and Eve smiled at each other.

"They'd be crazy not to use this place," Eve said.

Grace sighed. "I know. It's beautiful, isn't it?"

"Amazing. How'd you find it?"

"A neighbor showed me around. Cole Rawlins?"

Eve shook her head. "I don't know him."

"He works on the ranch." Grace braced herself, thinking Eve was going to follow up with more questions, and Grace wouldn't know how to answer them. But Eve's frown had nothing to do with Grace.

"All right, let's make this happen. I'm already sending the files." She glanced down at her open laptop. "Production needs to get out here and approve the site and the money. They'll take care of the legal stuff this time. I don't have the experience. But you and I will deal with the county, since I know the council members. But it's private land. There shouldn't be any issues."

There were egos to stroke and payments to negotiate. But hours later, production finally gave the go-ahead. By 9:00 p.m., when Eve dropped her off at her apartment, Grace was exhausted, and the next day would likely be busier. But she realized she hadn't been worried about the mess she'd left behind in L.A.

This felt like good, honest work, even if she couldn't call herself a good, honest person. It felt…nice.

Despite that her bed was no more than a cheap sleeping bag on a wood floor and she hadn't had dinner, Grace drifted almost immediately into sleep. But she promised herself an air mattress the next day. She deserved it.

SWEAT SLID DOWN his neck as Cole pushed himself to finish his last twenty lunges. His muscles burned and his leg ached, but there was no sharp pain, which was an improvement. At first the pins in his leg had made him nervous. He'd been afraid to push it. Afraid something would come loose, afraid his femur would break into four pieces again, and it would be over. He hadn't realized that the leg wasn't the problem. It was the cracked pelvic bone that might not heal right. Some sort of separation that might need more plates, more screws. And maybe no more riding.

That couldn't happen. It wouldn't.

He had to ride again. He was going to own land. Run his own ranch. Live exactly the way he wanted to and answer to no one. He'd been saving for thirteen years, ever since he'd woken up to the knowledge that he'd become someone else, and his father had died disappointed in him.

After that time in L.A., he'd had a little money in the bank. He'd rather have burned it than use it as a foundation. It was tainted. And ugly. But it was also fifteen thousand dollars, and he wasn't naive or idealistic. Ranch work didn't pay much. Hell, it really didn't pay anything at all. The only saving grace being that room and board were provided if you were willing to live in a bunk.

But now, the money was trickling out of his account. He had to get back to work.

He pushed himself to do ten more lunges, even though his muscles shook and his shirt was soaked with sweat.

"Four," he ground out past clenched teeth. "Three."

He had to ride again.

"Two," he grunted. "One." He groaned through the last lunge and then stood straight and hung his head.

Two weeks. Two weeks and then he'd be cleared to ride.

He grabbed some ibuprofen and did some stretches to loosen up, then headed for the shower.

Sighing, he tried to relax his shoulders under the hot spray, but the tension stayed. Another night when he didn't feel tired. Another night of lying there in the dark, his mind working and turning and trying to skip over the worry.

He had too damn much time on his hands. Grace distracted him, but there were only so many hours of the day he could spend thinking about her.

Jesus, she was bad news. Foulmouthed and bad tempered and itching to get out of Jackson the moment she'd set foot in it. She was also fascinating. The look on her face when she'd seen that river valley… He wished he'd been able to capture that moment. Ensure that he'd never forget the way her suspicion and wariness had softened into wonder.

That had been a surprise. How her lush mouth had

relaxed into a sensuous curve. How her eyes had lost their darkness completely. Not like when she laughed, and they sparkled for a moment as if she were surprised. The darkness had simply opened up. There was something pure there, past the pitch-black perfection of her makeup. Something young and untouched.

He wondered if she looked like that when she came.

"Shit," he muttered, wondering where that thought had come from. It didn't matter. It was there now. And his cock thickened at the thought of her beneath him.

What would she be like? Wild and rough? Quiet and solemn? He had no idea. He'd never so much as dared to stroke a finger over her skin. Hell, he'd hardly seen any of her skin at all. But he could imagine what she looked like beneath her clothes. She was small. Five-two or five-three without her heels. Delicate bones. Small breasts. But her ass… He'd checked it out, and his fingers curled with the need to cup her ass. Squeeze it. Pull her tight against his hips.

His cock swelled as he imagined her yielding to him. But any yielding on her part wouldn't last for long. She'd fight for her pleasure.

Cole ran the bar of soap down his body, then wrapped a hand around his hard shaft.

He'd strip off her sweater first, and then her jeans. He imagined her standing before him in black panties and a wife beater, her nipples hard against the thin fabric.

He'd get down on his knees for her, put his mouth to her and suck her right through the fabric. Tease her nipples until she was arching into him, her fingers clutching his hair. She'd be rough, and he'd love that. It'd give him permission to be rough in turn.

He'd shove up the beater and close his teeth over her bare nipple. Slide both his hands down the back of her panties and spread his fingers over the warm flesh of her ass.

Stroking his cock, Cole imagined shoving her panties down and putting his mouth to her pussy.

He groaned, putting one hand against the cold bathroom tile to support himself as he jacked off. Water beat against his back. His hand was slick and tight as he imagined her gasping at the way he'd suck her clit.

Christ, he'd love to do that. Make her arch and whimper. Taste her as she got wetter and wetter against his mouth. He couldn't imagine her still and quiet. No, he was pretty damn sure she'd writhe and moan and fight toward her climax. The way she fought everything.

He tightened his grip on his cock and stroked faster, imagining the way he'd suck her. Lick her. Reach up and squeeze her nipples as he pushed her toward orgasm.

Heat swept over his skin. Steam filled his lungs. And in his head, Grace shook and screamed, and the taste of her flooded his mouth as she came. "Oh, fuck," he groaned as his own orgasm slammed into him.

Afterward, he spread his fingers against the tile and took a deep breath. He rolled his shoulders. Stretched his neck. And realized he felt great.

He was going to get some sleep tonight. Finally. And tomorrow he'd go back to work. It'd be a good day. He could feel it.

CHAPTER EIGHT

Cole stepped out of his truck and straight into chaos.

The ranch yard was usually quiet, aside from the sound of horses and a few men, but now it was packed. With vehicles. Equipment. And people. Strangers doing strange things in this familiar place.

Suddenly, the chaos coalesced. The random pieces joined together to become something solid, and Cole recognized what was happening. Ice swelled from deep inside him and turned his skin cold.

This was a movie set.

He shook his head and looked around again, disorientation making it hard to process what he was seeing.

It looked like a movie set, but there were key parts missing. Cameras and cranes and huge light towers. And crowded as it seemed, there weren't enough people. There was only one trailer, parked next to the barn. If this were a real movie set, there'd be a dozen trailers and a couple of awnings set up for the lower-level actors, not to mention all the space for wardrobe and makeup.

What the hell was going on at the Easy Creek? This was a bad dream. It couldn't be real.

His pounding heart helped to drown out the noise, but Cole still flinched at the sound of something hydraulic firing up behind him. More equipment. Maybe they were just starting the setup. Maybe a caravan was coming down the dirt road like a circus arriving in town. A circus from hell.

He cursed and set off across the yard, heading straight for the big house. There were more people inside.

"Where's Easy?" he asked the first familiar face he saw. Manuel tilted his head toward the kitchen. The guy didn't talk much, which was fine with Cole at the moment. There was only one person he wanted to talk to.

"Easy," he ground out when he spotted the old man seated at the kitchen table. Papers were strewn about him like evidence of a crime. "What the hell is going on here?"

Easy's body might be giving out on him, but his mind was sharp as hell, and he sent Cole a warning look that would've felt like a knife if Cole had been able to feel anything. But adrenaline meant he didn't feel a thing except anger.

"Easy—"

"You'd better watch your tone when you talk to me in my own kitchen, boy."

Cole crossed his arms and glared. Easy had been around since Cole was in diapers, but that didn't mean Cole liked being reminded of it.

"Your kitchen, huh? I guess I was confused because the whole damn place looks like a Hollywood soundstage. Why is that?"

"It's preproduction," Easy said slowly, as if that explained something. As if that explained *anything*.

"Preproduction?" Cole yelled.

"Yep."

"What do you think you're doing?"

"What does it look like I'm doing? I'm making an easy buck."

Cole waved his arm toward the front of the house. "Like *this?*"

"What do you mean, 'Like this?' They're not filming a porno in the barn, they're just shooting a few scenes for a big movie. A couple of weeks of distraction, and I'll have a few more dollars in my retirement fund."

Cole ground his teeth together. He knew Easy was close to retirement. In fact, no one knew that better than Cole, which was why Cole thought of this place as *his* ranch and why he didn't want these scavengers on it.

Damn it.

"This is a ranch," he made himself say calmly. "In the middle of summer, for godssake. How are we going to take care of the cattle and—"

"They're my stock, Cole. You think I'd do this if it put them in harm's way?"

Cole shifted and jerked his chin in acknowledgment, the most acquiescence he could manage at the moment.

"The stock's all up at summer grazing anyway. At worst, it'll inconvenience the men. You'll have to work around these folks, and they might be underfoot around the bunkhouse. But you don't even have to worry about that, so what's the problem?"

"You know what my problem is."

"This ain't the past, Cole."

"Isn't it? Because it sure as hell feels like you trucked in a scene from my life I'd rather forget and set it up like a damned surprise party for me!"

"This might be a good thing for you."

"Good?" he snapped. "How do you figure that?"

"You can't work full-time. Not on a horse and not doing physical labor. But this kind of thing is mostly waiting around. Maybe you can put in a few extra hours. You know about this film stuff. Maybe you could—"

"Easy! Jesus. You want me to jump back into this? Christ. We haven't talked about it much, but I'm sure my dad filled you in on it before he died."

Easy took a slow drink of coffee and kept his eyes on Cole. "I know he didn't like what you were doing," he eventually said. "He said it was trouble, but—"

"Trouble," Cole growled, wishing he could put everything he was feeling into that one word. Trouble. Right.

"You're not a kid anymore, Cole. And this ain't L.A. You don't have to piss your pants over it."

"Jesus. Are you kidding me?"

"I ain't gonna allow mischief out here, and if these people want to party, they'll go into town."

"Easy," he said, but the words he wanted to say slipped away. His face burned with shame. They'd never talked about it, not in anything more than the most general terms. The parties and money and sex. "I can't do this."

"Sure you can."

Just three words. A few letters each. But they went through Cole like a blast of heat. Easy didn't sound the least bit worried. And the surety in his words made Cole's stomach twist into a hard ache. "I'm not working with them."

"It'll make you money."

"I can earn money working the ranch. I can earn even more when I'm back in the saddle. Two weeks—"

"Farrah said it wasn't definite. Has anything changed since then?"

Goddamn it. He really wished he hadn't used Easy's niece as a physical therapist. After all, for a small town, Jackson had quite a few PTs. Skiing meant lots of broken bones and a high density of world-class athletes.

"I'll be fine," he managed to grind out.

"You might be, but if you ain't, then you need all the hours you can get without a saddle."

"You know why I don't want these people here. What the hell are you trying to do to me, Easy?"

"What the hell are you so afraid of, Cole?" Easy countered.

"Are you honestly asking me that question?"

"I honestly am. You went out to L.A. as a kid. And you screwed around. That's it."

"I screwed around?" Cole growled.

"Yes," Easy said. He wasn't shouting anymore, but his voice was still rough with anger. "You screwed around the way that kids do."

"My dad—"

"And you've been hiding from it ever since."

"I haven't been hiding from shit! I came back home. It's where I belong."

"Is it?"

The quiet words froze Cole to the bone. "Excuse me?"

"How do you know you belong here when you've never done anything else?"

He didn't like this at all. He didn't like the sad look

in Easy's familiar eyes. "Why are you asking me this, Easy?"

"Because you came back here to lick your wounds. Then you just never left."

"I didn't leave because this is where I belong."

"Maybe."

"Maybe, my ass. I've been saving up to buy this land for a dozen years. You need me to prove something now? *Me?*"

"Maybe I do. See, I was wondering how you'd react to our new friends out there in the yard. It's been a long time, Cole. Too long for you to look so spooked."

"I'm not spooked, damn it. I don't like these people. There's a difference."

"Is that what it was on your face? Dislike? Looked more like panic."

He didn't think he'd felt panic before, but he was starting to feel it now. What the hell was Easy trying to pull? None of this made any sense. They'd talked about this years ago. Easy would run the ranch until he couldn't, and then Cole would buy it from him at a fair price. Slightly below market, maybe, because Easy didn't have any kids and Cole was like family. But a fair price for the small ranch.

So maybe Easy had changed his mind. Maybe he'd decided not to retire or sell his land. Or maybe he'd gotten a better offer. "You thinking about selling to someone else, Easy?" Cole asked quietly, hoping it would sound like mild curiosity. Instead, it came out sounding like fury, even to Cole's ears.

"I haven't thought about selling to anyone else since the moment you told me you'd buy it."

"Until now?"

"This isn't about someone else. I took the offer from the producer because the money's good. I wasn't thinking much about you until you showed up here yelling. Now, if you haven't spent thirteen years hiding, show me that."

"I'm telling you I haven't."

"Yeah. You've also got a whole heap of pride and arrogance and stubbornness pushing those words out. So *show* me."

"How?" he snapped. "By playing lapdog to a bunch of Hollywood assholes?"

"Yep."

"Fuck you, Easy!"

"Nah, that won't help." There wasn't an ounce of tension in Easy's voice now. In fact, he sounded genuinely amused with himself.

Cole's shoulders fell. Hell, *Easy* was a misnomer. Oh, sure, he seemed laid-back and good-natured, but underneath that, the man was made of pure steel.

If he needed Cole to prove something, Cole was going to have to prove it. Why the man needed proof was another question. For another day. And Cole would damn well be asking it. But for now...

"Fine," he sneered. "I'll play your little game."

"It's not a game," Easy said softly. "And it's not a test. At least, I won't be the one grading it."

"If you're going to make me do this, at least don't speak in riddles. Christ."

"You're gonna do it?"

"Sure. Yeah. I'll do it. Just to prove you're being ridiculous."

"I might be. But it's better than watching you cripple yourself over something you may not even want."

This broken leg was ruining his life. First, he'd lost his brand-new position as ranch boss. He'd waited five years for Raoul to move back to New Mexico the way he'd been threatening. Finally, the position had been Cole's, and the little house that came with it. But that was gone, too. After all, someone had to be boss when Cole couldn't be, and that someone got the boss's house.

And now this broken leg might cost him his sanity. Maybe even his whole way of life.

"Just tell me what you want me to do, so I can do it."

"How would I know anything about it? Go talk to the lady in charge."

"Fine. Which lady?"

Easy said the name. It fell into Cole's ear and then expanded like an explosion. He hadn't been expecting to hear it and, strangely, the shock gave him the moment he needed to compose himself. Easy didn't see what Cole was really feeling, and that was damned good, because this time, it was definitely panic.

CHAPTER NINE

THE TRUCK TIRES SQUEALED as Cole took the turn into Jackson. He needed new tires. Hell, he'd needed new tires since last year, but he'd been trying to eke one more season out of them. Then that stallion had fallen on him and fifteen hundred dollars for a new set of tires had seemed an extravagance. More savings gone. More hours he'd have to work.

Now they were hours he'd have to work with Madeline.

Easy couldn't have known. He'd never have forced the issue otherwise. Maybe Easy knew Cole had worked with Madeline, maybe he even knew they'd had a fling, but he didn't know how badly it had ended.

"Damn," he bit out, rubbing a hand over his eyes as he waited for a stoplight to turn green. But when it turned green, no one moved. A buffalo had wandered onto the shoulder of the highway, and now tourists were getting out to snap pictures. By the end of the week, they'd barely even glance at a standing bison, but it was only Tuesday. It was still special. Cole would've smiled at them on any other day.

But not today.

Madeline had been off-site today, at least, so Cole had gritted his teeth and told the location manager that he was there to help if they needed it. There had been a few questions here and there about moving horses and parking trailers and finding a place to store lights, but that had been it. Maybe Madeline would stay off-site. There was a river location where they'd film an extensive action scene. Probably on the Snake. Maybe she'd stay put on that site. Maybe Cole would be spared.

But it didn't feel like mercy. It felt like torture, waiting for that woman to show up. His first eight-hour day back at work and he felt that he'd lost his mind. Actually, he felt that he *needed* to lose it. And fast. So when he finally got past the tourists, Cole drove too fast for home, then raced through his shower and headed for the Crooked R.

After the long day and too much tension, his leg throbbed, and if he couldn't have a beer—or four—he was just desperate enough that he might've given in and popped an oxycodone.

Not good.

During those first few weeks, he'd taken the pills the doctor had given him, but only sparingly. He'd tried to get by on nothing but high-dose ibuprofen and Tylenol, but sometimes he'd needed the serious stuff. Sometimes he'd suffered enough pain to fantasize about sawing off his own leg just to stop the deep, incessant throbbing. Ridiculous, of course. Amputation would've offered more terrible pain, but his whole body had felt like one giant, pulsing light of agony. He'd been hurt plenty of times. This time, he'd realized that the ruthlessness of sharp pain could overwhelm itself somehow. Burn through you until it was done. But that horrible, deep ache…that was something else.

Yet he'd made it through. The long hours of daylight when he'd pretended to be cheerful for his friends, when it had taken all his concentration not to grind his teeth to dust and scream in pain and rage. And the longer hours of the night, when he'd lain sleepless and sweating, and sometimes he'd let tears roll down his cheeks just for the relief of it.

He'd gotten through it, and he was almost clear of it now. No more powerful drugs. Just ibuprofen for a few more months, and he'd be fine. He had to be. And he'd be damned if he was going to let that bitch ruin him. Not again.

Cole walked across the yard, head down, lost in thoughts of what might happen the next day. His stomach turned with the knowledge that he'd see her. This woman who'd once been his lover. This woman who'd used him. Who'd convinced him to use himself.

His face heated at the thought. His shoulders screamed with a tension that traveled down his back to join up with the ache in his hip.

He didn't want to look at her face. He didn't want her looking at his.

Would she smirk? Would she sneer, looking him in the face and knowing what he was?

The panic that Easy had named reared up in full force as Cole rushed up the steps of the saloon.

He headed straight for the bar, but as he tipped his hat at Jenny, his gaze slid down the line of stools and caught on a sight he hadn't expected. His panic skipped briefly, like an interrupted song.

Grace was there, parked at the end of the bar, a drink in her hand, her purple hair gleaming under a neon sign. A beer appeared in front of Cole, and he murmured a thanks to Jenny before he downed half of it.

That helped ease his panic back a little. Then Grace looked up, caught him watching and smiled; Cole's panic tripped again, and tumbled into something else. Excitement. Distraction.

He'd never seen her smile like that before. Free. Happy. Maybe a little drunk. Jenny approached her and said something, drawing Grace's attention away. She smiled so hard that her nose crinkled.

Okay, maybe she was more than a little drunk.

Cole finished his beer and sauntered over.

"Miss Grace," he said, tipping his hat.

"Hey, cowboy," she drawled.

"Buy you a drink?"

She shot the last two inches of what looked like orange juice and held it up. "I just happened to be in need of one. Thank you."

Well. He'd half expected her to sneer and tell him she could buy her own drinks. She was different tonight, and it wasn't just the alcohol. She *looked* the same at first glance. Tight, worn T-shirt, this one with a British flag on it. Tight, dark jeans. Black combat boots. Shaggy hair that was a sexy mess of black and brown and purple. But her eyes shone with something new.

He tilted his head at Jenny. "Another round, Jenny. I think we're celebrating something."

"We are," Grace crowed.

"Are you going to tell me what it is, or is it a secret?"

"Just a good day. The new job is going really well."
She winked.

"Yeah? That's great."

"And with all these hours, I can afford to buy myself
a screwdriver. Or two. Thanks to Jenny running a tab.
I'll pay you on Friday, Jenny, I swear."

Jenny winked. "I know where you live."

"I guess it's hard to hide in a town this size."

She slid Grace another glass. "And there are only so
many places to drink."

"Cheers," Grace said, raising the drink toward Jenny.
Then she turned her smile to Cole. "Thanks, cowboy."

"My pleasure," he murmured, meaning every syllable.

"Hey!" a cranky voice shouted from behind them.
"You'd better not be giving my booze away, Jenny!"

Cole turned to grin at Old Rayleen, who was glaring
at them above the cards she held in her hand. "I bought
your niece a round, Rayleen."

"Oh, yeah? You didn't ask if I wanted anything. In-
grate."

Cole winked. "I'm sorry, Miss Rayleen. Can I buy
you a drink?"

"I can get my own drinks in my own place," she
groused. Then without looking up from her game, she
muttered, "Whiskey sour."

Jenny was already handing him the drink before he
got off the stool. Cole delivered it with a flourish. "I'm
sorry, Miss Rayleen."

"Pfft. No one notices an old lady sitting in the corner," she grumbled. She downed half the drink in one swallow. "Not even if I had purple hair."

"Your hair's beautiful and you know it," he scolded.

That brightened her up. She smiled and patted her gleaming white hair. "You're sweet to notice, Cole Rawlins."

"I'm always sweet to you, Miss Rayleen. You know that."

"Oh, shoot. Charmer. You brought me my drink, now go away."

"Yes, ma'am."

"You look better walking away, anyway," she murmured.

Cole was blushing even before he saw Grace's wide grin.

"Did my great-aunt just compliment your ass?"

"I'm sure that's not what she meant."

"Really?"

"No," he said and sighed. "That's exactly what she meant." He waited for Grace to stop snorting before he touched his glass to hers. "So you had a good day. Does that mean you're thinking of staying in Jackson?"

"Come on, now." She laughed. "You said yourself that I don't look like a Wyoming girl."

"No, but I think we could all get used to you."

"Yeah? Am I growing on you?" Her smile gleamed with flirtation. Cole felt lust curl through his body.

"Oh, you're growing on me, all right."

She laughed. "Flirt. I'm pretty sure I'm not your type, Cole."

"How would you know?"

"Because if I am, then you must have been awfully lonely in Jackson Hole. I'd guess your type is more like Jenny here."

"Oh, I… No…"

Jenny raised both eyebrows and waited to hear what he'd say. Shit.

"I don't…"

Grace looked from him to Jenny and her eyebrows rose, too. "Oh, God. Were you two… I'm sorry."

Jenny winked. "It was a casual thing, sweetie. No big deal. You two flirt away. I'll move out of earshot."

"Jesus, Cole," Grace muttered when Jenny moved away. "Well, at least I pegged you right. That's something."

He could tell his face was red, but he tried to shake it off, worried it looked like guilt. "We only went out a couple of times. That doesn't make someone my type."

"It doesn't make them not your type either. Pretty? Cute? Cheerful? Move along, Cole. I'm none of those things."

"That's not true. You—"

"Oh, please." She smiled. "Don't lie. If you're going to try to talk me into something, at least be honest about it."

His mind was spinning with a mix of frustration and hot interest. "What exactly do you think I'm trying to talk you into?"

She laughed again, bright, genuine amusement edged with bitterness. "Hmm. I wonder." When she leaned closer, Cole's skin prickled with awareness. "You know that honesty thing I mentioned? Why don't you try it out? What are you doing over here buying me drinks, stud?"

What was he doing? Trying to distract himself, certainly. Trying to add something good to this fucked-up day. But with what? Her body?

His own body answered that question with a surge of blood that left his cock feeling heavy. He hadn't had sex in a long time. A really long time. Nearly a year and a half. And something about her pushed his buttons. Buttons he'd forgotten about since he'd come back to Wyoming. That kind of attraction was best left alone, especially considering his current problems.

But his bad mood was making his lust sharper. More aggressive. And she was challenging him. Goading him. All she saw was a charming cowboy. But if she wanted honesty, he was in the mood to give it to her.

"All right," he murmured, leaning closer until he was only a few inches from her ear. Her smile faded a little. "You want honesty? You don't know anything about what my type is. But you're right about something. You're not pretty or cute or sweet."

She snapped back a little at that. She tried to keep her smile in place, as if she didn't care, but two bright spots of pink appeared in her cheeks and they had nothing to do with makeup. "Sure," she said quickly. "Glad to know I've got some things right."

"You're something different from that." He caught a strand of purple hair between his fingers. "You're fascinating. And interesting. And hot."

The pink in her cheeks deepened. The smile wavered.

Maybe she didn't like that. Maybe he'd said the wrong thing. But surely any woman wanted to know she was fascinating and hot. And if she didn't like that, well, she'd asked for it.

"Interesting, huh?"

"Yes."

"Because I have purple hair?"

He cocked his head and watched her smile fade. "Maybe. There must be a reason you do it. Isn't it because you want people to notice you? To wonder?"

"No. It's because I want people to know I'm not like them."

"Well, that's pretty interesting. But that's not what I meant, anyway. I meant that you're strong. And dark. And I want to know what made you that way. And I want to know what's underneath it."

"And you think you'll find out by fucking me?" she countered.

Cole flinched a little at the hard word, but he'd said he'd be honest, so... "Maybe. I figure it can't hurt."

"Can't hurt? Maybe you're not doing it right."

Oh, shit. Lust shot through him so sharply he almost groaned. Her eyes were dark and hard again, but her mouth had softened into a smile. A smile with a secret. Damn, he wanted to do it right. With her. Tonight.

But she was standing up, scooting off her barstool and away from him.

"Pardon me," she said with such politeness that he knew she was mocking him. "I've got to go to the little girls' room. See if I can make myself pretty."

Yeah, she was definitely his type.

GRACE KNEW SHE was drunk, but she wasn't stupid drunk. She was just very pleasantly, in-a-good-mood drunk. So why the hell was she thinking about sleeping with Cole Rawlins? It was a stupid idea from any angle.

Oh, she liked a one-night stand as much as the next damaged girl, but not with a man who lived next door. And not when she was still stinging from her last relationship. And not with a damn *cowboy,* of all things.

And definitely not with a man who didn't think she was pretty.

"Idiot," she sneered at herself in the mirror. She knew she wasn't pretty. Hell, she'd dared him to say she wasn't pretty. So why did it sting?

Without her makeup, she was fairly plain. A small girl with a pointy chin and dark eyes and pale skin. Her natural hair color was dishwater brown, as her mom used to call it. As plain as the rest of her. But she'd learned how to transform herself at a young age. To make herself look unapproachable and tough without veering into the pitiable, obvious outward hurt of the goth look. To make herself stand out just enough. Maybe even be striking on occasion. But not pretty.

Not that she couldn't force it. She was damn good at what she did, after all. She could pull off pretty, even for herself. In fact, for a while there, she'd been styling herself to fit in. She'd felt almost comfortable with it. Then Scott had started pushing her to be nicer. To kiss ass. To make herself into part of the Hollywood crowd. For *him.* And her one small rebellion had been going back to purple hair and black shadow. But she knew how to create the illusion that she was pretty.

She smiled at her reflection as she thought of pulling a transformation. Of showing that bastard just how cute and sweet she could be. The idea made her laugh, and she forgot her momentary hurt. She was who she was. And if Cowboy Cole wanted a way into her mysterious life, why not? He wouldn't find any answers that way. There were big differences between sex and intimacy. The first being that she'd had lots of one, and had never bothered with the other.

Grace worked her hands into her hair and scrunched it up, then tossed it around to make it even messier. She touched up her black eyeliner and added a faint hint of pink gloss to her lips. Her blush was fine. So subtle that you couldn't see it beneath the actual flush in her cheeks now.

No, she wasn't pretty. Or sweet. Or cute. But she was still going to get lucky tonight. Her first cowboy. And God, she hoped he'd be her last.

him, she put her mouth to his neck. She closed her lips over his earlobe and sucked.

Now he was the one who moaned. And when he turned to catch her mouth with his, triumph surged through her like a wave. Yes. Finally. Finally, his mouth was hers. His lips opening so she could taste him. His tongue hot against hers.

Somehow it didn't appease her. Grace tugged at one of her hands until Cole set her free, then she twisted her fingers into his hair and pulled him tighter to her. She sucked at his tongue and held him so he couldn't get away.

But now he had a free hand, as well. His fingers spread over her shoulder and then slid down. He cupped her breast, his thumb brushing over her nipple until she groaned into his mouth.

Normally, sex for Grace was about *her*. She took the pleasure she could glean from it. She took it for herself, a trick she'd learned early on from the men she'd slept with.

But as Cole slid his hand lower and snuck it beneath her shirt, she was suddenly very aware of him. Of what he might be feeling as his palm pressed the skin of her belly and he sighed. He sighed as if it was a relief to touch her. A blessing.

Grace pulled her head back to try to catch a breath, but it was impossible. Cole immediately put his mouth back to her neck, and his hand slid around to her back. Within seconds, her bra was unclasped and his big hand was against her bare breast. His skin was hot against her, and just rough enough to make her gasp.

"God, you feel good," he murmured. "So damn soft."

Soft. Not what she ever wanted to be, but her body arched into his touch at those words, as if it were proud of its weakness. He rolled her nipple between his fingers and she moaned at the pleasure.

"You like that?" His words were harder now. More urgent. "Tell me."

She didn't want to. Didn't want to admit anything. He squeezed her tighter, and Grace pushed her hips toward him, wanting more.

"Tell me," he urged.

The words rose in her throat, but she kept her teeth clenched, her head turned away from him, even as goose bumps chased over her skin. Why couldn't he just be quiet? Just take what he wanted and let her do the same?

"Please," he murmured just below her ear. Then he sank to his knees, and his mouth whispered against the curve of her breast. "Tell me."

She shook her head, but her jaw trembled and she couldn't keep her teeth clenched anymore. "Yes," she finally breathed. He sucked at her nipple and she groaned. Then his teeth pressed into her, and something snapped free inside her. "Yes," she urged. "God, yes. Please."

He'd let her go to put his hands to her hips, so Grace was free to clutch his head. To dig her nails into his scalp and offer the same pain as his teeth scraping over her sensitive breasts. He swept her shirt higher, both his big hands sliding up her back.

She pulled her shirt and bra off.

"Oh, Jesus," Cole rasped. "Look at you."

When she looked down, Cole had put his mouth to

the tattoo that snaked up her hip and waist. He slid his mouth along the black branches of the leafless tree that spread all the way to her ribs, stopping just below her breast.

But he didn't stop there. He caught her nipple in his teeth again, but his hands slid down to unfasten her jeans. Grace held her breath. She was aching and wet, and she felt as if he'd been teasing her for hours, even though he'd first touched her only a few minutes ago. Maybe it was the sight of him on his knees for her, his mouth worshipping her body. She liked that. She liked it a lot.

But when he rose up to his feet and slid his hand into her open jeans, she liked that even more.

His fingers rubbed along her slick sex and she cried out. "You're so wet for me," he said. "Does that feel good?"

He knew it did, damn him, because she was whimpering and pressing her hips against his circling fingers. "Tell me what you like."

She shook her head again, determined to resist this time. He wanted her to give something up. To give in. But she was only going to take. Take the pleasure of his fingers against her clit, rubbing her. Pressing. Her hips jerked in need.

"You like that?" he pressed. "Or this?" He slid his hand lower and suddenly his fingers were deep inside her.

Grace cried out, but she bit her lip, trying to stifle the sound.

"Tell me."

"No!"

He growled and then his hand was in her hair, turning her head away from him, holding her tight against the door.

Oh, God.

"Tell me." His mouth was against her ear, whispering. "Tell me what you want." His fingers slid out of her body, and Grace wanted to weep. She just wanted to get off. Just wanted that one simple thing, but now his fingers were too light against her clit. Just enough pressure to make her whimper, to drive her insane. Not nearly enough to get off.

"Like that?" he asked.

No. No. Not like that. She ground her teeth together. She tried to shake her head.

"More?"

Oh, God, she hated him. Hated him for wanting her to give him something. She wrapped a hand around his wrist and dug her nails in.

"That's it, honey," he murmured. "Show me what you like."

Bastard, she cursed in her mind. But she pressed his hand tighter to her and sobbed in relief when he rubbed her clit with just the right pressure.

"That's it. That's what you like."

Yes. Yes. Just like that.

But now she felt so empty inside. Tight and empty and needy. She wanted to be fucked, but she didn't want to give up his fingers. Her hips rocked, urging him on. Begging him in ways her voice never would. She pressed his hand down, tilting her hips up, and he obliged so nicely, his fingers sliding deep inside her again.

"God, yeah," he groaned into her ear, the hand that held her hair tightened to a delicious pain. "Show me. Show me what you like. I want you to come for me."

Grace wrapped both her hands around his wrist and showed him. She urged him into the rhythm she wanted, fucking herself with his fingers. The heel of his hand ground against her clit and she was panting.

"Oh, God. Like that, Grace? You like that? Deep and slow?"

Yes. Yes, she liked it just like that. Oh, God, yes. Yes. And then she was saying the words, her mouth beyond her control as he held her against the door and worked her just the way she wanted.

"Yes," she whispered. "Yes. Please."

"Tell me," he ordered.

"Yes. Like that. Fuck me. Make me come. Please. Deep and... Yes. *Please.*" Then the terrible words finally stopped because she was screaming, bucking against his hand, straining against the fist in her hair, because the pain made it that much sweeter as she came for him.

"Yes," she cried out. Not for him. She came for herself.

Her hips shook and trembled through the last waves of her orgasm. Her whole body was one weak mass of shivers and sighs. "Oh, God," she breathed. "Oh, God."

Cole was breathing almost as hard as she was. He'd worked hard after all, at breaking her down, at making her give in. She knew that once she'd sobered up, she'd be pissed as hell. But right now, she just wanted more.

She eased her nails from his wrist, wondering if she'd made him bleed. Even as she smiled at the idea, she reached for the buttons of his jeans. His grip on her hair loosened, so she watched as she pulled open each button, then slipped her hand under the warm fabric of his briefs.

"Ah," he rasped as her hand closed over his cock.

Ah, indeed. Her heart had started to slow to a normal rhythm, but it kicked into overdrive again at the feel of him. Hard and thick in her grasp. Really hard. And really thick. She stroked him, slowly. All the way down to the base, then up over the head, her thumb spreading pre-come over the tight skin.

"Grace," he moaned, and she felt powerful again. Back to herself. But that only lasted a moment. A moment to stroke him again. A moment while his eyes closed and his head fell back as air rushed from his throat.

But then he opened his eyes and looked at her, and the intensity made her gasp. There was nothing of the friendly cowboy in those blue eyes. He looked wild.

He turned her, walking her toward the couch. But whatever she'd thought he was going to do, she was wrong. Instead of laying her down or even sitting down himself, he turned her away from him and bent her over.

Her eyes widened as he tugged her jeans down. Was he really just going to… "Oh," she gasped as his fingers slid along her clit again. She was too sensitive and started to flinch away, but then he lightened his touch and she moaned.

"I could make you come all day," he said. "The sounds you make. God."

Grace braced her hands against the back of the couch and let him touch her. His fingers were surprisingly gentle now, but no amount of gentleness could hide the rasp of calluses on his skin. She could feel his tempered strength. Years of hard work with leather and metal.

She'd just come, and already he was pushing her toward tightness again. Emptiness.

His fingers moved away and she shook her head.

"Touch yourself," he said.

"No. You do it."

He laughed at her sharp words. "I'm busy with something else, darlin'."

She turned to glare over her shoulder and saw him pulling a wallet from his pocket. He drew a condom out of it and raised an eyebrow.

"Now touch yourself," he ordered.

A glance down convinced her. His cock looked even bigger now, and she wanted it inside her. So she bit her lip and touched herself, moaning at the touch of her own fingers.

His hand settled on her tattooed hip, holding her steady as he pressed the head of his cock to her. She gasped hard as he sank slowly into her, stretching her with his width.

"Oh, God. Cole…"

He never once paused. He gave her no time to adjust or relax. He just slowly pushed deeper. The perfect amount of force against the pleasure she spun with her own hand.

Yes, she said silently, unwilling to let him hear. *Yes. Yes.*

He didn't issue any more orders. He didn't speak at all. He just held her hip, and curved one hand over her shoulder, and he fucked her. No more demands. He simply took his pleasure. And she took hers. The way she wanted. Stroking herself, feeling every inch of his cock as he slid into her, then out.

Oh, God. Yes. He was steady and strong, holding her in place. "Yes," she breathed as the pressure built inside her. He must have heard her faint whisper, because his hand gripped her hip harder and he increased the pace of his thrusts. He thrust deep, and she loved it. She loved that he'd bent her over and simply taken her. He wasn't being careful. Wasn't treating her like she was small and soft.

Grace tipped her hips up to meet his thrusts, and he grunted. Now his hips slapped into her ass. Yes. Yes. "Oh, God, yes," she cried out, and then her body spasmed and she was screaming. A wordless scream of release and disbelief. She almost couldn't take it. Not on the heels of that last, powerful climax.

She would've pulled away, but Cole's hands were too strong, and he held her tight and fucked her until he groaned and slammed his cock deep into her one last time.

She couldn't…God, she couldn't believe it had been so intense. He was still inside her, filling her up so much she felt that she couldn't catch her breath. When he slid free of her body, she gasped and collapsed, her knees landing on the cushions.

Cole slapped her ass. "I'll be right back."

"Did you just *slap my ass?*" she screeched as he walked toward the bathroom.

"Yep."

"You…damn…" Her outrage gave her the strength to push to her feet, and she yanked up her jeans. "I can't believe—"

"Can't believe what?" he asked, strolling back in with an obnoxious grin.

"That you slapped my ass like you were dismounting a horse!"

"That's not how I usually dismount a horse, but that's just me. Where do you think you're going?"

She'd been spinning away, meaning to stomp over to the door and yank on her shirt, but Cole wrapped his arms around her waist and tugged her down to the couch.

"Hey!"

"Hey, nothing. You always walk out before the dew is dry?"

"The dew?" Grace found herself lying topless on a cowboy's naked chest, staring down at him in open-mouthed shock. "You didn't just say that, did you?"

His hands spread over her back and he smiled softly. "Stay for a few minutes, all right? I'm not quite done with you."

"Well, I'm done with you."

"Fair enough. Consider it a favor, then? Please? For a nice cowboy?"

"Nice," she muttered, but his hands felt sweet on her back. And her muscles weren't exactly strong at the moment. So Grace frowned to convey her ambivalence, but she slowly let herself relax into his chest. She laid her cheek to him, trying to ignore the tingle of pleasure she felt as her skin rubbed over his soft chest hair.

But she couldn't ignore the sweet rumble of his sigh. Grace closed her eyes and exhaled.

COLE WAS GLAD she wasn't looking at him anymore. He was having trouble maintaining his good ol' boy smile.

Holy crap, that had been…

Clearing his throat, he tried to search for the right word, but his mind was still reeling. Right now, Grace was a perfect, sweet weight against his body. But a few minutes before, she'd been a line of slim muscle, taut as a bowstring. All that deadly energy, caught up in a small body. Jesus, just touching her had driven him a little mad. Mad enough to—

"You're more intense than I expected," Grace said.

Cole held his breath for a moment, then said, "Yeah?"

"Yeah."

"I'm not usually. Maybe you inspired me. Should I apologize?"

She lifted her head to look at him, her eyes as dark and unreadable as they'd ever been. "Do you think you should?"

Did he? He studied her. Her face was still pale. Her hair still wild. And her dark eyes watched him as if she'd never trusted anyone. But her cheeks and mouth were the prettiest pink he'd ever seen.

Cole turned, easing her down to lie on her side, facing him. He dipped his head to kiss her, and for a moment she seemed startled and pulled away. He met her gaze, then tried again, moving slower, and this time, she held still as he pressed a kiss to those pink lips. After a few moments, he felt her body relax against him and her mouth offered a kiss of its own.

He trailed his finger along her jaw. "I don't want to apologize. Because I liked it and I think you did, too. Should I take that back?"

Her eyes slid away. When she moved, he thought she was getting up. It'd been intense, yes, but maybe he'd offended her. He'd gotten caught up in the scalding heat of the moment, and he hadn't thought about what it might mean to her. To have a man she barely knew take her as if he'd die if he didn't get deep enough.

Shit. But that's exactly what it had felt like. He should've—

She shifted one last time, and then stopped moving. She faced away from him now, but she was still lying down, still pressed to his body. Her ass snug against his hips. Her back to his chest. God, he wished they were naked.

"No," she said to the space in front of her. "I don't want you to apologize."

Cole let out the breath he'd been holding, exhaling as slowly as possible so she wouldn't be aware.

"I was just surprised," she added.

"Me, too."

She turned her head enough to shoot him an inscrutable look, then settled back down with her head on her arm. He wanted to curl his own arm under her and pull her tighter against him, but he had the feeling she might bolt if he did that. She'd barely let herself be kissed, which struck him as odd. After all, she'd just come twice for him.

Shit.

Twice.

But regardless of her prickly nature, Cole needed to touch her, so he put his hand to her waist, his fingers resting against the stark black lines of her tattoo. "When did you get this?"

"The tat? A few years ago."

"Will you tell me about it?"

She shrugged. "What's to tell? It's a tree."

"A dead tree?"

"Maybe. Or maybe it's bare for the winter."

"Come on. You must know. Tell me what it means."

Her laugh was just a humorless huff of impatience. "It means I dated a tattoo artist when I was twenty-three. That's all."

"I don't believe you. If that's all it was, you'd have a Celtic cross on your shoulder or a unicorn on your ass."

That got a real laugh out of her, at least. He didn't realize she'd gone stiff against him until she relaxed. "So you checked for unicorns when you were back there?"

"I did. That's one more horn than I'm comfortable with in these situations." He could practically feel her smile.

"You're funny, you know that? You have any tattoos? Maybe a lucky horseshoe or a spur?"

"A heart with 'Ma' written in elaborate script?"

"Something like that."

"You can check me over later. Be thorough, all right?"

"You wish."

"Oh, you've got that right, Miss Grace."

She laughed, and her body relaxed a tiny bit more. Maybe if he could get her to melt into him, she'd relax in other ways, as well. Maybe she'd tell him something about herself. Anything. Though if he couldn't get her to melt after two orgasms, the girl might be made of steel.

"I should go," she murmured, but she didn't move. If she didn't want to leave, he'd give her every reason to stay.

He smoothed his thumb along her ribs. "Tell me about your new job," he said, hoping he'd picked the right topic. It'd been a long time since he'd held a woman like this. Even longer since it had felt so natural. Strange that it was with someone who represented everything he'd run from.

"I'm working with a photographer named Eve Hill. I hoped she'd hire me to do makeup, you know? But she needed more help than that, so I'm working more hours than I expected, and trying out new things." She flashed a smile over her bare shoulder. "Clearly."

Clearly? Did she mean him? He pressed his mouth to her shoulder blade, amazed that her skin could be so soft when she did everything she could to make herself look hard.

"I didn't think I'd be so good at it, but it's working out. Thanks to you."

"Me?" he asked. "Are we talking about your job now? Or sex? Because yeah, you were damn good at that, but..."

She snorted. "The job, obviously."

"I'm not following you."

"The ranch!"

He'd just been putting his mouth to her skin again, but he froze at her words. "What do you mean 'the ranch'?" The warm press of her skin suddenly felt claustrophobic.

"Easy Creek! Obviously I couldn't have found that site for Eve unless you'd taken me there. Turned out it was perfect."

Shock washed through him like water through a sieve. "You did that?"

"Did what?"

"You brought those people to Easy Creek?"

"Yes! Apparently there was a location scout in town until last month. He went out of business, so Eve has been taking up the slack. Yesterday, when they described the kind of place they were looking for, I knew the ranch was perfect. So, thank you."

"Thank you?" He pushed up, trying to get away from her.

"Hey!" she protested when he nearly knocked her off the couch.

He finally managed to get to his feet and stalked away. "Are you kidding me?"

"What's wrong?"

He turned to see her standing next to the couch, arms shielding her breasts, expression wary at his sudden change of mood.

"What's wrong?" he repeated. "How could you have done that to me? That's my place of work, it's not some scenic stop on a damn tour, Grace."

Her jaw fell.

"I can't believe you," he said, but then he laughed. "Actually, I can. I don't know why I'd find it hard to believe that a girl like you would think it meant nothing to bring fifty assholes out to my ranch and let them run wild."

"*A girl like me?* Are you kidding me? What the hell does that mean?"

"It means you're one of them. It's so obvious. I should've known better than to think anything different. Jesus, I delivered Easy Creek to you with a goddamn bow!"

Grace stalked toward the door, brushing past him with a glare. "I don't know what your problem is, but I'm not it. You're way out of line."

"Did you not once think that maybe you should've run it by me before you dragged half of Hollywood out there?"

"No, as a matter of fact—" Her voice was cut off by the fabric of her shirt as she yanked it over her head. Cole looked away from the sight of her bare breasts.

"As a matter of fact, it didn't occur to me, because it's *not* your ranch. You don't own it. Hell, you don't even live there. So, no. It didn't once occur to me that I needed your permission. Asshole."

With that, she stalked out of the apartment. His door hit the wall and bounced back so hard that it closed. Cole wanted to go over and open it again, just so he could slam it himself. Instead, he had to be satisfied with the convulsive bang of her door slamming.

It had been her.

Her.

She was the one who'd done this to him.

He was breathing so hard he felt as if he'd just run a mile. He was an idiot. Getting involved with a woman like her. He should have known better. He *had* known better.

"Shit!" he roared. He wanted to punch something, but the last thing he needed was a broken hand on top of this broken leg. For once, that wasn't hurting. He was too fucking pissed to feel anything. Except the rage.

He paced to the door, then across the living room. He rolled his shoulders, trying to slough off the weight that had settled there. But he couldn't budge it. It felt like the air was pushing in on him. The walls.

Cole grabbed his shirt and his keys and walked out. And he finally got to slam the door. Somehow, it didn't make him feel any better.

CHAPTER ELEVEN

THERE WAS ONE LINE OF GROUT above the tub that was whiter than all the others. Grace knew this because she'd been standing in the shower staring at it for the past fifteen minutes. The room got steamier and steamier, but that one line still glowed white. A repair, maybe. Or just a defect.

Which brought her back to her life.

"God," she groaned, rubbing her hands over her face.

She'd taken a shower when she'd gotten home last night, but she'd hoped another long, hot shower this morning would clear the confusion from her head. So far, nothing. And she had to get to work soon.

Work. At the same place where Cole Rawlins worked.

"Great. Another superintelligent move, Grace Barrett." What the hell had she been thinking, sleeping with a *cowboy?*

"A girl like you," she muttered. That's what he'd called her. *A girl like you.* How had he dared to throw something like that at her after he'd had sex with her?

She'd known. That was the worst part. She'd known he'd only wanted her because she was different and dangerous. Known he'd wanted to have sex with her even though he'd avoided driving her all the way to the ranch.

The sex hadn't had anything to do with *liking* her. It never had anything to do with liking her.

Which was fine. Just fine. Because she'd taken what she wanted from him, hadn't she? She'd gotten off. Twice. That was a lot better than most one-night stands. And hell, as badly as it had ended, even that wasn't the worst post-sex exit she'd ever suffered. So screw it.

"Screw it," she assured herself, turning off the shower. Whatever his problem was, he could deal with it. She had work to do, and she'd be damned if she'd let some oversexed cowboy mess up her plans. She had a lot more riding on this job than her feelings.

It took ten minutes to do her makeup, and another ten to dry her hair and work in a tiny bit of her dwindling supply of styling product. She got dressed in the last of her work-suitable outfits and was out the door with ten minutes to spare. Thankfully, she got no glimpse of Cole on her way out.

Unthankfully, Shane was coming down the stairs as she locked her door.

"Morning, Grace," he drawled, tipping his hat.

"Shane," she said without inflection. Had Cole told him already? Bragged about banging the new chick? It was fine if he had, she just didn't like not knowing. And Shane wasn't giving anything away. He simply dipped his chin and strolled out the front door. He seemed like a nice enough guy, but she couldn't tell what he was thinking and that left her on edge.

At least Cole seemed honest about what he felt, whether that was lust or disdain. Though at the moment, on her way to a place where he'd be, that seemed less like a benefit.

Maybe she wouldn't be needed at the ranch site today at all. Or maybe Cole would be out on the range, or something.

While she was waiting impatiently for the bus to arrive, her cell phone rang. Merry's name popped onto the screen and made her smile.

"Hey, Merry," she said in relief.

"Hey, yourself. What are you doing? Have they crowned you rodeo queen of Wyoming yet?"

"No, but soon. I can feel it."

Merry laughed until she snorted. "What are you doing?"

"I'm on my way to work. You won't believe what I'm doing."

"Maybe I shouldn't ask. But is it strippergrams? I thought they told you they only hired girls with boobs."

Grace leaned against a streetlight and laughed so hard she had to close her eyes. "No, it's not any form of stripping, so whatever you were about to say about working the pole, drop it."

"Like it's hot?" Merry cooed.

"Yes. What I'm really doing is working with a location scout. On a Madeline Beckingham movie."

"Are you kidding me? Oh, my God. Are there robots and explosions and stuff?"

"No, this one is about monsters. And cowboys. Hence the location. But it's more than I could've hoped for. An industry job in Wyoming. And the pay is good."

"Speaking of—"

"I'm not moving to Dallas!"

"That's not what I meant. Scott called me."

Grace's heart dropped with such suddenness that she felt dizzy. She pressed her shoulder harder to the streetlight to be sure she didn't fall. "Merry—"

"He left a pissed-off message, asking if I knew where you were. He says if you don't call him, you'll be sorry."

"I…"

"What a dick," Merry snarled. "Oh, my God. I hate that guy."

"I know," Grace breathed. Lights danced behind her eyes. He hadn't said anything more. Merry didn't know.

"You should've left him a long time ago."

"I know," she whispered. "Listen, my bus is almost here."

"Okay, I just wanted to give you a heads-up. Call him if you want, but I don't think you should. I blocked his number, so it makes no difference to me. But I thought you should know he called."

"Thank you."

"Do you want me to call him back? Tell him to go to hell?"

"No!"

Merry laughed. "Are you sure? I could tell him he's no good at oral sex. Isn't that what you said? He tried that alphabet trick on you once?"

Relief made Grace smile. "Yeah. But I almost had him trained by the end. *Almost.*"

"Good for you."

"My bus is here," Grace said, relieved that it was the

truth and she didn't have to lie to her best friend any more than she already had.

"Okay. Have a great day. Say hi to Madeline Beckingham for me."

"Sure."

"I love you, Grace."

"Me, too," she said. It was the only response she ever gave. But Merry's words filled her up with a warm feeling. Such a warm feeling that by the time she stepped onto the bus, her panic had almost faded entirely.

She had nothing to be unhappy about, after all. It was a beautiful day, nobody on the bus tried to start a pleasant conversation, she had a roof over her head and she was earning money. Plus, she'd fucked out all her stress last night.

Heck, yeah, she had.

So when Grace stepped off the bus, she put a little extra sway into her step and clomped her way down the wooden sidewalk.

"'Stay gold, Ponyboy,'" she said with a smile as she opened the door to the studio.

"What?" Eve asked from behind the counter. She looked up from some prints she'd been reviewing. "What's a ponyboy?"

Grace flushed. Apparently Eve had never seen *The Outsiders*. Merry watched it once a year and made Grace watch it, too. "Nothing. Sorry. Just a movie joke."

"For...yourself?"

"Yes."

Eve just nodded and slipped the photos back into an envelope. "Ready for a long day?"

"I'm ready. Are we heading back out to the ranch?"

"Yes, I'll drop you off there. I'll be working at the river."

"Great," she said, not quite meaning it. She wasn't exactly worried about seeing Cole again, but she didn't want to put up with his glaring face first thing in the morning. Especially without caffeine. She still didn't have a coffeemaker, and she'd forgotten to stop for a cup at the gas station.

But Eve rode to the rescue. Or she drove to it, pulling up to a drive-through coffee place. Grace nearly wept with happiness at the smell. A real latte. My God. It had been weeks.

By the time they bounced over the last few yards of the ranch road, Grace was ready to face Cole. It was a good thing she'd braced herself, because as soon as she got out of Eve's car, he looked up from a conversation and his gaze caught hers.

She raised one eyebrow. He lowered both of his.

"God," she muttered. "Men."

"You already have man problems?" Eve asked from just beside her.

Grace winced, realizing she'd muttered out loud. "Kind of."

"One of these production guys bothering you?"

"Nobody bothers me," Grace said.

"Good for you. You know any of these people?"

She glanced around. "Probably not. They're mostly preproduction. Not a lot of call for makeup."

"All right. You've got my phone number if you need me. And if I get out of cell range, I'll be back in a couple of hours. The catering's been lined up, so we can grab lunch here when I get back."

And just like that, Grace was in charge again. Well, not in charge of much. Just her side of things. Clearing up problems. Making phone calls. She'd have to add more minutes to her phone. Maybe even get a real plan.

No, that was too permanent. When she went to Vancouver things would be tight, and money uncertain. But… For the first time, it occurred to her that she might have more options. Working in makeup was a pretty narrow field. Sure, there might be a perfect opening now, but there was a good chance she'd find nothing afterward, and she'd probably stay in Vancouver for a little while.

But preproduction stuff? Location work? That could open up a whole new world for her, at least until she could get settled and figure out her next step.

If Eve were willing to give her a recommendation, Grace might be able to slip in on the ground floor of a company. And Eve seemed to like her. In fact, she treated Grace like an equal, as if she weren't a stranger in a strange land. Maybe her time in Wyoming would be less like limbo and more like a season away from her real life. Nothing to be taken seriously, but nothing terrible either.

She looked up from entering lot dimensions into a laptop and caught Cole looking at her. She aimed her most emotionless stare at him.

Okay, not a season away from her real love life, apparently. That was as screwed up and nonsensical as ever.

Cole looked away first. Good. She didn't know what the hell he was so upset about. She hadn't taken anything from him. He was still at the ranch, still walking around in his tight, dirty jeans and button-down shirt. Still wearing his scuffed cowboy boots and worn hat.

He glanced up and found her still looking, then tugged the brim lower before turning away.

Grace smiled and bent back to her task.

Did he think she couldn't handle this? Sex without the niceness? Hell, that was the way she preferred it. He could call her anything he wanted; he couldn't take back her orgasms. And that was the point of sex, after all. Getting off. So, a complete success.

Ignoring the fact that she seemed to be trying to talk herself into something, Grace held her smile. But it fell away when her eye caught on a woman who looked familiar.

Grace looked down at the computer, then slowly up again. This time the young blonde woman was looking back at her, and Grace's heart sped up. She knew this woman, but how? Her ice-blond hair was cut into a symmetrical bob that framed her lush face. Her eyes narrowed on Grace, but this time, Grace didn't look away.

Who was she?

Grace suddenly placed her, picturing her lips painted red and her petite body encased in a skintight scarlet dress. She'd met this woman at a party once. But which one?

Though Grace looked back to the spreadsheet on the computer screen, she didn't see it. She was rifling through memories, instead. A year ago, there wouldn't have been nearly as many parties to remember, and few that a woman like that would've attended.

But Scott had made his mark on Grace's life. At first, his gentle suggestions about her career had felt like help. She'd been a great makeup artist, in demand with a certain population. Artsy filmmakers and independents had loved her. But Scott had pushed her to want more and try harder.

At first it had been thrilling, getting work on big-budget movies, but she hadn't quite fit in. And she'd rubbed people the wrong way. But Scott had been so happy. She'd been his ticket from TV to film. Introductions. Industry parties. He'd been thrilled. And Grace had been miserable.

She might've broken it off at that point, but then she'd been fired. And bad-mouthed by that asshole director. And Scott had let her move into his place. A favor. A blessing.

But after a while she'd become extraneous. Worse than that. She'd become a liability. An edgy girl in a world of glamour. A tough girl forced to rub elbows with beauties like that blonde.

Who was she? More important, did she know Scott?

Grace looked back up, trying to seem natural instead of nervous. The woman was gone. Grace slumped in relief.

Nothing to be worried about. Everything was fine.

She couldn't have been more wrong.

"Hello," a cool voice said from just behind her.

Grace spun around to find the blonde eyeing her with a less than friendly smile.

"You're with the scouting team?"

"Yes. Hi," Grace said.

"I'm Willa," the woman said, not offering a hand. "Willa James."

"I'm Grace."

Her fake smile tightened. "Grace," she repeated. "Of course. You're from L.A., right? We've met before."

Grace's heart began to pound, but she tried to tell herself it was fine. She'd met thousands of people during her career. Hell, she might have even met thousands of people at parties.

"I am," she finally said, and left it at that.

Willa. Her mind scrambled. *Willa.* Willa, who was the girlfriend of Malcolm? Who was a good friend of Diane. Who maybe knew Scott from—

"What are you doing in Wyoming?" Willa pressed.

"Working."

She sneered. "Aren't you a makeup artist? Are you here to make sure the crew look good?"

Adrenaline flooded her veins and she snapped, "Yes, exactly. I'm making the lighting guys pretty." But she immediately regretted it. This woman knew her somehow. And Grace couldn't afford to go pissing people off anymore.

Willa laughed, though her voice carried not even a hint of humor. "Well, interesting seeing you here."

The woman walked away, leaving Grace with a cold sweat prickling over her brow. What if Willa knew Scott? What if she'd heard rumors? What if—

Her darting gaze caught on Cole. Willa walked past and he glanced from her to Grace, as if he suspected the tension. Scalding heat rushed up to paint Grace's face red.

But it was okay. It was just a casual connection. No reason to be alarmed. Really, it was inevitable that she'd see somebody here that she knew. Hollywood was a strangely incestuous place. Sometimes it felt like some giant backwoods family. You were related to all of them, even the ones you'd never met.

It was fine.

But her face burned. Her ears and neck felt on fire. She wanted to sink into the earth. She wanted to run away. Again.

Would Cole try to stop her? If he did, then she'd have an excuse to turn on him. Slap his face, yell crude insults, confirm everything he seemed to think about her.

Damn, that would've felt good.

But she only finished entering the measurements of the ranch for Eve's site files, then emailed them to Eve and sent a copy to the location manager. By the time Grace looked up, Cole had disappeared, and so had Willa. In fact, the whole population of the yard seemed to have shifted toward the main house. A big black SUV with tinted windows and giant tires had pulled up. The crowd hovered nearby. Madeline Beckingham had arrived.

COLE'S BRAIN HAD FROZEN up, split down the middle, and was now insisting on sluggishly crawling along on two separate, equally unpleasant tracks.

On one side, he watched his old lover Madeline Beckingham slip from a shiny black SUV, as beautiful as if the past thirteen years hadn't happened. It made no sense. He'd aged from a smooth and happy twenty-one-year-old kid to a hard-worn thirty-four-year-old cowboy with plenty of lines around his eyes to mark the years.

If Madeline had aged at all, he couldn't see it. She looked just as bright and luminescent as ever. Her hair was vivid red and straight as silk. Her skin a slight golden color that should have looked unnatural with the red hair, but somehow, she made it look like the skin tone every redhead should have been born with. Not that she'd been born with any of it. What she'd been born with was money. And she'd made herself into exactly the beauty she wanted to be.

The sheen of her had blinded him to the hard edges underneath. She was still good at that masquerade, it seemed. After all, in the time that had passed, she could only have gotten harder.

The other half of his brain was keeping track of his new lover, which was probably not the right thing to call a woman he'd slept with once and then kicked out of his place.

Funny, but Grace seemed like the other side of the coin in this situation. Same danger as Madeline. Same hardness. But Grace put all her hard edges on display, and saved the softer ones for private.

Both of them made him feel like a goddamn fool.

Cole tugged his hat lower over his eyes and tucked his thumbs into his pockets as he watched Madeline's entourage surround her. He was a safe distance away: twenty feet or so, and leaning against the shady side of the tack house. He didn't think she'd see him, and at first, she didn't. But then she waved her assistants off, walked a few steps across the yard until she had a relatively solitary space, and spun in a slow circle, a wide smile overtaking her face.

"This is perfect," she crowed. "Perfect! Oh, my God, the pictures didn't do it justice. It's exactly what I wanted. We're going to have to do a quick setup here. The summer colors will only last another six or seven weeks. I—" Her spin came to a graceful stop. She was facing him. She was looking at him. "Are you kidding me?" she called. "Cole? Is that you?"

For a moment, he considered leaving. Just turning his back and walking away. It wasn't worth this. His land, his relationship with Easy, his plan for the future—none of it was worth facing this woman. But she rushed toward him, and he couldn't summon the will to run like a coward.

"Oh, my God," she said breathlessly. "Cole! I can't believe it's you. You're *here?*"

"Where else would I be?"

Her arms snaked around him and held him tight. The moment headed straight for discomfort and quickly tunneled into awkwardness when he only held his arms up and away. Madeline didn't seem to notice. She kissed his cheek and squealed.

"I had no idea! You didn't leave any word when you left. As a matter of fact…" She stepped back and crossed her arms. "I completely forgot that I'm furious with you. You just disappeared."

"I came home," he said gruffly.

She forgot her pose of anger and laughed, waving a

hand that seemed to dismiss everything, including him. "All right, it doesn't matter. Is this your ranch?"

"I work here."

"Perfect." She looped her arm through his and tugged Cole out into the sunlight. He'd spent a lot of the past hours worrying about this moment. About seeing her. About how he'd react. But it was so surreal that it didn't feel like anything at all. She was someone he'd known intimately. Someone who knew things about him that no one else knew, but she felt like a stranger. No, that wasn't it. *He* felt like a stranger when he was with her. A stranger he didn't like at all.

"This is *my* cowboy," Madeline was saying to a group of people who were too well dressed to be actual crew. "Be sure to get Cole anything he needs while we're here."

"Actually…" He pulled his arm free of hers. "I'm taking care of things for Easy during the shoot. So let me know if you need anything."

"Anything, huh?" Her eyes swept down him so quickly that he was almost sure no one else noticed. Almost. Before he could stop himself, he glanced toward the table where Grace had been sitting. She was still there, and she looked in his direction, but she was in the middle of a conversation with another woman and quickly looked away.

"I've got to check on the horses," he said, not looking back toward Madeline.

"You know…" Her hand closed over his wrist before he could move away. When he glanced down and saw her red nails against his skin, a cold sweat broke out at the nape of his neck. "We're going to get filming pretty quickly. Four weeks, I'd say, so we don't catch the fall colors. You up for another go-round?"

He'd loved the sight of long red fingernails back then. The scrape of them trailing down his skin. He raised his eyes and met her gaze. "Excuse me?" he said coldly.

She smiled as if she'd just eaten something delicious. "My God, Cole. You've only gotten more handsome. How is that even possible? You've got to be in the movie. Please."

The movie. She was asking him to be in the movie. Cole wanted to feel relief, but he wasn't that stupid. After all, that was what she'd said the first time. *Be an extra. Help us out. Tell me everything you know about ranch life.*

Jesus, that had been a rush. Being singled out like that. Being approached by Madeline Beckingham, a woman who'd been famous since she'd directed her first film at nineteen. A woman who'd been famous *before* that.

At first, he'd thought her interest had just been about his riding. His skills. When he'd realized she'd noticed more than that... Shit, that had been so much better.

Cole reached for the hand wrapped around his wrist and carefully removed it. "I've got to check on the horses," he repeated. But she didn't look the least bit discouraged as he turned away. No didn't mean no for Madeline Beckingham. It was just the opening volley. And somehow Cole had never managed to win a round. In the end, he'd lost every single one.

CHAPTER TWELVE

"I NEED YOU TO GO to the county offices to file the last of these permits," Eve said, tossing Grace the keys to her car.

"But..." Grace caught the keys even as she shook her head. "You need me here."

"Nope. You got us caught up on paperwork this morning. I'm going to spend the afternoon shooting photos for the production files. Finally."

So this virtual stranger was just going to let Grace take her car? "Okay," she said softly. "Right now?"

"Now!" Eve urged, making a shooing motion as she walked away.

"Okay." Grace looked down at the little Lexus icon on the key. It was a nice car. Not flashy, but very nice. She didn't understand these people. Eve knew she had nothing. No car. No family. Not even a halfway decent phone. Grace could just get in Eve's car and be out of Wyoming before she was even missed. When she was sixteen, she might have actually done that.

But maybe nice people didn't think that way.

"Grace!" Eve shouted. "One more thing!"

For a split second, she was sure Eve had realized how stupid she was being and changed her mind. But then she saw that Eve was walking toward her with Madeline

Willa? Let me take a guess. Is she the one who did Felicia's makeup for the Golden Globes this year?" She laughed at her own joke.

"No. I recognize Grace. She's from L.A." She sounded caught between delight and contempt.

"I'm aware of that," Madeline said wearily.

"I bet you don't know that she skipped town because she's a thief."

"That's not true!" Grace said, feeling as if she were playing a scene in a movie. This wasn't really happening. She knew it wasn't, because she should've felt mortified, but she didn't feel anything at all.

"It is true," Willa sneered. "I just talked to her ex. She's a thief. Not to mention the rumors of a little substance abuse problem."

Eve and Madeline both looked from Willa to Grace. "That's not true either," she said, her voice a little shaky. Did it sound as if she was lying?

Willa rolled her eyes. "Call Frank Edison and ask him why he fired her from her last job. Which was about six months ago, by the way, because nobody else will hire her. Her boyfriend kicked her out after she stole eight thousand dollars from him."

Grace shook her head, staring at Willa in shock. A defense formed in her mind, but it all sounded so stupid. She'd say the same things if she actually were a druggie thief, after all. *It's not true. I didn't do it. It's all a misunderstanding.*

But apparently she didn't need to say anything at all, because someone jumped to her defense. Not her defense, actually, but…

"Jesus, Willa," Madeline Beckingham scoffed. "A substance abuse problem? I'll be sure to fire the whole cast then."

"Ms. Beck—"

"I don't give a shit what her problem is as long as she can make me look good on HD film in natural sunlight. She can bathe in the blood of virgins for all I care." She smiled. "Maybe *that's* why she's in Wyoming. Virgins are few and far between in Southern California." She laughed at her own joke again, but nobody else in their little group laughed. That didn't bother Madeline. She just chuckled and shook her head. "Come on, Cole. Let's find Bill."

Cole. Great. Just great. Grace didn't turn around to look at him. She waited for their footsteps to fade away. She waited for Willa to huff and stalk off. And then she made herself meet Eve's gaze.

"It's not true," Grace repeated, her voice hoarse with emotions she still couldn't feel. "I swear. It's not true. I mean, I was fired by Frank Edison, but it had nothing to do with my work or alcohol or anything. It was a personal disagreement. And the other thing, the money, that's about an ex-boyfriend. We broke up and—"

"Okay." Eve's expression seemed purposefully blank. "We'll talk about it later in private."

"Sure. I…I'll be back in an hour then."

Eve's gaze touched on the keys in Grace's hand.

Oh, God. "I'm sorry. I can see if someone else could give me a ride. Maybe…" But there was no one else. Maybe if she asked Cole—

"Just be back in time to do her makeup. And charge production your normal fee for makeup work, okay?"

"Sure. Yes." They both stood there for a moment. Eve had to be wishing she hadn't volunteered her car, and Grace wished she could think of a way to let her off the hook. But she needed to get to town, and Eve couldn't lose two or three hours of her day driving her. "Okay," she finally said. "I'll be back as quickly as possible. Without speeding, I mean."

"No problem."

Newfound maturity or not, Grace hoped she ran into Willa alone sometime soon. She wanted to slap that bitch across the face. She wanted to hurt her. Because the feeling was returning to Grace's body and she felt like she might throw up. That'd be a nice, funny way to reinforce the rumors that she was some sort of addict. Thank God she hadn't eaten since eight that morning.

Face burning, she got into Eve's car and pulled carefully away, determined not to even stir up one piece of gravel. She just disappeared as quietly as she could and tried to decide if she should keep on driving. Because the worst part about the lies Willa had told was they were so close to the awful truth.

CHAPTER THIRTEEN

"I'VE GOTTA GET THIS," Cole ground out to the production assistant who was trying to get him to agree that the barn corral could indeed be easily moved to a place that got better natural light. "Excuse me."

Cole glanced at the screen of his cell phone, didn't recognize the number, and still breathed a sigh of relief. Whoever it was had to be better than this boy who looked eighteen years old and didn't have a lick of common sense.

"Hello?" He headed straight down the trail that led from the barn to the meadow corral. The background noise of two dozen people began to fade behind him. But there was no answer on the phone. "Hello?" he repeated.

"I didn't know who else to call," a rushed female voice said.

"Okay. Who is this?"

"There's no spare tire in her car."

"Grace?" he asked, feeling stupid even as he said it. Of course it wasn't Grace. She was... He glanced around, realizing he hadn't seen her since—

"I'm sorry to spring this on you, Cole, but I don't have a credit card to pay for a tow and the spare tire isn't in the trunk and I can't be late or they'll think..."

"Where are you?"

"I don't know. About halfway toward the ranch after I turn off the highway?"

"Okay, I'll be there in ten minutes."

"Really? You'll come?"

Cole looked at the people milling about. The crowd had thinned out, at least. But Madeline was still here, ruling over them all from the front porch of the big house. "Yeah. See you in a few."

Just like that, he escaped, the way he'd been wanting to all day. But the escape was bittersweet, because he knew he'd be returning in half an hour. But he had work to do. Real work. The horses were stressed from the ruckus and traffic, and Cole had decided they'd be better off at the meadow corral than in the barn. These were ranch horses. They could handle sleeping in the lean-to for a few nights during the summer. They didn't need blankets or even a roof over their heads, and they could take on coyotes with a well-placed kick.

But like Cole, they couldn't take these people with their earpieces and notepads and sunglasses and hard laughter.

As soon as he was out of the yard, Cole rolled down the windows of his truck and turned off the radio. He wanted some peace and quiet, and if rescuing Grace got him thirty minutes of peace, maybe she wasn't so bad.

Ridiculous, though. Apparently she was way worse than he'd imagined. A thief, huh? He wouldn't have guessed that. Though he hadn't liked seeing her tortured earlier. Humiliated. Ironic that she'd been slapped in the face by the people she'd brought here.

After all her tough talk, he wouldn't have expected

her to put up with that kind of shit. But it seemed she was just like everyone else in Hollywood—willing to give up every bit of herself to get near the dream. Kissing ass. Apologizing for someone else treating her like shit.

When he saw her ten minutes later, she looked too small. She stood at the side of the road, arms crossed and jaw set, and glared at his truck as if Cole was to blame for whatever had happened. He pulled over and stared at her for a moment, so small against the wide landscape.

Grace glared and motioned for him to hurry up. He wondered if she'd bother with a thank-you.

"Hurry!" she said. When he opened the door, she rushed to speak. "I have to get back as soon as possible!"

Nope. No polite thank-you. Not even an impolite one. But then her face softened. Just for a split second before she got control. "I'm sorry. Thank you for coming. I just…"

"What happened?"

"I don't know if it was a nail or a leak or… The tire's flat and there's no spare."

"No spare?" He walked toward the car. "Pop the trunk."

She rolled her eyes but opened the driver's door and popped the trunk. The well that should've held the spare was, indeed, empty.

"Oh, look!" Grace exclaimed in a saccharin-sweet voice. "I'm not an idiot woman! It's a miracle."

"I'm here to help, you know."

"Then help!"

He was surprised to find himself biting back a smile.

"Fine. We'll need to get the tire off and take it into town for a repair."

"No! I can't be late, Cole. Please. Not after that. Eve's car… She'll think… I just can't be late."

She wasn't angry, he saw now. Not at all. She was scared. Anxious. And a little panicked, too. Her dark eyes darted from the car to him to his truck. "All right," he said. "Get in. I'll drive you and then come back for the tire."

"Wait!" she yelled and jumped to open the back door. She pulled out what looked like a very fancy toolbox. "Okay. Let's go!"

"Yes, ma'am," he muttered. Christ, she was bossy. He should be happy to see her like this. Caught by the trouble she'd brought on them both. Nearly as tortured by these people as he was. She'd brought them here. She'd done this.

He opened the truck door for her before walking around to get in the driver's seat.

"I thought a herd of those antelope were going to swarm me at any time," she muttered.

"The pronghorn? You probably could've fought them off."

"Oh, one, sure. But a whole herd? And this is right where we saw them."

"Well, you made it."

"Yes. And, Cole—thanks for saving me. Really." She crossed her arms over her chest, and the movement made Cole think of her breasts. Naked. Small and tight and hot under his mouth.

He shifted. He didn't want to see her like this. Vulnerable and worried. He wanted her to be a bitch again. The woman who'd completely screwed up his life.

"You know Madeline Beckingham," she said out of the blue.

That worked just fine to get him pissed again. "Yeah? How would I know Madeline Beckingham?"

"You tell me, but it's as obvious as the fact that there was no spare in that car."

Fine. Now he knew what to feel. Anger. And discomfort. "She filmed a movie here a long time ago. I was an extra and I helped train some of the others in Western riding."

"Is that when you started hating girls like me?"

He shot a look at her and her eyes were back to normal now. Dark and mocking him. Yet something was different. She'd changed her makeup at some point. Instead of pure black, her makeup was smokier. Gray with a hint of violet at the corners. She looked softer. Maybe that was what was throwing him off. That, and the memory of her gasping into his ear as he got her off.

Jesus.

"Look, Grace. I'm sorry about last night. I was in a bad place when I went to the bar. This movie shoot, it's... Then I saw you, and..."

"And? What? You don't like girls like me. You've made that clear. So you saw me and, what?"

He shrugged. "I forgot about being pissed off. Forgot about the movie shoot. About my leg. My future."

"Your future?"

He waved off the question. "All the bullshit. And I

didn't expect that the person helping me forget was the one who'd screwed me over."

"Is that what I was doing? Helping you forget?"

He took his eyes off the road long enough to meet her gaze. Not that it did any good. She showed him nothing. It drove him crazy, that she could make herself so blank. "Isn't that what I was doing for *you?* Helping you forget?"

She stared at him until he had to look back to the road. When he broke the gaze, she laughed that jaded laugh again. "It was sex, Cole. What you were doing for me was the same thing I was doing for you. Getting off."

"I can get myself off," he said. "I'd bet a hell of a lot of money that you're perfectly capable of jacking off, too. So whatever it is for you, it isn't just coming."

"You're wrong," she whispered.

"No, I'm not. And I got really pissed because I thought you were one thing to me, and you turned out to be something else."

"Well, I'm so sorry, Cole!" she snapped. "I guess I wasn't the right tool for the job."

He clenched his teeth together, but she was making him see that maybe things weren't as black-and-white as he'd wanted them to be. She hadn't done anything wrong. Not from her perspective. She couldn't have known that what she'd done would stomp all over the most fragile parts of his life. The wounds that had healed all wrong. And if she couldn't have known that, if it hadn't been malicious, then Cole was being an asshole.

She'd slept with him. She'd been happy. And celebrating. She'd slept with him as part of that. And he'd thanked her for it by treating her like shit.

If she wasn't the woman he wanted her to be, that wasn't her problem.

Cole swallowed a curse and rubbed a hand against his thigh. "I'm sorry. I shouldn't have done that."

"Shouldn't have done what?" she challenged. "Fuck me?"

"No. I mean, that might be your take on it at this point."

"No. I got off, right? The rest of it hardly matters."

"You don't mean that."

"Don't I?" she asked. She offered a tight smile when he looked at her. "You've been honest, at least. You want my feelings to be hurt? You want me to feel like shit because you didn't walk me to my door and tell me I was special afterward? Well, sorry. I don't. It takes more than that, cowboy."

"Grace. I'm sorry. Even if your feelings weren't hurt. Even if you don't give a shit and I was nothing more than a fun ride for you. I'm sorry. I like you, and I shouldn't have—"

"You don't know anything about me," she said, her voice soft and yet somehow cutting through his words like a machete.

"I know a little. I wish I knew more."

"Ha. You've made pretty sure you're never going to know anything more. Girls like *me*? We don't give that kind of knowledge up easily. And if you know anything about me, anything at all, then that was accidental. That wasn't anything I meant to give you."

"Yeah. I get that." He knew she was trying to be tough, but she was breaking his heart. She didn't want to show him anything, which just made him want to see it all.

"But," she said carefully, "we can have sex again, if you want."

"What?" He exhaled the word on a shocked sigh.

"It was good. It'd be even better if you kept your mouth shut afterward."

They were almost to the ranch. The truck passed under the sign. Shadows flashed over his face and then disappeared. Cole had no idea what to say. He was half horrified and half aroused. The obvious answer was, "Yes. Let's do that." But instead, he heard his mouth say, "Why?"

Why? What the hell? He was losing his mind.

"Why not?" she answered.

He didn't realize he'd stopped, but Grace was opening the door. She hopped out, transferred her box to one hand and closed the truck door without another word.

If you want.

If he wanted? Jesus. He couldn't even get out of the truck now, not without embarrassing himself. And once again, Grace Barrett had managed to banish every one of his worries. Even the one that was watching from right across the yard.

FOR A MOMENT, Eve looked genuinely worried. Grace saw it clearly on the woman's face as she hurried down the steps of the porch and rushed over. "Where's my car?"

"A tire went flat and there was no spare."

"Oh," she said, then the worry was chased away by a grimace. "Oh, my God, I keep forgetting to replace it. I'm so sorry. Are you okay?"

"Yes, Cole gave me a ride and he's going back to grab the tire and get it patched."

"He doesn't have to do that. I'll call a tow truck."

Grace gestured toward the truck that was already pulling away. "Too late." She cleared her throat. "I'm sorry about the car."

"It's no big deal." No big deal, and yet they both lapsed into silence and stood in an awkward limbo for too many seconds. "It's not true," Grace finally said. "What Willa said about me. I know you don't have any reason to believe me, Eve. But I don't have a drinking problem. I don't do drugs. And I'm not a…a thief." The last word was hard to get out. It felt shameful just to have to say it.

She'd made herself back into that teenage girl who'd run from everyone, including the police.

And these days, she might set herself apart from other people in terms of appearance, but she did it on purpose. She tried very hard to walk a fine line between respectability and edginess.

As a kid, she hadn't had that choice. She'd lived on the streets. If her hair had looked wild then, it was because it had needed a good wash and a cut. And if her eyes had looked dark and angry, they had been. And those tattered clothes? They really had been dug out of a box outside the door of a soup kitchen. She'd lived like that for two years after she'd run away. She'd stolen things. She'd lied and schemed and done what she'd needed to for food. She'd never actually sold her body, but there'd been a constant, unacknowledged negotiation between her heart and her mind, hadn't there? Men whose interest had been more interesting because they had a place. Or a car. Or enough money to pay for dinner without even thinking about it. She'd rarely slept with a boy who'd been like her. A hustler. A street kid.

So she could say she'd never been a whore. She could tell herself that, but she couldn't say she'd never been a thief. Maybe that was why it stung so badly now. Because she really was one.

She swallowed hard as the silence pressed harder against her skin. "I'm sorry about that, Eve. And I understand if you think it's best if we…if I…don't…"

"Grace, I've lived alone since I was twenty-two. I've owned my own business for years. I've never had a business partner. Never been married. Every decision is my own, and I have to trust my gut. And my gut says I like you. It also tells me that Willa chick is a superficial bitch. So, let's leave it at that, all right?"

"But you must wonder—"

"Okay, I'll admit that I had a fleeting moment of thinking I was an idiot to hand a near stranger my car keys and wish her the best. But here you are. And my car is allegedly still intact." She smiled, and not for the first time, Grace noticed that sadness in her eyes. Maybe it was always there. Maybe it was only obvious when she smiled.

But whatever it was, she was choosing to give Grace a chance.

"I have a reputation in L.A.," Grace admitted. "It

might be my fault. I can have an attitude. I don't like to kiss anyone's ass, even if they're my boss. But I'm good at what I do, and I try to keep my head down. Still, there's always that one situation, you know? Where you have to say that something isn't right, even if speaking up will get you into trouble. I've made mistakes, but most of them I wouldn't take back."

"Good. I've worked at the edges of this industry for a while now. I see the bull that goes on. And, um, let's just say I see hints of inflexibility in your personality."

"Ha. That's a nice way to say it."

"Whatever it is, I can see how you might be like oil in their water sometimes. But let's see if you and I can manage to make it work. Just please remember that you're representing me right now. So if you get into one of those situations again? Maybe run it by me first?"

Grace felt a surprising rush of emotion. There was no reason for Eve to give her a chance. There was every reason for her to cut her losses and let Grace go. Grace felt grateful and touched, and that made her feel uncomfortable. Strangely, she would almost rather Eve had fired her. Then Grace could be mad. She could walk away and not look back and tell herself it hadn't been the right job for her anyway.

She knew how to handle people being mean to her, but kindness? That felt like a burden.

"Thank you," she said, hoping that would be enough.

"You'd better take care of Madeline. The film crew will be here anytime."

"Sure. Of course."

"And I'm still setting up the shots and camera angles for production. By the time we're done with that, it should be time to go. Oh, and your makeup looks nice, by the way. Good idea."

"Thanks."

Grace had redone her makeup when she'd stopped for her kit. She'd changed it subtly, softening it up to offer visual reassurance to the client. She could use her skills to put people at ease, just as carefully as she normally used them to keep people at bay. She was growing up. She could do this.

Still, she approached Madeline warily, half-sure that Willa would've been working her magic in the past two hours, feeding lies bit by bit into the ear of the director.

But Willa was sitting a dozen feet away, pouting and scrolling through something on her phone. She glanced up as Grace walked past and muttered, "Bitch."

Grace rolled her eyes.

"You made me look like a fool."

Grace didn't know what to say to a girl who'd throw someone under the bus and then accuse them of making her look bad. Under normal circumstances, Grace would probably walk over and call her every foul name in the book. But not today. Not here. She kept walking and swallowed back her anger.

Madeline Beckingham was on the porch, still ruling over a small kingdom, looking over sketches and issuing directions to the men gathered around her.

"Oh, thank God," she said when she looked up and saw Grace. "They're on their way from Jackson Airport right now."

"Don't worry. I'm quick."

"I want to look natural. Make me look as though my skin is naturally flawless, even in the sun. Got it?"

"Of course."

"And you may find a few stray scars near my ears from a medical procedure. Cover them up."

Madeline was only in her forties, but apparently she'd already had a face-lift. Maybe she had a soft jawline or too much sun damage. Whatever her reasons, the face-lift was a good one. Grace wouldn't have guessed, but scars were never hidden from makeup artists or hair-stylists.

By the time she'd finished Madeline Beckingham's makeup, Grace felt more herself again. Maybe not ready to take on the world, but ready to take on one shitty ex-boyfriend and a bitchy production assistant. And maybe even an irritable cowboy.

CHAPTER FOURTEEN

COLE WAS MUCKING OUT THE LAST of the stalls when the scuff of a boot told him he wasn't alone.

"You hanging in there?" Easy asked.

Cole didn't look up. "I'm still upright, ain't I?"

"Yeah. You don't look any worse for wear either."

"Probably because I haven't done any real work in days."

Easy snorted. "You're doing real work now."

"I'm doing the work of a ten-year-old. Should only take me about twenty years to work my way back up to ranch boss. Thirty if I stay part-time."

"Cole," Easy said, one syllable that chastised him for talking back like a child.

Cole heard the scolding in that word and shook his head. He set the head of the rake on the floor and steadied his arm against the handle. When he finally looked at Easy, Cole saw the same man he'd known his whole life. Worn and silver-haired. Small-boned but tough as nails. Nobody had ever given Easy anything. He'd worked for every damn thing he owned. Worked since he was six years old and left with a sick mom and no father.

Cole's own father had been a good man, but he'd been hard. Yet somehow still run over by life. Easy, on the other hand, had an inherent strength that had never turned brittle. It seemed as though he could make things happen by sheer will alone. Easy and Cole's father had met at twelve and been friends from then on. Both good men. Both good cowboys. But Cole's dad had been a bitter ranch hand who'd owned nothing more than his boots and his saddle when he'd died from a heart attack at age fifty-two. Anything else that had ever belonged to him, including Cole's mother, had been lost somewhere along the way. Even Cole hadn't been around.

He swallowed hard at that memory. It still made him sick. He'd been out in L.A. with people who didn't know him and didn't give a damn. His dad had died alone.

As for Easy, Cole had always thought he'd known Easy as well as he knew his own father. Better, even. But now—hell, he had no idea what he knew anymore.

They stared at each other. "What?" Cole finally asked.

"You want to tell me why you're so mad?"

He laughed, but the sound was pure anger. "You must be kidding. You've basically told me you think I might be a weak, frightened coward hiding out in the mountains from the things that scare me most."

"I said I'm afraid you—"

"Yeah. I get it. You're afraid I'm not the man you hoped I'd be. You're not sure. Fine. That makes me feel better, Easy."

"That's not how it is, Cole!"

"Then tell me how it is. Because right now, it feels like a big pile of shit, and I'm not talking about the muck in this stall," he snarled, tossing the rake on the ground, where it bounced and banged before settling. "A test to see if I'm a real man, huh? To see if I'm worthy of filling your shoes? You should've made this easier on yourself. You should've listened to my dad from the start. Then you wouldn't have had any doubt."

His words fell into silence. Cole felt his cheeks flush and looked away from Easy's calm stare.

"That's exactly what I'm talking about it," Easy finally said. "Your dad was a good man."

"I know," Cole said heavily, rubbing a hand over the ache in his chest. "I know that."

"But he was wrong about you, Cole. You were a hard worker, but you were still a kid. You deserved to take a little time to find your way in the world."

"I let him down, Easy. And I let myself down, so don't tell me he shouldn't have been disappointed. He was a good man, and I—"

"He *was* a good man. And he was scared to death. He didn't like seeing this place turn into a playground for rich folk. He watched them change things. He watched them come and go through here, and he was afraid one day you'd go with them."

Cole pressed his fingers into the ache under his breastbone. "And that's just what I did."

"You were gone for all of two months, Cole. That's a summer vacation."

"It was long enough to break his heart."

"You didn't—"

Cole cut his hand through the air. "I don't want to talk about this, Easy. I know what happened."

Easy glared at him, jaw set in a stubborn line. But Cole could be stubborn, too, when he wanted. He met

Easy's glare with his own. Finally, Easy sighed and shook his head.

"Fine. We'll talk about that later. The bigger issue here is that I don't want you to throw this opportunity away."

"What opportunity?"

"That last time, you loved working on that movie."

Even after everything else, this shocked the hell out of Cole. He felt his jaw drop. He laughed in complete shock. "Are you crazy? *Opportunity?* To work on a movie? What are you talking about? I'm a cowboy, Goddamn it!"

"You have been, yes. A good cowboy. A great hand. A man to be proud of. But you need to consider the worst here, Cole. Your leg—"

"My leg is fine," Cole snapped.

"Cole."

"It's *fine.* I can't even believe you're bringing it up. In a couple of weeks, I'll be back out there."

Not liking the way Easy was looking at him, Cole shook his head and picked up the rake again. "Come on, Easy. If that's what you're worrying about, set it aside. Jesus."

He felt a little strange. Dizzy. He didn't want to talk about this anymore, but Easy just kept staring.

Cole started to turn away to finish his work, but one of the ancient barn doors swung open and there she was. Madeline Beckingham herself stood in the doorway, hands on her hips.

Cole and Easy were both frozen for a moment, caught

by the dramatic sight of dust motes dancing in front of her gilded silhouette.

"Cole Rawlins, I've been looking for you everywhere. Are you hiding from me?" She laughed as if the idea were hilariously ludicrous. Cole didn't crack a smile. "Come on. I need to find a horse to ride out to that little bridge past the tree line."

"I thought that's what all the trucks were here for."

"Documentary shoot," she said. "A horse is going to look a whole lot better than an SUV. Plus it's been nearly a year since I've ridden, and you know how much I love horses."

Yeah. She loved horses. Or she loved the romance of them. The drama and style. The same way she loved the cowboy boots and tasseled belt she was currently wearing. Her family had owned a home here when she was a kid, but that didn't make her a local.

"Come on!" she said, waving both her arms.

Cole glanced at Easy. "You letting her use the horses?"

"If she can ride, I don't see a problem with it."

"Great."

Though everything inside him told Cole to move away from Madeline, he walked toward her.

"You're a lot more serious than you used to be," she said, looping her arm through his to turn him toward the distant corral. Seemed they were going to take a leisurely stroll.

"I'm not a kid anymore," he said darkly.

"Yeah? I thought you were pretty nicely grown-up

back then. But I have to admit, I kind of like your new dark and dangerous side."

He clenched his teeth and kept walking.

"We never got to say goodbye, you know."

"Somehow, I didn't think you noticed."

"Oh, come on, Cole." She squeezed his arm tighter against her, making sure his muscles pressed into her breast. "You know how much I liked you."

He did know, as a matter of fact. Because she'd discussed it with her friend during sex. With him. With both of them.

Jesus, he'd thought he'd died and gone to heaven when he'd figured out exactly what the "special date" was. Her girlfriend was in town from London to discuss financing a film, and apparently they liked to have fun together. Lots of fun. Cole had been more than willing, but it had also been…surprising. And strange. They'd talked about him as if he wasn't there, even as they'd used his body. They'd commented on him, cracked private jokes, told him what they wanted and when they were done.

Strange or not, he'd been happy to contribute. But once the thrill had worn off…

She nudged him to get his attention. "I have a dinner tonight, but why don't you come by afterward. We can have drinks. Get reacquainted."

"No," he said immediately.

"Are you seeing someone?"

He thought of Grace. "No."

"Then come see me. It's been a long time. Too long."

He didn't say anything in response. He'd already said

no. That was the end of it. But Madeline didn't hear no very often.

"It was good, Cole. God, it was so good. I missed you when you left. So, tonight when you're not seeing anyone and you start remembering how good it was…" She laughed. "Well, you know where I'm staying."

He almost asked how many other people would be there. But that would reveal too much. He was damned if he was going to reveal anything at all.

"Oh, I want that pinto!" she said suddenly. "Can I have him?" And that was about as much consideration as she gave men, too.

"Sure. The pinto's fine. He's young. He'll probably be grateful for the exercise."

The joke went over her head. Or maybe it just hadn't been very funny.

CHAPTER FIFTEEN

GRACE WAS RELIEVED she didn't have to ride home alone with Eve. One of the preproduction photographers recognized Eve from a photography retreat they'd attended years before. He asked if she wanted to grab dinner, so Grace had ridden home in the backseat, happy to shrink into the corner and pretend she wasn't there.

Despite her new boss's reassurances, Grace was still self-conscious about that scene. Out of all the messes she'd managed to get herself into over the years, that confrontation had been the most mortifying moment. Because there was truth in it this time. Because she'd done something really stupid.

She hadn't meant to take anything from Scott, only what he'd promised her. And then… God. She'd always been able to be arrogant about things people had thrown in her face, because she made very sure that no one ever knew enough about her to injure her. People could say anything they wanted, nobody knew the real Grace Barrett.

But now people knew something real enough to hurt. Lots of people.

When they got to the Stud Farm, Grace murmured a good-night and slid quickly out of the car.

What the hell did it matter anyway?

This place was only a temporary resting point. She didn't really know these people and never would. She'd leave and they'd remember her as a purple-haired chick with a shady reputation and a grumpy disposition. Hell, a few years ago, the idea would've delighted her.

"Must be getting old," she said as she hurried up the front walk.

"Grace!" a female voice called from the blue dusk beyond her sight. "Is that you?"

"Jenny?"

Jenny emerged from the shadow of the pine tree and waved. "Hey, I'm off early tonight, so I'm glad I caught you! I already left a message for Eve, but I didn't have your number. Want to get together Sunday evening?"

"Eve?" she asked nervously.

"Yes, we both have birthdays next week, so I thought this would be a fun way to celebrate."

"By getting together with me? I don't think so."

"You promised we'd do makeovers!"

"Oh. I don't..." She clutched the handle of her makeup kit tighter, afraid her suddenly sweaty hand would lose its grip. "Eve's my boss. I don't think she'd want to hang out with me."

"This is a small town." Jenny laughed. "It's pretty slim pickings as far as girlfriends go. Boyfriends, too, for that matter. If we didn't fraternize, we'd all just stay home. Where's the fun in that?"

"Oh. I..." Crap. This would be awkward. Even if Eve would've said yes yesterday, she wouldn't say yes today. Why would she want to hang out with someone like Grace? Someone she had to worry might steal her car?

"*Please?* Come on. You owe me. And you promised. And Sunday's my only night off this week."

It would be fine, she told herself. Eve would say no. Of course she would. "Okay. Sure. It sounds like fun."

"Yea! I'll give you my address later, all right? I can't wait!"

"Happy birthday," Grace said as Jenny waved and disappeared back toward the saloon. "Almost." She heard Jenny calling goodbye to the people lingering on the saloon porch, and then she heard the distinctive sound of the woman's muscle car starting. Grace didn't know enough about cars to know the make, but it was definitely American and old and it was definitely yellow.

That kind of car was almost exclusively driven by men, and Grace liked that about Jenny. That she drove a loud car that looked like it should be used for drag racing. Maybe Grace would buy a car like that someday. Or maybe a motorcycle. She'd like that. She'd wear leather pants and a shiny black helmet. She'd go anywhere she wanted. Fly across the country like a bird.

The idea took hold of her. It grabbed her and held her heart in a fist.

She could buy a bike. As soon as she paid Scott back. She could buy something cheap and go anywhere. Chicago. New York. Toronto.

Anywhere.

The idea of getting back to a big city loosened the fist squeezing her heart. God. She could fade back into the crowd. She could work during the day and then sink into a life apart at night. Where she never saw the same people and never knew anyone. And no one ever knew anything about her.

"God, yes," she said and sighed. That was what she needed. To be *unseen*.

For now, she just wanted to get inside and take a shower and collapse. On a secondhand sleeping bag. Well, it was better than a park bench any day. There was a door that locked. Walls to keep her safe.

She glanced at Cole's door as she walked to her own. She thought of knocking. Thought of simply announcing to him that she needed some stress relief. But she walked to her own door and went inside. She had something to do first.

Grace took out her cell and carefully dialed Scott's number.

"Yeah?" he answered impatiently.

"What are you trying to do to me?" she ground out.

"Well, hello, Grace." His familiar voice was tinged with an equally familiar self-satisfaction. "I thought you might decide to finally call."

"Are you kidding me?" she asked. "Is that what this is about? A phone call?"

"No. This is about getting my money back."

She bit back the curses she wanted to rain down on him and made herself speak calmly. "I already promised to pay you back. I have a plan, and—"

"Somehow when I found out you'd skipped town without a word, I doubted whether or not your promises were sincere."

"They were. I swear. I'm working, damn it."

"In Wyoming?"

"Yes, in Wyoming! And if you want your money back, it's probably not a good idea to tell the people employing me that I'm a thief!"

"Grace," he said as he sighed, sounding exhausted. "You skipped town. You haven't paid back a dime. And you haven't worked in months."

"I'm working right now, and I told you I have another job lined up in a few weeks. And I'm not a thief!"

"I don't know what you think you are, but my eight thousand dollars is gone and you took it."

Grace rubbed her hand over her forehead. "I told you, I didn't mean to. You'd offered to loan me a thousand, and I thought the envelope—"

"I offered that loan when we were still together. Don't play dumb."

She swallowed. Whatever Scott's faults were, he wasn't stupid. She'd known when she'd "borrowed" that money that the loan offer probably didn't still apply. That's why she'd grabbed the envelope and slipped it into her purse without stopping to look at it. He'd never kept more than twelve or thirteen hundred dollars around before. It was just household cash, not a savings account.

"I believed you," he said. "I didn't want to think you'd steal from me, but now I find out you're partying in a ski town—"

"It's the middle of summer and I'm working! My great-aunt lives here and she gave me a place to stay."

"I've never heard of this aunt before."

"Yeah, we don't hang out a lot. She's seventy."

"Look, Grace, I'm sorry, but..."

She tried to make herself breathe slowly, but her heart was racing. "But what? Did you file charges?"

He was silent for so long that her hands started shaking.

"No," he finally said. "But I will if I have to."

"I gave up a lot for you," she said past numb lips.

Scott's laugh sounded genuinely confused. "You got fired and I let you move in. What did you give up?"

"That's not what I meant." But even to her, the words sounded weak. He couldn't know what she'd given up. And it had been her job to say no to it in the first place. "I'll send you some money in a few days, all right? And I'll send all of it as soon as I can."

She hung up before he could say anything else.

She had given up a lot. The only reason she'd been working on that film set in the first place had been because of Scott. He'd wanted her to be more successful, more mainstream. He'd convinced her that it was the next logical step in her life. She'd gotten off the streets. She'd found her gift and gone to school. And she'd slowly found some measure of security in her life. But it had never *felt* secure. Crappy apartments, crappy cars. Fun jobs with independent films that didn't pay much. She'd supplemented by working some print jobs, but she'd still lived pretty close to the bone.

But she'd lived on her terms. Her life had been good. Then she'd met Scott and he'd started asking questions. *Why don't you push yourself? Where will you be in five years? Don't you want to challenge yourself?* He'd tapped into her insecurities about money and safety.

He'd convinced her that her life wasn't enough. And she'd let him.

She'd changed for him, like those stupid girls with low self-esteem she'd spent years mocking. Like her *mother*. She'd changed for a man and she'd lost everything. Just the way she'd deserved to.

She'd never, ever do that again. Subvert her own needs. Make herself small. Keep her head down in fear that she'd piss a guy off and he'd kick her out.

Her mom had done that. Over and over. As far as Grace knew, her mom was still doing it. Making herself into a meek partner for one man after another.

Grace was just about to power down her phone when it rang. Her thumb hovered over the red button as she waited for the caller ID to pop up. When it did, it wasn't Scott's name. It was Cole's.

"Can I interest you in a drink?" he asked as soon as she answered.

"A drink," she repeated, glancing toward her door.

"A drink. As a peace offering, maybe?" He sounded as if he was trying to be charming, but there was a strain in the friendly drawl. Some rough edge that snuck into the ends of his words. He was stressed out, and so was she.

"You already apologized," she said. "And I accepted. So I don't need a peace offering."

"Right."

Her hands were still trembling. Her head screamed with tension. She took a deep breath. "But if what you're really calling about is my proposal that we have sex again, then yes. Let's."

Silence greeted her words. In fact, he was silent so long she had time to walk to the kitchen and open the peanut butter.

"Now?" he finally said.

She grabbed a plastic knife. "In a few. If you want to."

Another pause. Briefer this time. "Yes," he said.

"Good. I'm going to take a shower. See you soon." She hung up and felt a tight smile stretch her mouth. Men were so funny. They never knew how to react to a woman who approached sex the way a guy did. They thought it was a trick. A mirage. As if she couldn't want it as much as they did.

She liked that. Men always thought they were the ones doing the using. They thought they were taking advantage or breaking you down. There was nothing better than making it clear that with her, that wasn't the case. She needed a release right now, and she'd take it.

Half a peanut butter sandwich later, Grace realized she could hear water humming distantly through pipes. Cole was getting in the shower. This time, she wanted to see him naked, not just half-dressed. She wanted his whole body under her hands.

The thought turned her on with immediate and startling thoroughness. She wanted him naked and hard right now. She liked that she'd shocked him. Liked that feeling of wicked power. She wanted more of it.

Grace tossed the last of her sandwich, too turned on to think about anything but getting ready. For sex. With a big, rough cowboy who made her say and do dirty things for him.

Hell, yeah. After this shitty day, that was just what

she needed. She showered and shaved and used the last of her favorite body cream, loving the silky feel of her skin as she rubbed it in. She wanted him to moan when he touched her. Wanted him turned on by the barest brush of skin.

She'd just finished drying her hair and touching on some eye makeup when she heard a knock on the door. Cole. He couldn't wait.

Grace stared at her reflection for a moment. He was right that she wanted to use him to forget. She wanted the pleasure of his body to erase everything, just for a little while. She'd never tell him that, but it was just what she needed. Hot, hard sex with a guy who didn't even want to like her. Bring it on.

She turned off the light and walked slowly to the door.

"Want something?" she asked as she opened it. And then his mouth was on hers, his body against her. Yeah, he wanted something. He wanted it badly. Almost as badly as she did. She was just curling her fingers into his hair when the noise of a man clearing his throat interrupted.

Grace opened her eyes to see Shane standing in the entry of the building, closing the door behind him.

"Pardon me," he said, tipping his hat. "I'll give y'all some privacy."

"Fuck off, Shane," Cole growled against her mouth. He turned her, putting her back against the wall, and shut the door with his foot. "Now, where were we?"

"Right here," she answered, sliding her hands down to his ass to pull him tight against her.

"Perfect," he murmured against her jaw, his mouth going to her neck to tease her.

God, she could get hooked on that. His mouth on her neck, sucking, scraping, biting. It made her moan and whimper in ways she wished she could hide. But screw it. It didn't matter. Physical pleasure was just that. He made her feel good, and there was no shame in it. She obviously turned him on, too. Good times all around.

He pushed her T-shirt up, and she did the same for him. She hadn't bothered with a bra, so their naked chests pressed together, their body heat seeming to double with the contact, until her skin felt seared. Burned straight through to the bones beneath.

She reached for his belt and had his pants unbuttoned and open within ten seconds flat. "I want your clothes off," she said.

"Absolutely," he answered, but he wasn't doing what she wanted. He was busy running his hands down her back, pressing his mouth to her shoulder. It felt good, but she *needed* him naked.

"Your boots," she complained. "Your jeans. Take them off."

"Okay," he said, but his hands slid up to cup her breasts. She moaned at the touch, but pushed him away.

"Naked. Now."

She shoved her own jeans down to encourage him, and that seemed to work. He toed off his boots and ditched his jeans, his gaze locked on her body the whole time. She returned the favor, her eyes devouring him, taking him in. He was so hard already. Completely ready for her.

As soon as he was naked, he reached out to touch her, but she pushed his back against the wall.

"I love your body," she whispered against his collarbone as she spread her fingers over his chest. The hair on his chest was softer than she'd expected and feeling it again made her smile against him. And the feel of his thick cock pressed to her belly. That made her smile, too.

She slipped her hands down his sides and around to his ass. She pulled him tighter against her and listened to him moan in response. Oh, God, she loved that. She wanted more of it. More moaning. More loudly. She wanted gasping and groaning. Hell, she wanted to make him shout with lust. For her.

Grace went to her knees.

"Oh, Jesus," he breathed.

For a moment, she just pressed her cheek to his abdomen. She held his ass and turned her mouth to his belly. She loved the taste of him. The scent of his skin. The heat of his flesh against her. There was something about him. Some chemistry between them. Just the smell of him made her wet.

She wrapped one hand around his cock and dragged her mouth over that delicious line of muscle that started at his hip.

He gasped and she smiled, trying to decide if she should tease him or give him what he wanted. But it was what she wanted, too. And if she was good at anything, it was taking her fair share.

She tightened her hold on him and slowly slid her open lips over the head of his cock.

"Grace," he rasped.

She glanced up and found him watching her, eyes narrowed, jaw flexing between granite and steel.

Grace narrowed her own eyes. "Tell me what you want," she challenged, knowing her breath whispered over his wet skin.

"You know what I want."

"Really?" She let her bottom lip glide over him and she could taste him, salty and slick against her mouth. "How am I supposed to know what you want if you won't tell me?"

"Grace," he said darkly, the word barely a rumble of sound.

"Mmm?" She kissed him again, with the cruelest whisper of pressure.

He was silent for a moment and she had to bite back a smile. He didn't want to play this game. Well, neither had she, but he'd persuaded her, finally. And she'd persuade him. She stroked her hand slowly up his shaft and flicked her tongue out to lick the tiny bead of liquid she'd inspired. "Mmm."

"Oh, God," he moaned. "Please."

"Please what?"

He took a deep breath and a shudder moved through his body. "Please…take me in your mouth."

She laughed a little, but it was mostly shock. Shock that his words felt like a blow. Like a violent shove of lust that nearly shattered her. This was a secret she hadn't known. No wonder he'd pushed her so hard that night. This was magic, a power over another person's body, over their voice and their will and pride.

God.

Grace parted her lips and pressed her open mouth to him. She let her tongue touch him and heard him suck in a breath at the heat.

As the taste of him spread over her tongue, her heart pounded hard and the tension between her legs wound tighter. She let him slide over her tongue until her lips were around the head, and then she sucked at him and heard him moan. She wanted to laugh again with the sheer joy of it, but she just slid off and then took him in again, a little deeper this time.

"Yes," he hissed, his hips bucking a little. She teased him with her tongue, rubbing and sucking, then looked up to flash laughing eyes at him. He didn't look amused. "More," he ordered.

Another push of lust into her veins. He was a big man. Big and confident and overwhelmingly masculine. And she liked him issuing orders more than she would've expected.

She took more. Her lips stretched over him as his breathing roughened. She'd never be able to take him all, so she tightened her fist around the base of his shaft and worked it in time with her mouth.

"Oh, fuck," he moaned. "Like that. God, that feels good. Just like that."

She hummed her approval into his cock and worked him in and out of her mouth. On her knees. Taking more, just as he'd ordered.

"Grace. Jesus. Just...like that. Please." His hand touched her head, barely grazing her hair. She knew he wanted to take her now. Twist his hand into her hair and make her take everything. Strange that she could feel so powerful in this pose, but she did. She felt like she could make this grown man weep for her.

She was so turned on. Nearly desperate. She slid her mouth slowly from him, marveling at how much of him she'd managed to take.

He was panting now, staring down at her, eyes glittering and dazed.

"Come here," she whispered.

For a moment, he didn't seem to understand what she meant. His gaze was blank, confused. But then he slid down to his knees and kissed her, his wet cock pressing hard into her belly. She pushed him until he sat down, then climbed onto his thighs and pushed him to his back.

"Condom?"

"Right. Yeah." He turned his head and stared at his jeans for a moment, as if he weren't quite sure of his movements. But he finally reached out just as Grace reached for him.

"Christ," he cursed, as she wrapped a tight fist around his wet cock. He fumbled with the wrapper as she pumped her hand, thoroughly enjoying the way his hips jumped up in eagerness.

"Does that feel good?" she asked coyly.

"You know it does, damn it." The plastic finally tore open, but he paused to watch her fist slide up and down him.

"What do you want now?" she asked, rising up on her knees to look down at him.

"You. Please. I want you riding me."

"Yeah?" She stroked him again and reached for the condom.

"Yeah." His voice was a little broken now. A little strained.

She slid the condom on and eased higher on his body. Then, holding him, she lowered her hips until the tip of him rubbed against her swollen sex. She sighed in relief and tilted her hips so that he slid over her clit. "Mmm."

He watched every movement with eyes that looked like blue flame. His big hands wrapped over her hips, but he didn't push her down. Instead he slipped her back and forth a little, letting her sex slide along the head of his cock. Now she was the one panting. But this time she didn't have to beg for anything. She was in control. So she notched him against her opening and eased herself down.

"Oh," she said and sighed as his thickness pressed her open. "Yes."

His jaw was ticcing again. The muscles of his neck pressing tight against the skin.

"Yes." She sighed. She felt full and tight and he was only halfway in. Grace rose back up, the pleasure of it making her hum again. His fingers squeezed hard on her hip, but he let her control the movement even when she rose high enough that he slid out completely. He muttered something so low and broken that she couldn't hear it. Something angry or desperate, she couldn't be sure. But he didn't push her down.

As a reward, she let her hips sink and took him back inside her body. Deeper this time. Deep enough that she gasped, her lips parting with the delicious pressure of it. This time when she rose up it was just a little, and when she sank again, she took him all the way inside her.

His eyes were closed now, his jaw tight and solid with muscle, his brow furrowed as if he were concentrating.

She liked this. With him. She wanted to simply take from him, but she liked his part in it just as much as her own.

"Cole," she said. He opened his eyes, and she began to ride him. Slow at first, feeling every millimeter of his cock as it slid inside her, caressing her, stretching her. Slow enough to rise all the way to the tip before sliding down again. His fingers dug in so hard that the skin felt numb beneath them, but she didn't mind. She liked the reminder of his power. Not that she needed much of a reminder. His chest was wide beneath her. His hips narrow and muscled. Hair spread from just below the hollow of his throat all the way down to a narrow line of fur that trailed to his cock.

She slid a hand down her own belly, through the hair of her sex. She touched her pussy, letting her fingers brush over his shaft as it slid out of her, wet and hot. Then she touched her clit.

Cole's eyes blazed as he lifted his head to watch.

She smiled. "You want to watch?"

"Fuck, yes."

Now he took control of her hips, and she was glad. She concentrated on touching herself, rolling her clit beneath her fingers while he eased her hips up and down his shaft. Faster as her body yielded to him, getting even wetter.

"Tell me," she ordered. "Tell me."

"Fuck. You're so gorgeous. So perfect. And your pussy's so hot around me. Squeezing my cock. Jesus."

She panted as his words worked through her.

"Are you going to come for me like this?" he asked. "Are you going to come while you ride my cock?"

His words wound around her like some wicked vine, squeezing tight, pricking thorns into her skin with a pain that just pushed her pleasure higher.

"Yes," she whispered. "Yes, yes, yes."

"Good. I want to watch you." He began to thrust up as he pulled her hips down, and Grace gasped at the brutal invasion. "I want to watch you come while I feel you squeeze around me."

"Yes. Oh, God. Cole. I…"

She leaned forward, putting her free hand to his chest. She dug her nails into his skin and clenched her eyes shut as she got closer to coming. "Oh, fuck." God, he was so big. Too much. And as he said her name and urged her on, telling her exactly what to do and how to feel, Grace felt every tight sensation inside her body loosen for the briefest instant. And then it all wound painfully back again, turning and turning until… "Oh, God!" she screamed, as her body broke apart on a violent spasm. He slammed his hips up and held himself deep within her as she came. Then when the last of the clenching waves gripped her, he pulled her down to his chest and slowly turned them both until he was cradled between her legs.

"Grace." He smoothed her hair off her face, the damp strands making her aware that her whole body was slick with sweat. He kissed her with surprising sweetness for a man who hadn't come yet. But Grace was still catching her breath when he grew more urgent again.

He pressed her hands down, just as he had that first night. Only this time his hands held her wrists.

She moaned, half in surprised lust, and half in denial that she enjoyed it. But when Cole started moving in her again, she couldn't deny how devastatingly good it was. To be filled with him and held down by him at the same time. It felt like more than being fucked. It felt like being taken.

He thrust slowly, but without any mercy, sinking himself as deep as he could. His hands felt like an extra connection, but when he shuddered and came, Grace suddenly wished her wrists were free. She wished she could put her arms around him and feel the muscles of his back straining as he came. That strange, stray thought scared her in a way his roughness never could.

CHAPTER SIXTEEN

COLE FROWNED AS HE CAME OUT of the bathroom, his eyes roaming over the small apartment. He could see almost every corner of it from this vantage point. It wasn't as if there was any furniture blocking his view.

"Where's your stuff, Grace?"

She buttoned her jeans and didn't look up at him. "Thanks for that."

"'Thanks for that'? Really?"

"Yes, really. It was just what I needed. I had kind of a shitty day, in case you didn't notice the fun at the ranch."

He wanted to find out more about that. Who that woman had been, spouting nasty things about Grace. Whether any of them were true.

"You want that drink now? I've got beer at my place."

"No, thanks."

"Are you going to hang out here?" He very pointedly looked around the room. "Maybe do some meditating? You've got a hell of a feng shui thing going on here."

"Screw you, Cole." She opened the door and held it wide, raising her eyebrows in cool expectation. Cole was relieved not to see any of his friends out there this time, especially because he was buck naked.

"Uh, Grace? You want to close the door until I get my clothes on?"

She swept an impatient look down his body, but she closed the door.

"You're really not much for pillow talk, are you?"

"No."

Cole reached for his clothes. "So, you didn't actually have anything to move in, did you?" He kept his voice calm, hiding his growing shock.

"I came here on a bus. There wasn't a lot of space for furniture."

"You just left it behind."

"Something like that." Her eyes dipped down as he stepped into his underwear. "That scar—that's where you broke your leg?"

He glanced at the scar. "Come over to my place. Have a drink. Please?"

"I don't want a drink."

"Then just come over to my place." What the hell did she do in here all evening? No wonder she was so quiet. There was no television. No stereo. Just a pile of books next to a sleeping bag in the bedroom.

He tugged on his shirt and shoved his feet into his boots. "Come on. Did you have dinner?" he asked, opening the door and trying to scoot her through.

"Yes," she snapped. "I'm not a stray cat. I don't need you to feed me."

"Fine. Then just get naked and get in my bed. I don't give a shit."

That made her laugh, as usual. An insensitive jab. She even smiled as she willingly followed him to his apartment. But once she was in the apartment, she stood there, arms crossed as if she was uncomfortable again.

Cole tilted his head toward the bedroom. "Go on. You know where it is."

"I thought you were offering a drink."

"Oh, I'll bring you a beer once you're in bed, but not until then."

Amazingly, she actually headed for the bedroom. He'd only been teasing. Mostly. But she just rolled her eyes and laughed her husky laugh and sauntered toward his room. He thought he saw her hands reach to unbutton her jeans, and Cole swallowed hard.

Shit. She made no sense to him. She was a mystery. A mystery inside a minefield. Somehow he couldn't help but work his way through it, waiting for the violence to erupt at any moment.

He'd thought she was a typical artsy city girl starving herself to stay thin and lounging in a minimalist apartment. But he'd let his prejudice blind him. She didn't have any furniture. She'd didn't have real food, probably because she had no way to cook it. Or just no money at all.

At least he had his answer about whether she'd stolen that eight thousand dollars. He doubted she had eighty dollars.

Cole grabbed two beers, popped the tops and headed for the bedroom.

Yeah, she'd taken off her jeans but kept on her faded blue T-shirt and bright yellow panties. That was a good thing, Cole assured himself as he handed her a beer. He wanted to talk, and if she were naked, he'd likely be distracted by her ass. Or her breasts. Or that tempting triangle of perfect hair between her legs.

Yeah. This was good.

But just in case she preferred a bit more skin, he stripped down to his briefs as she climbed up to the bed and rested her back against the headboard. He took the other side and clinked his beer against hers. "Here's to a fine evening."

"Hell, yeah."

He was taking a drink when he felt her hand on his thigh. She touched him lightly and then lifted her fingers to hover over him. "Does it hurt?"

"Yeah. But not when you touch it. The incision is long healed."

Her hand lowered again, the warm pads of her fingers brushing cautiously over the ugly slash of scar tissue. "What happened?"

"You already heard. A horse panicked. A fresh-broke stallion. Somebody started a diesel engine right next to the corral. He panicked and reared and backed into a horse I was leading. The stallion lost his footing and came down right on top of me."

"Yeah, but this is a surgical scar."

"The femur was shattered. They had to put plates and screws in."

She traced the longest scar, then lightly touched each of the round white spots that looked like bullet holes. "But it's okay now?"

"Not quite."

"But it will be?"

"There's a good chance."

Her eyes rose to his as she pressed her hot palm to his thigh. "You'll be okay."

He smiled, entranced to see her being sweet. "You think?"

"I do. You're a big, strong cowboy."

"Not as strong as I used to be."

"Mmm. But just as big." Her fingers dragged playfully over his cock, which already felt pleasantly heavy from all the attention in such close proximity.

"Flatterer," he murmured.

"I can be charming when I have to."

He leaned in to touch her hip and press a kiss to her neck. "Charm comes in a lot of different packages."

"Don't expect too much."

"All right." He pushed the hem of her shirt up just enough to let his thumb graze the black lines of her tattoo. "Tell me about your tattoo."

"I already told you about it."

"No, you didn't."

She tilted her head a little, a hint that she wanted another kiss. So he kissed her again, then caught her earlobe between his teeth for just a second.

"Someday you're going to tell me, you know."

"No, I don't know." But her body relaxed into him with a sigh.

"All right. Tell me about that woman. The awful one who was trying to get you in trouble."

Her sigh this time was rough with frustration. "Oh, God. I don't know anything about her. I think I met her at a party in L.A. She obviously knows my ex."

"You think that's why she did it? Because of him?"

Grace frowned. "I don't think so. It seemed like she was just showing off for Madeline."

"Ah. Of course. People have told lies for less."

Grace sat up again, her back to the headboard of his bed. She took a sip of beer. "What if it's not a lie?"

"Which part? You already told me you weren't into drugs, and I know you're not a big drinker. Are you a thief?"

"What if I said I was?" she asked, her chin edging out.

"I don't know," he said honestly. "I know you didn't take eight thousand dollars, anyway."

"How?"

"You're spending your nights in a sleeping bag on hardwood. Either you're the most frugal thief ever or it isn't true."

"But if it was? If I were a thief?"

"What are we talking about here? Cars? State secrets? Your ex-boyfriend's kinky porn stash?"

She managed a small smile. "No. Anyway, it doesn't matter. It was just a misunderstanding. And now he's being an asshole."

"Why'd you break up?"

Her smile faded and she crossed her arms. "We weren't really getting along, that's all." They drank their beers in silence for a while. He wondered at the edge in her voice that warned him away from the subject, and finally decided to dare it.

"Why weren't you getting along?"

She shook her head. "I'm sorry, but why do you think I'd tell you my deepest, darkest secrets after the way you treated me last night? What kind of a fool do you think I am?"

"I'm sorry," he said softly. "Again. This whole film thing…it's a sore spot with me."

"It's all right."

"No, it isn't."

"It doesn't matter. You got back in my pants, didn't you? Just let it go."

Yeah, he'd gotten back in her pants, but he had this need crawling through him, tunneling under his skin. He wanted to get her to reveal more than just her body. He had no idea why. Her dark eyes drove him mad. And her cool smiles. And the way she'd seemed so unsurprised at the way he'd treated her.

It fascinated him and made him feel like shit at the same time.

He needed to know more. Maybe if he offered something, she'd tell him more in return. "I worked for Madeline Beckingham when she was shooting a film here thirteen years ago. I got caught up in the attention. I didn't like what it brought out in me."

"Were you an actor?"

"At first I was just an extra. Then I helped with some of the training on riding issues. I worked with the stuntmen. And I got a small part."

"That doesn't explain your anger."

Here was the delicate part. Telling the truth without coming close to all of it. He sat back against the headboard with a sigh. "I got caught up in it. Arrogant. Madeline promised me a lot of things, and I believed her. I was stupid enough to give up my spot at the ranch I'd worked at for four years. I walked away from my friends during the busiest part of the season. Left the girl I'd been in love with for two years. I acted like I was better than all my old friends. In general, I behaved like a self-satisfied, conceited asshole."

"And what does that have to do with girls like me?"

He watched her hands as she slowly rolled the bottle back and forth between them. "You're not like those women. I shouldn't have said that to you."

"How can you be sure?"

"You're not polished like that."

"No? I'm all rough around the edges, huh?"

She was rough around more than the edges, but he knew better than to say that. "No, I mean they've been polished into something fake. They're smooth and beautiful like plastic. Perfect. High heels in the dirt."

She turned to look at him, her expression as blank as a white wall.

"You don't create yourself into something meant to attract."

"Uh, did you just say that?"

"I don't mean sexually. Obviously, I'm attracted to you."

"Or it's the age-old allure of free sex right next door."

"Come on. You know that's not true."

She laughed at him, shaking her head. "Sure I do."

"I meant that you present yourself as a warning. That's honesty, isn't it? You want people to think you're not soft."

"I'm not," she said quickly.

He put his hand on her white thigh, marveling at the sight of his scarred, tanned skin against her perfect leg. "You feel pretty soft to me."

"Don't be fooled. I'm not and I never have been."

"Why?" he asked, trying to sound as casual as possible. As if he didn't really give a shit at all.

It worked. "My life's been pretty screwed up. That's all. I had to take care of myself."

"Did you always live in L.A.?"

"Not always, but nearby. Long Beach. Riverside. San Bernardino. And little places out in the desert. We moved a lot when I was young."

"You and your family?"

"Me and my mom." She finished her beer and got up to walk to the kitchen. "You want more?" She brought back two more and lay back down beside him. When she repositioned herself, her shirt hitched up a little, and Cole took the opportunity to slide his hand up her hip.

He watched his fingers spread over the tattoo, fascinated by the contrast. Her fine white skin, untouched except for the startling blackness of the ink and, covering them both, his brown fingers. After years of clashes with leather and steel and wood and barbed wire, his hands looked like they'd been chewed up by a machine. But her skin was flawless. As if she'd never been touched, much less damaged.

A dangerous illusion that only added to her mystery. He shouldn't try to solve it, but he couldn't seem to help himself.

"You must have been a tiny kid," he murmured.

She tried to ignore the way his hand felt on her sensitive belly. She tried to pretend she didn't feel tiny again.

"Yeah," she answered. "I didn't look tough, so I had to be tough."

"Bad neighborhoods?"

She paused, staring at her beer and seeing a dozen different apartments in a dozen different cities. "My mom wasn't around a lot. That's all."

"And your dad?"

That was an easier answer. That one didn't even hurt. "I never met him. What about your parents? Did you grow up on *Bonanza?* Or…what was that other one? *Gunsmoke?*"

"Are you asking if my mother was an Old West whore?"

She convulsed and pressed a hand to her mouth to keep the beer in. "Oh, God," she finally gasped. "Don't do that when I'm taking a drink."

"You're the one who said it."

"Okay, I forgot about Miss Kitty. Sorry. I didn't mean to imply anything."

"At least she had a heart of gold. But no. My dad was a ranch hand his whole life. My mom left when I was ten. She's married to an insurance salesman out in Casper. They used to make me go stay there during the summer, but I kept running away, so that stopped. That's it. Pretty boring."

"That sounds sad, actually."

"Naw, it wasn't bad. Normal kid stuff."

She turned to meet his gaze, and he was watching her so carefully, his blue eyes clear and pure. "Are you sure?"

"Everybody has stuff like that in their lives. Things other people don't see."

Whether it bothered him or not, the story made her sad for him and she didn't want him to see that in her eyes, so she put her hand over his and stared at their entwined fingers. "Maybe," she murmured. "People never do look very hard."

"They don't. But I like looking at you, Grace. I don't think you're as tough as you seem."

She chuckled. "That's not true. Don't think things like that. I can't be soft. For anyone."

"No?"

"No," she whispered.

He turned his hand up and folded her fingers into his, and she felt as if her hand could disappear into his larger one. She wasn't sure if that comforted her or scared her to death.

"Why?" he asked.

"That's a ridiculous question. *Why?* Because people suck. Haven't you ever noticed that?"

"Not everybody sucks."

God, what was this? More Old West shit? "No? How about you, Cole? How do you think I would've felt after that first time if I were a sweet, soft girl? If I'd let you bend me over your couch like you'd paid for me, and then you threw it all in my face before I even got my clothes back on?"

Blood rushed to his face as quickly as if she'd slapped him.

She smiled. "Because if I trusted people, I probably

would've trusted you not to do that. But I don't trust people, so I was fine. You see how it works?"

"I'm sorry," he said. "I didn't… You're right. That was awful."

"Sure it was. But we're all awful, Cole. I'm awful, too. We may as well have a good time together."

"You're not awful."

"Oh, God." She laughed. "Really? What that bitch said about me today, even if that wasn't true, it used to be. I used to steal things. Shoplift. I used to take clothes and food and shoes, because I thought I had a right. I didn't have anything and those people did, so why not? And I did drugs when I needed to forget what my life was. When I wanted to pretend I was only hanging out at the park with my friends instead of living there."

"That's—"

"And I've told men I loved them just because it seemed easier than not saying it back. Because it might buy me a few more weeks of not being alone. But I've never loved anyone, Cole. Not the way you're supposed to."

"None of that is bad, Grace. You just…"

"It was all bad. All of it." She laughed to hide the new huskiness in her voice. "But strangely, I only ever get ruined by the good stuff I do. Standing up for myself. Speaking up when something is wrong. Trying to make my life better. So I just want to start over. Reset. Go somewhere where no one knows me."

"Are you running away?"

"Maybe. Does it matter? It's all semantics. I don't

care. I'm not more or less ashamed of myself because of it. I've got plenty of other shit to be ashamed of."

"Like what?"

She thought of Scott and felt her throat thicken. Not because she'd loved him. She hadn't. But because she'd given up things she'd believed about herself. Important things. For *nothing*. If she'd loved him, maybe she could use that as an excuse when she looked back. Then again, she was awfully glad she hadn't given him her heart.

She didn't answer Cole's question.

"You're right, you know," Cole said quietly.

"About what?"

"We're all awful. If you've made mistakes, you don't have to be ashamed of that. And you don't have to be ashamed about being soft sometimes."

"I'm not soft," she said again, but when his fingers slid between hers and tightened, she had to swallow hard. He plucked the beer from her other hand and set it on the bedside table. Then his fingers settled on her cheek and turned her toward him. But she didn't look at him. She closed her eyes and pretended he really meant it as he pressed a soft kiss to her jaw, then her chin, then her mouth.

"Grace," he whispered.

She wanted to tell him to be quiet. To stop talking and let her pretend. Pretend he was touching her that way because he knew her and cared.

His fingers whispered over her skin, down her neck and over her shoulder until he eased her down to lie on the bed. Leaning over her, he kissed along the same path, then down to her breast. His mouth closed over her nipple, wetting the thin fabric of her shirt until she could feel his heat through it.

She arched into the pleasure as he sucked at her gently, then turned the same attention to her other breast. By the time he pushed her shirt up and exposed her, she was panting.

His lips whispered against her bare breast. "I love seeing you like this. Like nobody else does."

She shook her head as he pressed another gentle kiss to her nipple. "Plenty of people have seen me," she growled, wanting to shut him up.

"Not like this," he whispered. "Not here or now. Not in my bed."

Oh, God. Her throat tightened. His tongue traced her with the lightest touch and his breath cooled the wetness and made her want to groan.

When his hand slipped down her belly, she was relieved. She could give up the fantasy that this light, slow touch had something to do with cherishing her. But he didn't shove his hand down her panties and get her off. Instead, his fingers dragged over the cotton, and he simply cupped her heat in his hand, holding her as he carefully sucked one nipple between his teeth.

"More," she said. "Harder."

He paused. She felt him lift his head and look at her, but she kept her eyes closed and turned her face away. His fingers curled a little tighter against her, but when he bent his head again, his mouth was just as gentle. He teased her, tempting her to feel something more than just sexual need.

His lips slid down to her ribs, lingering over the tattoo

he couldn't stop asking about. It was as if he wanted to collect details about her for his own amusement. Why?

"Harder," she rasped, sliding her hand over his to push his fingers more firmly against her. "Cole."

"Shh," he whispered against her skin. "It's okay."

But it wasn't okay. She didn't want it like this. Even though the cotton grew wet under his fingers. Even though her skin bloomed with warmth under his mouth. She didn't want this.

She pulled his hand higher and forced it beneath her panties. She wound her free hand into his hair and squeezed her fist tight. "More," she ordered.

"No." He twisted his hand up and captured her wrist.

She pulled his hair tighter until he pushed her down into the mattress.

Grace turned her body, turning away from him, struggling, forcing him to treat her roughly. He yanked her back against his body, her ass pressed to his cock.

When she pushed away, her flesh only pressed more tightly against his thickness.

She wouldn't be soft for him. No matter what he thought. No matter what he asked for.

When he shoved her to her stomach and fucked her, Grace was smiling. She didn't need gentleness from anyone. She just needed this.

CHAPTER SEVENTEEN

HEAVEN ENVELOPED HER in fluffy warmth, and Grace burrowed into it with a sigh of wicked pleasure. She curled her legs up and snugged her hands beneath her chin, finding a perfect little pocket of heat and softness to hide in. Oh, God. It felt so good that goose bumps chased over her skin despite the delicious warmth.

She felt safe. Cozy.

Then she smelled bacon. And toast. And coffee.

It was too good to be true, and her half-comatose brain managed to sound an alert. *Something's wrong.*

Her eyes popped open, wide with alarm before she was even fully awake. She sprang up, ready to fight.

Yes, something was definitely wrong. She'd fallen asleep in Cole's bed.

"Oh, shit," she whispered as she jumped down from the bed and looked frantically around for her clothes. Her panic twisted higher when she couldn't find them. Where were they? She reviewed the night in her mind. Yes, she'd definitely had clothes on when she'd come over. And then...

Yanking the covers back, she spotted the bright yellow cotton of her underwear and then the blue of her T-shirt. Thank God. But once she had those on, she couldn't find her jeans. Keeping one eye on the corner of the short hall that fed into the living area, Grace searched the room. She could hear Cole moving around in there. Heard the clink of plates as he set them down.

Was he going to feed her breakfast in bed now? Maybe tell her how special she was and ask what she wanted to do today?

She didn't know why the idea felt like a mortal threat. She wasn't *that* screwed up. She'd had boyfriends. Men who'd loved her in whatever small way people were truly capable of love. So, why did the idea of sleeping in Cole's bed terrify her?

Just as angry tears were pricking her eyes, she dropped to her knees and spotted her jeans under the bed.

"You up, Grace? Breakfast is ready. Come on out and I'll feed you."

Jeans in her fist, Grace crouched on the floor. Her head popped up and she glared down the hallway.

That was it. She remembered now. She'd been falling asleep last night, Cole's arms wrapped around her, and he'd whispered something. Something about staying the night. "Don't go back there. You don't even have a bed. Stay with me for a while."

Stay with me for a while.

A few years ago—hell, a few weeks ago—those words would have sent a secret thrill through her. Not because of love or affection or desire, but because those words would've offered a reprieve. Another reprieve in a long line of them. Another few weeks or months when she knew she was okay. Alive and fed and clothed and warm and not alone. Not really.

The thought scared the hell out of her. She sprang to her feet and stalked out of the bedroom.

"Morning, beautiful," Cole said, looking as happy as she'd ever seen him.

Beautiful. Whatever her issues, she didn't need that kind of bullshit platitude. She had no idea what she looked like, but she knew it wasn't beautiful.

She kept walking all the way to the door. "I don't need to be taken care of, Cole," she snarled.

His smile blanked to shock. "What?"

"I don't need you to feed me or offer me a place to sleep."

"Okay," he said carefully.

Her hand on the knob, she took a deep breath and managed a tense smile. "Thanks for the beer. I'm sure I'll see you later. I just… I can't stay."

She opened the door and took three steps into the hallway and nearly walked straight into a man she'd never met before. He was talking to Aunt Rayleen.

The woman turned with an automatic scowl that quickly pulled into a sneer when her eyes traveled down Grace's body. Then she looked pointedly at the door Grace had just closed behind her.

"Well, well, well."

Grace rolled her eyes and moved to walk around her aunt and the man.

"Couldn't keep it in your pants, huh?" Rayleen snarled. "That's because you're doing it wrong. The pants are supposed to be on your ass, girl, not dragging along behind it."

Grace just barely managed to bite back a suggestion about exactly what Rayleen could do with her opinions.

The man tried to step out of her path at the same time Grace tried to get around him, and they ended up stepping back and forth several times.

Rayleen snorted. "Old Cole is pretty popular, you know. You'd better watch it, or you'll end up with the clap."

Grace sighed heavily and stopped to glower at her aunt. "The clap? Really? What decade is this?"

The man snorted, and Grace threw him a glare. "Who are you?"

"I'm Lewis."

"He's your upstairs neighbor," Rayleen clarified. "You telling me there's a bed you haven't tried to crawl into? Not that you'd have much success with this one. Still, I knew letting a woman in here would be nothing but trouble. You're using up all the good ones."

Grace could only assume that meant Lewis wasn't a good one, though that obviously had nothing to do with appearances. He was wide-shouldered and dark-haired with a smile that set the bar for wickedness.

"Anyway," Grace finally said, "nice to meet you."

He stuck out a hand, cutting off another attempt at escape. Grace switched her jeans to her left hand and managed the briefest of handshakes.

"Okay, you stay right there, and I'm going to..." She kept him in place with one hand while edging around him and closer to her door. "I'm going to take my pants-less ass behind closed doors now. Bye."

"Hussy," Aunt Rayleen said, not quite under her breath.

"Witch," Grace responded.

"Ha! Which one of us is slinking through a shame walk? You do keep your chin up, though. I like that."

"Years of practice," Grace muttered.

Rayleen's laughter followed her through the door. Grace threw her jeans on the floor and stalked straight to the bathroom to start the shower. She tried not to look in the mirror, not out of worry for what she looked like, but out of worry for what she'd see in her eyes.

She used people. It was an ugly thing to see in one-self. That sometimes people were no more than shelter for her. No more meaningful than a roof and walls and a warm bed to wake up in. Not always, but often enough.

And it wasn't just other people. She used herself, too. After what had happened with Scott, she couldn't ignore it anymore.

Oh, she'd pretended it had been a real relationship. Maybe it even had been, at the start. But three months after she'd moved into his place, she'd suspected he was cheating. A month after, she'd known for sure. And as tough and proud and self-respecting as she'd always imagined she'd been, Grace had said nothing.

She'd put her head down and pretended not to know. Not because she loved him. Not because it hurt too much, but because she hadn't had anywhere to go.

The worst part, the part that ate her up on nights when she couldn't sleep, was that Scott had known. He'd looked at her as if she was dirt. Less than dirt, ac-tually, because when you walked all over dirt, it wasn't the dirt's fault. But Grace—she'd let it happen. So he'd walked a little harder. And then when he'd tired of even that horrid little game, he'd kicked her out.

He'd known. And she'd looked straight into his disgusted eyes and begged him not to break up with her. But he hadn't needed her anymore. She'd ruined any chance that she could help advance his career, and his career was all he cared about.

Grace got into the shower and scrubbed as hard as she could.

She'd never let that happen again. Ever. She'd never be dependent upon anyone for anything. And she wouldn't be so proud that she'd yell her way out of a job again either. What the hell did she have to be so proud of? She was nearly thirty, she had nothing, and she could barely support herself.

Yeah. You're definitely a kick-ass chick, Grace Barrett. The coolest of the cool.

The tears that had been hanging around for days finally won the battle and spilled down her cheeks. But it didn't count in the shower, did it? It never did. They weren't real tears when your face was already wet. So Grace let the water wash them away.

This wasn't who she'd planned to be. It wasn't what she'd worked toward. After a couple of years of being angry and lashing out at the world, she'd gone back to school to get her GED, and she'd put herself on a path to do something she'd really loved. For a while there, she'd been so proud of herself. She was good with makeup. More than good. She'd called herself a makeup artist, and she'd meant it.

But then she'd found that the perfect place for her wasn't so perfect after all. And the space she'd carved for herself was too small. And the anger she thought she'd left behind was still in there, bubbling over at the worst times.

For a while there, she'd been a success. A small one, maybe, but someone who could be proud of herself. Now she was a failure by any stretch of the word. A weak person who'd thought she was strong.

But this was the moment. This was her chance. She could make something of herself, or she could keep being a tragic story. The typical tough girl who was really bleeding inside, pretending she didn't need anyone when she really just wanted to be wrapped up in strong arms.

"Yuck," she muttered, wiping tears from her eyes. It didn't matter. More tears immediately replaced them.

God. She'd come all the way to Wyoming, several worlds away from L.A., and she was doing the same damn thing. Fighting with people, falling into bed, letting a man offer a helping hand. Except it was never a hand, was it?

That thought made her snort with wet laughter, and the tears stopped.

She was going to do this. She was going to go into work today and do a great job. She'd kiss a little ass if she had to, because she was strong enough to do that. She could deal with people who treated her like shit, because she wasn't shit. And she could walk away from a man who told her she was beautiful and tried to take care of her, because being taken care of and lied to wasn't love or security or anything but being treated like a wounded bird.

She didn't need that. Not anymore. She'd pay Scott the money she owed him. Somehow. And that would be the end of her old life. She was moving on.

COLE COULDN'T BEGIN to guess what had gone wrong this morning. Well, aside from the fact that he was sleeping with an incredibly prickly, difficult woman who couldn't even cuddle after sex without getting tense about it. So, after standing in the kitchen, stunned, for a few minutes, he'd figured it out. She'd woken up, panicked at the idea of having spent the night and she'd bolted. No big surprise, really. She was more vulnerable than she wanted him to know. He'd already figured that out.

But then she hadn't answered the door when he'd knocked on his way out. And when neither she nor Eve had shown up at the ranch, he'd tried calling, and she hadn't bothered answering the phone. Not the three other times he'd called either.

So not a momentary panic, but something deeper.

But what? It had been good last night. Hot and sweet and intense. And even after…she'd finally relaxed in his arms and fallen asleep. For once, he'd been happy for his insomnia, because he'd gotten to see Grace, relaxed in sleep. Her blackened eyelashes resting on pale cheeks. Her wide mouth warm and soft.

She'd looked so young, and it made him wonder what she'd been like as a teen. A runaway, he suspected from what she'd told him, living on the streets sometimes. It made him feel odd and uncomfortable, imagining that.

She was so small. How in the world had she made it out of that okay?

Or maybe she wasn't okay. There was that darkness in her eyes.

Not always, though. Not when she needed him. Not when she was coming.

At the thought, Cole shifted, telling himself not to go there. Because just that hint of a memory had blood rushing to his cock, a pleasant, dull—

"Cole." A hand curled around his biceps. He hoped it was Grace, but he knew before he even looked that it wasn't. She'd never touch him that way in front of other people. She'd never deign to slide a possessive hand around his arm as if she were claiming him. But Madeline would.

"Are you avoiding me?" she asked.

Yes. He looked down at her hand on his arm, but she didn't bother taking the hint.

"You didn't come by last night. I was a little surprised."

"I'm not your boyfriend anymore, Madeline."

"I know, but…for old time's sake?"

"Old times," he murmured, shoving away from his place against the barn so that her hand would drop. "But I wasn't really your boyfriend then either, was I?"

"Hmm. Are you sure? You felt like my boyfriend."

"Madeline," he said, hoping she'd hear the warning in his voice and back off.

"It's lunch break," she said. "Come ride with me."

His shoulders snapped to instant, utter tension, and

his leg suddenly began throbbing. "I can't. I've got work to do."

"Work, like holding up the barn? It's lunchtime, Cole. And I know for a fact that Easy told you to keep me happy. Isn't that your job?"

For a moment, he couldn't hear anything except the blood rushing in his ears. His heart hammered with twin storms of anger and alarm. He started to say, "My job is being a ranch hand," but he cringed away from it. A few months ago, he'd been the boss. He couldn't make himself say it. Not to this woman.

Maybe that was the worst part about all this. If he had to see this woman again, he wanted to be whole, strong, successful. He wanted to be in control and he wanted her to know it. But here he was, playing the part of her crippled errand boy. Her toy again, just as he had been before.

"Please?" she pressed. "Pretty please?"

And then there was a memory. Lying in her bed, spent and naked and sweaty. He'd been starry-eyed in love with her and floating in a cloud of satisfaction. And then she'd asked him to go spend the night at her friend's hotel. *Pretty please? She really liked you, Cole. And you obviously liked her a lot, too.*

He'd said no at first, and Madeline had lost her powers of cute persuasion and been immediately irritated. "Are you kidding me? You already fucked her. What difference can it possibly make?"

"It doesn't seem right. If you're there, it's one thing. But this feels like cheating."

"She's a very powerful woman, Cole," Madeline had

said, her voice caught somewhere between a coax and a threat. She'd shoved her arms into a robe and gone to light a cigarette and glare out the window.

He'd said yes, finally, and headed out the door to a waiting car.

His throbbing leg pulled him back to the present.

"It's just a quick ride, Cole. Why are you being such an asshole?"

He had a few choices. Walk away and admit defeat. Explain that he couldn't ride. Not yet. Or tell her that he hated her guts because of what she'd done to him. Emotional wounds or physical ones?

He went for something less drastic. "I broke my leg last year. It's still acting up. No pleasure riding right now."

Her anger dropped away and she smiled. "Pleasure riding, huh? Is that why you didn't come by last night?"

He didn't respond, but he was damn glad she'd changed the subject.

"Well, will you at least saddle my horse for me?"

"Sure."

Riding high on relief, he grabbed her tack and started up the trail to the corral, doing his best to hide any limp. She was right behind him, just a step back. As they moved away from the yard, the noise of people faded and they were suddenly very alone in the breeze. Leaves rustled. Their boots crushed the occasional patch of dried grass. Cole felt every step like a knife of hot steel.

"You know," Madeline said, "I'm a little surprised to find you here still playing cowboy, Cole."

His head snapped up and he glared at the far tree line. "Excuse me?"

"I expected you were still in L.A. somewhere. Or at least not here. You had big plans."

He actually laughed, her statement was so outrageously awful. "Madeline, I don't even know what to say to that. I did have big plans. Yes. You've got that part right."

"So, what happened?"

He adjusted the saddle he'd balanced on his shoulder, hoping the shift would take some of the weight off his injured leg. "I came to L.A. for you. Did you forget all that?"

Madeline moved past him with a shrug. "It got too complicated. Even you said that."

"It got complicated because you were sharing me with your friends!"

"Sharing. Exactly. It's not like you weren't willing."

"I didn't know what I was getting into. And I didn't enjoy it."

"Hard to believe that when you managed to perform. Chelsea had nothing but good things to say about you. Not that I needed to be told. Your body is a work of art, Cole Rawlins."

"Am I supposed to say thanks?"

She waved a hand. "Look, I'm sorry about how it ended. After that argument, I just assumed you wouldn't want to stay in L.A. and work for me."

"Are you fucking kidding me? You banned me from your estate. You stopped taking my calls!"

Now she was the one who stopped, her boots sending up little arcs of dust. "I did no such thing."

"I tried to call that night."

"I remember that. I was busy."

"Busy with Chelsea," he snapped. That had been the end of it. When she'd gotten pissed that Cole had said no to another threesome. She'd accused him of being an unsophisticated hick.

She put her hands on her hips. "I didn't ban you from the estate."

"I showed up the next day. God, I even brought flowers, as if *I* had something to apologize for."

"You called me a psycho slut."

He just raised an eyebrow, daring her to argue that point. "I was told I was no longer needed. When I said I needed to talk to you, Diane said I wasn't allowed in and if I stayed she'd call the police."

For a moment, Madeline frowned in confusion. Well, her eyebrows dipped a little, but her forehead stayed smooth as silk. Then her eyes widened with some sudden understanding. "Oh," she said.

"Is it starting to come back?"

"I may have mentioned something to Diane about never wanting to see you again. It was late at night and I was still mad. When you left, Chelsea and I argued, too."

"I'm sorry to hear that," he snapped.

"I don't think she wanted me at all. She's the one who asked if you could join us."

Cole let his head fall back and stared at the sky. One lonely cloud floated at the edge of his vision. "I have no idea why you're telling me this."

"I just meant that I didn't intend to make you disappear from my life. I lost my temper. I was complaining about you. That's all."

"And the phone calls? Was Diane in charge of ignoring those, too?"

Her gaze slid away. She shrugged again. "Look. It was obviously not going to work for us, Cole. You were a small-town boy with small-town ideals. I spent my college years in Europe. I have different ideas about sex and love. I didn't need you hanging around and making me feel like there was something wrong with me."

"Yeah? And you decided that after we'd been together for a month? That realization came to you after I gave up everything and moved to California? For *you?*"

"You gave up a minimum-wage job," she snapped.

"I gave up a girlfriend and a life and my family!"

She flushed a little and started moving toward the corral again. "You wanted to come. You needed some excitement. Isn't that what you said?"

He followed her, anger taking away any of the pain he'd normally feel from moving so quickly. "I also said I loved you. Do you remember that?"

"Cole, we gave it a go. I had a life in L.A. and you didn't like it. That's it."

"Right. A life. And an image. And other people you wanted to sleep with."

She reached the fence, but she couldn't go in. There were too many horses still in the corral, and she was a Hollywood girl, but she knew enough not to go barging in on unfamiliar horses.

She put her hands on the raw wood of a railing and

watched as one of the mares came closer to sniff her. "I'm playing a man's game here, Cole. In a man's world. And if I have to do twice the work that any man does to be taken seriously, then I'm going to play just as hard as they do, too."

Cole let out a slow breath. "Wow," he murmured.

"I didn't lie to you, you know. I wanted you there. But after a few weeks, I knew it wasn't going to work. You and I were nothing alike. We didn't want the same things."

"Like Chelsea?" he spat.

"Yes. Like Chelsea, and art films and those parties I'd take you to where you didn't understand half the subjects being discussed. You were a cowboy, for godssake."

Cole huffed out a laugh, but he knew it sounded more like he'd been punched in the gut. "You know what? That would honestly hurt my feelings if I thought that was really the reason you blew me off. But you're a damn liar. You never intended for me to be anything more than your personal toy. After all, you weren't going to take me to London and introduce me to that actor you were living with there, were you?"

She turned and met his gaze, and he couldn't quite believe how untroubled her eyes were. She wasn't ashamed. She didn't feel guilty. "So?" she said. "It was good between us while it lasted. We had chemistry and excitement. We made each other happy for a few weeks."

"What the hell does that matter?"

"You know why it matters. I want to do it again."

Cole tossed the saddle onto the top rail and rolled

his shoulders. "This is unbelievable. I can't even talk to you."

"What else do you have going on? You have to hang out with me anyway. Why don't we both enjoy it to its fullest?"

"Why? Because you fucking humiliated me, that's why. I had to stand there with flowers in my hand and beg to see you while your little lackey smirked at me. And then I was alone in L.A. with no work. And after all that, my—"

He cut himself off. She knew nothing about his father, and he couldn't even blame that on her. That part was his responsibility.

"I apologize for embarrassing you, Cole. I didn't intend to do that. If that's what this is about, then let me make it up to you."

"No," he said. "That's not what this is about, Madeline. Excuse me." He pushed open the corral gate and tossed the bridle around the pinto she'd picked out as her own.

He could feel her eyes on his back. She was still looking for some weakness. Some opening to get what she wanted. She was good at that. He hadn't realized it back then, and he knew now that he'd been shamefully easy to manipulate. A twenty-one-year-old kid who'd felt as if he was staring at the sun when he looked at her. Hell, he'd been all ego and testosterone and sex drive. A good ol' country boy, just as she'd said.

He'd even told her that he loved her after she'd pulled a trick with her mouth he'd never experienced.

That was what he hated about her. Not for what she'd

done to him, but for what he'd done to himself. What he hated about her was that she knew all of it. She knew that he'd bad-mouthed his friends. That he'd scoffed at the idea of being a cowboy for his whole life like his father. That the moment Madeline had crooked her little finger, Cole had walked away from a sweet girl who'd loved him.

"God, you're a delicious treat," Madeline had said that first night. He should've paid attention to her words. A treat. Not even a real person. Just something to be consumed.

He checked the cinches on the saddle and led the horse to the gate. "Need a hand up?" he asked gruffly.

"Sure." She sounded subdued, but she'd slipped on her sunglasses and he couldn't read her eyes.

"Bring him back to the barn."

"Got it."

Cole watched her ride off and told himself this would be over in a few days. Granted, they'd be back. But by then, Cole would be in a saddle and out on the range. No way was he taking on this job for actual production. Easy could take that idea and shove it up his ass.

And if he wasn't able to ride…

"That's not going to happen," he muttered as he flipped open his phone. No signal out here at the corral, which was no surprise. Half the time he couldn't even get one bar back in the yard. And he was less and less convinced that Grace would call anyway.

Maybe she'd tired of him the same way Madeline

once had. Maybe he needed to find a girl who'd never known anyone but cowboys. He wouldn't be such a damned disappointment then.

CHAPTER EIGHTEEN

SHE'D MANAGED NOT TO THINK about him today.

Okay, that was an out-and-out lie.

Grace grimaced as she thanked the caterer who'd given her a ride home and headed for the ol' Stud Farm.

The truth was that she'd managed not to think about him when she was too busy to think, so she'd volunteered for every single bit of work that Eve had mentioned even as an idea. Their duties on-site were winding down, but there was still paperwork to babysit and copies to make and forgotten items to run out to sites.

Eve had been taking pictures for the production team at the river, so luckily, most of Grace's hours had been spent there. She'd only had to stop at the ranch once, and she'd happened by at a lucky moment. Cole had been walking away with Madeline, heading out toward the horses.

Things were no better between those two, it seemed. Their body language had been tense as they'd talked.

Thank God his back had been turned, because the sight of Cole had caused Grace to nearly stumble to a stop. How could she already know the shape of him and the way he moved his hands in the barest of expression as he talked? How could she immediately recognize the way he held his jaw, despite the fact that his face was shaded by the brim of his hat?

And why did that recognition set off some awful resonance inside her chest? It was a terrible, subtle vibration that traveled through her belly and turned her on like a switch.

"Damn," she murmured as she let herself into her apartment. It wasn't quite six yet. Eve had sent her home early. Good thing, because she could relax for a little while without worrying about running into Cole.

And relaxing was just what she planned to do. But first, she had some errands to run. Starting with the bank, to cash her first check. An hour later, she was the proud owner of a used air mattress and folding chair, a tiny two-cup coffeemaker, one saucepan and ten packs of ramen noodles. The fifteenth was payday, it seemed, and she needed to use a tiny bit of the money to take care of herself.

Grace cooked up a big bowl of noodles and sat in front of her open window in her new chair to watch the world go by as she ate.

Well, not much of the world. But at least six cars passed, and a pack of motorcycles rolled by. Two of them parked in front of the saloon. Wednesday was five-dollar pitcher night.

"I have five dollars," she said to her empty bowl. She smiled, not at the thought of beer, but at the thought of having a choice. Music glided over as the wind shifted, tempting her further.

"Oh, what the hell." She'd started the day off in her

underwear in a hallway. That seemed like the kind of day that should end with a beer.

She carefully cleaned up her kitchen, setting up her tiny coffeemaker in a corner as if she needed to conserve counter space. Then she changed into a T-shirt and her heeled boots and touched up her makeup before heading over to the Crooked R.

The place was packed.

A man was behind the bar for a change, though Grace caught a glimpse of Jenny weaving between crowded tables. "Hey, girl!" she called when she spotted Grace. "You sure got Rayleen riled up today!"

Grace groaned and shook her head. Jenny couldn't hear her, but apparently Grace's expression was clear enough, because Jenny laughed so hard, her tray nearly tilted into disaster.

Smiling, Grace looked around for a place to sit, and her eye caught on Shane, who was standing at the bar. He held up a pitcher and pointed at it, offering to share. She almost shook her head no.

But she didn't know anyone else in the place, so Grace tilted her head and began to work her way toward him. Too late, she saw that Aunt Rayleen was at her usual table. And the man Grace had met that morning in her underwear was standing just behind Shane.

Shane seemed to read the foul word that formed on Grace's lips, and his eyebrow rose in question. Well, if he hadn't heard the story, she wasn't going to inform him.

But that was wishful thinking, of course.

"Hey, Grace," he said, "you putting on daily shows

in the hallway now? I can't wait to see tomorrow's performance."

"Funny," she muttered as she took the beer he offered. "Thanks."

Rayleen gathered up a stack of cards and glanced up as she shuffled them. "Well, there she is. Miss America."

"Aunt Rayleen," Grace said and sighed.

"I see you're not too big for your britches after all. Guess there must have been a mix-up this morning."

"Hey," Lewis interrupted, stepping around Shane to offer a hand. "I thought I'd reintroduce myself. I'm Lewis MacIntosh. It's good to meet you, Grace. Again."

She shook his hand and murmured hello.

"Sorry we weren't introduced before today. I was down in Denver for a few days. I'm actually moving next month."

"Good riddance," Rayleen interrupted. "Go on. Perpetuate a fraud on some other old woman."

Grace leaned a little closer to Lewis and lowered her voice to a whisper. "I see she doesn't like you much either."

Shane laughed, apparently hearing every word. "That's the understatement of the year."

"How so?"

Rayleen snorted. "Don't bother flirting with that one, you hussy."

"Why not?" Grace snapped. "I am a hussy, after all."

"No use. He's gay as the day is long."

"Who?" Grace asked in surprise. "Shane?"

"Nope. That one's straight as an arrow. Ain't ya, Shane?"

"So they tell me," he said with a drawl.

"I'm talking about Lewis. Bet he could suck the chrome off a trailer hitch. A goddamn disappointment."

"Not such a disappointment for his partners, I'd guess," Shane said in a low voice, lifting his glass toward Lewis.

Grace inhaled half a mouthful of beer and spent a full thirty seconds coughing. Maybe she could like Shane after all, if only for the sour expression on Rayleen's face.

Lewis was grinning, but his cheeks had gone fantastically red.

Shane winked. "His ex-boyfriend used to hang around here and lament all the things he missed about Lewis. I can tell you for a fact that his cooking skills were not number one on that list. Not after a few drinks, anyway."

"Jesus, Shane," Lewis said on a laugh. "Shut the hell up."

"Yeah," Rayleen grouched. "It's enough to make a woman weep."

Grace shot her a glare. "Aunt Rayleen, stop being mean."

"It's all right," Lewis said. "She's mean to everyone. If she were nice to me, I'd know she really had a problem with it."

"Oh, I've got a problem with it!" she barked, but Lewis just rolled his eyes.

"I love you, too, Rayleen. I know you're secretly going to miss me."

Her mouth screwed up into a bitter pout. "If I do, it's only because you're as gorgeous as you are useless."

Lewis's laughter boomed through the bar. "Don't pout. You'll be fine. You've still got Shane and Cole."

"Shane, maybe. I don't take sloppy seconds." She scowled at Grace, who tried not to shudder.

"Oh, good Lord," she prayed, trying to purge that image from her mind.

"How do you think I feel?" Shane said, offering her a refill of beer. She took it gladly.

"She hasn't actually slept with any of her renters, has she?"

He lowered his voice. "I can't speak for anyone in this millennium, but as far as I know, she keeps her hands to herself. Actually, she's never even disrespectful unless she's showing off around here. But she always makes a big Thanksgiving dinner and drops off a plate for any of the guys who happen to be alone. Christmas, too."

Grace fell silent at that. Maybe the old woman really was just lonely. She'd been married once, a long time ago. A *really* long time ago. Her husband had died in a car accident. She hadn't always been this person.

Grace tentatively approached Rayleen's table and took a seat as the old woman eyed her.

"What did you do before this, Aunt Rayleen? You haven't always owned this place, have you?"

Rayleen shrugged and slid a pristine cigarette between her lips. Grace had never seen her actually smoke one. As a matter of fact, she smelled of fabric softener, not smoke. "I raised horses when my husband was alive.

Owned a gas station in Alaska for a time. Lots of different things."

"Alaska? Wow. What was that like?"

"Cold," she snapped.

"I hear there are a lot of men up there."

The cigarette bobbed. "There were enough."

"How did you end up here?"

"Sold my place in Alaska for a pretty penny after the pipeline went in. Then I just started driving."

"I can see why you stopped here."

Rayleen glanced at the cowboys gathered around the pool tables. "Place has its charms."

"It does," Grace agreed, almost against her will. Too much charm. She hadn't wanted to like it here as much as she did. "So, you don't think you'll ever end up in Florida with Grandma Rose? She says she keeps trying to talk you into moving."

"Oh, God. That place old people go to die? Please. The scenery's a lot better here." She eyed the cowboys again, making clear she wasn't talking about mountains.

"They do grow 'em strong," Grace agreed in an attempt at a drawl.

"Yeah, they do. Go on, now."

Grace, who'd been feeling a little warm and fuzzy about reaching out to her aunt, frowned at the sudden dismissal. "What?"

"Go on. You're sitting too close. It makes me look old. The lighting in here is dim, but it ain't that dim."

"You're saying you don't want me sitting close to you?"

"Well, not on five-dollar pitcher night. Beer goggles aren't infallible, girl."

Half exasperated and half amused, Grace moved back to the bar. Maybe if Rayleen learned how to be a little nicer, she'd have real friends. Realizing how close to home that little bullet struck, Grace reached for her beer. She had friends. Well, she had Merry. One really good friend. At that moment, Grace felt a sudden urge to reach out to Merry. Maybe to assure herself that she wasn't as far gone as Rayleen. Yet.

Making quick work of her beer, Grace tapped Shane on the shoulder. "I'll be back in a few, and I'll buy the next round, okay?"

She worked her way back toward the front, passing close enough to the jukebox to be tempted. She'd loved jukeboxes since she was little. Too many hours spent parked at seedy bar-and-grills as a kid. The jukebox had looked like a carnival to her. Flashing lights, promises of fun, a riot of noise.

She didn't know a lot of country songs, but she knew a little of the old stuff. George Strait. Dolly Parton. Her mom had gone through a two-stepping phase with an old boyfriend, and the music had played at their apartment around the clock.

Trying to calculate if she had a dollar or two to spare, she slipped out onto the porch and sat in the corner with her phone.

"Hey, Merry."

"You're still alive! I was worried you'd been eaten by bears or something."

"Not yet, but there's some really creepy antelope here that are out to get me."

"Are you drunk?"

"No. I'm serious about the antelope. They're called pronghorn. Look them up. There's something wrong with them."

"That's not what I meant. You just sound so relaxed. And I hear music in the background."

"I'm at the saloon," Grace said, smiling at the absurdity of it all.

"Yeehaw!" Merry yelled.

"By the way, did I tell you my apartment building is called the Stud Farm?"

"What the hell? Are you sure you aren't accidentally living on an Old West porn shoot? It's an easy mistake to make."

"No," Grace said quietly. "But I am fucking a cowboy."

"What?" Merry squealed, the word disappearing into peals of laughter. She was just as delighted as Grace had expected. "Since when?"

"A couple of days ago."

"I should hang up just to punish you for not telling me sooner. But I can't miss this. What cowboy? What do you mean? This sounds like a continuing project!"

"Actually I'm not sure if it'll continue anymore, but it's happened a couple of times."

"Oh, it's *happened?*"

Grace could practically hear her friend making air quotes.

"As in, 'I'm sorry, was that your penis I just sat on several times in quick succession?'"

"Something like that." She giggled. Maybe she was drunk. She certainly felt warm and loose and happy. She leaned against the corner post and hung her legs over the side of the porch.

"Details," Merry ordered. "God knows it's as close as I'll have been to an actual penis in months."

Grace looked around to be sure no one was near. "Look, he's not right for me. *Obviously*. He's an actual cowboy. On a ranch."

"No," Merry breathed. "No! Shut up. I can't take it. Does he wear a cowboy hat?"

"Yes."

"Does he wave it in the air when he's breaking you like a wild horse?"

"Shut up."

"Oh, my God, he does, doesn't he? Does he call you his filly?"

"Do you want to hear this or not?"

"Okay. Sorry." There was a sound like a hand slapping flesh. "I'm covering my mouth," Merry said, her voice muffled and muted. "Go ahead."

"He lives across the hallway from me. He's hot. And he's really, really good in bed."

"Oh, my God," Merry whispered.

"But I think it's over."

"But why?" Merry wailed.

"It's too complicated. I'm not at the point in my life where I can get serious. A couple of nights? Sure. But every night? That's asking for trouble. And I truly, honestly can't handle any more trouble right now. Not for a while. I really…can't do it."

"Hey," Merry said softly, her voice clear again. "Are you okay?"

"I'm good."

"Are you sure?"

"I'm just…" Grace's eyes burned, and then she felt the cool welling of the tears that spilled past her eyelids. "I'm tired, Merry. That's all."

"Oh, Grace. Don't—"

"No, I'm good. I just need a break, you know?"

"A break from what?" her friend pressed.

Grace wiped the tears from her cheeks and raised her gaze to the deep blue sky to stop any more from falling. She let her head fall to rest against the corner post. "I don't know. Struggling. Fighting everything. I just want it to be easier."

"Come to Dallas," Merry said with such urgency that Grace laughed.

"No, I'm good here. I'm working. I'm saving money. I go to Vancouver in a few weeks. I'll start over there. I'm almost thirty now. I can't be pissed off and rebellious my whole life. It's not as charming once your tattoos start to sag."

"You're not saggy."

"No, but I will be. And I'll hopefully have more to my name by then than a makeup kit and three pairs of black boots. Oh, and I also own a coffeemaker," she said, hating that she felt pride at something so stupid.

"I'm worried about you," Merry said softly.

"Don't be worried. Nothing's ever broken me. You know that. And nothing ever will. I promise."

"I knew you should've left Scott a long time ago. I can't believe he just threw you out. And—"

"This is a good thing, Merry. I'm enjoying this new work. It gives me more options. Everything's good."

"All right." Merry sighed. "While you're there, try out a few more things. Cowgirl. Rodeo queen."

"Rodeo clown!" Grace shouted, then looked around, startled by her own outburst.

"Hell, yeah!" a cowboy said from the far side of the saloon porch, but he was already bleary-eyed with drink, and his friends didn't even glance at her.

"So are you going to go back to L.A. eventually?"

"I don't know. I thought I was done with it. But I feel better about it here. Maybe it's the distance. Or maybe it's just that I'm out of the makeup trailer. I don't feel cornered. Or it's because I'm bringing something to them instead of them directing me."

"You don't like being bossed? Is that what this is about?"

Grace collapsed into laughter, swinging her feet against the weeds growing under the porch. "Maybe."

"God, you are a hot mess."

"Maybe," she said, laughing.

"But I love you."

That sobered her up every time Merry said it. Merry's life had been nearly as unstable as Grace's. The big difference being that Merry's mom had always been there. She even tried to take care of Grace when she visited. So Merry was used to saying that. Grace wasn't.

"Me, too," she said.

"Chicken," Merry said softly.

"Whatever. You're just trying to distract me, anyway. We need to address the problem of these penises you can't seem to get near."

Merry laughed, and everything was normal again, thank God. "You make it sound like I'm chasing them around the neighborhood."

"Why aren't you?"

"I'm no good with guys. Not like you are."

"Oh, Jesus." Grace sighed. "If you think I'm good with men, you're further gone than I thought."

"They don't think I'm sexy, Grace. Not the way you are."

Grace got angry the way she always did when she thought of people not being nice to Merry. "You are sexy! And you're the sweetest person I know. Any man would be lucky if you even looked at him."

"Sweet," Merry groaned. "That's the problem. I'm the perpetual little sister. The buddy. Once a guy ruffles your hair, your vagina has ceased to exist for him. And," she said and sighed, "a lot of guys ruffle my hair."

Despite her frustration for her friend, Grace laughed. "It's going to happen. Someday you'll meet a guy who thinks you're sweet *and* wants to see your vagina."

"You think?"

"I know. And hey, if not, you've always got a nice rack to fall back on."

"That's true," Merry agreed grudgingly.

"None of those guys are good enough for you anyway."

"Which guys?"

"All of them," Grace said. She meant it. Despite the fact that she'd grown up with no money and no dad, just as Grace had, Merry had somehow come through with her sensitive soul intact. Grace would kill any man who changed that.

"I'd better go," she finally said.

"All right. But call me again soon. I miss you, Grace."

She got off the phone, but she stayed where she was on the porch. It was another perfect evening in Wyoming. Cool in the shade. Crickets just starting to chirp. No mosquitoes. No smog. Just the breeze on her skin and the falling dusk. She took a deep breath. And another. And then Cole walked out their front door.

And all her good intentions, all her strength of conviction and determination—everything crystallized. Right there where she could see it. She watched as it all went clear and bright. And then it broke apart and collapsed into sharp shards of lust. They stabbed into her, impossible to ignore.

God, she wanted him again. She wanted him to want her again. The idea was sweet somehow, despite that it was all animal heat and need. It was sweet and strong and devastating. But she closed her eyes and told herself it wasn't real. He was just a man. It was just sex.

She pushed to her feet and disappeared into the saloon before he could corner her alone. It was safer this way, surrounded by people. She could disappear among them, then slip away without a fight. Or whatever it was that he wanted. He'd called several times today. He probably thought they should talk. Probably wanted to know what she was feeling. But she never told anyone what she was feeling. As far as she was concerned, no one deserved to know what she was really feeling, deep down inside. The idea of admitting that she was scared or worried or hurt to a man... No. Her mouth went dry.

At least it was perfect timing. Shane had already ordered another pitcher.

"I told you I'd get that."

He shrugged. "Next week."

"What if I'm not here next week?"

Shane paused in the act of raising the pitcher to pour another glass. One eyebrow rose, disappearing beneath his cowboy hat. "You planning on leaving soon?"

"Sooner rather than later."

His gaze focused past her shoulder. "Does Cole know that?"

"I have no idea."

"Right. I see." He poured her glass and slid it over. "Maybe I'd better order another pitcher, then."

"Oh, we're all big girls here, aren't we?" She shrugged off the flat doubt in his eyes. "It is what it is."

"Sure," he answered, managing to convey a lot of doubt in that word.

When Cole joined them, Shane lifted his chin in greeting and offered a beer. "How's it going?"

Cole just grunted in that way men did when they were friends. Some shorthand that other men didn't seem to find rude. He tipped his face toward Grace. "Can we talk?"

"Sure," she said without making any sign that she was willing to move.

Cole's mouth flattened, but he leaned closer after shooting a look at Shane. Shane cleared his throat and turned away.

"What's going on?"

"Nothing. I'm just enjoying the evening."

"What happened this morning?"

"I left."

"In a huff."

"It wasn't a huff. I was genuinely pissed. I didn't mean to spend the night."

"Why not?"

She took a sip of beer and let her gaze wander around the room. "Regardless of what you might think, I don't need your help."

He leaned closer and spoke through clenched teeth. "What the hell did that have to do with help? We had sex. You spent the night. That's what people do."

"Oh, yeah? Do you spend the whole night with a lot of girls you pick up at bars? Make them breakfast? Ask them to *stay* with you?"

"First of all," he growled, "I didn't pick you up at a bar. Second, that very obviously wasn't a one-night stand, since it's happened for two nights now. Third, I asked you to stay because I like you in my bed. And you seemed to like it, too, considering the way you were snuggled up against me this morning."

"You were warm," she snapped, as if she remembered anything about it.

"I was *warm?*"

Shane darted a look over his shoulder at Cole's raised voice, but his face was carefully blank.

Grace was starting to feel a little guilty, and she didn't like that. Maybe she had been curled up to him because he was warm, but that wasn't the half of it, and she knew it. She liked touching him. She liked his skin and his hands and his scent. Just the thought of it opened up an ache in her body. It felt like a flower blooming, spreading red-hot petals through her insides. It was need, but not just that. It was want, too. And yearning. And she hated it so much. It felt like weakness.

She lifted her face and looked into his eyes. "I don't need help."

"If you think that's true, maybe you should look around. You don't even have a bed. You don't have a place to eat your dinner. A place to sleep. You *came* here for help!"

Good. He'd pissed her off now, and that thing spreading inside her closed up again, squeezing itself small and invisible and meaningless. "Not from you. I don't need or want help from you. Got it? Your dick isn't some rescue line I need to hold on to. It was just sex. Deal with it."

She stalked away, but not toward the door. She wouldn't retreat, as if he bothered her so much she couldn't be in his presence. He didn't. He was nothing to her. But she was still aware of his eyes on her as she stopped in front of the jukebox and flipped through the selections.

Considering it a good bargain, she spent two dollars for three songs and nearly five minutes worth of time choosing them. Almost all of her anger had sunk back to its normal place by then, below the surface, accessible but not out of control. And her neck no longer burned with awareness. She discovered why when she turned around.

Cole was no longer watching her. Instead, he was watching Rayleen's table. And no wonder. Seated with Rayleen was Cole's boss, Easy. Cole didn't look happy to see him. Rayleen, on the other hand…

Oh, the woman wasn't doing anything so obvious as smiling at Easy, but her eyes were bright and her back straight and she looked ready to fight. It was the same way she looked when she was flirting with her young studs.

Interesting. Had they dated sometime back in the 1900s?

Grace worked her way back to the bar to ask Jenny.

"Oh, Easy comes in here a couple times a month on pitcher night. They play gin rummy for cash."

"Is that all they do?"

"As far as I know," Jenny answered. "And that's all I ever need to know about it."

Grace wanted to stay there with Jenny, talking and hiding, but pitcher night was busy, and Jenny was too slammed to hang out. "Sunday!" she promised as she rushed away.

"Sunday," Grace whispered. But she needed the break tonight.

At this point she had three choices: run away, sit here alone or move back to the other end of the bar. Sitting here alone was nearly as bad as running off. Nearly everyone she knew in this town was seated just a dozen feet away. Sitting alone was like a terrible limbo. Too afraid to face Cole, too afraid to leave.

Plus, her beer was over there.

"Screw it," she muttered and pushed off her barstool to face the tension she'd caused.

This was the problem with small towns. She'd only been here a few days, and already people knew her. And in a small town, they'd be there even if she tried to avoid them. In L.A. there were a thousand neighborhoods, a thousand bars.

Oh, there were a few bars in Jackson, but most of them were geared toward tourists. There were a few grocery stores, a few banks, a few apartments she could afford. And people she would know even on those days when she didn't want to know anybody.

There had been a lot of those days. Days she didn't want to be seen. Days she didn't want anyone to look at her and find her lacking. Or days when she was so full of everything—life and anger and hurt and fear—that she wouldn't be able to hide it, and everyone would see.

But she'd had time to compose herself, so she stopped next to Cole and reclaimed her beer. "Why do you hate your boss so much?" she asked.

He looked down at her, his gaze tense and far away for a moment. He blinked and shook his head. "I'm sorry for what I said."

"About what?"

"About you coming here for help. About needing it. I shouldn't have said it."

"You say a lot of things you shouldn't say but really believe. I'm getting used to it."

"It's just you," he said, his cheeks flushing a little.

"Just me, what?"

"I lose my temper with you. I don't know why. I'm sorry."

She waved off his apology and watched Rayleen and Easy both lay cash on the table.

She knew why Cole lost his temper with her. Because she had some sort of supernatural ability to piss people off. Everybody lost their temper with her. She was abrasive or unlikable or irritating. Probably all three.

"I really am sorry."

"It's fine," she said. It was always fine, because she wouldn't let it be any other way. She wouldn't let it hurt her that he said things to her he wouldn't say to anyone else. Or that he was rougher with her in bed than he was with other girls. She wanted him to think she was tough—to *know* she was tough—so it only made her happy that he treated her as if she wasn't fragile. Right?

It was fine. She cleared her throat. "I'm sorry I didn't explain why I left," she murmured. "This morning, I mean. I'm sorry." He didn't say anything, so Grace finished her beer and gestured for Jenny to bring another pitcher to replace the one Shane had just finished off. "Did Rayleen and Easy date at some point?"

"Not that I know of," Cole said.

"I think she likes him."

Rayleen hooted and scooped up a pile of dollar bills. "You'll have to find some other way to pay for your little blue pills, old man. I'm gonna bleed you dry."

"You certainly know how to suck the life out of a man," he answered.

"That's what my dear departed husband used to say."

Shane snorted in amusement as Easy's neck turned beet-red. Cole didn't crack a smile.

But Rayleen grinned. "Don't tell me nobody ever told you about the ol' fellatio, Easy. Why, these young cowboys tell me it's all the rage."

"You're incorrigible, woman."

"That comes with the fellatio, you fool."

Even Cole snorted at that.

Easy adjusted his hat and shuffled the cards, his neck still ablaze. "You been hanging out with your young studs too much, Rayleen. You should spend some time with a real man who'll teach you some manners."

Grace nudged Cole with her elbow. "See?" she whispered.

Rayleen's smile slipped back to her normal sour sneer. "If you hear about any real men, you be sure to let me know."

"You attract a lot more flies with honey, you know."

"There's the problem right there. Who the hell wants a bunch of flies buzzing around? A damn nuisance."

Easy just grunted and dealt the cards.

"They've got something going on," Grace said to Cole.

"Jesus, I hope not."

"They're lonely, maybe. Both of them."

She watched as Rayleen pretended she didn't like playing cards with Easy. Then she acted like Shane was bothering her with his teasing. Rayleen was lonely. She was *alone*. And she was so scared to acknowledge it that she made a point of being mean. But this bar, the apartments, everything was designed to bring other people into her life. To force them near on Rayleen's terms.

Grace's heart began to pound hard and her mouth went dry. Suddenly Rayleen wasn't just some old, washed-up, lonely woman. She was Grace in thirty years. Grace, who lashed out when she felt vulnerable. Grace, who couldn't let herself need or want anything from anyone.

She poured herself another beer and drank it fast.

If she didn't change her life, someday she'd have to do this. Find some way to force people close. And by that time, it wouldn't be so easy to get the small things she needed. She wouldn't be able to use her body the way she did now, to touch men when she wanted and then push them away. To find release and pleasure at a moment's notice. And no one would take her in if she needed help. She'd just be another crazy old grouch who was too mean to have real friends.

She had to get out of here soon. She had to pay off her debt and start her new life. Make a new way for herself. She didn't want to end up like Rayleen any more than she wanted to end up like her own mother: weak and broken and used up and stupidly wondering why things weren't better.

Because you never make anything better, she'd said to her mom when she'd last seen her three years ago. *Because your one gift in life is being so malleable you bend like putty.* Her mom had simply looked confused and cried a few tears at Grace's meanness. The mean-ness that had gotten her through her mom's abusive boyfriends, and then a life of fear and violence on the streets.

But Grace could see what she'd done wrong now. She'd been so afraid of becoming her mom that she'd made herself too strong. She couldn't bend at all. She could only fall over and shatter, hurting anyone who got near.

There had to be a better way. She had to find it. If she was going to be alone, she didn't want it to be like this.

"I don't hate him, you know."

Grace blinked from her thoughts and saw that Cole was leaning against the bar, head bowed. "Who?" she asked.

"Easy. He's not just my boss. He was my dad's best friend. He's been like an uncle to me. Hell, maybe another father."

"So, what's wrong?"

"This thing with the movie production."

"Ah. You're pissed that he accepted the offer. It was a pretty fair price, you know. You can't begrudge him that. The studio was under the gun."

"He didn't do it for the money. He did it to teach me a lesson."

"What lesson?"

"Hell if I know. Something for my own good, I gather."

She watched the way his mouth flattened with anger. With his head tipped down, she couldn't see much more beneath his hat. "You must know."

His lips turned up into a tight smile and he finally met her gaze. "Easy doesn't have any kids. I'm supposed to buy his ranch when he's ready to retire. Close enough to a son, I guess. At least he'll know the person who owns his land. But now he's not sure."

"Not sure of what?"

"Not sure I'm the right man for the job anymore."

"Oh." She looked from Easy to Cole, aware she'd stumbled into a thicket of male ego and hurt pride. "Did he say that?"

"No, he said he wanted to give me more *opportunities*."

She wanted to ask why, wanted to ask what had happened, but she worried it would be like a tiny crack in a pressurized tank. One little tap and it would spread, bright and ominous notes of warning chiming that it was about to explode.

"He's worried about my leg," Cole said softly.

"But that'll heal eventually."

"Yeah," he said. "Probably."

Grace felt her skin go cool as she realized what he was saying and hoped he didn't mean it.

"It'll be fine," he said so softly that she barely heard it.

"What if it's not?"

"It will be."

She heard fear in those words, but more than anything else, she heard weariness. An unyielding weight of exhaustion that she immediately recognized. When you were looking straight at a wall and there was no way around it. No way under or over. She knew in that moment it seemed that there was nothing to do but lie down and give up the ghost. Just lie down and hope life was over with quickly instead of lasting too long.

She'd been there. Recently, but also many times in the past. Hell, she might even be there right at this moment, but she hadn't looked around and realized it yet.

She wanted to touch him. The thought hit her so suddenly and completely that it scared her. She wanted to touch him and feel his hands on her, too. A connection. Something to anchor two lost people.

His hands. His mouth. They'd make her feel real. And she could do that for him, too.

He glanced up and froze. His pupils tightened as if he could read the need on her face. She had to part her lips to get enough air.

Cole raised his hand as if he meant to brush a hair from her face, but instead he touched his thumb to her mouth. Grace closed her eyes and shuddered. That was all it took with him. One touch and she forgot her resolution to stay away. To be pissed. To never want anything from him.

His hand fell away, sliding down to her shoulder, then down her arm until he wrapped her fingers into his. "Come on."

Come on. The only words it took to seduce a girl like her. She let him lead her out of the saloon and back to his apartment. Grace walked to his bedroom before he'd even closed the front door.

COLE DIDN'T KNOW WHY he felt so desperate. He'd been entirely spent not twenty-four hours before and exhausted by a day of stress and frustration. But one look from Grace and his heart was pounding with so much need it felt like panic.

She pulled her shirt over her head and then they fell to the bed, hands grasping each other, mouths devouring. He was hard as a rock already, and he gasped with relief when he ground his cock against her. Her legs wrapped around him, her hips rocking.

He wanted to be inside her already, but he couldn't conceive of letting her go long enough to get her jeans off. So he just pushed himself against her and listened to her moan in approval. Her hands crept beneath his shirt. Her nails dug into his skin and scratched at his lust until it howled.

He wanted to fuck her until she screamed. He wanted to make her sorry she'd left the way she had. Sorry she'd even wanted to leave.

"Cole," she groaned. Her hands slid beneath his jeans and forced his hips tighter to her. "Fuck me. Please. God, just fuck me."

He laughed in angry pleasure. He'd do it when he was good and ready. She could wait the way she'd made him wait for her call today.

When he didn't respond, her nails dug into his skin and then her teeth were at his neck, biting hard.

"Damn it," he barked, startled at the pain. But more than that, he was shocked at how much it pissed him off. And how close he felt to coming as rage surged through his blood.

"Now," she ordered. *"Now."*

Cole sat up to tear off his shirt. "Take off your jeans," he growled. Her triumphant smile turned his heart into thunder. He felt like a stallion that'd do violence to anything that tried to interfere with his goal. He unbuttoned his own jeans and pushed them down just far enough to draw out his cock.

Her eyes blazed with victory.

As if she'd won.

Cole growled and yanked her jeans off with rough hands. Grace laughed as if he couldn't be rough enough to do anything more than amuse her. He slipped on a condom and lowered himself over her. And when he grabbed her wrists and pressed them to the bed, she laughed again, taunting him. She thought she was about to get what she wanted.

But Cole had other ideas. He pressed his hips tight to hers, pushing his cock against her just as he had before. Only this time there were no clothes between them. It was just his cock sliding against her clit.

She wrapped her legs around him again, and the heat of her pussy seared his shaft. But he didn't shift his hips. He didn't slide lower so he could sink inside her. Instead, he pressed his cock against her clit again, rocking until she moaned.

For a moment, he almost forgot why he was doing this. He was overwhelmed with the thought that he could shift one inch down, just one tiny inch, and his head would slide into her. She was so wet. It would be so easy. He'd slip right into place and then press a little and he'd be in her. Inside that tightness and heat. Surrounded by her body as she took him in. He'd—

"Fuck me," she pleaded. "Fuck me."

He remembered, suddenly. Remembered that he'd meant to make her pay.

"No," he said. He slid lower, but he didn't stop where she wanted—where *he* wanted. Instead he put his knee between her thighs and bent over to suck her nipple between his teeth.

"No!" she gasped, even as she arched up into his mouth. He pressed his teeth a little harder and she cried out, then whimpered when he licked at her to soothe the sting.

"Oh, God," she groaned. She tried to slide down, but his thigh blocked her way. He pressed his leg against her, loving the way she moved against him in desperation.

She seemed to remember that he held her wrists then, and when she struggled against him, he remembered, too. That he had her beneath him, that her delicate wrists were in his grip, that she was fighting him, twisting her arms, even as she rocked against him, the heat of her pussy scalding his skin, driving him mad. He wanted inside her. He *needed* it.

She jerked her hands, trying to free them. He held her easily.

"Tell me you want me to let you go," he whispered against her skin.

"Do it," she ordered.

"No." He dragged his mouth up to her collarbone. "Tell me you want me to let you go, if that's what you want. Tell me to let you go and get off you."

She bucked beneath him, her arms straining.

"Or…beg me to hold you down and take you. Beg me."

"Fuck you," she growled.

He kissed her neck and now his body was pressed against her, his cock notched just *there.* He wanted to groan the way she was groaning. Wanted to beg her to let him. *Please, just let me.* She was so strong. So stubborn and angry and brave.

"I'll fuck you, Grace. All you have to do is ask me nicely. That's all. Ask for what you want from me instead of taking. I'll give you anything."

"I hate you," she sobbed. Her hips tipped up, dragging her sex against the head of his cock. Power turned to liquid heat in his veins and threatened to weaken his will.

He dragged her arms above her head and easily held both her wrists in one hand. He slid the other between them, and his fingers found the slick, hard bud of her clit easily.

"Oh, God!" she screamed. "Oh, God, please. Please, Cole."

He smiled, amazed that he could still be controlled enough to feel anything more than animal lust. "Please, what?"

"Please. Please, fuck me. Now. Please. Just…" She pulled against his grip and moaned louder as he rubbed her clit. "Hold me down," she rasped. "Fuck me. Hard. Please. I need it."

Her words transformed the power in his body to blinding need. Desperation. Whatever she needed from him, he needed it more.

He took her wrists in both hands one more time, pressing them hard to the mattress.

"Please," she whispered. "Please, please, please."

He pressed his hips forward slowly, easing into her heat. He held his breath, concentrating on the sweet tightness of her body.

"Yes," she urged as he filled her. "God, yes. Cole—" Her words died on a gasp as he surged deep. He took her slow and deep and hard. He held her down, watching her face as her eyes closed and her lips parted and the breath rushed from her throat. She gasped with each thrust, panting as he took her faster.

When he needed to feel her hands on him, he let her wrists go, grunting when she grabbed his ass and dug her nails in. "Yes," she urged. "Yes, yes."

He wanted to come right then. His body screamed with it. But he needed her to come. Needed it like air. Needed to feel her jerk beneath him. Needed to hear her scream. She hated to give him anything, which only made it sweeter when he finally felt her go taut beneath him.

"God. Oh, God. Cole. I… Ah!" She screamed then, her pussy squeezing him as she dragged her nails up his back.

"Ah, fuck," he breathed as the pain twisted around his pleasure and sank him deep into his own orgasm. He thrust hard, over and over. By the time he came back to himself, all he could hear was Grace panting into his ear. He smiled weakly and rose up to his elbows to kiss her.

"I'm sorry," she said after a deep breath. "Did I hurt you?"

"Yes. Did I hurt you?"

"No."

"Good." He kissed her nose and rolled off, sinking

into his mattress as if it were made of down instead of cheap springs and foam. His back burned. "I'm worried you're going to fuck me to death one of these nights."

"I might," she purred, a smile in her voice.

"Good," he said again. He looked over to find her lying there, smiling, her eyes closed and her face peaceful. He'd thought he might never move again, but he found the will to turn to his side and kiss her jaw. "You're so beautiful."

She opened one eye, then closed it again. "Nice try. You already told me I wasn't."

"I was wrong," he murmured, breathing in the scent of her warm skin. "Totally, utterly wrong."

"Spoken like a man who just had an amazing orgasm."

"Damn straight." He got up to go to the bathroom to clean up, then shucked his jeans before he got back into bed. When he felt the press of her whole naked body against his, Cole sighed and closed his eyes. Something about her relaxed him. The sex, obviously, but not just that. He felt peaceful with her, which made no sense. She was so tense and prickly and combative. Though not now. Right now, her body melted into his.

Her hand touched his hip. "Does it hurt?"

"Not at the moment."

Her fingers traced the lines which had finally faded from red to a sick pink. "But usually?"

"It depends. Sometimes I don't notice it. But at night, it aches like a bad tooth."

"God, it must've hurt when it happened. I've only broken my hand. And a couple of toes."

He lifted her hand to his mouth to kiss her knuckles. "Let me guess. A punch that landed badly? And, of course, kicking things that pissed you off?"

"No!" She jerked her hand away, but she was laughing. "Okay, maybe one of the toes had something to do with my bad temper. But the hand wasn't my fault. I got knocked down at a club and reached out to catch myself. I'm not sure if it was the landing or the boot on my hand that broke it."

"Nice club," he murmured.

"I could tell you some stories."

He put his hand to her waist, aware of the way her breath hitched a little. He propped his head up on his hand so he could watch her face as he spread his fingers over her skin. "But you won't tell me, will you?"

"No," she said, not a hint of tension in her voice, just honesty.

Sliding his fingers down over her hip, he covered half her tattoo with his hand, then pushed slowly back up over the stark shape of the black tree. The tips of its branches stretched up her ribs, coming to a stop just below her heart. His thumb brushed the bottom of her small breast.

"Will you tell me about the tattoo now?"

"Why would I?"

"Because I want to know. Because I care what it means."

"It's just a tree," she said, sighing.

"It's black and bare. Cold. Or dead. Which one?"

She sighed again, then finally opened her eyes to look up at him. The weary black of her gaze was almost as dark as the ink of her tattoo, but so much deeper. "I don't know."

"You must know."

"I don't. Maybe it's dead. Maybe it's bare for the winter, just waiting to wake up and live again. But... maybe not. Nothing much has changed in the five years since I got it."

"It's not right, then," he said. "That's not you. You're not cold and dead."

"You sound awfully sure for a man who hardly knows me."

"I know you well enough to see your heat. You're alive and fighting and strong."

He watched her throat work as she swallowed several times, then her face tipped slowly away from him. She stared into the dimness of his room as if there were a movie playing on the other wall. Finally, she shook her head. "Anger isn't strength. It isn't even living." She added a moment later, "It's like stars."

He slid his hand up, over her breast and her beating heart and her beautiful neck. He smoothed her hair back, but she didn't look toward him again. "What do you mean? What about the stars?"

"People look at them and see something beautiful. Something alive and bright." Her voice had gone so flat that he felt a momentary fear. "But it's just old light. Old and dead. Some of those stars aren't even there anymore, did you know that? You think they're alive and shining, but they died a long time ago. There's nothing there."

"Jesus, Grace. That's not you."

"It might be. I'm not sure. But I have to find out.

I thought I was tough when I ran away from home. I thought I'd seen it all and I could handle anything. But at sixteen, I was still too alive. I could still feel it all."

Cole realized his heart was beating harder. "What are you saying? You could feel what?"

When she finally looked at him, it had gotten too dark in the room to see much, but he thought he caught a glimmer of tears in her eyes. Grace laughed. "Nothing. I think I'm drunk."

"Grace. You could feel what? Were you hurt?"

She shook her head. When he tried to brush a hand over her cheek, she batted it away. "It doesn't matter."

"Of course it matters. You were just a girl. If you were hurt or raped or—"

"I was living on the streets. Of course bad things happened. To me and everyone else I knew. There were no doors to lock, and you can't call the police when you're a runaway. But at least when you're drunk or high, it fades. It doesn't matter. And eventually, you don't feel it anymore. It's the only way to keep going."

"Grace, I…"

"At least I got out alive. Some of us didn't. I try to feel grateful for that, but now…I don't even know what I want to feel anymore, but something's got to change."

Turning her face away, she fell into silence. Cole's chest ached, as if there was breath stuck and he couldn't make his lungs work. But he was breathing just fine. He took a deep breath and another, trying to ease the tightness.

"I can't keep going like this," she whispered, "but

what if I'm just old, dead light? What if it's only anger in there, making me seem alive?"

"You're alive, Grace." He kissed her forehead, then her nose, her wet cheek. "You have a right to be angry, but that's not all there is. Do you think anger makes me want to touch you this way?" He smoothed her hair back again, kissed her cheek, then her ear.

"That's not the only way you touch me."

"Oh," he said as all the air left his lungs. "That's not—"

"I know. And it's good. It's what I need. That's my point."

"I'm sorry. I'm not usually like that. If you don't want me to—"

"I do want you to. You know that."

"But if it reminds you of something bad… If it—"

"It doesn't," she said quickly. "I left all that behind. And I can't be soft, but I have to find some way to *bend*."

Cole didn't know what to say. He didn't know how to take back something they both wanted, but it killed him to think he might hurt her in ways he hadn't realized. "You're soft right now," he whispered as the room finally went fully dark. "The softest thing I've ever felt." She was. Her skin was hot beneath his hand, her limbs a languid line against him, and everywhere he touched was like silk.

"That's old light, Cole," she murmured.

"No. No, it's not. It's new. It's for me."

Whatever she said, he knew that was true. In public she was on guard, a bundle of tension and wariness and sharp claws. But in his bed, afterward, she was small and soft and warm. And so vulnerable it made him hurt for her. Not that he'd ever tell her that.

"What were you like as a kid?" he asked.

"Me? I don't know. Skinny and wary and restless. What about you?"

"Skinny and loud and covered in dirt."

She laughed. "I bet."

"So you're still skinny and wary and restless. Nothing's changed. You haven't gone supernova."

"You, on the other hand... You're not skinny and loud anymore."

"But I am filthy."

"Yes, you do still have that."

They subsided into comfortable silence for a while, the darkness settling around them. It was only ten, but he was already sinking into that weightless space between wakefulness and sleep when she spoke again. "I'm ready to change. To give myself a chance. I need to start over and make a life for myself. Settle down and stop running away. Stop living like I don't have anything valuable to lose."

The thought that she might stop fighting him and they could see where this might lead... Cole would never say it to her or anyone else, but that seemed like something he could hold on to. Something that might see him through the next few weeks.

She was so damn strong. She'd been through a hell of a lot more than he had, and she was still going, still fighting the world. But maybe he could help her leave the battle behind. At least with him.

He'd never tell anyone else she was soft. He'd keep

that secret safe. He'd even let her pretend she didn't need anything but sex. But there was no mistaking the way she curled into him. Or the way she sighed when he pulled her closer still.

Grace Barrett was soft for him, and getting softer every minute. He didn't want to go to sleep and miss it. "You want to watch TV? A movie? Anything?"

Her eyes opened. "What do you have?"

"Darlin', I was on bed rest for quite a while. I have everything. Cable, pay-per-view, Netflix, some sort of streaming contraption. You name it, I've got it."

She watched him for a long moment, and then she smiled. "Do you think you can get *The Outsiders?*"

"Is that a movie?"

"Only the best movie ever made. Assuming you like rumbles and hair grease. You've never seen it?"

He shrugged and grabbed the remote. "Nope."

Grace bounced up to her knees, a grin taking over her face. "All right, cowboy. You find the movie. And I'll…" Before he realized what she was doing, she raised her hand and smacked his naked ass. Hard. "I'll find some snacks. Do you have popcorn?"

"Jesus!" He rubbed a hand over the sting.

"What? I thought that was how you dismounted around these parts." Laughing, she walked naked toward his kitchen, flashing a smile over her shoulder that Cole would never forget. If he had anything to say about it, he'd make her smile like that every day from now on.

CHAPTER NINETEEN

GRACE WOKE TO AN OMINOUS SKY. She was in her own bed, at least, despite having fallen asleep at Cole's place during the movie. She'd snuck out at two, when she'd woken up dying of thirst and still a little drunk.

She wasn't sure exactly how many beers she'd had. She'd been nervous and stressed and angry. Four, maybe. Or six, counting the ones at Cole's.

Whatever the number, it had been too many, because she'd blabbed about her life as if she'd been on a therapist's couch. God. And all that *after* she'd begged him to fuck her.

As good as the sex had been, her face flamed at the memory. God, he must have loved that. Did he like her just because he wanted to see if he could break her down like that? Because it was a challenge to make the tough girl whimper and moan?

Grace stared at the lead-gray sky she could see from her air mattress. There were curtains in the bedroom, but they weren't long enough, so whoever had hung them—Rayleen, probably—had just positioned the little spring-loaded curtain rod six inches beneath the top of the window frame. She had privacy, but not a lot of protection from the morning light. Grace couldn't decide if it was ingenious or the tackiest thing she'd ever seen.

After a few minutes, she decided on ingenious. After all, rich people paid a lot of money for those top-down blinds and got the exact same results. This was practically like living in Beverly Hills.

Despite her bad mood, Grace laughed at that as she crawled to the edge of the air mattress and dismounted. She was low to the ground, but the thing was as wobbly as a water bed, and she wasn't quite at full strength yet. At least she'd had the brains to drink a huge glass of water when she'd returned to her apartment, or she'd be nursing a serious headache, instead of just a case of embarrassment.

"This time," she whispered to herself, "you're really not doing that again. Even if he is the best sex you've ever had." And he was, damn it. He really was. And if she didn't like him at all, she'd probably go ahead and indulge for the next few weeks. Scratch that itch until she left. But she did like him. He was sweet and strong and likable. The kind of guy she'd think about really dating if she were going to be around for a while. If he weren't a cowboy. And if they had anything in common besides the sex. But she wasn't going to be around for long, and they were nothing alike. And frankly, she wasn't even sure he liked her. Oh, he liked the sex. He was a man, after all. But men didn't fuck nice girls that way.

He took her the way she deserved to be taken. It was rough and brutal and intense. It was good. But it wasn't sweet. It wasn't gentle. Thank God. It was just what she wanted. But it wasn't the way you made love to someone you liked.

By the time she showered and dressed and left for

the bus stop, the sky seemed to have fallen lower. She ducked her head against a few raindrops and wondered if she was about to get the day off. The clouds looked really nasty. A sick gray-green she'd never seen in the sky in L.A., like something straight out of the Weather Channel. Maybe she was going to see her first tornado. The idea both thrilled her and scared her half to death, but she kept her head down and waited for the bus. Still, by the time it dropped her off near the studio, the air was so charged Grace found herself jogging down the wooden walkway, the hair on her arms standing on end.

"Hey!" she said too loudly when she burst through the door. "Are we going to the site today?"

"Sure," Eve said, frowning at her laptop. "Why not?"

"There's a big storm." She gestured toward the windows.

"Oh, that'll blow over any minute."

"Are you sure?"

"Yep, look how fast the clouds are moving."

She edged back to the window and cast a doubtful eye toward the sky above the restaurant across the street. The clouds were scuttling pretty quickly past the roofline. "I don't know," she murmured.

"Come on. By the time we get out there, it'll be blue skies. First the river location, then the ranch. I'm doing final framing shots. Normally preproduction would take care of all of it, but with this much CGI, they want backup. It's half science, half art, and lots and lots of panoramic shots. You up for being my assistant?"

"Sure."

Eve's usual habit was to put on music when she drove,

and today was no exception. She was quiet. Quieter than most women, but she sometimes forgot Grace was there and sang softly along with the music. She had a beautiful voice, husky and soothing. It matched her eyes, somehow.

"You don't have to come on Sunday," Grace said. "If you're uncomfortable with the idea."

"Uncomfortable?" She turned down the music. "Why would I be uncomfortable?"

"After what happened. I'm sure you didn't want to say anything to Jenny."

"Grace, I don't know that production girl from Adam."

"You don't know me either."

"No, but you've never given me a reason not to trust you."

Grace suddenly felt guilty. Or maybe she just wanted to start cutting her ties. "I'm not planning on staying in Jackson. Not for more than a few weeks. Maybe less."

"Ah. Well, I can't say I'm surprised. But a lot of people say that when they move here. Even I did."

"You're not from here?" Grace asked.

"No. I moved here from Oklahoma when I was twenty-eight. I thought I'd be here for a ski season, then I'd move on to a real life somewhere. Settle down."

"But you never settled down? I mean, you don't have kids, right? You're not married?"

"No," she said, simply. "Never. But I guess I'm settled after all."

There was a story there. Grace could feel it, swelling beneath the surface, but Eve didn't so much as offer a glance of warning. She just stared straight ahead at the road, her hands loose and relaxed on the steering wheel. Whatever it was, Eve had no urge to share it. No need to get it out. She kept it close on purpose.

She'd meant to move on and she'd never left, and now she was settled by default. Grace wouldn't make that same mistake.

"I've got a makeup gig in Vancouver," she said. "In five weeks. The local film industry is pretty vibrant."

"You know people there?"

"No. No one. Someone called a friend and set up this job. I don't actually have anyone there." Which was just the way she wanted it. "I thought, if everything works out well between us while I'm here, could I use you as a reference? I might look into working with a scout. It's been really interesting. I think being in a trailer all day makes me grumpy."

Eve laughed. "I can imagine. You're quick. I think you thrive on action."

"Maybe," she said, realizing it was true even as she spoke. She was good at makeup. She was great with it. But maybe that wasn't the only important thing.

"Definitely," Eve said. "I can tell, because I'd much rather be locked up in my office, working on proofs."

"Huh." How had she never considered this before? That maybe her gift was a curse, keeping her locked in a small trailer for weeks at a time, in close proximity to the exact types of people she liked least. The production team was one thing. Some assistants and creative types were hard to deal with, but the equipment guys and preproduction crew were as varied as any other population. But in the trailer, it was the talent and the bigwigs, and the gossipy types that made them all beautiful. Sometimes she felt as if she was going to explode. Sometimes she did.

But this work, being outside, working with locals and the people who did the strong work on the set—it felt so much more natural. Maybe she'd just have to work her makeup skills on friends and extras.

"You think I could do this? Every day?" she asked Eve.

"Absolutely. You seem very sure of yourself. People like that. Of course, if you go to Vancouver, you'll have to work your way up the totem pole. It could be lean for a couple of years."

"I think I can handle that."

"I bet you can."

"Did you always know you wanted to be a photographer?"

Eve smiled and shook her head. "No. I played at it for a while, but I majored in business in college. I figured photography wasn't a real job—it was a hobby. But after college, I wasn't very inspired by my life. I worked in real estate, then banking. When my company was bought out, I was laid off, and I decided I needed to take a little time to figure things out."

"And you ended up here? I always thought people went to L.A., but maybe Jackson is the second stop on the road of confusion."

Eve laughed. "Maybe."

"So what happened?"

"I got a job at an art gallery here in town. It's gone

now. The owners moved away. But one of them was a photographer. He convinced me I had real skill and I deserved to give myself a chance to do something I loved."

"And you did it. That's pretty amazing."

She nodded. "I did it."

"So you're happy you stayed?"

"Yes," Eve answered. "I'm happy." But her words were stiff with logic instead of light with joy. Did she wish she'd moved on? Was her gift also a curse?

Grace was thinking about asking more, but Eve leaned over and turned up the music, though she smiled as if to prove she wasn't trying to avoid the conversation. She needn't have bothered. Grace could respect a woman who liked to keep her problems to herself. She'd never understood people who wore their pain like a medal, showing it off to anyone who met their eyes. How could you want people to know your hurt? That only taught them what your weak spots were. Why not just draw an X over your heart and ask the world to take its best shot?

So Grace let the music fill the car and watched the mountains slide past as they drove toward the narrow dirt road that led to the river. She watched the sky, and just like magic, the clouds eventually slid on after only the sparest of rain showers. Their departure revealed a painfully blue sky, surrounded by the dark horizon of the storm.

God, the place really was beautiful. The whole valley of Jackson Hole was just one amazing sight after another. She wondered what it would look like in winter when it was deep under snow and frozen through.

Beautiful and frighteningly stark, she imagined. She'd seen snow, but she'd never lived in it. How strange to have to bundle up and dare the ice every single day.

She supposed she'd find out in Vancouver, but it wouldn't be like this: isolated and brutal. Maybe she'd come back in the winter sometime to visit. To see people who could've been old friends if she'd stayed long enough. Maybe even hook up with Cole if they were both unattached.

Her heart swelled at the thought of seeing him a couple of years from now. The sweetness of it. The anticipation. But it hurt, too. She didn't know why. It hurt to think of those years passing.

Frowning, she turned her head away from Eve and watched the golden meadows slide by her window. She wanted to see the elk, she thought, when they came down in the winter. She wanted to know what that looked like.

But not this year. Some other time, far from now, when everything was better.

SHE'D RUN AWAY AGAIN. But that was fine. If that was what she needed to feel safe, Cole could live with that. It would only make it that much better when she finally woke up and turned toward him instead of trying to escape. And she would. Soon. He was sure of it.

Still, he kept an eye out for Eve's car all morning. Last night, Grace had pulled away from him, throwing insults when he hurt her feelings. But when he'd revealed his uncertainty about his leg, she'd reached out.

Sure, she'd say it was just sex, but it had been comfort. Hard as she was, she didn't like to see other people hurt.

What had she said about Rayleen and Easy? *I think it's sweet.* Sweet to watch two lonely people together, when she couldn't even admit to being lonely herself.

God, he wanted to take care of her.

Then again, he shouldn't think like that. At this point, he couldn't even take care of himself. Or the ranch. Or any of his responsibilities.

A young hand who'd been sent to the corral to retrieve Madeline's horse returned, and Cole saddled it. She wanted another ride to try to find the perfect place for a nighttime-sky shot. One of the monsters could fly, apparently. "She's a good rider," he explained to Jeremy, "but try to keep her under control. She tends to take more risks than she should."

"Got it," Jeremy replied, dusting off his jeans and tucking in his shirttail. This boy was her new cowboy toy, maybe. He was young. Nineteen or twenty. Agreeable and enthusiastic. She liked that.

Cole didn't feel any twinge of jealousy, but he felt a little bitter, remembering when he'd been young like that. Stupid and carefree. Invincible.

He caught sight of a vehicle coming down the drive and turned over the reins of the pinto to Jeremy. But it wasn't Eve's car. It was a big silver pickup with a logo painted on the side. The Idaho animal handler they'd been waiting for since yesterday. He'd bring in horses for the actual film shoot. Trained ponies who'd do exactly what Madeline wanted.

Cole smiled without any amusement as he walked

over to meet the handler. It was his job to show the guy around and work with what he might need for the shoot.

Two hours later, he'd dealt with the handler, approved locations for fake fencing to be put up that wouldn't interfere with the day-to-day operations of the ranch, and rescued a production assistant from an angry rooster.

He would've lost his mind if he hadn't walked into the yard and spotted Grace. He smiled before he could stop himself. The purple strands of her hair glinted in the sunlight, completely at odds with the pastoral scene behind her—the mountains still striped with snow at the highest peaks, even in July. The wild grass, golden and rippling like waves in the distance. And just behind her, the spring house lurked, its dark wood frame leaning precariously to the south, just as it had for the past twenty years. And in the foreground of it all was Grace, wearing her tight black jeans and some sort of tunic with a flirtatious nude girl painted on the side. Grace frowned, of course, unhappy about something, but her black eyelashes curled up in cheerful sexiness against pink eye shadow. Her lips were lush and rosy against her white skin.

She was so out of place. And exactly where she should be.

"Mr. Rawlins?" a young man asked. He was carrying a clipboard and looked about seventeen.

"Just a second," Cole said absentmindedly. "I'll be right back." He headed across the yard, straight toward Grace. She was talking to Eve now, nodding, still serious.

"Are you sure?" Grace was asking.

"Absolutely. I would have mentioned it sooner, but I forgot that Michael had moved to Vancouver. I'll call him tonight when I get back to the office if you think you'd be interested."

"Of course I would be. Thank you so much."

"When do you plan on going?"

Cole stopped short a few feet away.

Grace was turned half away from him, but he could hear her clearly. He could see her mouth forming the words. "If I can get a job lined up, I'll move on in a week or two. But not if you still need me. I wouldn't do that to you."

"No, once preproduction is done, I'll be…" Eve's words died as she met Cole's eyes. "Is everything okay?"

No. No, everything was not okay. His ears were filled with a rushing sound that seemed to have nothing to do with the breeze lifting Grace's hair off her shoulders.

"Hey, Cole," she said casually.

What had she been saying? She was leaving? *But not if you need me.* Her? Eve? "What the hell's going on, Grace?"

"Uh," Eve said. "I'll leave you two alone. If that's what you want, Grace."

Grace nodded, though she kept her glare straight on Cole as Eve moved away.

She hadn't been saying that, had she?

"I'm in the middle of a business conversation, Cole. What's wrong with you?"

"What's wrong with *me?* You're *leaving?*"

"What do you mean?"

"You're leaving Jackson," he said, more certain of

what he'd heard now. His pulse tripped and tumbled. "After what you said last night, you're just standing here talking about taking off."

"What did I say last night?"

He couldn't believe this. It was happening again. Promises and lies and then a casual goodbye as if he barely even had a right to that.

"Cole—"

"You said you were going to stay."

"I did not. I didn't say anything like that."

"You're kidding, right? Do you not remember anything we talked about last night?"

She crossed her arms and looked at him as if he was the bad guy. "Of course I remember. I whined about my life and then I said I was going to change it. I didn't say anything about staying in *Wyoming!*"

"Staying in Wyoming," he murmured, not quite able to draw enough breath. She said it as if it was the most absurd phrase ever spoken. The most ridiculous idea ever posed. Staying in Wyoming. With him. "Right. Of course. Why would you ever stay here? Unless, of course, Eve Hill needed help. Then you might stay. Or if your aunt offered you a place to live. Or if you had nowhere else to go. Other than that, why would you even *think* of staying, Grace?"

She shook her head. "I don't get what you're upset about. I'm going to Vancouver. I told you that before."

"Yeah, you did. And then last night, I thought… Jesus, what does it matter? You're going. That's it, right?"

She shrugged one shoulder. "Eve thinks she might be able to find me a job."

"Well, then, you'd better run as fast as you can, Grace. You've got a job waiting for you out there. Anything else? Or is it just the job? Nothing more meaningful than that? Just like this vacant apartment in this shitty little town. One little dot on the map to keep you going. One more meaningless physical connection to the earth since there's nothing else holding you down."

Her eyes blazed for a moment, showing amber in the depths of brown. But she shook her head and blew out a slow, deep breath. "I'm sorry if you misunderstood me."

"I didn't misunderstand shit. I see you, Grace. I see you and I thought I liked the real girl inside you. Last night, you were honest. For once. And I thought I liked you. But now you're back to lying and running. You're back to fear."

She glanced around as if she were afraid someone might hear. She stepped closer and lowered her voice. "I'm not afraid. I'm looking for something real."

"A job?"

"Yes, a job! And hope. A future. Eve thinks maybe she has an in with a scouting company. So, I can do the stuff I've been doing for her."

"Listen to yourself. You want to go all the way to Vancouver in hopes of what? The same job you actually have here?"

"This isn't the place for me," she said on a furious whisper.

"Why?"

"You already said it yourself. I don't belong here. I don't fit in."

"You don't belong anywhere," he snapped.

Grace gasped and stumbled back from him.

"You don't want to belong. You have no idea who you'd be if you fit in. People accept you here, Grace. You want to talk about Wyoming like it's some backwater, but people *like* you here. So if you don't fit in, it's because you're throwing your arms out and yelling that you won't be made to. Stop pretending like it's everyone else. It's you."

"I know it's me, damn you," she snarled. "You don't get to throw that at me like it's going to hurt."

He shook his head. "What you said last night—I'm not the one who misunderstood it. You are."

"I know what I meant!"

"Do you? Because you said you were ready to stop running. Ready to stop living like you didn't have anything valuable to lose."

"I'm not running," she snapped.

"And not losing anything either, I suppose?"

She raised her chin and stared him down. He held her gaze, trying to force her to show him something. Anything. But her eyes were black and depthless.

New pain bloomed in his body, and it had nothing to do with his leg. "Okay, then. I guess you were right. You'd better go on and build something real somewhere, because you sure as hell haven't pulled it off here."

Thunder rumbled from the east as he turned and stalked away. She didn't stop him. She didn't even make a sound.

Something valuable. Right. That wasn't him. It hadn't been him when he was young and whole, and it sure as hell wasn't him as a broken-down cowboy. She'd made that clear from the start. She was right. He was the one who'd misunderstood.

Jesus. He hadn't learned a damn thing.

He stalked past the boy with the clipboard, ignoring his outstretched hand.

"Mr. Rawlins!"

"It's Cole," he barked, still moving toward the big house. He was done with this shit. Done with Easy and his sadistic manipulation. Either Cole was good enough to run this place or he wasn't. Either he was a man and a cowboy and a boss, or he wasn't.

"Mr. Cole!"

"Christ." He paused on the front porch, one hand on the door. "What the hell is it? Somebody in urgent need of a lasso demonstration? Or can I offer to walk you to the bathroom trailer and wipe your ass for you?"

The kid blinked, his eyes huge in his face.

Cole sighed. "I'm sorry. What is it?"

"Ms. Beckingham! She was supposed to be back an hour ago and she's still gone."

Great. Just what he needed. A stubborn director lost on an adventure. "I'm sure she and Jeremy lost track of time. You can't reach her on the phone?" But he already knew the answer. If you could get a signal up here, it dropped off as soon as you got into the trees.

"Let's give it another fifteen minutes—" Thunder fell in from the east again, rumbling and rolling like stones. Cole looked up to see a bolt of lightning light up the next hill. Not good. It looked like dusk out there and it was only 3:00 p.m. "Maybe you should let her security detail know."

"I already did. They took a truck in the direction she went, but it ends in a trail."

"Okay, I'll talk to—"

This time it wasn't rolling thunder that cut him off but the gunshot crack of lightning close by. Several of the crew members shrieked, and everybody sprang into action to gather up equipment or cover their work with tarps. The wind shifted and suddenly went cold.

Cole rushed through the big house and found Easy in his office. "Have you seen any of the guys around?"

"Most of the men are doing a pasture move today."

"All right." He rushed out and checked the barn just to be sure, then grabbed his saddle and chaps. The kid with the clipboard followed behind him.

"You're sure?" Cole asked. "They're that late?"

"Yes. She was supposed to be back at two o'clock. We're going to the river one last time. Ms. Beckingham's plane is chartered to leave at five-thirty."

"Okay. I'm heading up to look for them." Lightning flashed over their heads. A deafening crack followed. He tried to remember when he'd first heard the thunder, even if he hadn't registered it. But he had no idea. He'd been distracted. And heck, half the sky was still blue. Unfortunately, it was the wrong half. The clouds moving from the east were nearly black.

Cole shouldered his saddle and headed for the corral. His big mare looked at him warily when he approached, but gave a shiver of satisfaction when he laid the blanket over her back. Cole would've shivered, too, for a different reason. But adrenaline was working through his bloodstream, keeping him from thinking too much about what he was doing.

"You ready to ride, girl?" he asked as he went through the familiar motions. Watching his own hands was like watching a movie. He could've done this in his sleep, yet it felt as if he'd never seen it before. His pulse was heavy and loud, but strangely slow.

He snugged the front cinch, then finished up quickly before patting her rump. "Be gentle, all right?"

She turned her head toward him and then away. He was slipping his boot into the stirrup when another bolt of lightning blasted the hill. She danced and snorted, and he slid his foot free. Now his pulse sped up. Just a little. Just enough to make him nervous.

"All right," he murmured. "Nothing we haven't done before." Cowboys didn't turn in every time it rained. On cue, a drop hit his hand. Then another, so heavy it stung almost like hail. He put his boot back into place and mounted his horse. At first, it felt fine. A little stretch in his hip. Nothing more. He felt a stab of relief so sharp that the breath flew out of his lungs like he'd been punched.

They'd been wrong. The doctors and therapists and specialists. They'd tortured him for nothing. They'd been wrong and he'd been right.

But once he moved off the wide, flat dirt around the corral area and started the climb up the trail, he settled into the saddle and felt a deep twinge in his hip.

He shifted and tried to relax into it, but that just made the pain worse.

Cole took a deep breath and tightened his thighs, trying to transfer his weight forward. That helped. A little. But he was barely into the trees and he could feel every shift of the mare beneath him, every terrible thump of her hooves. The pain moved deeper into his pelvis. Then his spine.

He shouldn't have done this. This would make it worse.

Then again, if he wasn't healed now, he was never going to be right again. He knew that. He could see it in the faces of every person who brought it up. *How's your leg, Cole? How's your hip?* That concern he pretended not to see. The sorrow they tried to hide.

Cole grunted and put his head down and told himself it didn't hurt as much as it did.

As the trail got steeper, he gave up his fight and let his body ease back until he was leaning back farther than he normally would. That wasn't bad, actually. It put a lot of the weight on his tailbone instead of his hips. In fact, aside from the sharp stretch of unused muscles, it felt almost fine. Until another crack of lightning broke the day and his mare stumbled. She caught herself quickly and settled back into a walk, but the jolt sent fire up his bones.

Cole cursed and gritted his teeth. Fear began to eat his adrenaline and, between that and the pain, sweat broke out and the wind turned it to ice. But it hardly mattered. Another flash of lightning seemed to be the starting gun for the rain, and it fell in a sudden explosion of sound. He was slightly protected by the trees, but not from the branches that slapped into him, dragging over his chaps and trying to knock his hat free.

At one point his mount startled and lurched forward, but she was a damn good horse, and even with his weight balanced so strangely on her, she only raced a few feet before slowing again.

She picked her way confidently over rocks and didn't hesitate for a second when the trail skirted along an exposed cliff. Cole wasn't so sure, though. He made himself sit upright, despite the pain. He didn't want to throw her off in any way, and he needed to be able to see over the edge. Likely Madeline and Jeremy had been caught in the storm and taken shelter. But just in case, he kept his eyes on the ridge of rock fifty feet below.

The trail continued on for more than three miles, but Cole knew where Madeline had been headed and he couldn't see any reason she'd have wanted to go down the other side of that split in the ridge. Then again, her mind didn't work like his, and maybe the view wouldn't be enough for her. Maybe she'd decided she needed to head down into the next valley to see what the view was like from the other side.

No way would Jeremy have the backbone to say no to a woman like Madeline.

For the first time, it occurred to Cole that there could be another reason they were late returning. His eye twitched. He shifted in the saddle again and couldn't find a position that didn't make it feel as if hot steel was jammed into his hip.

Madeline Beckingham was a woman of passion

and drive, and not just for her work. Even when he'd been twenty-one and she'd been thirty-two, she'd been nearly too much for him, needing sex more often than he had. And on rides like this, she'd sometimes been overwhelmed with the beauty of the place, and the ideas swirling violently through her head, and she'd almost been manic in her need.

"Jesus," he cursed, hoping like hell that he didn't round a corner and find her riding Jeremy like some crazed pagan, naked in the rain and wind.

Cole had thought she was a legend. An artist. A force of nature. And the truth was, no matter how much she'd hurt him, she was all those things. He'd been a fool to think she'd settle down with a man like him.

The same fool he was being for Grace. If he wanted a wild woman who couldn't be tamed, then he'd have to learn to live with being left standing there, scratched and bruised and alone.

At three-quarters of a mile up, his hip felt as though it was going to disintegrate. It felt as if every step were splitting him slowly in two. The wind suddenly died down, and the trail edged around another rock face, the rain falling steady now, slicking the rocks. Cole breathed in the wet air and tried to ignore the pain, but in that moment, staring down at the seventy-foot drop, he knew. It was over. Despite all his brave words, despite his denial, his life on horseback was over.

He'd been in the saddle for half an hour and it took everything in him not to scream with each step. He'd never make it through an eight-hour day, much less the sixteen-hour days during a roundup or a drive.

This was it. He had the money to buy the ranch, but what would be the point? This was the end. All his plans were dead and had been for almost nine months. He just hadn't realized it until now, even if everyone else had.

He made himself keep his eyes sharp on the view below, but his shoulders slumped. He could find work around here. He knew too many people to find himself without a job. But what would he be working toward? What was he going to do with himself?

Rope tricks at a dude ranch? Cooking brisket at some tourist joint? Maybe he could work at a hole-in-the-wall bar and drink his way through his nights the way his dad had.

His father hadn't been mean or embarrassing or even particularly drunk. He'd just popped open a beer when he walked in the door at night, and pounded them back until bedtime. He'd been…numb.

Cole wouldn't mind a little numbness right about now.

Cringing at a particularly bad spike of pain, Cole rounded the last, long curve before the trail headed up toward the break in the rock above. He didn't see any sign of Jeremy or Madeline yet, or the horses.

Thunder rumbled, and after the violence of the lightning strikes, the sound was almost soothing. But as he rode higher and higher toward the summit of the trail, Cole began to worry again. He'd expected to find them just at this point, sheltered beneath the overhangs of rock nestled in the aspen.

Lightning struck again, farther away this time, and Cole dared to urge the mare all the way to the split in the rock that the trail edged through.

He fought the urge to close his eyes against the pain in his hip. Every step the mare picked out was a brutal reminder that he was doing more damage. He reached the split in the rock and tightened his fingers just the smallest bit. The mare still knew him, and his sense of her was coming back. Cole patted her neck and sat as straight as he could.

A small valley spread out below. They used it for grazing in the early spring, but the cattle were higher now, eating grass that didn't green up until late June. Rain sheeted in the wind, but it wasn't so heavy that he wouldn't have been able to spot two riders. No one was there. Where the hell were they?

There was nothing down there but a grove of aspen and an old sheep-camp trailer. The wind gusted, blowing the rain toward him for a moment. He ducked his head and let it drip off his hat, then tried again. Despite the wind, the rain was dying off again. Cole squinted into the valley, then caught a hint of movement. He looked again, back toward the old trailer. Something moved beneath it.

No, not beneath it. Behind it. A horse shifted and poked its head around the corner.

"Bingo," Cole breathed, and urged his mare past the rock and down the trail. He was a quarter of the way down when he realized maybe this was none of his business. If they wanted to snuggle up in a broken-down love hut, they were welcome to it. But Jeremy should've known better. He was on the clock, and Cole would be damned if he'd let the boy get paid for sex.

When he got to the bottom of the trail, he almost

kept riding. There was a creek at the mouth of this valley, and he could just follow it down to a dirt road that crossed it a mile up, then circle back to the ranch. But he'd still only seen one horse. There was a chance there was a problem. A small chance.

Cole set his jaw and rode across the grass. The sharp agony had faded into a strange buzzing numbness around the edges of the pain. Probably not a good sign, but it was a relief. He still kept the horse to a walk.

When they got close, the mare snorted and whinnied to the gelding hobbled behind the little camp hut. A few seconds later, the tin door of the hut flew open. "Cole!" Jeremy called. He seemed fully clothed, but his shirt was wrinkled and matted to his body.

"Is Madeline in there?"

"Yeah, her ankle's pretty swollen, though. Her mount spooked in the storm and took off. Luckily, she was already off and just holding the reins. Got yanked off her feet. She should be fine, but I didn't want to risk riding through the storm."

Cole glanced at the sky. "I think it's letting up."

Madeline hopped into the doorway as Jeremy stepped down to the grass. "I need to get back, Cole. Is it safe?"

Aside from the foot she held off the ground and some damp patches on her clothes, she looked totally unaffected by the adventure. Smoke puffed from the tiny chimney of the stove that heated the trailer. Jeremy had played the gentleman, it seemed.

"Hey!" Jeremy said. "You're riding!"

"Yeah."

"Do you want to take Ms. Beckingham back while I look for that horse?"

"I—" Cole cut himself off. No, he didn't want to ride back with Madeline tucked against his back, but he couldn't trot around for an hour or two looking for a lost horse. He met Madeline's eyes. He didn't know what she and Jeremy had been doing in front of that stove in the camp hut, but the good news was that he didn't care. "Hand her up," he said tersely.

Madeline grabbed the fur-edged vest she'd been wearing and shrugged it on, then Jeremy tossed her up to sit behind Cole's saddle. Her arms went around his waist. She put her chin to his shoulder. "Thanks, Cole," she said softly. She didn't offer a farewell to Jeremy.

"Come back along the creek," Cole ordered, then headed that direction himself.

For a while, he was so aware of this woman pressed against him that he forgot his hip. It felt strange to have her touching him. She'd once been his lover, and then he'd hated her. Now it just felt like a stranger was embracing him. He shifted and cleared his throat.

"You okay?" she asked.

"Fine. You?"

"I'm good." A few heartbeats passed before she spoke again. "How badly were you hurt?"

He hoped she didn't notice the way his muscles twitched at her question. The woman was too quick by half. He didn't answer.

"You said you'd hurt your leg, but the limp, the way you favor that side… Jeremy seemed surprised to see you riding, which made me realize I haven't seen you on a horse once since I got here. You were glued to one on that first set."

"This isn't a set. It's my life and my work."

"More reason to be on a horse, then. What's going on, Cole?"

God, his jaw ached with the strain of his teeth grinding together. It was none of her damn business. More than that, he didn't want her to know. He'd never thought he'd see her again, but if he'd had to choose, she wouldn't have seen him like this. The lowest point in his life. The weakest he'd ever been. She'd left him lying on the ground like trash, and here he was again, as if he'd been ruined by her. As if he'd never gotten up and moved on.

He imagined Grace coming through ten years from now. Imagined himself as his father, broken-down and numb and bitter.

Christ. That couldn't happen. He'd have to find some way. He couldn't let these people determine who he was and wasn't. Madeline, Grace, Easy, the doctors. He couldn't measure himself with their words, see himself through their eyes.

"I shattered my femur," he finally said. "Broke my pelvis. I haven't been on a horse in nearly nine months."

"Oh, Jesus, Cole. I'm sorry. But you're better now?"

"Maybe."

"Well, thanks for coming to my rescue. I think that boy was scared of me."

He grunted and eased the horse down a steep bank. Shifting again, he tried to find a way to stall the pain for a moment.

"We can walk if you want," Madeline said quietly.

Cole stared straight ahead. "I'm not sure that would work at this point."

She touched his hip, slid her hand over him with proprietary ease. He looked down to see her hand on his thigh, her fingers sliding slightly under the edge of his chaps. It reminded him of Grace touching him, so he let her do it. It hardly mattered at this point.

"You need help, Cole?" she asked.

"What do you mean?"

"I don't think cowboys have the best health-care plans, do they?"

"I had insurance," he said dully. "I'm fine."

Her hand rubbed up and down his thigh, and he hated that it felt good. "You're back in the saddle now. Are you just going back to being a cowboy, then?"

"Yes. This place will be mine soon," he said, not knowing if it were true anymore.

"That's why you've been so possessive about it."

He stayed silent, keeping his eyes on the creek as he led the mare along the shallow edges.

"Why don't you let me help you?"

Her hand slid to his inner thigh. Cole gritted his teeth against the feeling, but his cock began to swell. "What are you talking about?"

Her hand slid up. She chuckled and scraped her nails along the fabric that strained over his erection. He wanted to tell her it had nothing to do with her. Nothing at all. It was just an automatic response to touch. But that would sound pitiful, so he just moved her hand back to his thigh.

"I know what you must think of me, Cole. But I know

what I want and I go after it. And I want you. Again.
The way it was before. You were good then. I know
you're even better now. More mature. A man's touch.
A man's knowledge."

"Just say it," he growled.

"I'm leaving today. I'll be in L.A. for a few weeks
before coming back to film. Why don't you come out to
California with me? Like old times. You can recuper-
ate. Relax. Sit in the hot tub. I've even got a personal
masseuse. It'll be good for you. You'll be a new man."

A new man. He'd been a new man after his last trip
to L.A., too. He'd gone out there an arrogant kid, and
he'd come back a man, though not for the reasons she'd
think. When she'd kicked him out, he hadn't wanted to
go home. He couldn't have imagined it. Dragging back
into town with his tail between his legs. All that brag-
ging he'd done. All the friends he'd blown off. And his
girlfriend, whose family had once embraced him as one
of their own—he'd broken her heart. But more than anything else, he hadn't wanted to face his father.

His dad had been disgusted that Cole had even
wanted to work on the movie set in the first place. And
when Cole had decided to leave town, his dad had called
him a disgrace. The worst kind of son. And a man who
didn't know how to keep his word. "You're a fool if you
think those people want you," he'd said. "And you're a
fool if you think I'll want you back when they're done."

So Cole hadn't gone back. His pride hadn't let him.
Instead he'd stayed in L.A. with the money Madeline
had showered on him. He'd partied and slept around,
hoping the news would get back to Madeline and hurt

her. He'd gotten drunk and popped pills so he wouldn't have to see what he was doing to himself.

A few weeks later, his father had died. Alone. A heart attack that Cole could easily blame on himself. His pride had meant nothing then. He'd come home to try to inch his way back into being a man his dad could've been proud of. Cole owed him that, at least.

He shook his head.

Madeline made a soothing noise and slid her hand back to his cock. "You didn't love me, you know."

He let her hand stay where it was this time, because he wanted her to feel that her touch wasn't working anymore. But he should have known better. She just stroked him and pressed her breasts against his back.

"You didn't love me," she repeated. "You loved the excitement. The newness. The adventure and the sex. You didn't know me well enough to love me. So whatever you tell yourself about what happened, know this—when you whispered that to me, it wasn't true, and that's what I had to live with. That's what I've always had to live with, whether it was you or someone else. People want things from me, Cole. Even when I was a little girl, my friends knew who my father was. And their parents knew."

She stroked him the whole time she spoke, and when he finally swelled against her hand, she hummed approvingly.

"People want things from me. Sex, excitement, money, power, fame, glamour. And you weren't different from anyone else. But you were sweet, at least. I've never forgotten that."

He finally admitted to himself that he couldn't steel his body against her touch, and he moved her hand away again in defense. "I wasn't using you," he said, but her words had changed his certainty.

"You were," she said softly. "But I liked you. And I have to admit, I half hoped you'd turn down my offer to come to L.A. that time. I kind of wanted you to say no. To tell me it wasn't about that. It wasn't what you wanted from me. But you did come. And it was fun. But it wasn't love."

Cole wasn't ready to concede anything yet. He'd been damn sure he loved her, but when she put it like that... What exactly had he known about the woman? "If it didn't mean much, what is it you want from me? Just sex?"

"Well, the sex was good, make no mistake. But it's not just that. I know you. Money can buy a lot of things. It can buy sex. But it can't make it good. And it can't make it sweet. You were sweet, Cole. I want that again for a few weeks. That's all."

"I'm not sweet anymore, Madeline."

"Yes, you are. Look how you came out to rescue me, a woman you have every reason to hate. You're sweet." She kissed his shoulder. "And strong." Then his neck. "And big."

This time when she cupped him, Cole closed his eyes and tried to imagine it. Sex with Madeline again. He could do it. But did he want to? After what he'd had with Grace... Hell, brief as it had been, that affair had rocked his idea of what intensity was.

With Madeline, it wouldn't be the best sex he'd ever

had, but sex was sex, and it couldn't all be the best. He knew it wouldn't be bad with Madeline, it would be fine. But afterward—there was the problem. Afterward, could he live with himself?

It wasn't as if he'd be betraying anyone. But Grace immediately invaded his brain. Her face, her dark eyes, her body melting into him. Except there'd be no more melting in Vancouver. Not with him, anyway.

And there was the real truth. The reason he hadn't said no out of hand. Because Grace was going to leave him behind. In a few weeks, she was going to walk away while he watched. But her memory would stay here. At the ranch. In his bed. In the saloon. She'd leave, but she wouldn't take her ghost with her. She'd leave that behind, tucked up against Cole like a shadow.

But in L.A., he could forget her. Just for a while. Long enough to ease this need for her, maybe.

Madeline's hand slid up to his belly and she kissed the back of his neck again. "Think about it," she murmured.

That was the terrible part: he already was.

CHAPTER TWENTY

HE WAS HAVING AN AFFAIR with Madeline Beckingham.

Grace watched as Madeline slid off the horse and immediately turned back to smile up at Cole. Her hand went to his knee, then a little higher. She touched him as though she'd touched him before. As if touching was the least of what they'd done.

Grace couldn't see Cole's expression beneath the hat, but he didn't edge the horse away or move the woman's hand. In fact, he nodded at whatever she said, and Madeline laughed.

Something shifted inside Grace's chest, something swelled and twisted and burned a hole inside her. She'd thought the sex between her and Cole had been honest. Not meaningful, maybe. Not tender. But honest. She'd understood it, and she'd trusted it.

But no.

No. Of course not. Of course it hadn't been any more honest than the rest of this fucked-up world. He'd been sleeping with Madeline, too. Probably holding her like some cherished china doll while he did her.

Grace felt herself sneering in his direction and made her mouth relax. She didn't care. She didn't care enough to show him anything.

It'd just been sex. She'd told him that over and over

again. Just sex. He hadn't owed her anything. He certainly didn't owe her anything now.

Still, he'd tried to make it into something more. That bastard. He'd tried to make it more, and he would've hurt her if she'd believed him.

Her gut instinct had been the last thing she'd been able to trust in this world, and now that was gone, too. First her pride in her own strength, now the basest of animal instincts. She had nothing.

She watched him move the horse back to the barn. Apparently he could ride again. Apparently he was just fine. Had that been another lie?

Despite all her resolutions about starting a new life, Grace wanted to kick something, hit something. She wanted to scream and rage and ruin.

But not here. She glanced around, relieved that no one was watching her, because the violence must show on her face. She caught sight of Cole disappearing behind the barn, and Grace moved in that direction.

Her rushing breath seemed to take her over until it was all she could hear or feel. The air straining through her throat, her lungs fighting to make space for it. There wasn't enough oxygen in this godforsaken place. The air was thin and meaningless. Despite her light-headedness, she walked on until she reached the barn.

When she turned the corner, she saw him standing next to his horse, his wide back facing her. His shirt was wet and tight against his muscles. His legs wrapped with dark leather chaps. He looked invincible.

Grace's rage swelled up until she could feel it saturate

her skin and then expand beyond it. She was cocooned
in it now. Shielded from anything else.

"How long have you been fucking her?" she snarled.

His head rose and he glanced at her over his shoulder. He didn't bother turning around. In fact, he turned
back and pressed his forehead to the leather of the saddle. "Go away, Grace."

"How long?" she repeated.

"It's none of your business."

"You bastard."

"What the hell do you care?" he asked, his voice
strained.

"I don't *care,* Cole. I've never cared. But I don't like
being lied to. I refuse to be one of those stupid girls,
you understand? *You* were the one trying to make it
into something more. What if I'd taken you up on that?
What if I'd believed all your bullshit?"

"You didn't, so it doesn't matter, right?"

"How long?" she yelled, hands curling into fists.
"Tell me!"

He raised his head, but he didn't look toward her.
"Thirteen years, I guess."

Thirteen *years?* For a moment, it made no sense.
That didn't even— "Oh," she said dumbly, seeing it
all now. Thirteen years. That was why this whole situation had been so volatile for him. Because Madeline
was his lover, and Grace had caused all their paths to
intersect, and then he'd been sleeping with Grace and
answering to Madeline in a place he'd considered his
own. And then trying to keep it all contained, trying to
keep his lies straight.

"I see. So I guess I was the interloper here. I was the girl on the side this time."

"No," he murmured, dropping his head again. "It wasn't like that." She thought she heard a pained laugh. "It wasn't like that at all."

"No? You can't even look at me."

"Yeah, you've got that part right."

"Damn it, Cole. Why would you do that?"

He sighed. "Why are you even asking? You made it clear we meant nothing. You didn't even *want* us to mean anything."

"That doesn't mean—"

"Can you just leave it alone?" he snapped, the words cracking as the lightning had earlier. "Please? I can't do this right now. Just…leave it alone."

Grace huffed out a shocked breath. "Oh. Sure. I'm so sorry I inconvenienced you."

"Grace—"

"No, it's fine. You're right. None of it meant anything. Goodbye."

She spun and walked away, swallowing compulsively against the boulder that had taken over her throat. Her cheeks burned. Her eyes stung. She needed to cry. She hadn't cried in front of anyone in years, and now she needed to sob. She couldn't do it. Not here. Not anywhere. Ever.

There wasn't even a reason to cry, for godssake. After everything that had happened to her, everything her life had been, *this* was what made her want to break down? A brief affair with a near stranger?

God, it was laughable. But instead of a laugh, a sob

snuck out. She inhaled sharply, trying to take it back.
Trying to grab it before it dragged more sobs from her.

Oh, God. Oh, God.

She veered away from the groups of people gathered in the yard and headed blindly in the direction of
the house. She didn't know why. She'd chosen the path
in panic, and now she didn't know what to do. If she
spun around and moved in the opposite direction, the
movement might draw attention, and she couldn't bear
that. So Grace kept going toward the house, then skirted
around the corner and rushed toward the backyard.

Once she was hidden from view, she pressed her
back to the wall of the house and tipped her head up.
She'd read somewhere that looking up could help stop
tears. That trick had worked before, but it failed her now.
These were more than tears. This felt like another person inside her, another *her,* trying to push out through
her throat. Trying to get free of this mess she'd made
of her life.

She pressed her shaking hands to her mouth to hold
it back. Her breath rushed past her fingers as she stared
up at the roiling sky. Why couldn't it rain now? Why
couldn't the sky open up and bury her in water?

This was terrible, whatever it was. She didn't want
this. Why did it hurt so much?

"Miss?"

Grace jerked away from the wall and dropped her
hands.

"You okay?" Easy asked from the back step of his
house.

"I'm good," she croaked, as if a person in good shape

would be hiding behind a house with her hands pressed to her mouth to hold back sobs.

"You look real pale, Miss…Grace, is it?"

"Yes," she said on a breath. "Just a little professional drama, Mr. Easy. That's all. I'm fine."

"Come on in for some lemonade."

"No, thank you. Really." The pressure was easing, thank God. She could almost speak normally.

"A beer, then."

The fact that she could fake a smile surprised her. "No. I'm fine."

"You want me to get Cole?"

"What?" she gasped. "No!"

"Sorry. I saw you with him last night."

For a moment, she flashed back to what she'd done with Cole the night before, then realized Easy was talking about the saloon.

"Oh. No, don't get him. I'm fine."

"If you and Cole—"

"Did you know Rayleen is my aunt?" she interrupted, desperate to change the subject.

His chin drew in. "What?"

"Rayleen is my great-aunt."

"Well. No, I didn't know that. I didn't think she had any family to speak of."

"Oh, she seems like she might've sprung from the depths of Hades, but she has a family. Her sister—my grandmother—she lives in Florida."

"Huh." He rocked back on his heels.

"Anyway. She's sweeter than she seems. Just thought you should know that." Actually, she had no evidence that Rayleen was sweet at all, but she'd needed to say something. Grace's feet moved backward. "I'd better get back. Thanks."

She'd controlled the tears, anyway. She hadn't broken down. She was going to walk away from this the same person she'd been when she'd arrived.

Somehow, the thought didn't comfort her as much as she'd hoped.

IT TOOK NEARLY twenty minutes of slow breathing before Cole could walk. Twenty minutes of trying to convince himself to take that first step.

His leg had simply given out when he'd dismounted, folding up with one last blast of pain. He'd caught himself on the pommel, and he was damn grateful for that, since Grace had come around the corner not thirty seconds later.

What did she want from him? Was she just stone-cold crazy? He was in too much pain to puzzle out a woman whose soul must look like a maze. If she had a soul. She probably didn't.

The tension of dealing with her and her anger hadn't helped his leg, but after a time, he'd been able to relax enough to stretch his muscles, then rub some of the ache away.

Cole kept his left hand on the pommel when he finally dared to take a few steps. His leg held him this time, despite its stiffness. Or maybe because of it. He stretched his back and led the mare toward the gate of the small corral. He moved slowly until he was sure he could put his weight on the leg. It hurt. But it held.

He tied off the mare to wait until he had the strength to look after her, then walked very carefully toward the big house. When he got to the porch steps, he stopped for a long moment, staring at the three steps before he took them.

"Easy?" he called when he stepped inside.

"Yep."

Cole followed his voice to the kitchen, where Easy stood at the back door, a cup of coffee cradled in his hand.

"I need to know if you have a plan for this place that doesn't involve me."

Easy immediately looked impatient, his face creasing in a frown. "I already told you I wasn't thinking of selling to anyone else."

"That's not what I mean. I mean, have you considered what you'll do if I can't ride again?"

Easy's frown immediately smoothed into shock, his pale eyes going wide for a moment before he remembered to hide his dismay. "Cole, why don't we leave this discussion until you hear what the doctor has to say? There's every chance—"

"I rode today."

"*What? Why?*" Easy's eyes fell to the chaps Cole still wore.

"Jeremy was stuck out at the spring pasture with Madeline Beckingham during that storm. We weren't sure what had happened, and I was the only one around to go find them."

"You should've told me! It's my ranch and you're my hand. I could've called in—"

"It doesn't matter, Easy. The point is I rode. And it wasn't... I don't think..."

"Cole," Easy said, his voice rough with emotion.

"I don't know if I'll be able to ride again. And I know you've been trying to tell me that, but I didn't want to hear it."

"Now, listen," Easy said, "you don't know anything. And I talked to Farrah after that dinner she made for us a month ago. She couldn't tell me any details about you, of course, but she said there were other surgeries. If that crack doesn't heal right, they can put plates in, just like in your leg."

"They might be able to, yes. But that'd be almost another year of healing, plus rehabilitation. And there'd be no guarantees. And no assurances it wouldn't put so much strain on the bone it'd cause more problems in the future. I already heard all this. I just wasn't listening. I wanted it to not be true so badly that I—"

"We don't need to discuss it now. Jesus, we've waited this long. Let's see what they say."

"No, I need to know you'll be all right, whatever the outcome."

"Me?" Easy practically shouted. His neck turned red, then his ears, but Cole saw the way his eyes glinted. "You're worried about *me?* Jesus Christ, boy."

"I know you don't want to sell this place to just anyone. You've worked too hard to—"

"I am not discussing this with you," he ground out.

"This is all you wanted to discuss before!"

"If you can't ride... If that happens... Well, we'll figure it out. I hardly ride at all myself anymore. There's no reason you can't—"

"Easy," Cole said quietly. Easy immediately closed his mouth, his gaze falling to his hands, clasped tight around the coffee mug. "I can't stay here. Not if I can't ride. I can't spend fifty years watching men ride out to do the things I can't do. When I'm seventy, sure. I'll have earned my place on the porch. But not like this."

"Damn it, Cole," Easy whispered.

"Isn't this what you've been trying to get me to see?"

He blinked rapidly, then cleared his throat. "That doesn't mean I like it."

"I don't like it either. But I've got to think about it. Away from here maybe. Because when I'm here, all I can see is this place, this land, what I've wanted to be my whole life. My father and…"

"Your father was wrong. This isn't the only life for you."

"I guess I'd better hope it isn't."

"That woman, for instance. She might be another life."

His head snapped up. "What?" Easy didn't know. Did he? About Madeline and their history and…

"That purple-haired girl."

"What?" Cole repeated stupidly.

"Grace. I found her hiding in the backyard a few minutes ago, awfully upset."

"Grace? Hiding? You must have that wrong."

"Did you do something mean to that little girl?"

"Mean? *Me?* You've got it all wrong, Easy. That *little girl* has the heart of a damn mongoose."

"She didn't look very ferocious when I saw her."

"That's because she'd just used it all up tearing a piece out of my hide."

Easy eyed him with disapproval.

"I'm serious!"

"A woman doesn't like to be picked up at a bar and used like a two-bit whore. You're grown enough to know that."

Apparently he was more grown than Easy, because Easy was being naive. Cole was the one who'd been used. "Forget about Grace," he muttered. He took off his hat to rub the ache from his forehead, then shoved it back on. "She's got nothing to do with my future."

"All right," Easy said. "If you say so."

"I'll help clean up after these folks tonight, but tomorrow…"

"Take the time you need. But your father was wrong. This isn't what makes you a man. This place or this work."

"No, he was right. Everything he said to me that night… He was right."

"He was *wrong*," Easy growled. "He didn't mean it."

"You must be kidding. He meant it enough to push me out of the house. To shove me through the door and tell me not to bother coming back because I wasn't his son anymore."

"He was scared, Cole. He was terrified he was losing you for good, and he lashed out."

Cole shook his head. "I broke his heart. That's what killed him. He was fine. Never been sick a day in his life. And then—"

"He broke his own damned heart, acting a stubborn fool!"

"You're wrong. But it doesn't matter. If I can't make him proud being a cowboy, I'll have to think of another way."

"We'll figure it out, Cole."

He would, because he had no choice. He'd figure it out. But not here. This place was him and his dad and Easy all pushed into one small space. He'd been thrown off by the endless sky and the lonely trails, but he could see now what Easy had tried to say. He'd boxed himself in here, like a kid building a fort.

He needed to get away. To think. Maybe California wasn't the place for that. Or maybe he needed to face it. Get it out of his system. Leave it behind on his terms.

But more than anything, he just needed not to be here.

CHAPTER TWENTY-ONE

IT WAS OVER. MADELINE Beckingham and all her people had left. Eve's studio was back to normal. And Grace had nothing to do. Nothing. For days.

She'd finished Cole's books, but she couldn't make herself knock on his door to give them back. And she couldn't leave them on his doorstep. It'd look like she was tossing his stuff on the floor in a huff.

So she read them again and told herself she wasn't done with them yet. She read and went for walks and tried her best to avoid any chance of seeing Cole.

On Sunday, when her phone rang and showed Scott's number, she blocked him. She'd purchased a money order on Friday and put it in the mail. Maybe he'd received it already. Maybe he was calling to tell her it wasn't enough.

Maybe he could kiss her ass.

They all could. The next time she needed to scratch an itch, she'd use a vibrator. Well, once she had the money to buy one, anyway. Until then, she'd freehand it. Not her preferred method, but desperate times and all that.

But she wasn't desperate, she told herself. She was good. She was fine. Things were looking up. Eve had heard from her friend in Vancouver, and he'd said to have Grace stop by his office whenever she made it to town. But even better, she had steady work for at least another week with Eve, who needed help getting her office back in order after the insanity of the week before.

Things were good. In fact, tonight she was hanging out with friends. People who liked her. So why did her chest ache like fire when she forgot to keep her guard up? Why did she want Cole so much?

Just admitting it made her angry. She wanted to slap him. Scratch him. Push him until he took her down to the floor and made her feel pleasure instead of this awful pain.

Grace put down the book she wasn't reading and curled up into a ball on her mattress. She crooked her arm over her eyes to block out the afternoon light and breathed as slowly as she could.

It didn't hurt. There was no reason it should. So it didn't. She wouldn't let it.

But why had he asked for so much from her? Why had he wanted more? His hands sliding over her back as if she were fragile. His mouth against the ink on her skin, asking what it meant.

That bastard.

None of that mattered. Because he touched her more truthfully than that sometimes. He touched her rough and cruel. That was what he'd really meant, she told herself. That was real. Nothing else.

Her phone rang again. This time it was an unfamiliar number.

"Hey, girl," a woman said. "It's Jenny. Are you ready for the makeover party?"

"I'm ready! But 'makeover'? Does that mean more than makeup?"

"Well, I keep buying hair dye and not using it, so I'm hoping you'll help me pick a color. You must be good with color even if it's hair, right?"

"I'm not bad." Regular trips to the salon were expensive. She'd done her own hair color for years.

"Thank God. I need help. So I was thinking six, if that's not too early for you."

"Perfect. Should I bring anything?"

"Nope. I'm making lasagna, and Eve's bringing wine, so I think we're covered. Just bring makeup and your amazing skills."

"Sure," Grace agreed, but she was stopping for a cake anyway. She didn't make new girlfriends often, and she wanted to do everything *right*.

Grace felt horribly nervous when she jumped into the shower to get ready. She was confident with men. She knew how to handle herself, she knew what they wanted. But women? Well, assuming they were straight, Grace was never sure what they were looking for.

She did her makeup very carefully, taking it a little softer with purples and deep gray. She wore her black jeans and a soft, off-the-shoulder blue sweater that made her look slightly more approachable than her other clothes. It was probably the most feminine thing she owned, and hopefully that would put Jenny and Eve at ease.

Stealing a look out the front window, she saw that Cole's truck was still missing from the driveway, and wondered if it would be safe to sneak over to the saloon to ask Rayleen about a bakery.

But if Cole were at the saloon… The thought made her stomach lurch. She didn't want to see him. The very idea of seeing him left her cold with dread.

That decided it. She wasn't going to hide in her apartment all weekend, afraid of *him*. Afraid he'd try to explain. Afraid he'd reveal more and make it so much worse. She didn't want to know. She just wanted to escape.

But if she was going to be here for another week or two, she'd have to face him.

Brave words, considering his truck wasn't outside.

Grace grabbed her makeup kit and walked outside before the fear could take over again. "You taking your show on the road?" Rayleen shouted as soon as Grace walked in.

Grace shook her head as she walked to her aunt's table in the corner. "Do you ever leave this place?"

"Not unless I have to."

The chair in front of Grace slid an inch as if Rayleen had moved it with her foot.

"Am I allowed to sit down?" Grace asked. Rayleen shrugged as if she didn't care, but the chair scooted out a little more, so Grace sat.

Rayleen nudged the kit Grace had put on the floor. "What's in the toolbox?"

"It's my makeup kit."

"You working tonight?"

"No, I'm going over to Jenny's. She wants a makeover."

"Oh," Rayleen muttered. "A girl's night, huh? Poker would be better."

"Maybe."

"Are you good with that makeup stuff?"

"I'm pretty good," Grace answered.

"Yeah? Well, I know your grandma's proud of you."

That surprised her. First, that her grandmother had said that. The only thing she'd ever said to Grace about it was that L.A. wasn't a safe place for a young woman on her own. Second, she was surprised that Rayleen would repeat it. "Thank you for telling me."

"The last time she visited, she brought two movies and made me watch the whole damn credit reel after each one, just because your name was there. Silliness, I say. You get paid for your work. I don't see why you have to get a written thank-you, too."

"She did that?"

"Sure. Damned obnoxious."

Her grandmother wasn't as hard as Aunt Rayleen, but she wasn't exactly the kind of granny who baked cookies and offered them with an indulgent smile. She was supportive more than loving, and worried more than affectionate, but maybe that was how she showed love.

How did Rayleen show love? With insults? With muttered complaints? Was that even possible?

Rayleen seemed to be done talking, so Grace finished her drink and stood. "Okay, I'd better head over to Jenny's. Can you recommend a good bakery that's not too expensive? It's Jenny's birthday in a couple of days. And Eve's, too."

"The one at the small market is all right. Next to the park."

"Perfect. Thank you."

She shrugged again.

"Have a good night, okay?"

Rayleen just grunted, and Grace headed out and down the block, grateful the bakery wasn't very far.

Using the last of her spare cash, she picked out a girly-looking cake that already said *Happy Birthday* in purple frosting. Not Grace's style, but it did match her hair.

She walked slowly toward Jenny's place, hoping the walk would calm her nerves. And it did, despite the fact that every time she heard the engine sound of a big pickup she worried it was Cole's truck. It never was. So Grace relaxed.

The sight of the pretty bakery bag in her hand made her happy. And the story Rayleen had told about Grandma Rose…that helped, too. She wasn't as alone as she sometimes felt. And tonight she wouldn't be alone at all. By the time she climbed the stairs to the condo and knocked, her nervousness had been left behind somewhere, lost on the streets of Jackson.

"Hey, girl!" Jenny shouted when she opened the door. She hugged Grace one-handed, the other hand occupied with holding a glass of red wine. "I'm half-drunk already. Eve drove, so she's insisting I drink one of the bottles by myself. The other one's for you."

"I did not insist!" Eve called. "I said it was an option."

Jenny snorted. "Option, shmoption. Time to get beautiful!"

Laughing, Grace let herself be pulled in. She held up the bag. "Happy birthday, ladies. I brought cake."

"Oh, my God!" Jenny squealed. "Cake! I love you!"

Grace felt heat climbing up her cheeks and quickly changed the subject. "Okay, if we're going to do hair color, we should do that first. Before makeup."

"But not before lasagna," Jenny insisted. "Or cake. Or wine!"

Eve groaned as she took a seat at the small kitchen table. "I should've taken the bus."

"You can always spend the night. I only have a double bed, but after a bottle of wine, I bet you won't mind cuddling."

"No, I'm fine with my two-glass limit."

"Oh, I'm just kidding. You can sleep on the couch."

Eve laughed, her cheeks turning as pink as Grace's had felt a moment before. "I'm honestly no good with alcohol. The last time I got drunk, I got sick on my stairs. If there's anything worse than being hungover, it's being hungover and having to clean up vomit."

Grace gratefully accepted the very full glass Jenny offered. "I can't imagine you drunk," she said to Eve. "You're so dignified."

"I'm just quiet and boring. Dignified is a trick us boring people pull."

Grace eyed her for a moment. "Are we coloring your hair?"

"Oh, God, no. I'd feel too conspicuous. People comment on that sort of thing. I hate it."

"I'll ask you again after the wine. I'd love to—"

"No," she insisted. "Absolutely not."

"You can do me any way you want," Jenny said as she picked up a big plastic bag and began pulling out boxes of hair-coloring kits.

"Oh, my God." Grace laughed. There was now an impressive row of boxes on the table. "How many do you have?"

"Nine. No, ten. Don't laugh! Every once in a while I get brave and tell myself I'll finally do something different, and then I get home and pull my hair back into a ponytail and go to work, and that's it. I chicken out. Plus I bought two more today. What do think?"

"Well…"

Jenny set the lasagna on the table and passed out plates while Grace moved the boxes around.

"Definitely not the browns. You've got a great skin tone for your natural blond. But this one…" She pushed forward a gorgeous, warm blond permanent color. "Maybe with a few lowlights with this coppery one." She moved another box toward Jenny. "That might be amazing."

"Really?" she asked, bouncing up and down on her toes. "You think so?"

"Yes. Do you have good scissors?"

Jenny slapped a hand to her long hair. "Why?"

"I'll just trim the ends. Then we can color it and straighten it. You'll look amazing."

An hour later, half the lasagna was gone, the cake had been massacred, Eve had given in and started her third glass of wine, and Jenny's head was deep in the kitchen sink as Grace washed the dye from it.

"This is so exciting," Eve said. She picked up a box

of chestnut-brown and eyed it wistfully. "I can't wait to see it dry."

Grace wrapped Jenny's hair in a towel. "That one's a temporary color, you know. It only lasts six weeks. It would just add some shine and a little depth to your natural color."

Eve put the box down.

"Come on. You're a photographer. You know how amazing a little color depth can be. Let's do it. It's six weeks. No big deal."

"I don't know."

"Do it!" Jenny shouted. "Do it, do it, do it!"

Eve refilled her wineglass, even though only half was gone. "Okay. Fine. Yes. Let's do it."

Jenny screamed so loudly that Grace was worried her neighbors would complain. Then she decided maybe they were used to it.

"Come on," she said to Eve. "Head in the sink, then."

Grace was just putting the last of the color into Eve's hair when someone knocked hard on the door. Maybe the neighbors had complained, because that sounded distinctly like the unforgiving knock of a policeman's fist.

Apparently Jenny was a good enough person that she'd never heard that knock, because she breezed over with her wet hair and a smile and swung the door wide open. And revealed a sight more alarming than the police.

Standing in the doorway, scowl already in place, was Aunt Rayleen.

"Good Lord," Rayleen barked, looking from Jenny

to Eve. "I thought she was supposed to make you look better. You ladies look like a pair of drowned rats."

"Sweet as ever," Jenny announced.

"I am sweet. I brought you the sunglasses you left on the bar yesterday."

"Oh, thank you." Jenny took the glasses, but Rayleen didn't give up her post.

"Why's your hair wet?"

"Grace colored it."

"Hmph. Some normal color, I hope."

Grace had been too shocked by her aunt's arrival to know what to think, but as Rayleen craned her neck to see in, Grace realized what was going on. Jenny seemed to see it at the same time. She tossed a helpless look toward Grace.

Did she want Grace to find a way to get rid of her boss? Or was she asking permission to let Grace's great-aunt crash the party? Knowing that Rayleen had dug up an excuse and walked all the way over here in the hopes of being invited in… Grace might be tough, but she couldn't be cruel. Not to this lonely old woman.

"Want a glass of wine, Rayleen?"

"Maybe," she barked. "But you're not getting your crazy hands on my hair."

"Okay. I'll leave your hair alone. Promise."

Sorry, she mouthed to Jenny once Rayleen had settled in at the table.

"Hell, I'm drunk," Jenny whispered. "The more, the merrier. I'm going to go dry my hair for the big reveal."

Grace was just finishing up towel-drying Eve's hair when Jenny started to scream. Grace's heart dropped, and Eve actually looked as if she might start crying. But then Jenny leapt from the bathroom and screamed again. "Oh, my God, it's beautiful! I love you, Grace Barrett! Look at it! Look at my hair!"

Grace laughed. Jenny's hair did look beautiful, shiny and textured and warm. But it was a subtle change for such a strong reaction. Still, when Jenny threw herself into Grace's arms, Grace hugged her back. Hard.

"I want to dry my hair," Eve said calmly, but she gave up her solemn look when Jenny grabbed her hand and dragged her into the bathroom. They were both giggling madly.

This felt like…high school. But the best part of high school. The kind of girl parties you saw in movies. The kind Grace had scoffed at in disbelief, because her teen parties hadn't been lighthearted at all. They'd been about forgetting. And treading the line between danger and despair.

"Good Lord Almighty," Rayleen muttered. "That girl screams like a monkey on fire."

"Yeah," Grace agreed, but she couldn't make it sound like a criticism. She could only wish she had that kind of joy. Maybe Rayleen felt the same, because she fell silent.

Grace joined her at the table and shuffled through the remaining boxes of hair dye. There was a deep walnut-brown that caught her eye. It was almost her natural color, just a little darker and richer. When was the last time her hair had been that shade? A year ago? No, two years ago. Before she'd met Scott.

Back when she'd been…happy? Was that possible? She'd had her own place, her own car. Merry had been in

Texas already, but Grace had had a few friends. People to go out with. People to laugh with at work.

Then she'd been with Scott for a while, and that had been fine. But it had felt off, somehow. She'd felt confined, even as she'd sunk deeper into it. She'd made her hair darker, then added bleached layers. Then more black. Then pink and red and finally purple. Going wild again, as she had in the years before. A small rebellion against growing up. Against giving in. Or giving up.

"Ta-da!" Jenny called, sweeping back through the door.

Eve's response was more subtle, but she was beaming. Jenny had dried her hair straight, and the length shone beneath the lights. "I love it," she said simply. "Thank you. So much."

"Let's do makeup now," Jenny said, clapping her hands. "I already feel like a new woman."

"Okay," Grace agreed, but then she looked back to the box in her hand. "But… Would you be willing to wait a little while? I think I'm going to change my hair up a little."

"But your purple!" Jenny said.

"It's starting to fade. These bright colors only last a few weeks."

Rayleen snorted. "Good riddance!"

"Well." Jenny sighed. "I suppose it'll be fun to see you with nonpurple hair. But maybe you'll dye it another wild color for me sometime."

"For you?" Grace laughed.

"Yes! You take all the risks, and I'll enjoy pretending I'm marginally involved."

"Okay. Deal. Let me get the color on my hair, and then I'll start your makeup. It's going to take a while for this brown to set anyway."

By the time she sat down at the table to do Eve's makeup, Grace had lost even the memory of being nervous. And doing makeup relaxed her even more. All her unhappiness faded, receding until it was only the faintest background buzz in her mind. She couldn't even credit it to the wine. She'd been too busy to do more than sip hers, unlike everyone else in the room. Even Aunt Rayleen had cracked a goofy smile or two.

Knowing Eve would be horrified by anything garish or even glamorous, Grace used a light hand with her makeup. Tinted moisturizer and translucent powder paired with a hint of warm pink on her cheeks and lips. She dusted her eyes with a neutral sand color, then smudged an espresso-brown shadow along her lash line. Finally, she used a light coat of mascara and darkened her brows with pencil.

With a smile, she turned Eve around to look at herself in the full-length mirror Jenny had brought from the bedroom.

"Oh," she said softly, her eyes widening. "Oh, my God. How do you do that?"

Jenny clapped. "You look so pretty!"

"When I put on my own makeup, I look like a clown!"

Grace laughed. "Just use neutral colors. Your skin is amazing, so you want to brighten it up a little, not cover it."

"My turn!" Jenny squealed. "Do mine like I'm going

to a party. I want to look like a sexy beast! Or, you know, as close as I can get to that."

"You're plenty sexy." Grace laughed, then shot Rayleen a glare when the woman snorted.

Fifteen minutes later, she turned Jenny around with a flourish. "Ta-da! Sexy beast, as requested."

Even though she braced herself for Jenny's squeal, she still wasn't ready for it. Amazingly, the mirror didn't shatter, though Grace's eardrums trembled.

"Look at my eyes!" she screamed. "Oh, my God, will you show me what you did?"

Grace gave her a quick demo, showing her how to brush a medium color nearly all the way up to her brow to disguise the fact that her Scandinavian eyes didn't have much of a crease. "Then a lighter color here, just beneath your eyebrow."

"I look so hot! We have to go out, ladies. We *have* to. I'll never look like this again."

"Yes, you will. You can do your makeup exactly the same way. I'm not a magician. It's just powder and cream."

"Blah, blah, blah. Finish your hair. We're going to the saloon! I want to show off to all the people who normally see me covered in beer stains after an eight-hour shift."

Grace quickly rinsed her hair and dried it, surprised when it turned out almost exactly as she'd planned. The black layers were still there, but the browns were deeper, and the purple was now a dark auburn-brown.

She carefully applied her own makeup, taking special care as she changed it to enhance the new hair color.

Instead of blacks, she chose deep browns that made her eyes look softer, and a pretty pink lip gloss.

When she was done, she packed up her makeup kit and wiped down the counter. But she didn't open the door. Instead she took a deep breath and looked at herself. She looked almost pretty now. Younger and softer. More like her natural self and less like an angry warning. She looked like a girl who might try to fit in if she found the right place.

It was scary. She felt stripped of her armor. Exposed. What if she saw Cole?

A terrible thrill coursed through her, and she glared at her reflection. She wanted him to see her like this. Wanted him to think she was *pretty*. How weak was that? How pitiful?

But it didn't matter. Good for him if he thought she looked pretty. He'd just have to live with wondering whether he'd really known what kind of girl she was, after all.

Reaching for the doorknob, she hesitated for another long moment, then took a deep breath and opened the door.

This time, the girls didn't scream. They just stared in openmouthed shock.

Rayleen recovered first. "Well, look at that. Maybe you'll stop scaring off my customers now."

Jenny pressed her hands to her mouth to try to suppress a squeal. It didn't work. "You look so pretty!"

"Thanks. Are we ready to go?"

"Look at you!" Jenny continued, undeterred. "Oh,

my God. Cole is going to swallow his tongue when he sees you."

"Cole!" Rayleen barked. "That cowboy's long gone."

"What?" Grace asked in utter confusion. How did Rayleen know they weren't seeing each other anymore?

Rayleen rolled her eyes. "I hope you two weren't serious."

"We weren't," Grace answered quickly.

"Good news, because Cole took off."

"For where?" Jenny asked after a few heartbeats of awkward silence.

"Not sure. He paid rent early and said he'd be gone for a couple of weeks. But considering the timing, I'd guess the boy went back to California for a little more time in paradise."

"What?" Grace breathed. "*More* time?"

"He lived in L.A. for a couple of months when he was young," Jenny said. "It was a long time ago."

Grace's mind was spinning. He'd lived in *L.A.?* That couldn't be right. Why wouldn't he have told her that?

Rayleen snorted. "There's more to the story than that. Rumor has it he was shacking up with Ms. Madeline Beckingham in her Hollywood mansion."

Jenny gasped. "What? I've never heard that." Her gaze slid nervously toward Grace. Grace found herself looking blankly into Jenny's worried eyes.

"Oh, the talk died down when he came back so quickly. I don't even know if it was true. He said it wasn't."

"Then it probably wasn't," Jenny cut in.

Rayleen shrugged. "Maybe not. But he left with her

last time, and he's gone again. I'm just saying, it's suspicious. That's all."

Suspicious. No, that wasn't the word for it. Because Grace knew he was sleeping with Madeline. And now she knew why he'd never mentioned his time in L.A. He'd let Grace tell stories about her life there as if he knew nothing about L.A. He'd let her talk about it like a fool. No, the timing wasn't suspicious. It was damning.

"Who cares about him?" Jenny said brightly. "All the more reason to go out and have fun with the girls. We'll flirt with more men than we could ever need. Right? Let's go!"

"No," Grace said softly. Everyone froze. Even Aunt Rayleen lost her scowl and finally seemed to realize that her gossip might have been unwelcome.

"Eh," she muttered. "I'm sure it's not true. He's probably camping."

"No," Grace repeated. She blinked her eyes, trying to clear the dizziness from her brain. When her vision cleared, she found herself looking at her aunt and seeing her with new eyes. Rayleen looked worried and a little guilty. And, truth be told, she looked frail without her scowl and her whiskey sour and her unlit cigarette. She was lonely. She was *alone.* Because she'd done too good a job of protecting herself from love and hurt.

That might be Grace someday, but even if it wasn't, she could understand what Rayleen had done. She could admire that the woman had had a tough life, and she'd had to make herself hard. But Rayleen deserved more than that. She deserved to be happy someday, and not hurt. Just as Grace did.

"Grace…" Eve started, but Grace shook her head.

"That's not what I meant. I meant, we need to do Aunt Rayleen's makeup first. That's all. She's one of the girls, right?"

"Oh, poo," Rayleen scoffed. "Nobody'd notice my makeup even if you made me look like a whore."

"What about Easy?" Grace asked.

Rayleen's eyes went wide as saucers.

Grace couldn't help but smile, despite the hurt banging around inside her. "Would Easy notice if you looked especially whorish?"

Her papery cheeks flushed. "What?"

Jenny giggled. "Oh, come on. We've all noticed the way you two flirt."

"Flirt? I wouldn't flirt with that old cowhand if he was the last man on earth." She cleared her throat. "Why? You think he's flirting with me?"

"I think he is," Grace said. "But even if he's not, I'd love to do your makeup."

"Makeup," she huffed. Then she shrugged as if she didn't care. "Sure. Knock yourself out. But don't make me look like some old fool."

"Got it." She used a creamy foundation to hide fine lines without looking cakey, and a bit of concealer to brighten under her aunt's eyes. But as Grace moved on to powder and blush, her mind wandered back to Cole. She'd felt betrayed before, and told herself she had no right to. But this…this felt worse. As if she'd known nothing about him from the start. He wasn't who he pretended to be. She might not be a wonderful person, but at least she'd warned him right away.

Biting back the hurt, Grace smudged a neutral color over Rayleen's eyelids to cover the pink that showed through her thin skin, then she carefully dusted a dark gray shade along her lash line and finished up with mascara.

"There. Easy as pie."

Rayleen scowled, as usual, but when she turned to look in the mirror, her scowl fell away. She didn't smile, but her eyes lit up. Just a little. "All right," she finally conceded. "It's fine."

Eve and Jenny exchanged amused looks. It was more than fine. Rayleen looked almost ten years younger, and her white hair only looked more beautiful against the careful palette of coral and gray.

Rayleen didn't smile, but she did look at herself for a long time before she finally slapped her knees and stood up. "Let's go."

"Wait!" Jenny shouted. "I need to take a picture. Girls' night out!"

Grace made herself smile for the picture, but as they left the condo, her heart was sinking. She couldn't do this. Go out and act as if she didn't have a care in the world.

It was stupid to feel so betrayed. He was a man she'd had sex with. He couldn't betray her, because he hadn't promised anything. So maybe it wasn't him. Maybe it was herself. There'd been a connection. A chemistry. Something that had made it feel different. But it hadn't been different. It had been the same in the very worst possible way.

She realized that she was planning excuses with every

step. Planning a way to escape from these women and lock herself in her apartment to lick her wounds alone. But what if she didn't? What if she swallowed all this strange grief and went to the saloon?

Despite the short length of time she'd known them, Jenny and Eve had given her a chance. They seemed to like her, or at least to want to like her. They might be friends. Actual friends. If they didn't want sex or money or connections, maybe they just wanted *her*.

Grace crossed one arm over her chest in defense. She held tight to her opposite elbow and tucked her head, startled at how frightening it felt to consider having friends. To trust that they genuinely liked her.

They turned the corner and Grace realized they were coming up on the Crooked R. "I need to drop off my makeup kit," she said.

"Sure," Eve said. "We'll wait for you."

"No, go ahead and go in. I'll meet you there."

Jenny rolled her eyes, and everyone kept walking past the saloon and toward the Stud Farm. "Don't be silly. We'll wait here and then go in together to make an appearance. Four beautiful women walking in at once? They won't know what hit them."

This was Grace's chance to make an excuse. To say she wasn't feeling well and she wanted to turn in. But instead, she nodded. "Okay. I'll be right back."

But as she headed up the sidewalk toward the porch, headlights flashed over the lawn and she glanced back to see a sheriff's truck pulling up to the curb.

Oh, God.

The SUV stopped and two deputies got out. As Eve

and Jenny and Rayleen watched, the men started up the walk toward Grace.

Oh, no.

It was an apartment building with four apartments. They might not be here for her. Or maybe it was something that didn't have anything to do with—

"Grace Barrett?" the shorter deputy asked.

"Yes," she breathed. Her pulse suddenly swelled to a booming beat inside her skull. Her entire body went tight and numb.

"We have a warrant for your arrest," the same guy said.

And there it was. This was it. "Oh," she said, not really speaking, just letting air escape from her lungs. They hadn't turned their lights on, at least, but she could still see flashes at the edges of her vision. "Oh," she said again as the deputy approached with his hands raised in a calming gesture.

She glanced toward her new friends, though she tried not to meet their gazes. All three women stood wide-eyed, lips parted in shock. "Can I set down my kit?" Grace rasped.

The deputy nodded, and she set it down slowly, more than familiar with how jumpy cops could be. But these officers were a little more Zen than the average L.A. cop. When she held her arms up, the deputy didn't snatch her wrist and twist it behind her back. Instead, he calmly slipped the cuffs over one wrist, and then the other. Grace couldn't help but wonder if he would have been kind enough to cuff her hands in front if she'd still had purple hair and wild makeup.

The thought of her hair brought tears to her eyes. Despite everything—the misguided affair with Cole, the knowledge that she was moving on soon—this had felt like a new beginning. A new start. She'd been shedding her skin. Letting go of her defenses. And she'd meant it. But now...

She dared one last look at Eve and Jenny and Aunt Rayleen, but they were blurry. She was protected from whatever she'd see in their faces.

"Grace?" Jenny called tentatively.

Grace just dropped her head and let the deputy lead her to his truck. She wondered if anyone else was watching. Wondered if half the saloon had come outside to watch her perp walk. It hardly mattered. All the important people were right there with front-row seats.

She felt the deputy's hand on top of her head guiding her into the truck. Grace just closed her eyes and let him push her under.

CHAPTER TWENTY-TWO

HE'D MEANT TO BE GONE for weeks. Meant to stay away until his CT scan. What was the point, after all? Why work at the ranch toward something he might not have again? So he'd driven away, meaning to stay gone. To take a roundabout way toward California. To consider whether that was what he wanted. Maybe even what he needed.

But that first night, he'd stopped at a campground in Idaho, and he'd slept under the stars on nothing more than a pallet and a sleeping bag. And as he'd stared up at the same sky he'd seen a thousand times before, he hadn't seen the stars at all. What he'd seen was fear. The new fear of what he'd do if he couldn't ride, sure.

But old fears, too. The nagging fear of becoming his father. That was part of what had driven him to L.A. the first time. And then the awful fear of letting his dad down, which had come after the possibility had passed with a startling finality.

The fear of letting down a dead man. Is that all that had driven him for the past thirteen years? It didn't seem possible.

No, it wasn't possible. He loved the work. Loved the land and the sky. The beautiful days and the weeks that were so brutal you wished you could lie down and die.

He loved the men he worked with and the simple dignity of the work.

But now...

Now there was a new fear.

And as he'd lain under those stars praying for sleep to claim him, he'd remembered the first time he'd let Grace see it. That moment when he'd confessed that he might not ride again. She'd reached for him. Reached for a connection. It wasn't the sex he remembered now. It was that moment when she'd *looked* at him. When she'd understood. She knew what it was to face fear, and she'd wanted to take it from him. Or share the burden, at least.

She'd been afraid before. She was still afraid.

Cole felt ashamed now. Hard as she was, she'd seen his fear and felt compassion. But when she'd turned her defenses on him, he'd lashed out. He'd hurt her more, and that was exactly what she'd expected. What she'd wanted, even. Because if he hurt her, she didn't have to fear it anymore. It was done.

The second day, Cole had turned north instead of west. He'd camped in Montana that night. A different forest. The same stars. This time next to a creek that danced through the dark, adding enough sound to the night that he hoped it would let him sleep.

His hip had recovered more quickly from the ride than he'd expected, and it was back to the familiar dull ache that had slept with him every night since the accident. It shouldn't keep him up, but he couldn't close his eyes.

In the end, his insomnia had finally made itself useful. By the next morning, Cole had figured it out. He'd faced the reality of where he was and he'd made a decision. If his ability to ride was what made him a man, then he wasn't much of a man at all. And if he couldn't keep Grace from leaving, at least he could let her go with the respect she deserved. He needed to step up to the plate and be the kind of person he could be proud of. Nothing to do with his dad or Easy or the ranch. Just himself.

He took the long way home, stopping for one more night along the Gallatin to let everything settle in his mind. For once, the ranch felt far away. But California had ceased to exist as anything but a harmless memory.

His dad had been wrong.

Whether it had all been a grand mistake or not, it had been Cole's to make and his to live with. He only wished he'd found a way to say that without screaming. He wished he'd made his peace with his father. But better late than never.

That night he slept for eight hours straight. And then he headed home to Jackson. Maybe even to Grace.

CHAPTER TWENTY-THREE

"She's not there."

Cole looked up to see Shane coming down the stairs. "Hey, man." He dropped the hand he'd raised to knock for the third time on Grace's door. "She's probably still at work," he murmured.

"Um…" Shane's gaze slid from Cole to the front door, then down to his feet. "Did you just get back?"

Cole shifted and narrowed his eyes. "What's going on?"

Shane grimaced.

"Where's Grace?" Cole pressed.

"You should ask Rayleen."

"Ask Rayleen *what?*" he growled.

Shane finally stepped off the last stair and stood there awkwardly. "I'm pretty sure Grace is gone."

"No. She was supposed to stay another week or two."

"Right." Shane ran a hand through his hair and glanced at the front door as if he wanted to bolt. "Something happened."

All the peace he'd managed to gather over the past days crumbled and slipped through his hands. He could almost hear it crash onto the wood floor. "Jesus Christ, Shane, do I have to beat it out of you? What the hell is going on?"

Shane took a deep breath. "Fine. Grace was arrested on Sunday night."

"What?"

"I gather that whatever the charges were, they were dropped. She was released this morning. She packed up and left a few minutes later. That's all I know."

Cole cursed and headed for the door.

"I'm sorry, man," Shane said, the words barely audible over Cole's pounding heart.

Cole pushed out the door and rushed to the saloon. Jenny and Rayleen were both behind the bar, their backs turned to the room. Jenny was hammering a nail into the wall, but they both spun to face him when he called Rayleen's name.

"Cole!" she said in surprise, nearly dropping the framed picture she held. She set it down carefully on the bar and crossed her arms. "What are you doing here? Thought you'd taken off for California."

"What?" He shook his head, then squinted at Rayleen. She looked different somehow. Younger? He waved the stupid thought away with an impatient hand. "I don't know what you're talking about. Where's Grace? I need to speak to her."

"Probably in Montana by now."

"Montana? You let her *go?*"

"She wanted to leave."

He ground his teeth together, unable to see the connection between those two things. "How did she get from here to Montana?" he made himself ask calmly. "She doesn't have a car."

"I dropped her off at Flagg Ranch this morning for the Yellowstone bus."

"So. You drove her. All the way up to Flagg Ranch. So she could leave. This morning."

"Cole," Jenny said. "Something happened with—"

"I heard about that. I don't give a shit. I just need to talk to her."

"The charges were apparently dropped, but she wouldn't listen to us. Eve thinks it has something to do with an issue in California. Grace just wanted to leave. She didn't—"

"Just—" He held up a hand to stop her from talking. "Hold on." His heart beating too hard, he called up her number on his phone and hit Call. He couldn't stop picturing how small she'd looked on the side of the road that day, when she'd been so worried about getting the car back to Eve. *I can't be late.... Not after that. She'll think...*

An arrest. Everybody knowing. She must be devastated.

He held his breath as the phone clicked. Then a mechanical voice told him the subscriber wasn't available.

"Shit," he ground out. "Where's she going? Vancouver?"

"Yes," Rayleen said quietly. "She said something about going through Bozeman." She looked up finally, meeting his gaze. "I'd guess the bus follows I-90."

The bus follows I-90. Right. Of course. It probably only left once a day. Bozeman wasn't exactly a hot travel spot. Maybe he could...

"If she gets in touch, *call me,*" he tossed over his shoulder as he headed for the door.

"Tell her we miss her, okay?" Jenny shouted.

He should've come straight home yesterday. He should've at least called.

If Grace needed to run, he could let her. He was almost sure of it. But not like this. Not when she thought he'd been sleeping with Madeline. Not when she was convinced that what she and Cole had meant nothing.

Because it had meant something. Something so big that it filled him up until he could barely breathe.

Cole got into his truck and headed north, hoping he could manage to catch a girl who meant to disappear for good.

CHAPTER TWENTY-FOUR

THE DINGY FLUORESCENT LIGHTS twitched around her as Grace struggled to keep her eyes open. She'd been on three buses already today and the fourth one wouldn't arrive until 1:00 a.m., which was... She flipped open her phone. Three hours from now.

Three hours. She could stay awake until then.

She eyed the dead coffeemaker sitting on the counter of the bus station. Bus *room* would be a more accurate description. But she couldn't complain. The clerk had left the door unlocked when he'd gone, allowing Grace to stay inside instead of waiting on the curb. Once again, Grace wondered if that would've happened with the purple hair.

She decided to stick with brown and black for a while. As bad as her luck had been, she wouldn't dare the distrust of strangers right now.

At least today had been the nicest bus ride she'd ever been on. She hadn't expected Yellowstone to look like the landscape of an alien planet. Steam and geysers and strangely colored rock. And amidst it all, animals roaming everywhere, as if there weren't tourists following just behind them, snapping pictures. Grace had seen elk, finally. More elk than she could have dreamed of, and now she saw the difference that Cole had laughed about. She wouldn't mistake them for deer again.

And bison just wandering around as if it were normal. She'd even spotted a moose, and once, a fox trotting along next to the bus.

If she had any money to spare, she would've hopped off the bus and stayed. For days or weeks. She would've stayed and seen things she'd never imagined. The geysers erupting in the distance. The bears she remembered from old cartoons. Staring out the bus window, the signs in the park had been nearly painful to see, knowing she'd never discover what they named. Mud pots and waterfalls and lakes. Lookouts and rivers. Those things weren't for her. She was only passing through.

But she was in Montana now. This was someplace she'd never been. That was something good.

But not good enough to offset the past few days. Nothing could make that better.

Grace dragged her duffel bag closer on the row of seats and pulled one end of it onto her lap so she could lay her head down. She stared at the torn edge of a promotional poster and told herself not to go to sleep. Not yet.

But she was so tired. Jail wasn't exactly a restful haven. And fury and mortification had kept her awake since then. She still couldn't believe Scott had actually done it. He'd had her arrested. Sent her to jail. This man she'd once shared a bed with had put her through the fear and shame of being arrested and strip-searched and processed like a felon.

That first phone call had been easy. She'd called Scott

and told him exactly what she thought of him. "How could you?" she'd yelled. "I sent you money! I was doing what I promised!"

"I just got the money today," he'd answered, sounding more subdued than she'd expected. "I didn't think—"

"I told you I'd pay you back."

"I know, but Willa got back and she came right over here to tell me you were lying."

Grace hadn't even been shocked at that. "What would Willa know about it?"

"She said you were driving around Jackson Hole in a nice Lexus, partying with—"

"No. No! That was my boss's car! My ex-boss, because there's no way I have a job now, since I was *arrested in front of her,* you asshole."

"Grace, look—"

"I'm paying you back," she'd said, the words breaking into a sob. "That woman was just pissed because I embarrassed her in front of Madeline Beckingham. I sent you money and I'll send the rest as soon as I can. Please don't do this. Scott..." Hating herself, hating him, she'd begged him to drop the charges. She'd wept and she'd begged him.

It had worked, anyway. And being out of jail was a sweeter victory than salvaging whatever pride she'd had left. She'd showered and packed and then taken the tattered rags of her ego and she'd run as fast as she could. She hadn't seen Eve, at least, and Aunt Rayleen had held her tongue. Out of kindness or disgust, Grace wasn't sure, but she'd been thankful for the reprieve from insults.

It already felt far away. Jackson Hole. A different world. She was alone in a state where no one knew her. She could walk out the door and disappear and no one would even know she'd been here. She would've found that comforting a few weeks ago. Now it scared her. As if she were barely tethered to the earth. One wrong move and she'd float into space and never be found.

Grace held tighter to the rough canvas of the bag. She wished it was 1:00 a.m. She wished she could go to sleep and open her eyes and be anywhere else.

The door whooshed open beside her, and Grace sprang upright with a gasp. She'd fallen asleep. The bus was here. The driver would—

"Grace?"

At the sound of Cole's voice, she shoved the bag off her lap and lurched up.

"Grace?" His confused gaze drifted up to her hair, but he quickly shook his head. "Are you okay?"

"What are you doing here?" She hadn't expected to ever see him again, and her heart sped to an alarming pace as she took in his scruffy jaw and weary blue eyes. When he stepped forward, she held up a hand in panic. "Did Jenny call you? Did... You were in California. What are you doing here? I—"

"I wasn't in California. Who told you that?"

"Everybody knows you went to L.A. with Madeline," she snapped, backing away.

Cole's cheeks burned bright red at her words. "I'm not sleeping with Madeline."

She remembered, suddenly, why she was so mad. Why she hated him so much. She stopped retreating.

"You lived with her!" She stabbed her finger toward him. "You lived in L.A. with that woman."

"That was a long time ago. I haven't... I'm not..."

"You lied to me."

"I didn't lie. I swear I'm not sleeping with her. That was thirteen years ago. I was a—"

"Yes," she ground out. "Thirteen years ago when you lived in L.A. A little fact you forgot to mention. Why? Because you thought it was funny to keep me in the dark?"

"No, it wasn't like that. I never talk about that time. I'm not proud of it. Listen..." He moved forward, reaching for her shoulders.

Grace pushed his hands away. *What are you even doing here?*

"Grace." He looked stunned. She was stunned herself. Everything was bubbling up. Fury. Betrayal. And awful humiliation. She didn't want to see him. Didn't want him to know. She panted, her hands squeezed to fists with the urge to hit him. For *seeing* her.

"I'm here for you," he finally said, his voice soft. "I didn't want you leaving this way."

"What way? In complete disgrace?"

"No. Thinking the wrong things about me. About us. It wasn't like that, Grace. I only let you think that because I was pissed. You'd bruised my pride. But I wasn't seeing Madeline. I didn't *want* to see her. Literally. Jesus, that's why I was so mad about the film. Because I never wanted anything to do with her again."

She shook her head, trying to buy time. She didn't know what to think. He'd popped out of the night like an apparition. Maybe he wasn't real. Maybe she was dreaming. The thought calmed her a little. "I don't know what to believe, Cole. And it doesn't even matter."

"Of course it matters. I don't want you to leave, but if you have to... You need to know that you mean something to me. I need you to know that, and take that with you."

Grace felt her heart calm a little more. He didn't know about the arrest. No one had been morbid enough to tell him. That was the only explanation. He didn't know what had happened and he thought everything was the same. "Cole, it doesn't matter, because I'm leaving. I don't belong here."

"What if you do?"

"I don't. It's obvious to everyone."

"Grace," he said quietly. "What if you do?"

The words snuck inside her as if she had no defenses. They curled up in her chest and *hurt*. "You don't know me."

"That's what you're afraid of, isn't it?"

"I'm not afraid of anything," she snapped back.

"Liar. You're afraid to let your guard down. You're afraid to be soft. You're afraid to let anyone know you. Why?"

"That's ridiculous."

"It is ridiculous." He smiled, showing his dimples, and the hurt in her chest swelled larger.

"Please go," she whispered, throwing a desperate glance at the door. Escape was right there, but she'd never get past him. "You have to go now. Please?"

"Why?"

"Because I'm leaving, and none of it meant anything."

"Liar," he said.

"You have to go." She heard the desperation in her own voice. She heard the fear and she hated it.

"Are you running away, Grace?"

Yes. Yes, she was running like hell.

He nodded as if he'd heard her. "Go on, then. If that's what you want. But know that you're leaving me behind."

She set her jaw and said nothing.

"I'm not afraid to say that now. If you go, you're leaving me, because I want you to stay. With me."

She nodded and managed to meet his gaze without flinching. "Goodbye, Cole."

His smile faded. "Yeah? You're going to run?"

"Yes," she said.

"All right."

All right. He'd go. Despite the wave of relief that swelled through her, the hurt stayed. "Goodbye," she said again.

"All right," he repeated, as if he were trying to resign himself to the truth. "There's a motel one block down. I'll be there. Call me if you change your mind."

"I won't."

Cole reached one hand up for a moment, as if he wanted to touch her, but then he let it fall. "Bye, Grace. You're not old light, you know. Not at all. You shine so bright it hurts my eyes." He reached for the door. "Oh, and Jenny says to tell you she misses you."

He left then, cool air gusting over her as the door hovered open behind him. When it finally shut, she took a deep breath. Then another.

She couldn't tell truth from lies anymore. She couldn't trust her own judgment. Did he know about the arrest? Was he lying about Madeline Beckingham? He had to be. Men lied about that kind of thing all the time. But if he'd just been playing Grace for a fool, he'd be relieved she was leaving, wouldn't he?

It didn't matter. None of it did. She couldn't go back. Maybe there would've been a chance of fitting in before, if she'd stopped throwing her hands out and claiming not to fit. But now, she may as well have been arrested in front of the whole town. Everyone would know. Cole would find out. And whether he'd lived in L.A. for a few months or not, he was still a nice cowboy surrounded by wholesome people. No one wanted a criminal in their midst. No one wanted a loser.

Jenny says to tell you she misses you.

More likely, she just felt sorry for Grace. But not as sorry as Grace felt for herself.

She dragged the duffel bag back up to the seats, then laid her head on it and waited for 1:00 a.m. to arrive.

WHEN IT STARTED raining, Cole found himself standing in the doorway of his motel room, staring into the wet night and worrying about Grace. He checked his phone a dozen times. She was only one block away, but if she called, he'd drive over to get her. He didn't want her walking through the cold rain. She might be tougher than him in a hundred other ways, but she wasn't used to the cold, and the temperature had dropped about twenty degrees in the past hour.

But the rain kept falling and his phone stayed dark and silent. At midnight, Cole closed the door and sat down wearily on the bed. And at one, he watched the bus drive by, taking her away.

He looked hard at the long line of windows as it passed, but they were pitch-black in the night. He couldn't see her in there no matter how hard he looked. All he saw were streetlights reflecting off the glass.

"Damn." He sighed as he sank into the bed. She was gone. He wasn't surprised. He hadn't seen much in her eyes except panic and anger. She'd wanted to go and he couldn't stop her. It was that simple.

There was no question it hurt, but the pain was simple loss. Grief for what he'd wanted with her, not anger or humiliation. She'd been running so long she didn't know how to stop.

Just a few days ago, he would've been too bruised and beaten to feel anything but rage. But he actually had Madeline Beckingham to thank for something. Hell, he might even owe her an apology. Because she was right. He hadn't really loved her. That love was a lie he'd lived with for thirteen years, painting himself as a heartbroken victim of a cold woman. But he hadn't truly known her. She'd been a shiny toy for a boy too young to know the difference between lust and love. And she'd been an easy name to give to the guilt he'd felt. The unyielding sorrow of knowing his last words to his father had been shouted with scorn and disrespect. Of knowing he could've reached out and hadn't. Granted, his dad had been wrong, too. But that didn't absolve Cole. Young as he'd been, he'd been a grown man, and he'd never forget that lesson.

Which was why he'd decided to lay his pride down and tell Grace how he truly felt. The fact that she'd gotten on that bus didn't change that. She was scared. And dark. And damaged. How could he hate that about her? She wouldn't have been strong and brave and passionate without that same past.

But fuck, it hurt.

At least he had a plan for his own future. At least he could concentrate on that.

Sighing, Cole toed off his boots and unbuttoned his shirt. His fingers were on the last button when someone knocked on his door. The tentative rap froze every muscle in his body.

It couldn't be...

She'd left.

Cole snapped from his shock and jumped up to open the door.

Grace stood there in the rain, hair dripping, shoulders bowed down by the weight of her bag. "I was arrested," she said quietly.

"I know."

"In front of everyone."

"Come here," Cole murmured, pulling her into his arms. She was ice-cold and shaking. Or maybe he was shaking. He turned her, pulling her into the warmth of the room before he shut the door behind her and tossed her bag aside.

"You're freezing," he said, rubbing his hands over her

arms before he pulled off her soaked hoodie. "I thought you were gone."

Teeth chattering, she let him undress her until she was wearing nothing but her panties and a tank top. Then he pulled the blanket off the bed and wrapped her in it. "Better?"

She nodded, still not meeting his eyes. "You knew?"

"Of course I knew. It was the first thing I heard when I got back to town." He smiled to take the sting away, to make it a joke, but she didn't answer his smile.

"I can't go back, Cole."

"Of course you can. You think no one in town has ever been arrested before? And you left so quickly, people probably think you're a fugitive. That only makes it more exciting."

"The charges were dropped," she rasped.

"I know." He sat on the bed and pulled her into his arms. "You want to tell me what happened?"

"I never meant for this to happen," she started, and then she told him the whole story. The cash she'd taken and lost. The way she'd fled L.A. in a panic that her ex might file charges. The money she'd sent and would have to keep sending for the next year or two.

"It'll be okay," he said. "It was a mistake. And bad luck. You don't have to be ashamed."

"But I do," she whispered. "You don't understand. When I was with Scott, I let him change me. I saw it happening and I went along with it, because…I let myself need him."

"Shit, Grace. We've all done that."

"That's not true. When have you ever needed anyone?"

"As a matter of fact, it's one of the reasons I don't tell anyone about L.A. I became someone I didn't like. I hated it and I didn't stop it soon enough. I know what that's like."

"You don't understand. It's not simple for me. My mother was—is—*weak*. And everything I am, everything I want to be, it's so I don't end up like her. Getting stepped on and spit on and used. Doing anything she can just to keep a man, because she thinks she can't make it on her own. Do you know what it was like to watch her do that? To change her looks and personality and interests every time some new boyfriend came to stay? She was a new person every year. Which one of them was my mother? Which one was real? I hated that. I hated her. And suddenly, it was me doing that. Because I needed him. Letting him treat me like shit."

"You didn't stay. You came to your senses."

"No," she whispered. "He kicked me out. That's the worst part, Cole. He kicked me out like a dog he didn't want anymore."

"Ah, shit, Grace." He kissed the top of her head and pulled her closer. "That's not you. You were going to figure it out. Be glad it ended the way it did. Because I know you, and if you'd stayed longer, you would have eventually exploded in a way that would've resulted in injury to that man's reproductive organs. And then you really would've gone to jail. And if you ended up on probation, how would you have come to Wyoming?"

He was relieved to hear a small, watery laugh. But she still felt too small in his arms.

"Listen, Madeline treated me like shit, too. And I left on my own. But then I went crawling back like a fool, only to find she didn't want me anymore. So, yeah, we have all done that. Everyone in this room, anyway."

She shook her head.

"I never thought I'd have the guts to beg again, but look. Here I am on my knees for you, begging you to stay."

"You aren't on your knees."

"No, but I would be, if I thought it would work. You have a job here. And friends. Just try, Grace. See how it feels."

She shook her head, but at least she didn't say no out loud. With her, that was progress.

"When I went to L.A. all those years ago, I didn't exactly receive a hero's send-off. I'd lived here my whole life. I had friends, a job, obligations. I had a girlfriend I walked away from. And my dad… We fought. We pushed each other. We said terrible things."

He felt Grace tilt her head to look up at him, but he didn't meet her gaze.

"I burned all my bridges and left everyone behind so I could hang out with glamorous strangers. Two months later, my dad died. That was what I came home to. No family. Friends I'd treated badly. Responsibilities I'd tossed aside. But I came back because this was my home. People forgave me faster than I forgave myself. And no one needs to forgive you for anything. You haven't hurt anyone. You don't have anything to be ashamed of."

"But it's not my home, Cole."

"Are you sure?"

She fell silent. He slid a hand over her hair, wondering why she'd changed it. He'd liked the purple streaks, but he was happy to have her back in his arms. He could get used to any hair color she wanted. He let her rest there for a long moment, hoping she'd change her mind. But she didn't speak.

"I'm scared, too, you know. I might never ride again. I'll find out in a couple of weeks."

"Find out what?"

"I'll have a CT scan, and then they'll tell me I can't ride again, and I have to figure out what that means."

Her hand spread over his chest. "You'll be okay."

"I won't be. That last time I saw you at the ranch, I'd finally realized it. I'd ridden and I couldn't even stand on my own afterward. It's over, Grace. But it'll be okay."

"But what will you do? If you can't ride…"

His throat felt thick, but Cole shook it off. "I've always been good with numbers. I've got the money I saved up for the ranch. I can take some classes. Go back to school. I can learn to manage the business side of a big place. Maybe one of these dude ranches. It's not my dream, but it could be my choice."

Her fingers pressed into him. He covered her hand with his.

"Maybe your leg is okay," she whispered.

"Maybe," he conceded, just because she sounded so sad. "But I don't think so. It scares the hell out of me, but that's okay."

"You're really scared?" she asked softly.

"I am. I'd be a fool not to be. So maybe fear means we're still alive. Maybe it means we haven't given up yet."

"Cole," she said. Just his name, and then she was silent for a long time. So long that Cole wondered if she'd fallen asleep. But she suddenly pulled away, shrugging the blanket off her shoulders as she sat back. She looked up at him with angry eyes. "Do you even like me?"

He blinked. "What? Of course I do."

"No. No, not 'of course.' I know you want me. That's not the same thing. Sometimes the things you've said, or the way you touch me…"

"Grace," he breathed. "I'm sorry. If you didn't—"

"I'm not saying you shouldn't have. I'm saying that's not the way you want a woman you love, is it? A woman you like and respect? You wouldn't want her that way."

He whispered her name again, stunned that she could think that. Heartbroken that he'd made her feel that way.

"You said it yourself, that you're not like that with other women."

Cole shook his head. "I'm not. You make me feel… out of control. Wild. I thought it was the same for you." He watched her eyes, feeling as if he might break apart if he saw hurt in them. But he could only see himself, reflected back in the darkness.

"It is," she finally said, and his mortification eased back a little. "I want you, Cole. So much. But I wonder if you only want me that way because of what I am."

"No," he answered.

"Because of *who* I am."

"Fine," he said harshly, his pulse quick with anxiety. "It is because of who you are. But not the way you mean. It's because you're beautiful and wild and brave and strong. It's because you seem invulnerable, but you melt for me. It's because I want you so damn much I feel like I need to bite down on a belt when you're close by. Sometimes I can't get deep enough or close enough. But other times…other times I want to touch you softly and you won't let me, Grace."

Her cheeks went pink and she looked away. Her makeup was gone, worn away by the day and the rain. She looked so young, as if all her defenses had vanished.

Cole reached for her, brushing his knuckles along her cheek. He tilted her face up, then slowly leaned closer. She didn't pull away, and he brushed his mouth over hers. "Let me touch you," he breathed, trailing his fingers down her neck. "Please."

She shook her head, but as he dragged his fingers down to her breast, Grace sighed into his mouth and her hands wove into his hair.

Her response ramped his arousal up toward that now-familiar wildness. He knew she'd respond with her own wildness if he pushed her. He'd felt the violent need shaking through her. But that wasn't what she needed tonight. So he touched her slow and soft, and she let him. Finally. She let him ease the last of her clothes off. Let him kiss her everywhere he wanted, until she was whimpering with need. And then she let him slide into her, careful and gentle, as if she were a virgin.

She said his name and dug her nails into his back, but he couldn't be goaded. Not tonight. He made love to her. He touched her and let her feel the way he wanted to take care of her. Not because she needed him, but because she didn't.

And in the morning, he took her home.

CHAPTER TWENTY-FIVE

"You don't need to be here," Cole grumbled, pulling the brim of his hat lower as he slumped into the chair. He looked around the doctor's office and found it suspiciously bare. What did the guy do in here? Just steeple his fingers and give bad news from behind his mahogany desk?

"I know I don't need to be here," Grace said. "I want to be here."

He looked over his shoulder at the closed door, impatient to get this over with.

Grace took his hand. "It's okay to be scared. Right? Isn't that what you told me?"

"It's fine. I know what he'll say. I won't be able to ride again. It's no big deal. I'll start classes in three weeks."

"No big deal," Grace repeated. "Sure. That's why you couldn't sleep last night."

He shot her an exasperated look. "You weren't even at my place last night."

"I heard you pacing around after I left."

"Maybe if you'd stayed, I wouldn't have been pacing around."

She rolled her eyes, but her fingers squeezed his. She stayed sometimes now. On the weekends, when she didn't have to get up for work. She'd sleep until he woke her with his hands and his mouth. He'd finally seen the miracle of Grace waking up smiling.

"If he gives me bad news, will you dye your hair purple again to make me feel better?"

"God, you're being a baby." She took any sting away by kissing his fingers. "Anyway, you said you were getting used to the new hair."

"It's pretty," he said carefully. It was. Beautiful, actually, but he wished he'd had a little longer with the purple. "If you've gone soft, I guess I'll have to accept that."

She might have bristled at that two weeks ago, but now he saw her mouth tighten in a smile she tried to hide. He'd tried to show her just how enjoyable soft could be. Not that she'd ever admit it.

The door opened behind them, and Cole's thoughts broke off as if they'd been chopped with an ax.

This was it. He was ready.

"All right, Mr. Rawlins." The doctor set down a laptop and pushed a few buttons. "I've taken a look at the images and the report."

Her hand tightened in his with far more power than he would have expected. He almost smiled at the thought. He almost forgot that he was about to hear the worst news of his life.

The doctor frowned at the screen for a moment and then looked up.

Cole braced himself.

"Well, everything looks great."

A heartbeat passed. And another. Then Cole's pulse blasted into overdrive. "What?" he breathed.

"It's looking good. The fracture in your pelvis has

finally started to mend. The plates in your femur will stay, of course, unless they—"

"But I don't understand," Cole cut in. "I was in the saddle two weeks ago. It felt like I was rebreaking everything all over again. I thought I was about to split in half."

"Well, what did you do? Ride up and down a mountain?"

"Uh…" He glanced at Grace and then back to the doctor.

"Listen, things are tender right now. The bone is still healing, and the ligaments and muscles are all tight. You have to ease slowly back into your old routines. I mean *slowly.* Five minutes in the saddle on a flat trail. Do that for a few days. Then ten minutes. You can't just pick up where you left off. Use ibuprofen. Ice it to stop the swelling. It might take a whole year, but you'll be back out there. No worries."

No worries. He said it so simply. No worries.

Jesus. *He could ride?*

"You're keeping up with physical therapy?"

"Yes," Cole answered, the word toneless even to his own ear.

"All right. Three more months of that, and I think we'll be done with you, Mr. Rawlins. It's been a pleasure."

He stood to shake the man's hand. The doctor closed his laptop and left, but Cole just stood there, dumbfounded.

"Cole?" Grace ventured. Her hand touched his back,

then slid up to his neck. He could feel each of her fin-
gertips as they brushed his skin.

"I can buy the ranch," he breathed.

"You can."

"My leg is okay. My hip…"

"It is."

He looked down to find Grace smiling at him. And
her eyes—for once, they were clear, deep whiskey-
brown and filled with hope.

"I guess you're just a big baby, huh?"

"I guess I am," he said hoarsely.

"I should've known. All that bitching about your leg,
but you didn't have any trouble taking me up against the
wall of the shower."

"Grace!" He looked around to be sure the doctor was
gone.

"What? It's true. You have all the strength in the
world when it comes to sex."

She was right. He was Superman out of sheer, stubborn will when it came to making love to her.

Cole finally relaxed. And smiled. And pulled her
into his arms. "Grace." He sighed. "Did you hear that?
I can ride again." He honestly hadn't expected it. He
hadn't even considered the possibility that maybe…
"My God," he whispered into her pretty hair. "Did he
really say that?"

"He did. Should we go home and celebrate?"

He blinked in shock and jerked upright. "Yes! We
should, actually. Absolutely. I insist."

Laughing, she pulled him out of the office and down
the hall. "You should probably call Easy first. Tell him

to pack his bags for Mexico. My poor aunt will be so disappointed."

"I think Easy can wait awhile," he murmured, thinking of exactly what he had planned when they got home. And what he had planned for the rest of his future.

GRACE FELT GIDDY. True joy coursed through her. Happiness for Cole, separate from anything she wanted for herself. It was a strange sensation. Something she wasn't used to. But she soaked it up, hoping that she could keep a little part of it tucked away forever.

Cole was going to be fine. Thank God.

He drove home quickly, his mouth occasionally revealing his happiness in a smile. She wasn't sure if he was happy about the prognosis or just anticipating what would happen when they got home, but it didn't matter. Either way, she was about to have her hands on him. His body made her feel safe, somehow. Even when nothing else could.

But right now, she had every reason to feel safe. She had come back to Jackson, and much to her surprise, her new friends had seemed relieved. Even Rayleen had hugged her, though she'd then proceeded to bitch about her apartment building being contaminated with estrogen. Admittedly, Grace had tried to avoid Jenny, at first, and even Eve. But Eve was hard to avoid when she'd immediately hired Grace back at the studio.

Things were okay. And now they were better.

She spread her fingers over Cole's thigh, loving the way his muscles flexed as he braked and accelerated. When he moved her hand away, she laughed. "Hey!"

"I'm too excited already," he growled.

Within seconds, he was pulling into the driveway of the Stud Farm, and Grace was grinning in anticipation. But when she hopped out of the truck, Cole grabbed her hand and led her toward the saloon.

"Hey! I thought we were going to celebrate."

"Oh, we will. But I thought I saw Easy's truck in the parking lot."

"Right. Okay. I'll be patient, then."

He grinned like a little boy. "You need to be patient, huh? It's hard to wait?"

"Shut up," she grumbled, embarrassed by how much she needed him. All the time. Every day. But it wasn't a scary need, somehow. It wasn't weakness. She couldn't understand it, but she was trying not to be afraid.

Just as they reached the saloon porch, Cole stopped. He turned to her, and Grace felt a sudden jolt of alarm at the serious set of his mouth.

"Cole…" she started. But then he smiled.

"Happy birthday, Grace."

"What?" she whispered.

"Happy birthday. I thought we'd need this to cheer us up. But I guess it'll just be something better."

"What?" she repeated, watching as his hand reached for the door. "How did you know it was my birthday?" She hadn't told him. No one even knew her birthday except…

"Merry told me," he said. And then he opened the door, and there she was. Merry.

And Eve and Jenny and everyone else, all of them yelling, "Happy birthday!" as she stared in shock.

"Merry?" she said, not believing her eyes. How could Merry be here, when…

"Happy birthday," Cole whispered into her ear. And then Merry was running toward her, arms spread, and Grace couldn't take it all in. There were a dozen people around her. Maybe more. Rayleen and Easy and Shane and Cole and…Merry.

Tears sprang to her eyes, and there was nothing she could do to stop them.

"What are you doing here?" she whispered.

Merry squeezed her tighter. "Cole flew me up to surprise you. Happy birthday, Grace."

"Happy birthday!" the whole room shouted again.

These people who'd only known her for a month. These people who had no reason to care.

"I love you," Merry whispered into her ear.

Grace shook her head just as she always did. But something was different now. Something wasn't so scary, and she somehow found the courage to say it back. "I love you, too," she said quietly. Joy filled her up as she spoke the words, so she said them again, into Merry's ear, but this time…this time she was looking into Cole's eyes.

His gaze fell. His cheeks flushed. And he smiled. And Grace knew it was the truth. She loved him. And she was finally home.

* * * * *

**Being one of the guys
isn't all it's cracked up to be....**

A charming and humorous tale from
New York Times **bestselling author**

KRISTAN HIGGINS

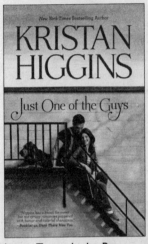

When journalist Chastity O'Neill returns to her hometown, she decides it's time to start working on some of those feminine wiles. Two tiny problems: #1—she's five feet eleven inches of rock-solid girl power, and #2—she's cursed with four alpha-male older brothers.

While doing a story on local heroes, she meets a hunky doctor and things start to look up. Now there's only one problem: Trevor Meade, her first love and the one man she's never quite gotten over. Yet the more time she spends with Dr. Perfect, the better Trevor looks. But even with the in-your-face competition, the irresistible Trevor just can't seem to see Chastity as anything more than just one of the guys....

Just One of the Guys

Available wherever books are sold.

www.Harlequin.com

PHKH703

HARLEQUIN Desire

ALWAYS POWERFUL, PASSIONATE AND PROVOCATIVE.

**A brand-new Westmoreland Family novel
from *New York Times* bestselling author**

BRENDA JACKSON

Megan Westmoreland needs answers about her family's past.
And Rico Claiborne is the man to find them. But when
the truth comes out, Rico offers her a shoulder to lean on...
and much, much more. Megan has heard that passions
burn hotter in Texas. Now she's ready to find out....

TEXAS WILD

"Jackson's characters are...hot enough to burn the pages."
—*RT Book Reviews* on *Westmoreland's Way*

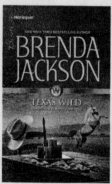

Available October 2 from Harlequin® Desire.

www.Harlequin.com

HD73198ST

REQUEST YOUR FREE BOOKS!

2 FREE NOVELS
FROM THE ROMANCE COLLECTION
PLUS 2 FREE GIFTS!

YES! Please send me 2 FREE novels from the Romance Collection and my 2 FREE gifts (gifts are worth about $10). After receiving them, if I don't wish to receive any more books, I can return the shipping statement marked "cancel." If I don't cancel, I will receive 4 brand-new novels every month and be billed just $5.99 per book in the U.S. or $6.49 per book in Canada. That's a saving of at least 25% off the cover price. It's quite a bargain! Shipping and handling is just 50¢ per book in the U.S. and 75¢ per book in Canada.* I understand that accepting the 2 free books and gifts places me under no obligation to buy anything. I can always return a shipment and cancel at any time. Even if I never buy another book, the two free books and gifts are mine to keep forever.

194/394 MDN FELQ

Name _____ (PLEASE PRINT) _____

Address _____ Apt. # _____

City _____ State/Prov. _____ Zip/Postal Code _____

Signature (if under 18, a parent or guardian must sign)

Mail to the Reader Service:
IN U.S.A.: P.O. Box 1867, Buffalo, NY 14240-1867
IN CANADA: P.O. Box 609, Fort Erie, Ontario L2A 5X3

Not valid for current subscribers to the Romance Collection
or the Romance/Suspense Collection.

Want to try two free books from another line?
Call 1-800-873-8635 or visit www.ReaderService.com.

* Terms and prices subject to change without notice. Prices do not include applicable taxes. Sales tax applicable in N.Y. Canadian residents will be charged applicable taxes. Offer not valid in Quebec. This offer is limited to one order per household. All orders subject to credit approval. Credit or debit balances in a customer's account(s) may be offset by any other outstanding balance owed by or to the customer. Please allow 4 to 6 weeks for delivery. Offer available while quantities last.

Your Privacy—The Reader Service is committed to protecting your privacy. Our Privacy Policy is available online at www.ReaderService.com or upon request from the Reader Service.

We make a portion of our mailing list available to reputable third parties that offer products we believe may interest you. If you prefer that we not exchange your name with third parties, or if you wish to clarify or modify your communication preferences, please visit us at www.ReaderService.com/consumerschoice or write to us at Reader Service Preference Service, P.O. Box 9062, Buffalo, NY 14269. Include your complete name and address.

Call it *Sense and Sensuality*…

An erotic and alluring new tale from
critically acclaimed author

JANET MULLANY

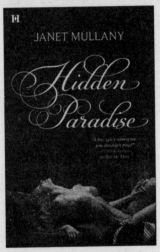

Louisa Connelly, a recently widowed Jane Austen scholar,
needs some relief from her stifling world. When a friend calls
to offer her a temporary escape from her Montana ranch,
she is whisked into a dizzying world of sumptuous food,
flowing wine and endless temptation….

Available now.

HARLEQUIN® HQN™
™ www.Harlequin.com

PHJM719